# A MURDER ON THE APPIAN WAY

## A MYSTERY OF ANCIENT ROME

### *Steven Saylor*

ROBINSON
London

Constable & Robinson Ltd
3 The Lanchesters
162 Fulham Palace Road
London W6 9ER
www.constablerobinson.com

First published in the UK by Robinson Publishing Ltd 1997

This paperback edition published by Robinson,
an imprint of Constable & Robinson Ltd 2005

A copy of the British Library Cataloguing in
Publication Data is available from the British Library.

ISBN 1-84529-247-2

Printed and bound in the EU

1 3 5 7 9 10 8 6 4 2

**Steven Saylor** is best known as the author of the *Roma sub Rosa* series set in ancient Rome and featuring Gordianus the Finder. His work has been widely praised for its remarkable accuracy and vivid historical detail as well as for its passion, mystery and intrigue.

Steven divides his time between Berkeley, California, and Austin, Texas. His web address is www.stevensaylor.com.

## Praise for the Roma sub Rosa series

'How wonderful to have a scholar write about ancient Rome; how comforting to feel instant confidence in the historical accuracy of the novel.'     *Sunday Times*

'Saylor has acquired the information of a historian but he enjoys the gifts of a born novelist.'     *Boston Globe*

'Saylor evokes the ancient world more convincingly than any other writer of his generation.' *Sunday Times*

'Saylor's scholarship is breathtaking and his writing enthrals.'     *Ruth Rendell*

## ALSO IN THE ROMA SUB ROSA SERIES

ROMA SUB ROSA

In ancient myth, the Egyptian god Horus (whom the Romans called Harpocrates) came upon Venus engaged in one of her many love affairs. Cupid, her son, gave a rose to Horus as a bribe to keep quiet; thus Horus became the god of silence, and the rose became the symbol of confidentiality. A rose hanging over a council table indicated that all present were sworn to secrecy. Sub Rosa ('under the rose') has come to mean 'that which is carried out in secret'. Thus 'Roma sub Rosa': the secret history of Rome, as seen through the eyes of Gordianus.

*To those who taught me history,*
*beginning with Iva Cockrell,*
*and at the University of Texas at Austin,*
*Professors Oliver Radkey, M. Gwyn Morgan,*
*Richard Graham and R. David Armstrong*

Men were eager to win office and even employed bribery and assassination to do so, but such was the state of affairs in the city that elections could not be held. With no one in charge, murders occurred practically every day.

Dio Cassius, *Roman History*, xl, 48

The Appian Way, which was made by Appius Claudius Caecus and honours his name, extends from Rome to Capua, a journey of five days. Its breadth is such that two wagons going in opposite directions can easily pass one another. This road is one of the noteworthy sights of the world, for the stones are so finely cut, levelled and fitted together, without mortar of any sort, that the unbroken surface appears to be not a work of man, but a wondrous phenomenon of nature.

Procopius, *Gothic Wars*, v, 14

'Stop quoting laws to us. We carry swords.'

Plutarch, *Life of Pompey*, x, 2

# CONTENTS

# A NOTE ON NAMES
# AND THE HOURS
# OF THE ROMAN DAY

For the names of certain historical figures in these pages, I have used familiar literary forms rather than the more authentic Latin. While their contemporaries never referred to Marcus Antonius as 'Marc Antony,' or to Gnaeus Pompeius Magnus as 'Pompey the Great,' these traditional versions carry such a magic that it seemed pedantic to resist them.

The ancient Romans did not number their hours as we do, in twelve-hour segments before and after midday, but rather beginning at daybreak, so that when a Roman spoke of the first hour of the day, he meant, quite literally, the first hour of daylight; and the first hour of the night was the first hour of darkness. The following table roughly approxi-

mates the equivalent hours of the day, as drawn from the historical sources and used in *A Murder on the Appian Way*:

| | |
|---|---|
| 7 a.m. | the first hour of the day |
| 8 a.m. | the second hour of the day |
| 9 a.m. | the third hour of the day |
| 10 a.m. | the fourth hour of the day |
| 11 a.m. | the fifth hour of the day |
| noon | the sixth hour of the day |
| 1 p.m. | the seventh hour of the day |
| 2 p.m. | the eighth hour of the day |
| 3 p.m. | the ninth hour of the day |
| 4 p.m. | the tenth hour of the day |
| 5 p.m. | the eleventh hour of the day |
| 6 p.m. | the twelfth hour of the day |
| 7 p.m. | the first hour of the night |
| 8 p.m. | the second hour of the night |
| 9 p.m. | the third hour of the night |
| 10 p.m. | the fourth hour of the night |
| 11 p.m. | the fifth hour of the night |
| midnight | the sixth hour of the night |
| 1 a.m. | the seventh hour of the night |
| 2 a.m. | the eighth hour of the night |
| 3 a.m. | the ninth hour of the night |
| 4 a.m. | the tenth hour of the night |
| 5 a.m. | the eleventh hour of the night |
| 6 a.m. | the twelfth hour of the night |

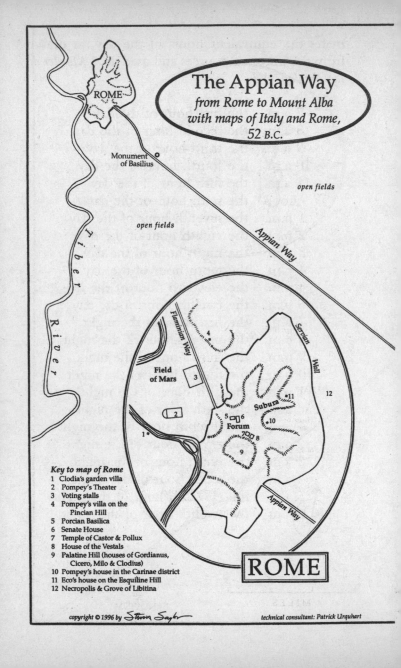

# The Appian Way
*from Rome to Mount Alba with maps of Italy and Rome,*
52 B.C.

ROME

Monument of Basilius

open fields

open fields

Appian Way

Tiber River

Flaminian Way

Field of Mars

Servian Wall

Subura

•11

12

3

2

5 6
Forum

•10

1•

8

9

Appian Way

**Key to map of Rome**
1 Clodia's garden villa
2 Pompey's Theater
3 Voting stalls
4 Pompey's villa on the Pincian Hill
5 Porcian Basilica
6 Senate House
7 Temple of Castor & Pollux
8 House of the Vestals
9 Palatine Hill (houses of Gordianus, Cicero, Milo & Clodius)
10 Pompey's house in the Carinae district
11 Eco's house on the Esquiline Hill
12 Necropolis & Grove of Libitina

## ROME

copyright © 1996 by Steven Saylor

technical consultant: Patrick Urquhart

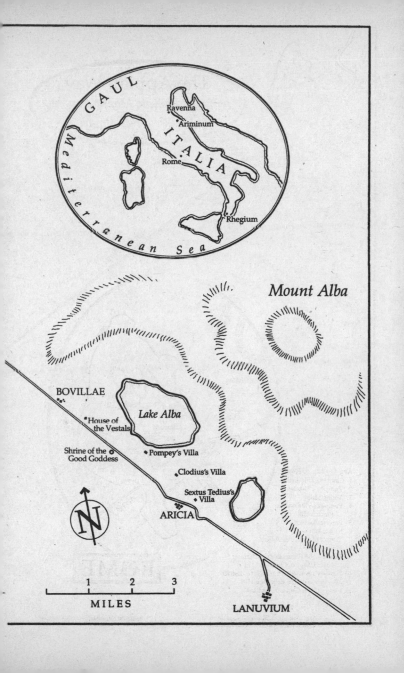

# Part One

## *Riot*

# I

'Papa! Wake up!'

A hand gripped my shoulder and shook me gently. I pulled away and felt cold air on the back of my neck as the blanket slid away. I snatched it back and snuggled against it, burrowing for warmth. I reached for Bethesda, but found only a warm vacancy where she should have been.

'Really, Papa, you'd better wake up.' Eco shook me again, not quite so gently.

'Yes, husband,' said Bethesda. 'Get up!'

What sleep is as deep as the sleep of a cold Januarius night, when the sky is a blanket of lowering clouds and the earth shivers below? Even with my son and wife yammering at me, I slipped back into the arms of Morpheus as easily as a boy slipping into a bottomless, downy bed of goose feathers. It seemed to me that two magpies were chattering absurdly in a tree nearby, calling me 'Papa' and

'Husband'. They swooped down, fluttered their wings, pecked me with their beaks. I groaned and waved my arms to fend them off. After a brief battle they retreated into the frosty clouds, leaving me to dream in peace.

The frosty clouds burst open. Cold water splashed my face.

I sat upright, sputtering and blinking. With a satisfied nod, Bethesda placed an empty cup beside a flickering lamp on a little table against the wall. Eco stood at the foot of the bed, gathering up the blanket he had just pulled off me. I shivered in my sleeping gown and hugged myself.

'Blanket thief!' I mumbled grimly. At that moment it seemed the foulest crime imaginable. 'Stealing an old man's rest!'

Eco remained impassive. Bethesda crossed her arms and arched an eyebrow. By the dim lamplight the two of them still looked suspiciously like magpies.

I closed my eyes. 'Have pity!' I sighed, thinking an appeal to mercy might gain me just one more blissful moment of sleep.

But before my head reached the pillow, Eco gripped my shoulder and pulled me upright again. 'No, Papa! It's serious.'

'What's serious?' I made a desultory attempt to shake him off. 'Is the house on fire?' I was irretrievably awake now, and grumpy – until I realized who was absent from the conspiracy to wake me. I looked around the room, blinking, and felt a sudden thrill of panic. 'Diana! Where is Diana?'

'Here, Papa.' She entered the room and stepped

into the circle of light. Her long hair, let down for the night, hung loose over her shoulders, shimmering like black water under starlight. Her eyes – the almond-shaped, Egyptian eyes inherited from her mother – were slightly swollen with sleep.

'What's the matter?' she said, yawning. 'What are you doing here, Eco? Why is everyone up? And what's all the noise from the street?'

'Noise?' I said.

She cocked her head. 'I suppose you can't hear it very well, here at the back of the house. You can certainly hear it from my room. They woke me up.'

'Who?'

'People in the street. Running. With torches. Yelling something.' She wrinkled her nose, which she does when she's puzzled. Seeing the blank look on my face, she turned to her mother, who stepped towards her with embracing arms. At seventeen, Diana is still enough of a child to appreciate such comforting. Meanwhile, Eco kept to one side, wearing the glum expression of a messenger in a play who bears ill tidings.

I finally realized that something must be truly, terribly wrong.

A short time later, I was dressed and walking at a fast clip through the dark streets at Eco's side, together with his four bodyguards.

I turned my head anxiously as a group of stern-looking young men came running up from behind and passed us. Their torches cut through the air with a whoosh. Our shadows danced crazily up and

down the street, growing huge as the torches passed close by and then dwindling like wraiths into the darkness as the torchbearers left us behind.

I tripped against an uneven paving stone. 'Numa's balls! We should have brought torches ourselves.'

'I'd rather my bodyguards keep their hands free,' said Eco.

'Yes, well, at least we have enough of those,' I said, eyeing the four formidable young slaves who surrounded us, one ahead, one behind, one to each side. They had the look of trained gladiators – stiff-jawed, flinty-eyed, alert to every movement in the street around us.

Good bodyguards are expensive to purchase and expensive to feed. My daughter-in-law Menenia had complained each time Eco added another to their household, saying the money would be better spent on kitchen slaves or a better tutor for the twins. 'Protection comes first,' Eco would tell her. 'It's the times we live in.' Sadly, I had to agree.

My thoughts settled on Eco's wife and children, whom he had left in his house over on the Esquiline Hill. 'Menenia and the twins . . .' I said, walking faster to keep up with him. My breath made clouds in the air, but at least the pace kept me warm. Even as fast as we were walking, another group of men came up from behind and passed us, their torches sending our shadows into headlong flight.

'They're safe. I had a new door put on the house last month. It would take an army to break it down.

And I left my two biggest bodyguards to look after them.'

'Just how many bodyguards do you own nowadays?'

'Only six – the two at home, and the four with us.'

'Only six?' I still had only Belbo, whom I had left behind to look after Bethesda and Diana. Unfortunately, Belbo was really too old to be an adequate bodyguard any longer. The other household slaves could hardly be expected to put up much of a fight, if something truly terrible were to happen . . .

I tried to push such thoughts from my mind.

Another group of men came rushing up from behind us. Like us, they carried no torches. As they passed in the darkness, I noticed Eco's bodyguards grow tense and reach inside their cloaks. Strangers without torches in their hands could be carrying something more dangerous, like daggers.

But the group passed without incident. Up ahead, someone flung open the shutters of an upper-storey window and leaned out. 'What in Hades is going on tonight?'

'They've killed him!' cried one of the men ahead of us. 'Murdered him in cold blood, the cowardly bastards!'

'Killed who?'

'Clodius! Clodius is dead!'

The shadowy figure at the window was silent for a moment, then let out a long, ringing laugh that echoed in the cold night air. The group ahead of us came to an abrupt halt.

'Trouble!' said Eco. I nodded, then realized the hushed remark was a signal to his bodyguards. They tightened their ranks around us. We pressed on at a faster pace.

'So where –' gasped the man at the window, barely able to speak for his laughter, 'where is everybody headed in such a hot rush? To a celebration?'

The group in the street erupted in angry shouts. Some raised their fists. Others stooped over, searching for rocks. Even on the Palatine Hill, with its immaculate streets and elegant houses, there are loose stones to be found. The man at the window kept laughing, then suddenly yelped. 'My head! Oh, my head! You filthy bastards!' He slammed his shutters on a hail of rocks.

We hurried on and turned a corner. 'Do you think it's true, Eco?'

'About Clodius being dead? We'll know soon enough. Isn't that his house, straight ahead? Look at all the torches gathered in the street! That's what brought me out tonight – we could see the glow reflected off the clouds. Menenia called me up on the rooftop to see. She thought the whole Palatine Hill must be on fire.'

'So you thought you'd come see if your Papa was singed?'

Eco smiled, then his face turned grim. 'On the way, down in the Subura, I saw people everywhere in the streets. Gathered at corners, listening to speakers. Huddled in doorways, talking in low voices. Some ranting, some weeping. Hundreds

8

of men heading for the Palatine, like a river rushing uphill. And all saying the same thing: Clodius is dead.'

The house of Publius Clodius – his new house, for he had purchased the place and moved in only a few months before – was one of the city's architectural marvels, or monsters, depending on one's point of view. The houses of the rich on the Palatine Hill grow larger and more ostentatious every year, like great preening animals devouring the little houses around them and displaying ever more sumptuous coats. The coat of this particular beast was of many-coloured marble. By the glow of the torches in the street one could see the glimmering sheen of the marble veneers and columns that adorned the outer terraces – polished green Lacedaemonian porphyry, Egyptian red marble mottled with white dots like the pelt of a fawn, yellow Numidian marble with red veins. These terraces, set into a hillside and planted with roses stripped bare by winter, surrounded the gravel-paved forecourt. The iron gate that normally barred entrance to the court stood open, but the way was completely blocked by the mass of mourners who filled the court and spilled out into the street.

Somewhere beyond that crowd, at the far side of the forecourt, was the entrance to the great house itself, which sprawled across the hill like a self-contained village, its various wings surrounded by yet more terraces and connected by porticoes

9

lined with yet more multicoloured marble columns. The house loomed above us, a miniature mountain of deep shadows and shimmering marble, lit from within and without, suspended dreamlike between the lowering clouds and the hazy reek put forth by the torches.

'What now?' I said to Eco. 'We can't even get into the forecourt. The crowd's too thick. The rumour must be true – look at all these grown men weeping. Come, best to get back home and look after our families. No telling what will happen next.'

Eco nodded but didn't seem to hear. He stood on tiptoe, straining to see within the forecourt. 'The doors to the house are shut. No one seems to be going in or out. Everyone's just milling about –'

There was a sudden pulse of excitement in the crowd. 'Let her through! Let her through!' someone shouted. The crush grew even greater as people stepped back to make way for some sort of conveyance coming through the street. A phalanx of gladiators appeared first, roughly shoving and elbowing their way forwards. People did their best to get out of the way. The gladiators were enormous, like giants; Eco's bodyguards were mere boys by comparison. They say there are islands beyond the northernmost reaches of Gaul where men grow that big. These had pale faces and scraggly red hair.

The crowd in front of us compressed. Eco and I were squeezed together, with his bodyguards still in

a ring around us. Someone stepped on my foot. My arms were trapped at my sides. I caught a glimpse of the approaching litter, supported on the shoulders of bearers who dwarfed even the giant gladiators. Suspended above the crowd, the red and white striped silk canopy shimmered in the flickering torchlight.

My heart skipped a beat. I knew that litter. I had been carried in it myself. Of course she would be here.

The litter drew closer. Its curtains were closed, as of course they would be. She would have no desire to see the mob, or to be seen by them. But for a brief moment, as the canopy passed, it seemed to me that the curtains parted a tiny bit. I strained to see above the heads of the litter bearers but was confounded by the play of light and shadows that rippled across the red and white silk. Perhaps it was only a shadow I saw, and not an opening at all.

Eco's hand on my shoulder abruptly drew me back, out of the path of the gladiators who advanced alongside the canopy. He spoke into my ear. 'Do you think —?'

'Of course. It must be her. The red and white stripes — who else?'

I was hardly the only man in the crowd to recognize the litter and to know who must be inside. These were Clodius's people, after all, the poor of the Subura who rioted at his command, the ex-slaves who looked to him to protect their voting rights, the hungry mob that had grown fat from his legislation to hand out free grain. They had always

supported Clodius, as he had always supported them. They had followed his career, gossiped among themselves about his sexual escapades and family affairs, plotted terrible fates for his enemies. They adored Clodius. They might or might not have adored his scandalous older sister, but they recognized her litter when they saw it. Suddenly I heard her name, whispered by someone in the crowd. Others repeated it, then joined in unison, until the name became a soft chant that followed in the wake of her canopy:

'Clodia . . . Clodia . . . Clodia . . .'

Her litter passed through the narrow gateway into the forecourt. Her gladiators could have cleared the way by force, but violence turned out to be unnecessary. At the sound of her name the mourners in the court drew back in a kind of awe. A pocket of emptiness formed before the litter and closed after it, so that it proceeded swiftly and without incident to the far side of the court and up the short flight of steps to the entrance. The tall bronze doors opened inward. The canopy was turned so that its occupants could not be seen as they alighted and entered the house. The doors shut behind them with a muffled clang.

The chanting died away. An uneasy hush descended on the crowd.

'Clodius, dead,' said Eco quietly. 'It hardly seems possible.'

'You haven't lived as long as I have,' I said ruefully. 'They all die, the great and the small, and most of them sooner than later.'

12

'Of course. I only mean —'

'I know what you mean. When some men die, it's like a grain of sand thrown into a river — there's not even a ripple. With others, it's like a great boulder. Waves splash onto the bank. And with a very few —'

'Like a meteor falling out of the sky,' said Eco.

I took a deep breath. 'Let's hope it won't be as awful as that.' But something told me it would be.

We waited for a while, trapped by the inertia that falls upon a crowd when something momentous looms. From those around us we picked up numerous, conflicting rumours of what had happened. There had been an incident on the Appian Way, just outside Rome – no, twelve miles away, at Bovillae – no, somewhere farther south. Clodius had been out riding alone – no, with a small bodyguard – no, in a litter with his wife and their usual retinue of slaves and attendants. There had been an ambush – no, a single assassin – no, a traitor among Clodius's own men . . .

So it went, with no sure truth to be found, only a single, unanimous point of agreement: Clodius was dead.

The lowering clouds gradually moved on to reveal the naked firmament – moonless, pitch-black, spangled with stars that glittered like ice crystals. The short, swift walk from my house had warmed my blood. The crush of bodies and burning torches had kept me warm, but as the night grew colder, so did I. I curled my toes, rubbed my

hands together, watched my breath mingle with the smoke in the air.

'This is no good,' I finally said. 'I'm freezing. I didn't bring a heavy enough cloak.' Eco seemed warm enough, I noticed, in a cloak no heavier than mine, but a man of fifty-eight has thinner blood than a man twenty years younger. 'What are we waiting for, anyway? We found out what the panic was about. Clodius is dead.'

'Yes, but how?'

I had to smile. He had learned his trade from me. Curiosity becomes a habit. Even when there's no money in it, a Finder can't help being curious, especially when there's murder involved. 'We won't find out from this crowd,' I said.

'I suppose not.'

'Come on, then.'

He hesitated. 'You'd think they'd send someone out to talk to the crowd. Surely someone will come out sooner or later . . .' He saw me shivering. 'Let's go, then.'

'You don't have to leave.'

'I can't let you walk home alone, Papa. Not on a night like this.'

'Send the bodyguards with me, then.'

'I'm not fool enough to stay in this crowd alone.'

'We could split them up, two for you and two for me.'

'No. I don't want to take any chances. I'll walk you home. Then I'll come back if I still want to.'

We might have haggled over these logistics for a while longer, but at that moment Eco lifted his eyes

to look at someone behind me. His bodyguards tensed.

'I'm looking for a man called Gordianus,' said a rumbling voice above my head. I turned to find my nose pressed against an extremely broad chest. Somewhere up above was a ruddy face topped by a fringe of red curls. The fellow's Latin was atrocious.

'I'm Gordianus,' I said.

'Good. Come with me.'

'Come with you where?'

He cocked his head. 'Into the house, of course.'

'At whose invitation?' I asked, already knowing.

'At the lady Clodia's command.'

She had seen me from her litter after all.

# II

Even with the red-haired giant leading us, I was dubious of the prospect of pressing through the crowded gateway and across the forecourt. Instead, he started off in another direction. We followed him down the street, past the fringes of the crowd to the foot of a narrow stairway tucked into the hillside beyond the outermost ring of marble terraces. The stairway was flanked by fig trees whose dense branches formed a canopy above.

'Are you sure this leads to the house?' said Eco suspiciously.

'Just follow me,' said the giant gruffly, pointing ahead to a distant lamp at the top of the stairs. Without a torch to guide us, the way was dark and the steps lost in shadow. We mounted them cautiously, lagging behind the giant, until we arrived at a narrow landing. The lamp was hung above a wooden door. Beside the door stood another

gladiator, who ordered us to leave our escorts outside and to remove our weapons. Eco produced a dagger and handed it over to one of his bodyguards. When I protested that I carried nothing, the red-haired giant insisted on searching me. Finally satisfied, he opened the door and led us inside.

We followed a long, dim hallway, descended a flight of steps, and at length emerged into a narrow room. We were in the foyer of the house, just inside the tall bronze doors, which were barred on the inside by a sturdy wooden beam. Through the doors I could hear the noise of the restless crowd from the courtyard beyond. 'Wait here,' the giant said, as he stepped through some curtains.

The foyer was lit by a hanging lamp, its flames reflected in the polished marble walls and floor. I stepped closer to the shimmering red curtains, fascinated by them. 'Do you know what these are, Eco? These must be the famous Attalic draperies. There's genuine gold thread in them. To see them by firelight, you'd think the fabric was woven of flames!'

I should explain that the house of Publius Clodius, and its furnishings, had a brief but remarkable history. The original owner had been Marcus Scaurus, who began building the house six years before. That was the same year that Scaurus was elected aedile, and was thus obliged, at his own expense, to entertain the masses with theatrical productions during the autumn festivals. Following the age-old tradition, Scaurus constructed a temporary theatre on the Field of Mars outside the city

walls. Two years later Pompey would build the first permanent theatre in Rome – Roman children would grow up thinking nothing of such Greek decadence in their midst – but Scaurus's theatre was built to stand for only a season.

I have been to many cities and seen many remarkable buildings, but never the like of Scaurus's theatre. There were seats for 80,000 people. The enormous stage was three storeys high, supported by 360 marble columns. Between these columns and tucked in various niches throughout the building there were a total of 3,000 bronze statues. These outlandish numbers were talked about until everyone knew them by heart, and they were not exaggerations; in slack moments during the plays, gawkers would count the columns and statues out loud while the poor actors emoted to no avail, upstaged by the decor.

The bottom storey of the stage was decorated with marble, the top storey with gilded wood, and the middle storey with astonishing constructions of coloured glass – not merely small windows but whole walls of glass, an extravagance that had never been seen before and will surely never be duplicated again. To decorate the stage there were enormous scenic backdrops painted by some of the finest artists in the world, framed by lavish Attalic draperies of red and orange cloth interwoven with gold thread, like the legendary golden robes of King Attalus of Asia; under the bright light of noon they seemed to be woven of sunlight itself.

When the festivals were over and the theatre was

taken down, Scaurus sold off some of the decorations and made lavish gifts of others. But much of the stuff he kept for himself, to decorate his new house on the Palatine. Marble veneers and columns were turned into terraces and porticos. The walls of coloured glass were transformed into skylights. Enormous crates full of statues and fabulous draperies and paintings were stacked up in the forecourt of the house and gradually taken inside. For his redesigned atrium, Scaurus decided to instal the largest columns from the theatre, made of black Lucullean marble, each eight times as tall as a man. The columns were so heavy, and hauling them so difficult, that a sewage contractor forced Scaurus to post a bond against possible damages to the city drains when the columns were transported across town to the Palatine.

The house of Scaurus excited almost as much comment as his theatre. People who had gawked at the theatre came to gawk at the house. His more conservative (and less affluent) neighbours considered the place an affront to good taste, a monstrosity of waste and excess, a defamation of stern Roman virtue. Those who complained should have remembered the old Trojan axiom: no matter how appalling a situation, it can always get worse – as when word got out that Scaurus was moving and had sold the place to the rabble-rouser Clodius. Clodius, the high-born patrician who disowned his pedigree to become a plebeian; Clodius, the bane of the Best People; Clodius, the Master of the Mob.

Clodius had paid almost fifteen million sesterces for the house and its furnishings. If the rumour was true – that Clodius was dead – then he had had little time to enjoy the place. He would never see the marble terraces bloom with roses in the spring.

I poked my head through the Attalic draperies into the atrium beyond, where the ceiling abruptly shot up to the height of three storeys. 'The Lucullean marble columns!' I whispered to Eco, stepping through the curtains and beckoning for him to follow, for here they were, soaring up in jet-black splendour to the ceiling forty feet above.

In the centre of the atrium was a shallow pool decorated with shimmering mosaic tiles of blue-black and silver, picturing the night sky and the constellations. High above the pool a corresponding square was cut into the roof, but instead of being open to the sky, there appeared to be a vast pane of glass across the skylight, through which the stars wavered as if they were underwater. It was a dizzying conceit: the skylight above appeared to be a pool reflecting the stars at our feet.

I took a slow walk around the perimeter of the atrium. Installed in niches in the walls were the wax masks of family ancestors. Publius Clodius Pulcher came from a very ancient, very noble line. One by one, the faces of his predecessors stared impassively back at me. Most had been captured in maturity or old age, but one could see they were in general a handsome lot. Pulcher – the name of the family branch – means beautiful, after all.

Eco tapped my shoulder. Our escort had

returned. He gestured with a toss of his chin and we followed him more deeply into the house.

As we walked down hallways I peered into the rooms on either side. Everywhere I saw reminders that we were in a house that had only recently been moved into and was still unsettled. Boxes and crates were stacked mazelike in some rooms, while other rooms were empty. In some places there was scaffolding and the smell of fresh plaster. Even the rooms which appeared finished seemed somehow tentative – furniture was set at odd angles, pictures were hung in odd spaces, statues were placed too close together.

What had I expected to find inside the house? Women weeping, slaves running about in confusion, a sense of panic? Instead the house was quiet, with hardly a person in sight. The vastness of the place made the quiet seem all the more acute and uncanny, like a deserted temple. Occasionally a slave crossed our path, deferentially stepping out of our way and keeping his face averted.

When the body dies, a philosopher once told me, all the life within it contracts to a single point before expiring altogether. So it seemed inside the house of Clodius, that all the life had gathered in one place, for suddenly we rounded a corner and entered a room lit by many lamps and full of hushed voices. Nervous-looking men in togas paced fretfully about, conversing in groups, gesturing with their hands, shaking their heads, arguing in whispers. Slaves stood out of the way in corners, quiet but alert, awaiting instructions.

We came to a closed door at the far side of the room. Nearby a hulking brute of a man sat with his chin in his hands, wearing a miserable expression. There was a bloodstained bandage on his head and a tourniquet around one arm. A handsome young man in an elegant tunic hovered over him, berating him and barely pausing to let the brute answer in mumbles. 'I still can't understand how you could have deserted him like that. Why were there so few of you with him in the first place? What in Hades were they thinking when they took him to that tavern instead of back to his villa?'

Our escort gently rapped on the door with the side of his foot; someone had taught him good manners. The young man and the wounded man looked up and peered suspiciously at Eco and me.

The wounded man frowned. 'Who in Hades —?'

The young man stared at us dully. 'It must be that fellow my Aunt Clodia sent for.'

The door opened. A pair of feminine eyes peered out. Our escort cleared his throat. 'The one called Gordianus, and his son, Eco.'

The slave girl nodded and opened the door. Eco and I stepped inside. Our escort stayed behind as the girl shut the door.

The room had the feeling of a sanctuary. Thick rugs covered the floor and tapestries covered the walls, muffling the quiet crackling of the single brazier that warmed the room and cast long shadows into the corners. Against one wall there was a long table, like an altar, with a few women

clustered before it, their backs turned to us. The women were robed in black, their hair let loose to fall over their shoulders. They seemed not to notice our arrival. The slave girl went to one of them and touched her gently on the elbow. Clodia turned and looked at us from across the room.

I had not seen her for almost four years, since the trial of Marcus Caelius. Clodia had retained my services to assist the prosecution; things had not gone as she planned, and her miscalculations had ended badly for her. Since then she had led a much quieter, more private existence, or so one heard, on the rare occasions when her name was mentioned. But I had not forgotten her. One never forgets a woman like Clodia.

She walked slowly towards us, the hem of her black gown trailing behind her. Her perfume reached us a moment before she did, scenting the air with the essence of crocus and spikenard. I had always seen her with her hair pulled back and held in place by pins. Now she wore it down for grieving, giving a lustrous black frame to the strik-ing angles of her cheekbones and the proud line of her nose. She was past forty now, but her skin was still like white rose petals. Her smooth cheeks and forehead seemed to glow by the flickering light of the brazier. Her eyes – those famous, glittering green eyes – were red from weeping, but her voice was steady.

'Gordianus! I thought I glimpsed you in the crowd. This is your son?'

'My elder son, Eco.'

She nodded, blinking back tears. 'Come, sit with me.' She led us to a corner and gestured for us to sit on one couch while she sat on another. She pressed one hand against her forehead and shut her eyes. She seemed on the verge of sobbing, but after a moment she breathed deeply and sat upright, folding her hands in her lap.

The light from the brazier was interrupted by a shadow. One of the others had crossed the room to join us. She sat beside Clodia and reached for her hands.

'My daughter, Metella,' said Clodia, though I hardly needed to be told. The young woman was unmistakably her mother's child. Perhaps she would even become as beautiful as her mother, given time. A beauty like Clodia's was not something a woman could be born with. It consisted of more than what the eyes could see, of a mystery behind the flesh which accrues only with the passage of time.

'I seem to remember that you have a daughter the same age,' said Clodia quietly.

'Diana,' I said. 'Seventeen.'

Clodia nodded. Metella suddenly began to weep. Her mother embraced her for a moment, then released her and sent her to rejoin the others. 'She loved her uncle very much,' Clodia said.

'What happened?'

Her voice was strained and colourless, as if any display of emotion would make it impossible for her to speak. 'We don't know for certain. He was down south, at his villa past Bovillae. Something

happened on the road. They say it was Milo, or Milo's men. A skirmish. Others were killed, not just Publius.' There was a catch in her voice. She paused to compose herself. 'Someone passing by just happened to find his body in the road – there wasn't even anyone standing guard over him! Strangers brought him back to the city. His body arrived here just after sundown. Since then some of his bodyguards have come straggling in. The ones who survived. We're still trying to make sense of what happened.'

'I saw a man in bandages being questioned in the other room.'

'A bodyguard. The man has been with Publius for years. How could he have let this happen?'

'And the young man questioning him?'

'My nephew, I imagine. Our brother Appius's oldest boy. He came with me in the litter, along with Metella. He loved Publius like a second father.' She shook her head. 'Publius's own little boy was with him down at Bovillae. We don't know what's become of the child. We don't even know where he is!' This was suddenly too much for her. She began to weep. Eco looked away. It was a hard thing to watch.

Her weeping subsided. 'Clodia,' I said quietly, 'why did you send for me?'

The question seemed to baffle her. She wrinkled her brow and blinked back tears. 'I'm not sure. I saw you in the crowd, and so . . .' She shrugged. 'I don't know, really. But something will have to be done. You know about that sort of thing, don't

you? Inquiries. Investigations. How it's done. Publius knew how to go about that kind of thing, of course. But now Publius . . .'

She drew a deep breath and slowly exhaled. Her tears had run dry. 'I don't know why I called for you, really. To see an old, familiar face? We parted friends, didn't we?' She touched my arm and managed a wan smile. The effort produced only a small fraction of the charm of which I knew she was capable. The feebleness of the attempt made it all the more poignant. 'Who knows what will happen now? The world has turned upside down. But something will have to be done to set things right. Publius's children are too young to see to it. It will fall to others in the family. We may need you. It may come to that, you see.' She sighed wearily. 'There's nothing to be done right now, except to seek what comfort we can. Metella needs me.' She stood and looked bleakly towards the women across the room.

The interview seemed to be at an end. I nodded to Eco. Together we rose from the couch.

The slave girl came to show us out. Clodia walked away from us, then turned back.

'Wait. You should see him. I want you to see what they did to him.'

She led us across the room, to the altarlike table where Metella stood along with two other women and a child. At our approach the oldest of the women turned and scowled at us. Her face was gaunt and haggard. Her hair was almost entirely grey. Unpinned, it hung to her waist. There were no tears in her eyes, only anger and resentment.

26

'Who are these men?'

'Friends of mine,' said Clodia, her voice taking on an edge.

'What man isn't?' The woman gave Clodia a withering look. 'What are they doing here? They should wait in the outer room with the rest.'

'I asked them here, Sempronia.'

'This is not your household,' said the woman bluntly.

Metella went to her mother's side and took her hand. The older woman glared at them. The fourth woman, whose face I had not yet seen, kept her back turned. She reached down to touch the head of the little girl pressed against her. The child craned her neck and looked up at us with wide, innocent eyes.

'Sempronia, please . . .' said Clodia in a strained whisper.

'Yes, Mother, let's try to be peaceable. Even with dear Clodia.' The fourth woman finally turned. In her eyes I saw neither tears nor anger. There was weariness in her voice, but it was the weariness of exhaustion, not resignation. There was no emotion to be read in her voice or on her face, only a kind of steady determination. One might have expected to see a stronger reaction from the widow of the dead man. Perhaps she was simply numb with shock, but her gaze was keen and unwavering as she appraised us.

Fulvia was not a great beauty, like Clodia, but her appearance was striking nonetheless. She was younger by at least ten years; I guessed her to be no

27

more than thirty. As her little daughter clung to her, I saw where the child's curious, luminous brown eyes had come from; there was a sharpness in Fulvia's gaze that indicated a formidable intelligence. She lacked her mother's grim harshness, but one could see the seeds of it in the hard lines around her mouth, especially when she turned her gaze to Clodia.

I could see at a glance that there was no love lost between the two sisters-in-law. Clodia and her brother had long been famous (or infamous) for their mutual devotion; there were many who thought they were more like man and wife than siblings. Where did that leave Clodius's real wife? What had Fulvia thought of the intimacy between her husband and his sister? From the look that passed between them, I gathered that the women had learned to tolerate one another, but not much more than that. Clodius had been the link between them, the mutual object of their affections as well as the cause of their mutual animosity; perhaps Clodius had also kept the peace between them. Now Clodius was dead.

Quite dead, I thought, for beyond Fulvia I could see his corpse laid out on the long, high table. He was still dressed in winter riding clothes – a heavy, long-sleeved tunic cinched with a belt at the waist, woollen leggings, red leather boots. The filthy, blood-soaked tunic was torn open across his chest and hung in rags, like the streamers of a tattered red flag.

'Come,' whispered Clodia, ignoring the other

women and taking my arm. 'I want you to see.' She led me to the table. Eco pressed close behind me.

The face was undamaged. The eyes were closed and the bloodless lips and cheeks were marred only by a few smudges of dirt and blood and a slight grimace, like that of a man suffering from a tooth-ache or having an unpleasant dream. He looked uncannily like his sister, with the same finely moulded cheekbones and long, proud nose. It was a face to melt the hearts of women and make men prickle with envy, a face to taunt his scowling patrician colleagues in the Senate and win the adoration of the rabble. Clodius had been strikingly handsome, almost too boyish-looking for a man nearly forty. The only signs of his age were a few strands of grey at his temples; even these were mostly lost in his thick mane of black hair.

Below the neck, his strong, lean body was elegantly proportioned with square shoulders and a broad swimmer's chest. A gaping puncture wound pierced his right shoulder. There were two smaller stab wounds in his chest, and his limbs were marked with numerous lacerations, scrapes and mottled bruises. More bruises ringed his throat, as if a thin cord had been tightened around his neck; indeed, had he shown no other wounds, I would have said that he had been strangled.

Beside me, Eco shuddered. Like me, he had seen many dead bodies, but victims of poison or a dagger in the back present a less gory spectacle than did the corpse before us. This was not the body of a man

who had died from quick and furtive murder. This was a man who had died in battle.

Clodia took one of the corpse's hands in hers, pressing it between her palms as if she could warm it. She ran her fingers over his and wrinkled her brow. 'His ring. His gold signet ring! Did you remove it, Fulvia?'

Fulvia shook her head. 'The ring was gone when they brought him. The men who killed him must have taken it, like a trophy.' Again, she showed no emotion.

There was a gentle rapping at the door. A group of slave girls entered with cloths folded over their arms. They carried combs, jars of unguents and pitchers of heated water that sent trails of steam into the air.

'Hand me a comb,' said Clodia, reaching out to one of the girls.

Fulvia frowned. 'Who sent for these things?'

'I did.' Clodia moved to the end of the table and began to comb her brother's hair. The teeth caught on a tangle of dried blood. Her face stiffened. She pulled the comb through, but her hands were shaking.

'You sent for them? Then you can send them away,' said Fulvia.

'What do you mean?'

'His body doesn't need to be bathed.'

'Of course it does. The people outside want to see him.'

'And they will.'

'But not like this!'

'Exactly like this. You wanted your friends to see his wounds. Well, so do I. Everyone in Rome is going to see them.'

'But all this blood, and his clothes hanging from him like rags —'

'We'll take off his clothes, then. Let the people see him exactly as he is.'

Clodia continued to comb, keeping her eyes on her work. Fulvia stepped towards her. She seized Clodia's wrist, snatched the comb and threw it on the floor. The gesture was sudden and violent, but her voice remained as impassive as her face. 'Mother is right. This isn't your household, Clodia. And he wasn't your husband.'

Eco tugged at my sleeve. I nodded. It was time to take our leave. I bowed my head in deference to the corpse, but the gesture went unnoticed; Clodia and Fulvia stared at one another like tigresses with flattened ears. The slave girls scattered nervously as we made our way to the door. Before I left the room I turned and took a last look at the women, and was struck by the tableau of Clodius dead upon the table, surrounded by the five females who had been closest to him in life, their ages spread over the range of a lifetime — his little daughter, his niece Metella, his wife Fulvia, his sister Clodia, his mother-in-law Sempronia. I thought of the Trojan women mourning Hector, with the attendant slave girls for a chorus.

The brightly lit outer room seemed like another world, with its fretfully pacing men in togas and hushed masculine voices. The atmosphere was just

as tense, but of a different nature – not of mourning but of crisis and confusion, like a military camp under siege or a desperate gathering of conspirators. The room was more crowded than before. Important newcomers had arrived, and with them their retinues of freedmen and slaves. I recognized several well-known senators and magistrates of the populist stripe. Some stood in pairs, quietly conversing. Others were gathered in a circle, listening to a wild-eyed man with unkempt hair who kept striking his palm with his fist.

'I say we mount an assault on Milo's house tonight,' he was saying. 'Why wait? It's just a stone's throw away. We'll drag him into the street, set the place on fire and tear him limb from limb.'

I whispered into Eco's ear, 'Sextus Cloelius?'

Eco nodded and whispered back, 'Clodius's right-hand man. Organizes mobs, stages riots, breaks arms, slits noses. Not afraid to get his hands dirty.'

Some of the politicians nodded at Cloelius's suggestion. Others scoffed. 'What makes you think that Milo would dare to come back to the city, after what he's done?' said one. 'He's probably halfway to Massilia by now.'

'Not Milo,' said Cloelius. 'He's boasted for years that he'd kill Publius Clodius one day. Mark my words, he'll be down in the Forum tomorrow to brag about it. And when he shows his face, we'll slaughter him on the spot!'

'There's no point in a slaughter,' said the handsome, elegantly dressed young man I had noticed

32

on the way in, Clodius's nephew Appius. 'We'll press for a trial instead.'

'A trial!' cried Cloelius, exasperated. There was a collective groan.

'Yes, a trial,' insisted Appius. 'It's the only way to expose the bastard and his friends along with him. Do you think Milo alone was behind this? He hasn't the wits to stage an ambush. I smell Cicero's bloody maw! Uncle Publius's enemies didn't kill him on a whim. It was cold, calculated murder! I don't want just revenge; a knife in the back could accomplish that. I want to see these men discredited, humiliated, jeered out of Rome! I want the whole city to repudiate them, and their families with them. That means a trial.'

'I hardly think it's a matter of choosing whether to stage or not stage a slaughter,' said a calm, shrewd-looking young man at the edge of the crowd.

'Gaius Sallust,' Eco whispered in my ear. 'One of the radical tribunes elected last year.'

Heads turned. Having gained the group's undivided attention, Sallust shrugged. 'Well, what makes you think we can control the mob one way or the other? Clodius could, but Clodius is dead. There's no telling what will happen tomorrow, or tonight for that matter. A slaughter? Perhaps a bloodbath. We'll be lucky if there's enough organization left in Rome to stage a trial.'

At this there was another round of groaning and scoffing, but no one challenged outright what Sallust had said. Instead they turned uneasily away and resumed their argument without him.

'A trial!' Appius insisted.

'A riot first!' said Sextus Cloelius. 'The mob won't settle for anything less. And if Milo dares to show himself, we'll chop off his head and carry it through the Forum on a stick.'

'Then the mood of the city will surely swing against us,' argued Appius. 'No. Uncle Publius understood the way to make use of the mob — as a dagger, not as a bludgeon. You're wrought up, Sextus. You need some sleep.'

'Don't tell me how Publius used the mob,' said Cloelius. 'Half the time, I was the one who plotted his strategies for him.'

Appius's eyes flashed. They reminded me of Clodia's eyes, glittering and green like emeralds. 'Don't try to rise above your station, Sextus Cloelius. Save your vulgar rhetoric for the mob. The men in this room are a little too sophisticated for your style of blustering.'

Cloelius opened his mouth to answer, then turned and stalked off.

There was a tense silence, broken by Sallust. 'I think we're all a little wrought up,' he said. 'I'm going home to get some sleep.' A large coterie of retainers shuffled out of the room with him, leaving more space for those who remained to carry on with their pacing and gesticulating.

'We should do likewise,' I said, nudging Eco. 'I need my sleep. Besides, it's as Sallust says: there's no telling what may happen in the streets tonight. We should be home with our families behind barred doors.'

34

The gladiator who had escorted us earlier had been keeping an eye on us. As we moved towards the door he joined up with us and insisted on showing us out. He turned back only when he had delivered us into the protection of Eco's bodyguards on the landing outside the secluded side entrance.

We descended the steps to the street. The crowd gathered outside the forecourt of Clodius's house had grown even larger. Men stood in groups, arguing, like their leaders inside the house, over what should be done, only in louder voices and cruder language. Other men stood alone and openly sobbed, as if their own brother or father had been murdered.

I meant to walk straight on, but the crowd was like a force, an undertow at my feet that held me back. Eco was content to stay and observe, and so we lingered, fascinated by the torchlight, the floating bits of conversations, the shifting mass of humanity, the mood of uncertainty and dread.

Suddenly the great bronze doors to Clodius's house swung open with a double clang. A hush of anticipation rippled through the crowd. Armed men appeared first. They descended the steps in a cordon, preceding and flanking the men in togas who carried the body of Clodius upon a long, flat bier.

A groan rose from the crowd at the first glimpse of the body, followed by a great rush forwards. The bier was set down on the steps, tilted upward so that Clodius could be seen. We were caught in the

crush. The crowd in the forecourt compressed, and those in the street were pulled in behind them, as if sucked into a vortex. Eco gripped my hand as we were carried through the gates and into the forecourt, like flotsam on a flood. His bodyguards struggled to stay close, shoving and pressing against us. I was jabbed in the ribs by the point of a knife concealed inside the tunic of the bodyguard beside me, and considered the mad irony if I should be accidentally gutted by the weapon of a man intending to protect me.

We came to a stop. The crowd was packed into the forecourt like grains of sand in a bottle. Through the reek of the torches, I had a clear view of Clodius propped up on his bier, surrounded in death as he had always been in life, by armed guards. To either side of the bier stood the men who had carried it. Among them I recognized Appius and Sextus Cloelius.

Clodius had been stripped of his bloody garments and retained only a loincloth around his hips. The puncture at his shoulder and the wounds in his chest had been cleaned, but only to show them clearly; there was still plenty of gore and blood smeared across his pale, waxy flesh. His hair, I noticed, had been lovingly combed and untangled. It was pushed back from his face, as he had worn it in life, but a stray tendril had fallen forwards over one eye. To look at his face alone, one might have thought that he was merely asleep and frowning because the hair was tickling him, and that he might at any moment reach up to push it away. To see

him naked under the stars on such a cold night made me shiver.

Around us men moaned, cursed, wept, stamped their feet, shook their fists, buried their faces in their hands. Another tremor of apprehension rippled through the crowd as Fulvia appeared on the steps.

Her arms were crossed over her chest, her head bowed. Her long, dark hair hung straight down, merging with the long black line of her gown. Hands reached towards her from the crowd, but she seemed oblivious of these gestures of comfort. She stood for a long moment beside her husband's body, staring at it. Then she lifted her face to the sky and let out a cry of anguish that turned my blood cold. It was like the cry of a wild beast rending the cold night air; if any still slept on the Palatine, surely it woke them. Fulvia tore at her hair, lifted her arms to heaven and threw herself across her husband's body. Her nephew and Sextus Cloelius made a fumbling attempt to restrain her, then stepped back in awe as she shrieked and beat her fists against the bier. She framed the corpse's face with trembling hands and pressed her face to her husband's, covering his cold lips with a kiss.

Around us the mob raged like churning water. I thought of what the tribune Sallust had said: No one controls such a mob; it takes on a will of its own. It can maim or kill a man without meaning to and for no purpose at all, crushing the life out of him or trampling him underfoot. I grabbed Eco and by some feat of will we managed to push our way back through the gate. The crowd that overflowed

the courtyard now filled the street as far as the eye could see. All up and down the block, houses were lit up as brightly as day with anxious-looking guards posted on the roofs. I pressed on, forcing a way through the crowd while Eco and his bodyguards struggled to keep up.

At last we passed beyond the edges of the crowd. I never slowed my gait until we rounded a corner and found ourselves on an empty, darkened street. I stopped to catch my breath, and Eco did the same. His hands were trembling. I realized that I was shaking, too.

Hearing only my own breath and the pulse in my temples, I didn't notice the approaching footsteps. But the bodyguards did. They stiffened and drew themselves around us. Men were coming up the darkened street, heading in the direction of Clodius's house. As they passed, their leader signalled for them to stop. He peered at us in the dim starlight. His face was in shadow, but I could see that he had curly hair and a prominent nose, and a strong physique beneath his cloak. After a moment he stepped away from his bodyguards and approached us.

'Do you come from Clodius's house?'

'Yes,' I said.

'Is it true, what they say?'

'What do they say?'

'That Clodius is dead.'

'It's true.'

The man sighed. It was a quiet, gentle sigh, very different from the raging laments we had just left

behind. 'Poor Publius! It's the end of him, then, for good or ill. All over.' He cocked his head. 'Don't I know you?'

'Do you?'

'I think so. Yes, I'm sure of it.'

'Can you see in the dark, citizen?'

'Well enough. And I never forget a voice.' He hummed to himself, then grunted. 'You're Meto's father, aren't you? And this is Meto's brother, Eco.'

'Yes.' I tried to get a better look at him. I could make out his rugged features – the strong brow, the flattened boxer's nose – but I still didn't recognize him.

'You and I met last year,' he said, 'briefly, when you came to visit Meto in Ravenna. I serve under Caesar, too.' He paused for a moment. When I gave no sign of remembering, he shrugged. 'Well, then, what's happening around the bend? That glow in the sky – not a house on fire?'

'No. Just a great many torches.'

'There's a big crowd gathered at the house?'

'Yes. They've come to see the body. His wife, Fulvia –'

'Fulvia?' He spoke the name with an odd intensity, as if it had a secret meaning for him.

'She grieves. You might be able to hear her from here.'

He sighed again, a deep, rich sigh. 'I suppose I should see for myself. Farewell, then, Gordianus. And you, Eco.' He rejoined his companions and moved swiftly on.

'Farewell —' I said, still unable to remember his name. I turned to Eco.

'As he said, Papa, we met him last year, at Caesar's winter headquarters up in Ravenna. A bit modest, the way he says, 'I serve under Caesar, too.' One of the general's top men, according to Meto. We were barely introduced. I'd forgotten about it myself. I'm surprised he remembers us. But then, the man's a politician, of course. He's been back in Rome for several months, running for office. I've seen him in the Forum, canvassing for votes. You must have seen him, too.'

'Have I? What's his name?'

'Marc Antony.'

# III

Over breakfast, Bethesda and Diana demanded to know everything. I tried to soften my description of Clodius's corpse in deference to their appetites, but they insisted on all the gruesome details. The wrangling of the politicians was of less interest to them, but they listened attentively to my impressions of the famous house and its furnishings, and they were especially curious about Clodia.

'Can it really be four years since the trial of Marcus Caelius?' Bethesda blew gently on a spoonful of hot farina.

'Almost.'

'And to think we haven't had a glimpse of Clodia in all that time.'

'Not surprising, really; we hardly move in the same exalted circles. But I don't think anyone's seen much of her. The trial took something out of her. She seemed a changed woman to me.'

'Really? It sounds like she made quite a show of inviting you into the very heart of her brother's grand house, as if she were doing you a great favour, making you feel privileged and special. She wants something.'

'Really, Bethesda, the woman was distraught.'

'Was she?'

'I told you, she could hardly keep from weeping.'

'To weep is one thing. To be distraught is another.'

'I don't follow you.'

'No?' Bethesda sat back from the table. 'Be careful of the farina, Diana. You'll burn your tongue.'

Diana nodded absently and gulped down a heaping spoonful.

'What do you mean, Bethesda? About Clodia?'

'Well, I have no doubt that she was very upset about her brother's death. We all know how close they were, or at least the way people talked about them. And such a bloody death, from the way you describe his body. Awful!' She stirred her farina. Little puffs of steam rose from the bowl.

'But?'

Diana cleared her throat. 'I think that what Mother is trying to say is –'

'Well, it's obvious, isn't it?' Bethesda looked at Diana and they nodded in unison. 'Her litter, her bodyguard –'

'And using the main entrance. Yes.' Diana pursed her lips sagely.

'What in Hades are the two of you talking about?'

'Well —' Bethesda tried another spoonful of farina and finally deemed it cool enough. 'From your description, it seems that there's the main entrance to the house, and also the secluded little side door that you took.'

'Yes . . .'

'And they both end up in the same place.'

'Yes, in the main foyer.'

'Well, I can't speak for Clodia, but if I were distraught, I should have no stomach for facing a huge crowd. I'd want to avoid that if I possibly could. And Clodia could have done so, quite easily, simply by entering through that side door. She could have avoided the crowd completely. Am I right? Her litter could have deposited her and Metella and her nephew Appius at the foot of the steps, and they could have gone up to the landing and into the house without anyone even knowing they'd arrived.'

'I suppose so . . .'

Diana picked up the thread from her mother. 'Instead, she went through the thick of the crowd in that huge litter — the one with the red and white stripes that everyone knows is hers — with a veritable army of big redheaded gladiators.'

Bethesda nodded. 'Where everyone would be sure to notice her arrival.'

'And talk about it long afterwards,' said Diana.

'What is your point?' I said, looking back and forth between them.

'Well, Papa, only that grief was not the only thing on Clodia's mind.'

'Exactly,' said Bethesda. 'Making an entrance – that was the point.'

'Oh, really!' I shook my head. 'If you'd been there, if you'd felt the mood of the place, the despair, the anguish –'

'All the better to heighten the drama,' said Bethesda. 'I don't doubt Clodia's grief. But you see, she must have considered the circumstances ahead of time. She realized that she wouldn't be allowed to appear publicly alongside her brother's body when it was shown to the crowd. That privilege was reserved for Fulvia.'

'So Clodia made an impression in the only way she could – by making a grand entrance,' said Diana.

'I see. You're saying she wanted to upstage her sister-in-law.'

'Not at all.' Bethesda frowned at my obtuseness. 'She only wanted what was hers.'

'To claim the portion of public grief that she feels belongs to her,' Diana explained.

'I see,' I said, not at all certain that I did. 'Well, speaking of doing things for show, of course I was quite struck by the inconsistency of Fulvia's behaviour –'

'Inconsistency?' said Bethesda.

'What do you mean, Papa?'

'I told you how stiff she was in the inner room, how she showed virtually no emotion, even when she put Clodia in her place about cleaning the

body. And then her hysterical shrieking in front of all those people when they showed Clodius to the mob!'

'But where's the inconsistency, Papa?' Diana looked at me curiously, as did her mother. I almost thought they were making fun of me.

'It seems to me that a woman should grieve in private and show restraint in public, not the other way around,' I said.

Bethesda and Diana looked at each other and wrinkled their brows. 'What would be the point of that?' said Bethesda.

'It's not a matter of having a point –'

'Husband!' Bethesda was shaking her head. 'Of course Fulvia didn't want to show her grief to you, a stranger, in the intimacy of her home, and especially not in front of Clodia. She comported herself with dignity – to make her mother proud, to show her little daughter how to be strong, to confound her weeping sister-in-law. And for the sake of her husband as well, since you Romans believe that the lemur of a dead man may linger for a while in the vicinity of its vacant corpse. So for you she put on her most dignified manner. But the crowd outside, that was a different matter. Fulvia wanted to stir them up, as much as she could, just as her husband had stirred them up so many times before. She could hardly do that by standing next to his bloody corpse and behaving like a statue, could she?'

'Then you think her display of public grief was calculated and disingenuous?'

'Calculated, most certainly. But disingenuous? Not at all. She simply chose the most suitable time and place to release the grief that was inside her all along.'

I shook my head. 'I'm not sure you're making sense. I'd rather try to figure out what sort of schemes the politicians in the anteroom were up to.'

Bethesda and Diana shrugged in unison to show that the subject bored them. 'Politicians are usually too obvious to be very interesting,' said Bethesda. 'Of course, it may be that I've misjudged Clodia and Fulvia. I wasn't there to see with my own eyes. I can only go by what you've told me.'

'Am I such an unreliable observer?' I raised an eyebrow. 'Men do call me the Finder, you know.'

'The thing is,' said Bethesda, oblivious to my point, 'that one never quite knows what some people are really up to. Especially with a woman as complicated as Clodia, or Fulvia. How does one ever know what she really thinks, really feels? What she really wants?' Bethesda exchanged a thoughtful look with Diana. Simultaneously they lifted spoonfuls of porridge to their lips, then abruptly lowered them as Belbo came into the room.

For many years the straw-haired giant of a fellow had been my private bodyguard, and had saved my life on more than one occasion. He was still as strong as an ox, but as lumbering as one, too; as loyal as a hound, but no longer fit for the chase. I

still entrusted my life to him on a daily basis – I let him shave my neck – but I couldn't rely on him to protect me from daggers in the Forum. What does one do with a loyal bodyguard who has outlasted his usefulness? Belbo could read only a little and do only the most rudimentary sums. He had no special skills at carpentry or gardening. Aside from performing an occasional feat of prodigious strength – toting a heavy sack of grain or lifting a massive wardrobe single-handed – he served me well enough as a doorkeeper, a job which chiefly required him to sit in a warm patch of sunlight in the atrium for most of the day. Lethargy suited his bovine nature and enhanced that equable temperament which strangers often mistook for stupidity. Belbo's wits might be slow, but they were not dim. It was his way to smile at a joke after everyone else finished laughing. He seldom grew angry, even when provoked. He even more rarely showed fear. As he stepped into the dining room, however, his oxlike eyes were wide with alarm.

'Belbo, what's wrong?'

'Out in the street, master. In front of the house. I think you'd better come see.'

As soon as I stepped into the garden at the centre of the house, I heard the noise carried on the open air – an indistinct mingling of cries and stamping feet. It sounded like a riot. I hurried through the garden and the atrium to the foyer at the front of the house. Belbo pulled open the little sliding panel in the door and stepped aside to let me press my eye to the peephole.

I saw a blur of movement from right to left – a mob rushing by, all dressed in black. I heard the roar of the crowd but couldn't make sense of it.

'Who are they, Belbo? What's going on?' I stared through the peephole. Suddenly a figure broke away from the mob and ran directly up to the door. He put his mouth to the peephole and began screaming, 'We'll burn it down! Burn it down!' He banged his fists against the door. I jerked back, my heart pounding. Through the peephole I saw the man step back, his face frozen in a maniacal grin. Even with the door between us, I shivered. Then, just as suddenly as he had rushed up, the man turned and rushed away, disappearing into the mob.

'What in Hades is going on?'

'I wouldn't advise going outside to find out,' said Belbo earnestly.

I thought for a moment. 'We'll go up on the roof to have a look. Fetch the ladder, Belbo, and bring it to the garden!'

A few moments later I found myself settled precariously on the slanting tiles along the front roof of my house. From here I had a view not only of the street below, but of the Forum beyond, with its temples and public spaces clustered close together in the valley between the Palatine and Capitoline Hills. Just below me the mob continued to surge through the street. Some of them ran straight on. Others broke away and took the short-cut called the Ramp that leads down to the Forum and empties into a narrow space between the House of the Vestals and the Temple of Castor

and Pollux. Some of the rioters carried sticks and clubs. A few brandished daggers, in open defiance of the law that forbids such weapons within the city. And though it was well after daybreak, a few carried torches. The flames whipped and snapped through the cold air.

The mob eventually thinned, but was soon followed by an even larger, slower group of mourners. If it was a funeral procession, it was certainly a strange one. Where were the mummers doing parodies of the dead man to lighten the mood? Where were the wax effigies of the dead man's ancestors, taken from their places of honour in his foyer to witness his passage to join them on the other side? Where were the hired mourners, weeping and clawing at their tangled hair – indeed, where was there a woman to be seen?

But there was music – mournful horns, wailing flutes and shivering tambourines, making a noise that set my teeth on edge. And there was a body – the corpse of Clodius carried upon a wooden bier festooned with black cloth. He was still naked except for a loincloth, and still filthy and smeared with dried blood.

Some of the mourners broke away to take the Ramp down to the Forum, but the main procession with the corpse of Clodius kept to the street in front of my house, which runs along the crest of the Palatine. They were making a slow, deliberate circuit of the hill, I realized, passing by the houses of the rich and powerful in a sombre procession, letting his friends and foes alike take a final look at

49

the man who had caused so much disruption to the orderly life of the Republic.

A few houses farther on, their course would take them directly past the front door of the man who had been Clodius's most implacable enemy in the Senate and the courts. Clodius had made himself the champion of the lowly, of foot soldiers and freedmen; always against him there had been Cicero, the loyal spokesman for those who proudly called themselves the Best People. The funeral procession seemed orderly, but in the mob that preceded it I had seen men with daggers and torches. I held my breath, wondering what might happen when they reached Cicero's house.

When I looked towards Cicero's house, I saw that I was not alone in my apprehension. Intervening houses and trees blocked my view of the street, but of the house itself I could clearly see some shuttered windows in the upper storey and a portion of the roof. Two figures were perched there, as Belbo and I were perched on my roof, peering over the edge at the street below. By the glare of the slanting morning light I instantly discerned the thick-necked, grim-jawed silhouette of Cicero. Crouching close behind him, reaching out to make sure that his master did not lean too far, was the slighter silhouette of Cicero's lifelong secretary, Tiro. They were still for a long moment, as if frozen by the cold morning air; then Cicero reached back for Tiro's shoulder. They put their heads together and anxiously conferred. From the way they drew back and craned their necks, trying to see but not be

seen, I gathered that the bizarre funeral cortege was passing directly below them. The dirge of the horns and flutes became shriller, the shivering of the distant tambourines more manic. Intent on the spectacle below, Cicero and Tiro took no notice of my scrutiny.

The procession apparently came to a halt before Cicero's house. Cicero bobbed his head forwards and back, like a nervous quail. I could imagine his dilemma – he was afraid to take his eyes away from the mob, and yet the merest glimpse of him might incite them to violence. Horns blared, flutes trilled, tambourines rattled.

At last the cortege moved on and the dirge faded away.

Cicero and Tiro sat back, sighing with relief. Then Cicero winced and gripped his stomach. As the heel to Achilles, so the belly to Cicero; his breakfast had turned against him. He rose, still crouching, and moved crablike up the roof with Tiro following behind. Tiro turned his head and saw us watching. He touched his master's sleeve and spoke. Cicero paused and turned his face towards us. I raised my hand in neighbourly greeting. Tiro waved back. Cicero stayed motionless for a moment, then clutched his stomach and hurried on, disappearing over the edge of the roof.

Meanwhile, below us in the street, more men in black kept running by in parties of two and three, stragglers rushing to catch up. Most of them took the Ramp. I tried to see where they were all headed, but my view of the Forum was mostly

of beaten copper roofs gleaming in the sunlight; every now and again I could catch a glimpse of tiny figures moving in the spaces between. They all seemed to be gathering before the Senate House at the far end of the Forum, where the sheer rock face of the Capitoline Hill forms a natural wall.

From my position, I had a clear view of the front of the Senate House. Broad marble steps led up to the massive bronze doors, which were closed. I could see only a tiny portion of the open space in front of the Senate House, but this included a clear view of the Rostra, the raised platform from which speakers address the populace. Already the space between the Rostra and the Senate House was filled with a crush of black-clad mourners.

The funeral dirge, which for a while had faded out of hearing, now returned, rising from the Forum. Echoing up from the valley, the harsh music sounded more confused and discordant than ever. Suddenly it was overwhelmed by a great shout from the crowd. The body of Clodius had arrived. A little later I saw the bier as it was carried onto the Rostra and propped up for the crowd to see, just as it had been displayed on the steps of Clodius's house the night before. What a tiny thing it looked, and yet even at such a distance there was still something shocking about that glimpse of naked flesh amid so many black-clad mourners and so much cold, chiselled stone.

A speaker mounted the Rostra. I could hear only faint echoes of his voice. As he paced back and forth across the Rostra, waving his arms, pointing to the

corpse of Clodius and raising his fists, the crowd broke into a thunderous roar. From that point on the noise of the mob rose and fell but never quite subsided.

'What's going on?'

I turned my head, startled. 'Diana, go back down the ladder at once!'

'Why? Is it dangerous up here?'

'Very. Your mother would have a fit.'

'Oh, I hardly think so. She held the ladder for me. But I think she's afraid to come up herself.'

'As well she might be.'

'And how about you, Papa? I should think an old fellow like you would be more likely to lose his balance than I would be.'

'How did I ever come to have such an impertinent child?'

'I'm not impertinent. Just curious. It's like the siege of Troy, isn't it?'

'What?'

'Like Jupiter up on Mount Ida, watching the battlefield down below. They're all so tiny. It makes one feel . . . godlike.'

'Does it? Jupiter could send down thunderbolts or messengers with wings. And he could hear what was being said. Having a view hardly makes me feel godlike. Quite the opposite. It makes me feel powerless, watching from a distance like this.'

'You could go down and join them.'

'Put myself at the mercy of that mob? There's no telling what they might do next −'

'Papa, look!'

Like a storm-churned flood, the crowd seemed suddenly to overflow the broad square in front of the Rostra, surging in wave after wave onto the steps and terraces of the surrounding temples and public buildings.

'Papa, look! The Senate House!'

The broad steps were inundated by the mob, which rose like a black flood tide to lash against the tall bronze doors. Bolted from within, they stood against the tide, but soon I began to hear a low, thudding, repetitive boom. It was hard to see exactly what was happening, but the mob seemed to be assaulting the doors of the Senate House with some sort of makeshift battering ram.

'Impossible,' I said. 'Incredible! What are they thinking of? What do they want?'

All at once the doors gave way. A moment later a cheer of triumph rose from the crowd. I looked back to the Rostra. The speaker was still ranting, striding back and forth and exhorting the mob with wild gestures, but the body of Clodius had disappeared. I frowned, puzzled, then caught sight of the naked body on its black-draped bier proceeding with odd, jerky movements towards the steps of the Senate House. It seemed that the mob was passing the bier from hand to hand above their heads. I suddenly had a vision of the mob as a colony of insects, and the corpse of Clodius as their queen. I shivered and felt an intimation of vertigo. With one hand I reached for Diana, putting my arm around her shoulder, and with the other I held more firmly to the tiles of the roof.

The bier reached the foot of the Senate House steps, stalled for a moment, then tilted upward and began to ascend. The mass of the crowd, able to see the body again, produced another loud roar of mingled triumph and despair. The bier reached the top of the steps and was propped upright. A man stepped up beside it, waving a burning torch. He seemed to be giving a speech, though it was hard to imagine that the roaring crowd could hear him any better than I could. Even at such a distance, I was almost certain that the speaker was Sextus Cloelius, Clodius's wild-eyed lieutenant, the man who had spoken of riots and revenge against Milo the previous night.

After a while, still waving his torch, he turned and entered the Senate House. The bier was carried in after him.

'What can they possibly be thinking?' I said.

' "Burn it down," ' said Belbo. 'Wasn't that what the fellow said, the one who pounded on the door?'

I shook my head. 'He was raving. Besides, he must have meant burning down Milo's house, or maybe Cicero's. He couldn't possibly have meant . . .'

Sometimes, uttering the impossible can suddenly make it seem quite possible after all. I stared at the roof of the Senate House, as if by concentrating I could see through it to perceive what Sextus Cloelius was up to. Surely not –

And then I saw the first wisps of smoke, streaming wraithlike from the shuttered windows set high along the walls of the Senate House.

'Papa —'

'Yes, Diana, I see. They must be cremating the body, inside the building. The idiots! If they aren't careful —'

'They hardly look to me like the sort to be careful,' said Belbo, tilting his head earnestly.

A little later the first flickering tongues of flame appeared at one of the windows. One after another the shutters caught fire. Heavy black smoke began to pour from the windows, then from the open doorway. Sextus Cloelius ran out of the building, waving his torch triumphantly over his head. The crowd fell silent for a moment, probably as awed as I was by the enormity of what had happened. Then they released a roar that must have been heard all the way to Bovillae.

It was heard in Cicero's house, at least. From the corner of my eye I saw a movement on his roof. He had returned, along with Tiro. The two of them stood upright, no longer crouching, and watched the spectacle in the Forum below. Tiro clutched his face. He was weeping. How many happy hours had he spent in that building, copying down his master's speeches in the shorthand he invented, ordering his army of clerks about, paying witness to the great career he had done so much to foster? Slaves can be very sentimental.

Cicero did not weep. He crossed his arms, set his jaw in a hard line and stared grimly at the orgy of destruction below.

'There!' said Diana. She was pointing at Cicero. 'There! That's what Jupiter must have looked like,

gazing down at Troy.'

Knowing Cicero far better than my daughter did, and certain that there was nothing remotely godlike about him, I was about to correct her when Belbo interrupted.

'You're right,' he said. 'The very image!'

Their shared certainty forced me to take another look. Diana was right. I had to concede it. As Cicero looked at that moment, watching the destruction of the Senate House by Clodius's mob, so great Jupiter might have looked when he brooded on Mount Ida and watched the mad clash of mortals below.

# IV

Whipped by the cold wind, the blazes shot higher and higher until the whole Senate House was engulfed by flames. The mob danced on the marble steps, hooting and laughing while they dodged cascades of cinders and ash.

The fire began to spread, first to the complex of senatorial offices to the south of the Senate House. The threat of the mob had already emptied most of the buildings, but after the flames started a few panic-stricken clerks came rushing out, carrying armloads of documents. Some tripped and fell, others zigzagged madly, dodging the taunting mob, dropping their burdens. Wax tablets scattered like tumbling dice. Scrolls unfurled and streamed like pennants in the breeze.

Then the wind changed. The flames spread west of the Senate House, to the Porcian Basilica. One of the great buildings of the Forum, it was a hundred

and thirty years old, the first basilica ever built. Its distinguishing features – the long nave terminating in an apse with colonnaded aisles on either side – are now duplicated in buildings all over the empire. Many of the wealthiest bankers in the world kept their headquarters in the Porcian Basilica. It took hardly an hour for the fire to reduce its venerable majesty to a smouldering pile of rubble.

It was the bankers, I learned later, desperate to salvage what remained of their records, who finally organized a large contingent of freedmen and slaves to battle the flames. Acting out of pure selfishness, they may have saved a large part of Rome from going up in smoke. The firefighters formed long, snaking lines across the Forum and through the cattle market all the way to the banks of the Tiber, where they filled buckets with water and passed them up to pour on the flames, then passed the empty buckets back again. From time to time a few rowdies broke away from the mourners' frenzied revelry to harass the firefighters, pelting them with stones and spitting on them. Scuffles broke out. A cordon of bodyguards, also sent by the bankers, arrived to protect the bucket-passers.

It was a mad day. Rome seemed racked with fever, delirious. With Clodius consigned to the purifying flames, and the Senate House along with him, his mourners carried on their unconventional funeral celebration. Could they have planned such madness in advance, or did they make it up as they went along, inspired by the dancing flames and the billowing smoke, invigorated by the charred tang in

the air? At mid-afternoon, they held a funeral feast. Before the smouldering Senate House they set up tables, covered the tables with black cloths and spread out a banquet.

While the firefighters continued their frantic efforts, the Clodians drank and ate in honour of their dead leader. The poor and hungry of the city came out to join them, at first meekly and then, seeing that they were welcome, in jubilation. Vast quantities of food arrived – great urns full of blood-black sausages, pots of black beans, loaves of black bread, all suitably black for a feast to honour the dead, washed down with blood-red wine. Meanwhile the confused, frightened, curious citizens of Rome – those who lacked the safe vantage of a Palatine rooftop to watch what was going on – skirted the edges of the Forum, cautiously peeking around corners and peering over walls, gawking variously in outrage, delight, disbelief and consternation.

I spent much of the day on my roof, watching. So did Cicero. He would disappear for a while, then reappear with various visitors, many of them senators, as I could tell from the purple border on their togas. They would take in the view, shake their heads in disgust or gasp in horror, then disappear again, talking and gesticulating. There seemed to be some sort of all-day meeting going on in Cicero's house.

Eco came by to see me for a while. I told him he was mad to venture out on such a day. He had stayed clear of the Forum, and though he had heard

the rumour that the Senate House was destroyed, he had thought it was only that, a rumour. I took him up on the roof so he could see the spectacle for himself. He headed back to Menenia and the twins soon after.

Even Bethesda overcame her distrust of the ladder and ventured up on the roof for a while to see what all the fuss was about. I teased her that the sight of so much rioting must have made her homesick for Alexandria, seeing that the Alexandrians were so famous for rioting. She didn't laugh at the joke. Neither did I.

The feasting and the firefighting down in the Forum continued until well after nightfall. Towards evening Belbo brought me a bowl of hot soup and climbed back down. A little later Diana joined me with her own steaming bowl. As we sat alone on the roof, the sky darkened to deeper and deeper shades of blue verging into black. In every season, twilight is the most beautiful hour in Rome. The stars began to show in the firmament, glittering like bits of frost. There was even a kind of prettiness about the flickering lights down in the Forum, now that darkness hid the ugliness of charred wood and blackened stone. The fires had largely died down, but the deepening gloom revealed smouldering patches of flame in the ruins of the Porcian Basilica and the senatorial office buildings.

Diana finished her soup. She put down the bowl and pulled a blanket over her shoulders. 'How did Clodius die, Papa?'

'From his wounds, I should think. Surely you don't want me to describe them again.'

'No. I mean, how did it happen?'

'I don't know, really. I'm not sure that anyone does, except whoever killed him, of course. There seemed to be quite a bit of confusion about it at his house last night. Clodia said there was a skirmish of some sort down on the Appian Way, near a place called Bovillae, where Clodius had a villa. Clodius and some of his men had an altercation with Milo and some of his men. Clodius got the worst of it.'

'But why did they fight?'

'Clodius and Milo have been enemies for a long time, Diana.'

'Why?'

'Why are two men usually enemies? Because they want the same thing.'

'A woman?'

'In some cases. Or a boy. Or a father's love. Or an inheritance, or a piece of land. In this case, Clodius and Milo both wanted power.'

'And they couldn't both have it?'

'Apparently not. Sometimes when two ambitious men are enemies, one of them has to die if the other's to go on living. At least that's how it usually works out, sooner or later. It's what we Romans call politics.' I smiled without mirth.

'You hate politics, don't you, Papa?'

'I like to say I do.'

'But I thought –'

'I'm like the man who says he hates the theatre but never misses a play. He claims it's his friends

who drag him along. Even so, he can quote every line of Terence.'

'So you secretly love politics.'

'No! But it's in the air I breathe, and I don't care to stop breathing. Put it another way: politics is the Roman disease, and I'm no more immune than anyone else.'

She frowned. 'What do you mean?'

'Certain diseases are peculiar to certain tribes and nations. Your brother Meto says that up in Gaul there's a tribe in which every person is born deaf in one ear. You've heard your mother say that there's a village on the Nile where everyone breaks out in hives at the approach of a cat. And I read once that Spaniards suffer a form of tooth rot that can only be cured by drinking their own urine.'

'Papa!' Diana wrinkled her nose.

'Not all diseases are grossly physical. The Athenians are addicted to art; without it they become irritable and constipated. Alexandrians live for commerce; they'd sell a virgin's sigh if they could find a way to bottle it. I hear the Parthians suffer from hippomania; whole clans go to war with each other to lay claim to a fine breeding stud.

'Well, politics is the Roman disease. Everyone in the city catches it sooner or later, even women nowadays. No one ever recovers. It's an insidious sickness, with perverse symptoms. Different people suffer in different ways, and some don't suffer at all; it cripples one man, kills another, and makes yet another man grow fat and strong.'

'So is it a good thing or a bad thing?'

'Just a Roman thing, Diana. And whether it's good or bad for Rome, I can't say. It's made us the rulers of the world. But I begin to wonder if it won't be the end of us.' I stared down at the Forum, no longer like Jupiter watching the plain of Ida – more now like Pluto surveying the fiery pits of Hades.

Diana leaned back. Her jet-black hair made a pillow for her head as she studied the sky above. Her dark eyes reflected glimmers of cold starlight.

'I like it when you talk to me like this, Papa.'

'Do you?'

'This is how you used to talk to Meto sometimes, before he left for the army.'

'I suppose.'

She turned on her side, propped her head on her hand and looked at me earnestly. 'Is something bad going to happen, Papa?'

'I imagine the people around Clodius think something bad has already happened.'

'To us, I mean. Are we in danger, Papa?'

'Not if I can help it.' I ran my hand over the side of her face and stroked her hair.

'But things are getting worse, aren't they? That's what you and Eco always say to each other, when you talk politics. And now it's worse than ever – Clodius dead, the Senate House burned down. Is something awful about to happen?'

'Something awful is always about to happen – to someone, somewhere. The only escape is to make a friend of Fortune, if she'll have you, and run the other way whenever you see a politician coming.'

'I'm serious, Papa. Are things about to – I don't know, about to fall apart? For us, for everybody?'

How could I answer her? Out of the past I suddenly remembered a scene from the Forum when I was a young man, after Sulla won the civil war: rows and rows of heads mounted on pikes, the enemies of the dictator paying gaping witness to his triumph. Afterwards, people swore that such a thing would never happen again. That was thirty years ago.

'I can't see the future, Diana.'

'But you know the past, enough to understand about Clodius and Milo. Explain it to me. If I could understand what's happening, perhaps it wouldn't worry me so much.'

'Very well, Diana. Clodius and Milo: where to begin? Well, we shall have to start with Caesar and Pompey. You know who they are.'

'Of course. Gaius Julius Caesar is the man Meto serves, up in Gaul. The greatest general since Alexander the Great.'

I smiled. 'So Meto says. Pompey might not agree.'

'Pompey cleared the seas of the pirates and conquered the East.'

I nodded. 'And surnamed himself Magnus – 'the Great,' just like Alexander. As I said a moment ago, sometimes when two men want the same thing –'

'You mean Caesar and Pompey both want to be Alexander the Great?'

'Yes, exactly, since you put it like that. And there can't be two at once. The world is not big enough.'

65

'But don't Caesar and Pompey both serve the Senate and the people of Rome?'

'Nominally, yes. They receive their commands and permission to raise their armies from the Senate, and between them they've conquered the world in the name of the Senate. But sometimes servants outgrow their master. Caesar and Pompey have both grown too big for the Senate. So far, the salvation of the Republic has been that the two generals have held one another in check – neither can grow too powerful for fear of riling the other. And there have been other factors figured into the balance.'

'Pompey married Caesar's daughter, didn't he?'

'Yes: Julia. Apparently it was a genuine love match. That marriage link smoothed over the two men's differences. Family connections mean everything, especially to patricians like Caesar. And another factor: the two rivals used to be three. There was Marcus Crassus.'

'The man who owned Meto when he was a little boy. He was the one who put down Spartacus and the slave rebellion.'

'Yes, but despite that victory Crassus was never much of a general. But he did manage to make himself the richest man in the world. Crassus, Caesar and Pompey formed what they called the Triumvirate, sharing power between the three of them. That seemed to work for a while. A table with three legs is steady.'

'But a table with just two legs . . .'

'Sooner or later has to fall. Last spring Crassus was

killed in Parthia, at the eastern end of the world, trying to prove his military prowess once and for all by conquering some of the same lands that Alexander conquered. But the Parthian cavalry defeated him. They killed his son, along with forty thousand Roman soldiers. They chopped off Crassus's head and used it for a stage prop to amuse their king. Exit Crassus.'

'Leaving the Triumvirate with only two feet.'

'But at least those two feet were still bound together by the marriage link between Pompey and Caesar – until Julia died in childbirth. Now nothing holds the two of them together, and there's nothing to keep them from coming to blows sooner or later. Rome holds its breath, like a hedgehog watching two eagles circle overhead, ready to battle it out to see which of them gets to eat the hedgehog.'

'I think you must be the first man ever to compare Rome to a hedgehog, Papa!' Diana studied the stars. 'Is there a hedgehog constellation?'

'I don't think so.'

'So you've told me all this about Caesar and Pompey the Great. But what about Clodius and Milo?'

'Caesar and Pompey are eagles up in the sky, soaring over mountains and seas. Down here on solid ground, it's Clodius and Milo who've been fighting over Rome itself – the city, not the empire. They fought with gangs instead of armies. Instead of mountain ranges and seas, they squabbled over the seven hills and the markets on the riverfront.

Instead of battles, they staged riots in the Forum. Instead of campaigning against barbarians, they campaigned against each other for office – bullying and bribing voters, pandering to their constituents, postponing elections, pulling every possible trick to get the better of each other.

'Milo represents those who call themselves the Best People – old families, old money, the most conservative elements in the Senate. The kind of people Pompey likes to associate with, so it's not surprising that from time to time Milo has more or less acted as Pompey's henchman here in Rome.

'Clodius is – was – a radical, despite his patrician blood. He appealed to the mob. When he was in the military, he staged an uprising of common soldiers against their commander, who happened to be his own brother-in-law. The year the plebeians elected him tribune, he promised to set up a free grain dole, and he did, by annexing Cyprus to finance the scheme. Clodius was always out to better the lot of common foot soldiers and farmers and the city poor, and in return they were always there to vote when he needed them, sometimes with ballots, more often with fists. The rabble loved him. And the Best People hated him.

'From time to time Clodius found himself on the same side as Caesar, another patrician with populist leanings, and so they assisted each other, mostly behind the scenes. People came to think of them as allies – Caesar and Clodius against Pompey and Milo. The two great men moving all over the

world, each allied with a lesser man with a gang at his disposal here in Rome to fight for control of the capital.'

'Like the heroes of the Iliad,' said Diana. 'The gods allied with mortals: one god looking out for Hector, another god on the side of Achilles. And Hector and Achilles each having an army.'

'All these references to Troy – I take it you've been reading Homer?'

'I need to practise my Greek. Mother helps me.'

'Your mother can't read.'

'Yes, but she speaks Greek. She helps me with pronunciation.'

'I see. Well, a little literary allusion goes a long way. But if I can compare Rome to a hedgehog, I suppose we can also compare our local gang leaders to Hector and Achilles. It's apt, in a way. The gods withdrew their favour from Hector in the end, didn't they? So fell the House of Priam, and Troy along with it. The gods can be fickle, like any ally; it's all politics in the end. Allegiances shift like sand underfoot. Loyalty slips through your fingers.'

'And a man dies.'

'Yes. Then more men die, usually.'

'And buildings burn.'

We watched the Forum in silence for a while.

'Caesar and Pompey, Clodius and Milo,' said Diana. 'Still, how did it come to this, Papa? The Senate House burned to the ground . . .'

I sighed. The young think there must always be a simple answer. 'You know how the elections are held, Diana, or at least how they're supposed to be

held: citizens gather on the Field of Mars to cast their ballots for the various magistrates who run the government. There are different elections, on different days, for the various magistrates. Most of the elections are held in the summer; good weather for gathering out of doors. The voters elect two consuls, who have the highest power. After the consuls come the praetors, and then the aediles and the quaestors and so on, all with different powers and duties.

'The old year ends. At the beginning of Januarius the elected magistrates take office. They serve for one year and then step down or move on to govern foreign provinces. So it's been, for hundreds and hundreds of years, going all the way back to the fall of the kings and the founding of the Republic.

'That's how it's supposed to work, anyway. But today Rome is a city without magistrates. We're halfway through the month of Januarius, and still there are no magistrates to run the state.'

'What about the tribunes?' said Diana.

I hummed, stalling while I thought of the answer. The Roman constitution is so damnably complicated! 'Technically, tribunes are not magistrates. The tribunate was established long ago when only patricians could be magistrates, and the plebeians demanded to have their own representatives. Nowadays the magistracies are open to both classes, but tribunes must still be plebeians. There are ten of them each year, chosen by a special assembly of plebeians only. They still tend to represent the

interests of the weak against the strong, the poor against the rich. Clodius himself served a term as tribune – that was the year he managed to get Cicero sent into exile and established the grain dole.'

'But Clodius and his sister are patricians.'

'Ah, but Clodius fixed that; he had himself adopted by a plebeian practically young enough to be his son just so that he could run for the tribunate. Even his enemies had to admire his ingenuity! It's a natural office for a rabble-rouser. I dare say some of our more ambitious tribunes are down in the Forum right now, haranguing that mob. Anyway, the selection of tribunes was carried out as usual last year, with no disruptions. But not so with the regular magistrates.'

'What happened?'

'Last year Milo chose to run for consul. Clodius ran for praetor. If each had won, they'd have cancelled each other out. Milo would have vetoed Clodius's radical schemes, and Clodius would have undermined Milo's efforts on behalf of the Best People.'

'Each would have been a thorn in the side of the other,' said Diana.

'Exactly. So each was determined to keep the other from winning. Yet each was a formidable candidate, likely to win his office. So every time an election was scheduled, something occurred to postpone it. An augur would read the signs in the sky and say the omens were bad – election cancelled. A new day would be chosen, but on the eve of the election someone in the Senate would

come up with an obscure point of calendar law to show that no voting could be held on that day after all. Much debate – a new date is finally chosen. The day arrives – riots break out on the Field of Mars. And on and on. In previous years' elections there have been gross irregularities – voters bribed or intimidated, lawsuits used to keep men from running for office or from serving out their terms, all sorts of manoeuvres to tilt and skew the process. But there's never been a year like this last one – pure chaos. A republic that can't even manage to hold elections is a very sick republic.'

As if to punctuate that sentiment, a smouldering pocket of flame down in the Porcian Basilica suddenly flared up. The fire must have eaten through to a cache of lamp oil and ignited it. The concussion reached the Palatine a moment later, like the muffled boom of a drumbeat. By the glare of the towering flames I saw the tiny figures of startled firefighters scattering. A cheer went up from the feasting Clodians. The snakelike line of bucket-carriers altered course to douse the new flare-up, which spat back at them with steam and tongues of flame. In the gathering darkness the struggle between the fire and those who fought it began to take on fantastical shapes.

'So it's no surprise,' I went on, 'if Milo should have killed Clodius. The only thing less surprising would have been if Clodius had killed Milo.'

Diana nodded thoughtfully.

A little while later Bethesda called up from the garden. It was nearly time for dinner. Diana went

down to help her mother. She seemed satisfied with the answers I had given her, though I was quite aware that I had not answered her most important questions.

Are we in danger, Papa?

Is something awful about to happen?

The fiery explosion down in the Forum seemed to have ignited a fresh burst of excitement among the Clodians. They finished their feast. Speakers mounted the Rostra again. Chants echoed up from the mob.

A strange ceremony began. Men marched in single file up to the smouldering ruins of the Senate House, then descended the blackened steps holding fiery torches aloft. After a while I realized what was happening: they were lighting their torches from the same purifying fire that had consumed Clodius's remains. Out of piety and devotion, they would take it home with them, to add to their own hearth fires. Or so I thought, until I saw that the mob had another use in mind for the sacred fire.

From the steps of the Senate House the torch-bearers headed towards the Palatine. It was easy to follow their progress; they moved like creeping rivers of flame between the temples and across the paved squares. They returned by the ways they had come, some heading up the Ramp, others disappearing from my sight around the edge of the hill, heading for the paths that would take them up the western flank of the Palatine. The torchlight in that direction made such a glow that over on Cicero's roof I could see the figures of Cicero and

Tiro in silhouette, their backs turned towards me as they put their heads together.

Those who ascended the Ramp turned west, away from my house, and ran in the direction of Cicero's house. I held my breath. I saw Cicero's silhouette stiffen. But the torchbearers ran on. Following the street, making a circumference of the crest of the hill, they would meet up with the rest of the mob at some point on the farther side.

Who had a house in that vicinity?

Milo.

With the same cleansing fire that had turned the bloody remains of Clodius to ash, the mob intended to burn down Milo's house, and Milo with it, if he had dared to return to the city.

Diana called to me from below. 'Papa! Mother says it's time to eat.'

'Yes, Diana. In a moment.'

Milo's house was far away, measuring by a stone's throw; not far at all, measuring by the speed of flames riding a cold breeze to jump from roof to roof. If the mob set fire to Milo's house, the blaze could easily spread all over the Palatine . . .

The safest course might be to take the family to Eco's house over on the Esquiline. But what would happen then if my house did catch fire? Who would fight the flames? And what reason was there to think that we could cross the Subura and reach Eco's house in safety on such a night, with such a mob on the loose?

'Papa, are you coming down? Do you see something?'

A few stragglers came running up the Ramp. Their torches crackled in the air like flapping pennants as they took the sharp turn towards Cicero's house and beyond.

'I'm coming,' I said. I took a last look in the direction of Milo's house. I seemed to hear sounds of conflict – clattering, shouting – but the echoes were confused and distant.

'Papa?'

I turned and stepped onto the top rung of the ladder.

It was a sombre meal. I tasted nothing. Afterwards, when Diana and Bethesda had retired for the night, I stole up to the roof again. I looked in the direction of Milo's house but saw no sign of flames. Still, when I was ready to come down, I called for Belbo to take my place. We took turns through the night, one fitfully dozing beneath a mound of blankets on a couch in the garden, one up on the roof watching the skyline for any telltale orange glow. But when it finally came, the glow was in the opposite direction. The sun came up, and my house still stood.

I went up to the roof to have a final look. In the cold, hazy morning air, the Forum was like a smeared painting. I could hardly make out any details at all. But when I took a deep breath I caught the scent of burned wood and baked stone, the smell of what had once been the Senate House, which had become the crematorium of the rabble's fallen champion.

# V

'Driven off with arrows,' said Eco, stretching his arms over his head and yawning; he had slept as poorly as I had. The haze had lifted. The sun was shining in the garden. We sat on folding chairs across from the statue of Minerva, soaking up the tenuous midday warmth.

'That's the word in the street, anyway,' he continued. 'The Clodians didn't anticipate so much resistance. They expected to find Milo's house more or less deserted, I suppose. They figured they could break in, kill a few slaves, loot the place, then burn it to the ground. Instead, they were met by a troop of archers posted on the roof. Expert marksmen, apparently. The battle didn't last long. A few casualties, and the Clodians turned and ran.'

'I should think they'd have had enough by that point, anyway – burning the Senate House, stuffing themselves sick, listening to all those speeches.

You'd think they'd have been ready to call it a day.'

'You'd think so. But then, so the rumour goes, after they were repulsed from Milo's house, the mob left the Palatine, ran through the Subura and outside the city walls to the necropolis.'

'The city of the dead? At night? I should think they'd have been as frightened of lemures as of arrows.'

'They stayed clear of the sepulchres and burial pits. They headed for the sacred grove of Libitina.'

'Goddess of the dead.'

Eco nodded. 'They broke into her temple.'

'In the middle of the night? But why? Surely the duty of registering Clodius among the dead falls to his family, not to the mob. And they can't have been looking to rent requisites for the funeral – they'd already done the job of cremating Clodius, without paying much heed to religious niceties.'

'It had nothing to do with that, Papa. For some reason, it's in the Temple of Libitina that the fasces are kept when there are no consuls. You know, those bundles of sticks with an axe projecting, carried by the consuls at ceremonies and processions.'

'Their badges of office.'

'Exactly. With no consuls in office, the fasces have to be stored somewhere, and apparently the official place is the Temple of Libitina. So the mob breaks into the temple, seizes the fasces, and then runs back into the city to seek out the men running for consul against Milo.'

'Publius Hypsaeus and Quintus Scipio.'

'Yes. Both supported by Clodius, of course. The mob goes straight to Scipio's house and shouts for him to come out and claim the fasces.'

'Forgo the election entirely? Become consul by appointment of the mob?'

'That must have been the idea. But Scipio wouldn't show his face.'

'Probably scared out of his wits, like everybody else in Rome last night.'

'Then the same thing at the house of Hypsaeus. Shouts of acclamation, but the candidate kept his door shut. Then somebody in the mob got the idea to offer the fasces to Pompey.'

'Pompey! But he's not even eligible. He's still a proconsul, in charge of running Spain. He commands an army; legally he can't even enter the city walls. That's why he's living in his garden villa out on the Pincian Hill.'

'The mob couldn't be bothered by such technicalities. They ran out the Fontinalis Gate and up the Flaminian Way to Pompey's villa. They waved their torches and lifted up the fasces. Some shouted for Pompey to become consul. Others shouted for him to become dictator.'

I shook my head. 'What in Hades are they thinking of? Probably most of them weren't even born the last time Rome had a dictator.'

'There are plenty of people in the street who think it's time we had one again, to put an end to all this chaos.'

'They're mad. A dictatorship could only make things worse. Anyway, I can't believe the leaders

of the Clodian mob came up with such an idea. Clodius and Pompey detested each other, and Pompey's never been a friend of populist causes.'

'He's popular with the masses, even so. The mighty general, conqueror of the East. The Great One, Pompey Magnus.'

I shook my head. 'It still doesn't sound right. The same people who provoked the mob to burn down the Senate House are hardly likely to want a reactionary like Pompey to be their dictator. Maybe it wasn't the same mob at all. Or maybe the mob was taken over at some point by infiltrators from Pompey's camp.'

Eco raised an eyebrow. 'So you think the incident might have been staged by Pompey himself? Do you think he wants to be dictator, then?'

'More likely he wanted a chance to publicly turn down the call. There are plenty of senators, especially friends of Caesar, who think Pompey might be plotting to take over the state. How better to reassure them than to turn down a mob of citizens offering him the fasces?'

'He didn't exactly turn them down. Like Scipio and Hypsaeus, he didn't show his face.'

I moved my chair a bit to keep up with the sun. Where the shade fell the air had a bite. 'What word of Milo, then?'

'Some think he sneaked back into the city last night, and is holed up in his house. They say that's why the archers were in place to fight off the Clodians last night, because they're part of Milo's

personal bodyguard. But it seems just as likely that he left them to guard the place in his absence, especially if he had planned to murder Clodius. He knew the mob would react with violence, so he left his house fortified. Others say he's gone into voluntary exile, off to Massilia or somewhere.'

'That's possible,' I said. 'It's hard to see how he could possibly be elected consul now, if and when the state finally does manage to hold elections. And if Milo can't be elected consul, he's finished. He's spent a fortune putting on shows and games, trying to impress the voters. He doesn't have the resources of Caesar or Pompey, or even of Clodius. He wagered everything on his run for consul, and now he's surely lost all chance of winning. Exile might seem the only honourable solution to him.'

Another voice joined us, from the direction of the statue of Minerva. 'But then why did Milo kill Clodius, if it meant ruining his own future?'

I looked towards the statue. The virgin goddess towered above us, painted in such lifelike colours that she seemed almost to breathe. In one hand she clutched an upright spear, in the other a shield. An owl perched on her shoulder. A snake coiled at her feet. Under the midday sun her eyes were shaded by the visor of her crested helmet. For just an instant it seemed that Minerva herself had spoken. Then Diana stepped from beneath the shade of the portico and leaned against the pedestal. She put her hand on the sculpted snake.

'A good question, Diana,' I said. 'Why would Milo murder Clodius, if he knew it would unleash

such a fury? Why kill his enemy, if that meant killing his own chances of being elected?'

'Perhaps he miscalculated the reaction,' said Eco. 'Or perhaps he killed Clodius by accident. Or in self-defence.'

'Do you mind if I join you?' said Diana. Not waiting for an answer she pulled up a little folding chair and sat. She shivered in her cloak. 'It's cold out here!'

'Let the sunshine sink in for a bit,' I said.

'And then there's a third rumour,' Eco said. 'Some say that Milo is plotting revolution, and the murder of Clodius was just the first stroke. They say he's stockpiled weapons all over the city – there must have been an arsenal of arrows at his house to fend off the mob last night – and now he's crisscrossing the countryside, gathering troops to march on Rome.'

'Setting himself up as another Catilina?' I raised an eyebrow.

'Only this time the revolutionaries would have men like Cicero on their side, instead of against them.'

'Cicero is the last man to support anything remotely like a revolution, even if it was led by his good friend Milo. But who knows, nowadays? I suppose anything is possible.'

'Oh, and some other news, Papa. This must have happened yesterday, while the mob was rioting down in the Forum. A patrician committee of the Senate met somewhere here on the Palatine. They finally appointed an interrex.'

Diana looked puzzled.

'See if I can explain it accurately, Eco,' I said. 'In cases where there are no consuls – say, if both should die on a battlefield –'

'Or if a whole year should go by with no elections,' added Eco.

I nodded. 'In such a case, where there are no magistrates at the head of the state, the Senate appoints a temporary magistrate called an interrex to run the government and hold new elections. Each interrex serves for only five days, and then a new one is appointed; that way they don't get too settled in their office. So on and so forth until one of them manages to get new consuls elected. The Senate should have appointed an interrex at the beginning of the year, since there were no new consuls when the old consuls stepped down, but friends of Hypsaeus and Scipio managed to stall the appointment, thinking Milo had the upper hand and wanting to hold off the elections a while longer. No interrex, no elections. Well, perhaps now there'll finally be elections and an end to this crazy talk of solving the crisis with a dictator.'

'Not for another five days, at least,' said Eco. 'You missed one technical point, Papa: the first interrex can't hold the election. That can only be done by a subsequent interrex.'

'Not by the first interrex?' I said.

'During his five-day term he simply oversees a sort of cooling-off period.'

Diana nodded. 'It should take at least that long for the Senate House to cool off.'

The first interrex had no authority to hold elections, as Eco had astutely pointed out. But the supporters of Scipio and Hypsaeus, sensing that the candidacy of Milo was done for, decided the time for elections had arrived. Even as Eco and I talked, they surrounded the house of Marcus Lepidus, the newly appointed interrex, on the Palatine. Lepidus's wife, a lady of irreproachable character named Cornelia, was busy setting up ceremonial looms in the foyer, following an ancient custom pertaining to the wives of interrexes. (No one knows the origin of this custom; perhaps it has something to do with the interrex's role in weaving the threads of the Republic's future.)

When Lepidus appeared at his door, the leaders of the crowd demanded that he hold elections at once. He explained to them the impossibility of his doing so. They repeated their demands. Lepidus, a very old-fashioned patrician, told them exactly what they could do with such a radical notion, in terms to make their ears burn. Then he slammed the door on them.

The crowd did not erupt in a riot, but they did tighten their cordon around the house, preventing anyone from leaving or entering. They built fires in the street to keep themselves warm. To keep themselves amused they passed wineskins back and forth and shouted their electioneering chants, many of which were obscene poems about Fausta, Milo's

notoriously unfaithful wife. When the wine made the convoluted lyrics too complicated to recite, they resorted to a simpler chant: 'Vote – now! Vote – now!'

The interrex, ostensibly the head of the Roman state (at least for the next few days), was a prisoner in his own house.

Of course, every man is a prisoner in his own house when the streets are unsafe and atrocities take place even in broad daylight. What is a man to do? Lock himself away like a cowering deaf mute? Or step into the fray, looking for a means to put an end to the violence around him?

I had actually seen worse times in Rome – the civil war that led to Sulla's dictatorship, for a start – but I had been a young man then. I moved through those crises following the instinct of the young, which craves adventure ahead of survival. Looking back now, I'm shocked at how little regard I seemed to have had for the risks I took. I wasn't especially brave or foolish, merely young.

Now I was no longer young. I was far more aware and more respectful of death and injury, having seen and experienced so much of both in the intervening years. With every passing year the fabric of existence seemed more fragile to me. Life seemed more precious. I was less amenable to taking chances with my own life or with the lives of others.

Yet I found myself in times that called for taking chances. The idea of shutting myself away and

disclaiming all responsibility offered no satisfaction to me. Like many a man in Rome that winter, the tumult in the streets sparked a tumult in my own heart.

The Republic was very sick, perhaps sick unto death. Its wrenching spasms presented a spectacle I could hardly bear to look at, but I found it even harder to look away.

Some years before I had tried to remove myself completely from the arena of politics. Sick of deceit and false promises, of the pompous vanity of politicians and the gaping credulity of their followers, of the vindictive arrogance of victors and the squalid backbiting of the vanquished, I declared I would have no more of it. I moved to a farm up in Etruria, determined to turn my back on Rome.

That attempt did me no good. Instead, I became more deeply embroiled in political intrigue than I could ever have imagined. I was like a fretting navigator who goes to great lengths to avoid a whirlpool only to find that he's plotted a course straight into the vortex. The episode of Catilina and his riddle had made me recognize the inexorable nature of Fate.

Rome is my fate. And the fate of Rome was once again in the hands of her politicians.

So, in retrospect, I justify to myself my reaction when later that day, after Eco had gone home, I received a visitor. He was an old, old acquaintance.

Such an old acquaintance, in fact, that Belbo, secretly peering out the peephole in the front door,

didn't recognize the man. I had told Belbo not to let in anyone he didn't know by sight, so he dutifully fetched me from my study to have a look for myself.

I saw a man past middle age, of medium build with an open, handsome face and a touch of grey at his temples. He had the well-moulded lips, the straight nose and the curly hair of a Greek. He carried himself with an almost haughty self-importance, like a philosopher or a scholar. The boyish young slave I had first met thirty years ago had grown into a distinguished-looking man. It had been a long time since I had seen him so close at hand. Usually, when I saw him at all, it was at a distance, as I had seen him on the previous night, putting his head together with Cicero up on the roof of Cicero's house. He was very nearly the last person I had expected to call on me.

I shut the peephole and waved to Belbo to unbar the door.

'Tiro!' I exclaimed.

'Gordianus.' He bowed his head and smiled faintly. Behind him stood a troop of bodyguards. I counted at least ten men, which seemed a bit excessive if he had merely walked the short distance from Cicero's house. On the other hand, anyone leaving Cicero's house was likely to be a target of the Clodian mob. With a wave of his hand he ordered them to stay outside. Belbo shut the door behind him.

I showed him to my study and gestured for him to take a chair near the flaming brazier. Instead he walked slowly around the room, examining the

86

scrolls in their pigeonholes and the decorative painting of a garden on one wall.

'You've prospered, Gordianus.'

'In some ways.'

'I remember your old house over on the Esquiline. That big, rambling place with the garden all gone to seed.'

'It belongs to my son Eco now. His wife has restored the garden to immaculate condition.'

'Time passes so quickly! Who would have thought that you'd ever have a son old enough to run his own household?'

'He's made me a grandfather.'

'So one hears.'

'Does one?'

A smile quivered at the corner of his lips. 'You are still spoken of from time to time in Cicero's house, Gordianus.'

'But not too fondly, I imagine.'

'Oh, you might be surprised.'

'I certainly would be, if Cicero has anything good to say about me these days. I should have thought that the trial of Marcus Caelius was the last straw between us.'

Tiro shrugged. 'Cicero bears you no ill will. He's not a man to hold grudges.'

'Ha!'

Tiro inclined his head thoughtfully. 'Cicero can make himself a formidable enemy, to be sure, against those who make themselves his enemies by their spitefulness and deceit, or by the danger they pose to the Republic. But that has never been

the case with you, Gordianus. Cicero understands that you're a complicated man, not always easy for him to understand, but at heart an honourable and honest man. Honourable. Honest,' he repeated, stressing the words. 'Like Cicero himself. If the two of you have sometimes come into conflict, it's because you've seen things in different lights. Honourable men can't be expected always to agree.'

I sighed. Tiro was obviously as devoted to Cicero as ever. It would be useless to point out to him the flaws in his master's character – the man's totally unscrupulous behaviour as an advocate, his pompous self-importance, his utter disregard for the truth (unless it happened to serve his purpose), the long string of victims he had destroyed in the cause of upholding the privileges and the power of the Best People.

'Are you sure you won't sit, Tiro? Belbo can take your cloak; it looks rather heavy, even for this weather.'

'I'll sit, yes. I tire rather easily these days. And yes, I suppose I can do without the cloak. The room seems warm enough. I have to be careful of catching a chill . . .'

I hardly heard what he said, because as he shrugged off his heavy cloak I saw what he was wearing underneath – not a slave's tunic, but a toga. Tiro was dressed as a citizen! I looked at his hand and saw, sure enough, that he wore the iron ring of a citizen just as I did.

'But Tiro, when did this happen?'

'What?' He saw the direction of my gaze and

smiled. He worked his fingers as if he was still not used to the ring. 'Oh, this. Yes, a change in status. Hardly more than a formality in many respects. I do the same work, serve the same man. It's easier for me to own property now, of course –'

'Tiro – no longer a slave! You're free!'

'Yes.' He seemed almost embarrassed.

'Well, it took Cicero long enough. You and I talked of such a possibility the very first time we met. Do you remember?'

'Not really.' His cheeks coloured a bit, and I realized how pale they had been before.

'What did you just say – about taking a chill and tiring easily? Tiro, is something wrong?'

He shook his head. 'Of course not. Not any more.'

I looked at him sceptically.

'I was ill,' he admitted, 'but that was last year. Very ill, to be frank. My health has been . . . somewhat erratic . . . for the last few years.' He smiled. 'I suppose that's one of the reasons Cicero made me a freedman last year; it looked then as if it might be a case of now or never. But I'm much better now. I could have wished for a faster recovery, but at least I'm not walking with the cane any more. The physicians say there's no reason I shouldn't regain my full strength and be as healthy as I ever was.'

I looked at him with fresh eyes. What I had read as a haughty expression was merely due to the gauntness of his cheeks. I reckoned in my head and realized that he must be fifty. He suddenly looked his age; there was more grey among the

tight curls than I had thought, and there was a bald spot at the top of his head. A kind of boyish enthusiasm still sparkled in his eyes, but the firelight also caught the haunted glimmer of a man who had known severe illness. Yet he also seemed a man who was comfortable with himself and his place in the world; his frank and easy manner exuded an air of sophistication and self-contentment. And why not? The boyish slave who had come to my door those many years ago as the messenger of an obscure master was now a free citizen and the invaluable right-hand man of the most famous orator alive. Tiro had met great men and travelled the world at Cicero's side. He had helped to run the government when Cicero was consul. He was famous in his own right, having invented a form of abbreviated writing whereby a copyist could take down a speech verbatim as quickly as it was spoken; every clerk in the Senate House was now required to learn Tironian shorthand.

'Why did you come to me today, Tiro?'

'On behalf of Cicero, of course.'

'He might have come himself.'

'Cicero is keeping indoors,' he said, stressing the last word only slightly.

'So am I. What could he possibly want with me?'

'He'll tell you that himself.'

'He can't possibly think I'll agree to help him.'

'But you don't know what he wants.'

'It doesn't matter. I paid back the favour I owed him for helping me acquire my Etruscan estate years ago, with interest. Since then – let me be candid

with you, Tiro — since then, with every passing year, Cicero has fallen lower and lower in my esteem, not that I imagine my estimation means anything to Cicero. But I have my standards, humble as they may be. I don't intend to come running simply because Cicero thinks he can make some use of me one more time.'

Tiro's face was impassive, which disappointed me. I suppose I expected him to wince, or sigh, or shake his head. He only replied, in a dispassionate voice, 'You're mistaken, of course, in your opinion of Cicero. You misjudge him. Many men do. That always confuses me. But then, I work with him every day. I understand every nuance of his thought. Others aren't so privileged.' He looked at me steadily. 'Well, shall we be going?'

I almost laughed. 'Tiro, were you not listening to me?'

His expression became more severe. 'I saw you yesterday, Gordianus, watching the fires down in the Forum from your rooftop. What did you think of all that? You were appalled, of course. But not everyone was appalled. Those behind the destruction were delighted. Say what you like about Cicero, but when it comes to certain fundamental matters, you and he are on the same side. Did you know they tried to burn Milo's house last night?'

'I heard about it.'

'Such a fire could have spread all over the Palatine. This room we're sitting in could have been a pile of smoking rubble this morning. You realize that, don't you?'

I looked at him for a long moment and sighed. 'You're really not a slave any more, are you, Tiro? You talk like a free man. You bully with words just like a Roman.'

His face tightened. He was trying not to smile. 'I am a Roman now, in every sense of the word. As much a Roman as you, Gordianus.'

'As much a Roman as Cicero?'

He laughed. 'Perhaps not quite.'

'What does he want from me?'

'There's a fire, Gordianus. No, not the fire down in the Forum; a greater fire that threatens to consume everything worth fighting for. Cicero wants you to help pass buckets of water, so to speak.' He leaned towards me with an earnest look. 'There are men who start fires. There are men who put them out. I think we know which kind you are. Does it really matter whether you happen to like or dislike the citizen standing next to you in the bucket-passing line? The point is to put out the fire. Come, let Cicero talk to you.'

I sat for a moment, watching the flames in the brazier. I waved to Belbo, who stood quietly in the corner of the room. 'Bring Tiro his cloak,' I said. The flames danced and wavered. 'And bring a cloak for me, too. Tell Bethesda I'm going out for a while.'

Tiro smiled.

The walk was brief. The air was bracing. The bodyguards were perhaps unnecessary; we didn't

pass a single person in the street. All the houses along the way were shut up tight.

I had never been inside Cicero's newly rebuilt house. Some years before, when Clodius managed to get Cicero exiled from Rome, the Clodian mob had celebrated their triumph by burning down Cicero's house; I had watched the flames from my balcony. When the Senate recalled Cicero from exile sixteen months later, he set about rebuilding. Clodius dogged him at every step, blocking his progress with legal manoeuvres. The property had been confiscated by the state and consecrated for religious use, he claimed. Cicero countered that the confiscation was illegal and that his rights as a Roman citizen had been grossly violated. It had been one of their livelier, uglier exchanges.

Cicero had won the case. The house had been rebuilt. Well, I thought, as we stepped across the threshold, Clodius would never threaten this home again.

Tiro led me through the foyer to the atrium beyond. The room was chilly. High clouds had gathered, blocking the sun's warmth.

'Wait here a moment,' Tiro said, and exited to my left.

After only a brief pause, I heard voices from the hallway to my right.

The first voice was muffled and indistinct, but I recognized the second voice at once. It was Cicero. 'Well,' he was saying, 'what if we tell people that it was Clodius who staged the ambush, instead of the other way around?'

93

I also knew the third voice. It was Cicero's handsome, fiery protégé, Marcus Caelius: 'Jupiter's balls! Who'd believe that, given the circumstances? Better to say, perhaps, that —'

The three men stepped into the atrium. Caelius saw me and fell silent.

At the same moment, Tiro returned from the opposite direction. He saw the situation and looked chagrined. Cicero gave him a brief, sharp look, rebuking him for leaving a visitor unattended. Had I heard something I was not intended to hear?

'Gordianus agreed to pay you a visit,' Tiro said quickly. 'I went to the study to announce him, but —'

'But I wasn't there,' said Cicero. His rich orator's tones filled the atrium. An unctuous smile lit up his fleshy face. 'I tend to think better on my feet. The more expansive the thoughts, the bigger the circuit — the study couldn't contain me! We've walked a mile since you left, Tiro, round and round the house. Well, Gordianus . . .' He stepped forwards. 'I'm honoured to welcome you to my home once again. You know Marcus Caelius, of course.'

I did indeed. Caelius crossed his arms and gave me a sardonic look. He was a creature of quick-silver, and always had been. He had begun as Cicero's pupil. Then he allied himself, or appeared to do so, with Cicero's arch-enemy Catilina; that was how I first met him. Eventually he drifted into the camp of Clodius and into the arms — some said the clutches — of Clodia. His falling out with those two had landed him in dire straits, a trial for murder

for which I helped gather evidence for the prosecution. He had been rescued by Cicero, who came to the defence of his errant pupil with a stirring oration. Now, to all appearances, Caelius was once again the faithful protégé. He seemed to bear me no ill will for having helped the opposing side at his trial; his ambition was of the freewheeling sort that has little use for grudges. He was famous for his sharp tongue, but equally famous for his charm and extraordinary handsomeness. He was now serving a term as a tribune, which meant he was one of the few currently operating officers of the state.

'But I'm not sure that you've met my other friend,' said Cicero. He gestured to the third man, who hung back, peering at me distrustfully. The fellow was short and stocky, with the kind of muscular, barrel-shaped body that looks even stouter in a toga. His fingers were short and blunt, as was his nose. His face was round, with a small mouth and deepset eyes under shaggy eyebrows. The shadow of his beard was so heavy that it gave his jaw a dark, greasy look. No wonder he had been the natural enemy of the lithe, long-limbed, effortlessly elegant Clodius. Physically, two men could hardly have been more opposite.

Milo was back in town after all.

# VI

'Of course I recognize Titus Annius Milo,' I said. 'But you're right, Cicero. We've never been introduced.'

'Well, then, it's about time. Milo, this is Gordianus, called the Finder, a man of great ingenuity. We became acquainted many years ago, when I took on my first murder case. You've read my defence of Sextus Roscius, of course; everyone has. But not many people know the part that Gordianus played. Thirty years ago!'

'Our paths have crossed from time to time since then,' I said dryly.

'And our relationship has always been . . .' The great orator searched for a word.

'Interesting?' I suggested.

'Exactly. Come, let's move to the study. It's chilly in the atrium.'

We retired to a small, well-heated room towards

the back of the house. The walk down the hallway and through the central garden gave me a chance to peruse the surroundings. The furnishings, draperies, paintings and mosaics were all of the finest; I had seen nothing more impressive even in Clodius's house. The scale of Cicero's place was more modest, to be sure, but in some ways that made it more pleasing. Cicero had always had impeccable taste.

He had always had enough money to indulge his tastes, as well, but he now seemed to have prospered well beyond merely keeping up appearances. It takes real wealth to have a fountain decorated with gold-dusted mosaics, or to hang a painting signed by Iaia of Cyzicus on the study wall, or to display on a table to itself, covered by a thick piece of perfectly transparent glass (which must itself have carried a handsome price), a scrap of an original scroll of a dialogue with corrections in Plato's own hand. Roman law forbids advocates from collecting fees for their services; every case is pro bono. Yet successful advocates manage to become rich nonetheless. Instead of mere bags of silver they are rewared with generous gifts of property or exclusive opportunities to invest. Cicero was one of the best advocates in Rome, and he had always known how to cultivate the Best People. His house was full of beautiful, rare, expensive things. I could only imagine the treasures that had been destroyed or looted when the Clodian mob burned his old house.

At Cicero's direction a slave pulled a circle of chairs closer to the flaming brazier. Before we had

settled ourselves, another slave brought silver cups and a ewer of heated wine. Instead of hovering nearby, Tiro joined us. He was a citizen now, Cicero's confederate, not his slave. Still, I noticed he held a wax tablet and a stylus on his lap, for taking notes.

Cicero sipped daintily from his cup. Tiro did likewise. The wine was well watered; Cicero was not a man for strong indulgences. The same could hardly be said of Marcus Caelius, or at least of the Caelius I had known before Cicero reformed him. He saw me watching him and made a show of following his mentor's example, pursing his lips and barely touching them to the rim. The expression gave him such a simpering look that I decided he was deliberately mocking Cicero.

Milo made no pretence at delicacy. He drained his cup in a single swallow and held it out to the slave for more.

'Gordianus, was that surprise I read on your face when you recognized Milo?' Cicero cocked his head. 'You weren't expecting to find him here, were you?'

'Frankly, I thought he must be halfway to Massilia by now.'

'Ha! Turn tail and run like a rabbit? You truly don't know my friend Milo if you could think him such a coward.'

'I'm not sure it's a question of cowardice; more of expedience. Anyway, the rumour of his flight to Massilia is widespread.'

Milo scowled but said nothing.

'You see, I told you,' said Caelius, finally speaking. 'Gordianus and his son hear everything. Between them their four ears catch every whisper in Rome.'

Cicero nodded. 'Yes, go on, Gordianus. What else are people saying?'

'Some say Milo slipped back into the city last night and barricaded himself in his house, and that he was there when the mob came to burn it.'

'So they think he's not a coward, just a madman! No, Milo spent the night here, under my roof, safe and sound. What else do they say?'

'That he plans to incite a revolution. He started by assassinating Clodius, and now he's gathering an army to march on Rome. His confederates inside the walls have stockpiled weapons and incendiary materials all over the city –'

'Well, you can see for yourself how absurd that rumour is! Milo is here, in my house, not out rabble-rousing. And does my house stink of sulphur and pitch? Of course not. A revolution, indeed! There's not a man in Rome more dedicated to the preservation of the Republic than Titus Annius Milo, not even myself! When I think of the abuse he's suffered, and the terrible risks he's taken . . .'

The weight of such sacrifices seemed to bear heavily on Milo, who finished his second cup of wine and looked at me glumly.

I looked around the room, at the many scrolls in their pigeonhole cases, at Iaia's painting of a scene from the Odyssey, at the priceless scrap of Plato under glass. 'You take an awful risk yourself,

Cicero. If the mob had known that Milo was here . . .'

'Yes, I know what you're thinking. This house has already been torched once. But that was because Clodius managed to drive me out of the city first. It would never have happened if I had been here to stop it. And it will never happen again so long as I'm present to defend to my last breath what belongs to me. It may come to that for you as well, Gordianus, before this crisis passes. You have a fine house yourself now. You have a family to protect. Think of those things, and then think of that howling mob we saw yesterday, running wild like a pack of dogs down in the Forum. Do you know how Sextus Cloelius built the fire in the Senate House? He smashed the consuls' chairs and the sacred tribunal and used the wood to build a funeral pyre for the monster. He ripped up scrolls for kindling. Unspeakable desecration! Like their dead leader, these useless freedmen and beggars have no respect at all for the majesty of the state, and no respect for simple decency. They're a menace to any man who stands in their way.'

Cicero sat back and took a deep breath. 'The important thing is, the Clodians were foolish enough to burn down the Senate House. They had the advantage up to that point – people were clucking their tongues about poor, pitiful Clodius. That was a masterstroke, parading his corpse in public like that, stripped naked with all the wounds showing. As an advocate, I have to admire their panache. If I could drag a stinking corpse into court

and shove it under the jurymen's noses, believe me, I wouldn't think twice! Shock and sympathy are two-thirds of the battle. But they overplayed their advantage.'

Caelius swirled his wine cup. 'They took the heat off Milo and lit a fire under their own feet.'

Cicero raised his cup to Caelius. 'Precisely! Oh, Caelius, the turn of phrase is exquisite! A metaphor that's also literally true. 'They took the heat off Milo and lit a fire under their own feet.' Bravo!'

Even Milo smiled, begrudgingly, and raised his cup. He too was an orator, after all, with an appreciation for rhetoric.

'You say that Milo spent the night here?' I said.

Cicero nodded. 'Yes. While the Clodians paraded Clodius's naked corpse all over the Palatine, Milo waited outside the city. Not afraid to come back, mind you, but cautious, sensible, testing the wind, like a general checking the lay of the land before he proceeds. When I saw that the Clodian fools were setting fires, I sent a messenger to inform him. If he wished to come back to the city, he should do so stealthily, I said, and stay away from his own house. I offered him my hospitality, but the decision to return was his. I rendered no advice either way. Milo saw the path before him and took it. Titus Annius Milo, I have never known a braver man than you.' Cicero gazed at the subject of his words with an intensity that would have made a more modest man blush, but Milo's only reaction was to stiffen his jaw and raise his head higher. His features did not appear to me remotely

heroic, as we are accustomed to seeing heroes portrayed in marble or bronze, but he did know how to strike a defiant pose.

'I could never have abandoned Rome in her hour of need,' he said, with a rhetorical quaver in his voice. 'I came back to save her!'

'Excellent!' said Caelius. 'Tiro, copy that down, will you? We must remember to use that.'

I thought he was being rude or facetious, but Milo took no offence. Instead he leaned towards Caelius with a quizzical expression. 'Or do you think it should be, 'I never abandoned Rome, not even for a day —' '

'No, no, it was perfect the way you said it the first time. Tiro, did you get it?'

Tiro scribbled and nodded.

I realized that the discussion was taking place at more than one level, and for more than one purpose. 'You're in the middle of writing a speech, aren't you?' I said.

'Not yet,' said Cicero. 'We're still working out the basic ideas. You can be of enormous help to us, Gordianus.'

'I'm not sure I want to be.'

'I think you do,' he said, giving me a look that must have been familiar to Caelius and to all the others who had been his protégés and pupils. The look said, Do not disappoint me. 'Look at us here, locked away in my study, unable to take a step out of doors without a troop of gladiators to protect us. We're blind and deaf. We have a fierce, brave heart – Milo here. An eloquent tongue – Caelius.

A hand to write – Tiro. And I dare say, a cool head – myself. But we have no eyes, no ears. It's a delicate business, gauging the mood of the people in the street. One must look. One must listen. Miscalculations, at moments of crisis like this, can be . . .'

He did not utter the word disastrous. To speak of disaster would invite an ill omen. Besides, everyone in the room understood precisely what he meant. From bitter experience Cicero knew only too well what the outcome could be when the mob turned against a man.

'I only want your opinion on a few things, Gordianus. The race for consul, for instance. It looks as though the elections may finally be held. How would you gauge the mood of the people towards Milo's candidacy?'

I stared at him, dumbfounded.

'Well? Are his chances better now than before, or worse? It's a simple enough question.'

'Yes, but I can hardly believe that you expect a serious answer.'

Milo nervously tapped his empty cup against the arm of his chair. 'He means to say that it's hopeless.'

'Is that what you mean, Gordianus?' Cicero peered at me earnestly.

I cleared my throat. 'Clodius is dead. Someone killed him, with great violence – I saw the body myself.'

'Saw it? Where?' snapped Milo.

While I hesitated, pondering whether to tell them about my visit to Clodius's house, Cicero spared me the decision by interrupting.

'Gordianus saw the body from his rooftop, just as I saw it from mine. I told you, Milo, how they paraded the corpse all over the Palatine.'

'Yes, I saw it from my rooftop,' I said. It was not, after all, a lie. 'And if any Roman didn't see it, he's certainly heard about it.'

'And what exactly are people saying about the matter?' said Cicero.

'What do you mean?'

'How do they think Clodius died? Who do they think was responsible?'

If Cicero wished to feign obtuseness, I would oblige him. 'The word on everyone's lips is that Milo killed him. Or Milo's men.'

'Where?'

'On the Appian Way. Somewhere near Bovillae.'

Cicero nodded thoughtfully. 'How?'

I paused. 'Judging by the wounds, I would say that daggers were used.' I thought of the puncture wound at the shoulder. 'Perhaps a spear, as well. And he may have been strangled.'

'You must have had a clearer view of the body than I did!' said Cicero.

'Perhaps my eyes are trained for such details.'

'But you've heard no actual details of the . . . fatal incident . . . and how it came about?'

'No.'

Caelius nodded vigorously. 'And neither have most people, I'll wager. How could they have heard details? Who could possibly supply them?'

Milo worked his stubbly jaw back and forth and

drummed his fingers against his cup. 'Still, rumours spring up like weeds in a crack. If a story has a hole in it, people will fill it up with anything that fits.'

'Have you heard rumours, Gordianus?' said Cicero. 'About a battle, an ambush, an accident?'

'I've heard all sorts of rumours. An ambush, a battle, a single assassin, a traitor among Clodius's men . . .'

'I think that's hopeful,' said Caelius, sitting back and raising an eyebrow. He held out his wine cup and a slave hurried to fill it. 'People haven't yet made up their minds. There's still a chance for us to tell them our side of the story. But we'll have to do it quickly. Gossip sets like mortar in people's heads. Once it's hardened you have to chisel it out. Best to pour your own gossip into their ears first.'

'And of course there's the fire,' said Cicero. 'Surely that's cracked open some hard heads. People who were hostile to Milo before will surely listen to reason now. Only the most lunatic radicals could take the side of that mob of pyromaniacs against Milo.' He sighed, exasperated. 'I don't understand why the death of Clodius should stir such a controversy, anyway, except among the small core of his most rabid followers. Any sensible man can see that Rome is better off without the scoundrel. It's so obvious! If we go before the people and say 'Yes, Milo killed Clodius,' aren't we simply saying that Milo is a hero? We're essentially proclaiming him the saviour of the Republic!'

Cicero looked to me for a reaction. I answered

carefully. 'I can't speak for most people, but I think there are plenty of Romans who are simply tired of all the chaos and disorder —'

'Exactly,' said Cicero, 'and it was Clodius who was behind all that disorder, fomenting unrest among the rabble, shaking up the natural order of things. Get rid of Clodius and you're halfway to getting rid of chaos. Tiro, take that down: 'Get rid of Clodius —' '

'You may be going too far,' said Caelius, shaking his head. 'It begins to sound like gloating. Even people who are glad to see the last of Clodius may have serious concerns about the circumstances of his death. You can't make Milo out to be a champion of law and order if at the same time you proudly assert that he broke the law by killing a man.'

'Ah, but it takes on a different light if you show that Milo was the victim of an ambush and merely defending himself,' said Cicero, waving a finger.

'Was it an ambush?' I said, looking from face to face. 'Was Milo the intended victim?'

Tiro, busy scribbling on his tablet, didn't look up. The others looked at me curiously.

Cicero brightened. 'Well, what do you think, Gordianus? Is it credible that Clodius might have set an ambush for Milo down on the Appian Way?'

I shrugged. 'Their hatred for one another was well known.'

Caelius looked at me sceptically. I felt like a witness under cross-examination. 'But then isn't it just as likely that it was Milo who set a trap for

Clodius? What would you say to that idea, Gordianus?'

'But surely it can't have been both ways. It must have been one or the other.'

'Must it?' said Cicero. 'What if there was no ambush at all? What if the two parties happened to meet on the Appian Way entirely by accident? Does that strike you as credible?'

'Perhaps. But people pass on the road all the time without someone ending up dead.'

Caelius laughed. 'He has a point!'

Cicero pressed his fingertips together. 'But accidents happen. A man can't always control his slaves, especially gladiators who've been trained to protect him and to react at the first hint of danger. Tiro, make a note: Milo needs to free certain of his slaves, who might otherwise be compelled to give testimony under torture. Slaves can be tortured, but not freedmen. If worse comes to worst . . .'

'If it comes to a trial, you mean,' I said.

Milo grunted. Cicero tapped his fingertips against each other. 'It's my conviction that Milo will yet be elected consul. He deserves no less for his service to the state! Still, we must be prepared for less happy possibilities.'

'A trial for murder, you mean. What would Milo have to fear from the testimony of his slaves?'

Cicero considered the question. 'Gordianus makes a good point. If Milo waits and frees the slaves at the wrong time, it could look bad. The earlier the better, I think.'

'You can always say they were manumitted out

of gratitude, as a reward,' Caelius suggested. 'They saved his life, after all.'

'Did they?' I said.

'Well, that's what we'll say,' said Caelius, looking at me as if I were a simpleton.

I shook my head in disgust. 'You're only talking about appearances, aren't you, and nothing more? About this or that hypothetical version of what might or might not have happened, and whether people will believe it. You might as well be writing a comedy for the stage.'

'Better a comedy than a tragedy,' quipped Caelius.

Cicero looked at me thoughtfully. 'We are advocates, Gordianus. This is what we do.'

I shook my head.

Cicero saw that I was not satisfied. 'How shall I put this?' he said. 'Your nature is different from mine. Truth has a different meaning to you; you seem to think it matters in and of itself. But the truth you crave is an illusion! Chasing after Truth is a fit pastime for Greek philosophers who have nothing better to do, but we are Romans, Gordianus. We have a world to run.'

He studied me for a long moment, and saw that I still resisted. 'Gordianus! The next few days and months are absolutely critical to the survival of everything decent and honourable that remains in this city. You saw what they did yesterday – the madness, the destruction, the wanton desecration. Can you picture yourself in that mob? Surely not! Can you imagine what Rome would be like if

people of that ilk were allowed to rule? A nightmare! Surely you can see where your own interests lie.'

I studied each of their faces in turn – Cicero radiant with purpose, Tiro busy with his stylus, Caelius looking sombre but ready to grin, and Milo thrusting out his jaw like a stubborn boy spoiling for a fight.

'But what really happened on the Appian Way?' I said.

I received only blank stares in reply, before Cicero smoothly moved on to some other subject and then quickly, graciously, firmly made it clear that my visit was at an end.

I left Cicero's house without a satisfactory answer to my question – and indeed, with no clear idea of why he had summoned me. Cicero himself didn't appear to know exactly what he wanted from me, but seemed merely to be feeling me out. I had a vague sense of opposing forces marshalling their powers, and wondered exactly where I stood in the scheme of things.

# VII

The siege at the house of the interrex Marcus Lepidus continued the next day, and the next, and the next, with the partisans of Scipio and Hypsaeus continuing to demand immediate consular elections.

Temples and business interests in the Forum closed their doors. Every day, great crowds came to gawk at the charred ruins of the Senate House. Some wept, some cheered; fights and shouting matches were common. Some of the visitors laid flowers on the steps, as if it were a sepulchre, in honour of the man who had been cremated there. Others scattered the flowers and trampled on them.

Affairs of state came to a standstill.

Life continued, however. Bethesda sent her slave girls down to the markets to buy the things she needed for dinner. It took them longer than usual, as they had to search harder, but they returned with

full baskets. Belbo went to fetch a pair of shoes that I had sent out to be repaired, and reported that work went on more or less as usual in the street of the shoemakers. People went about the day-to-day business of gaining a livelihood and feeding themselves, but with a sense of dreadful suspense. Rome had the distracted air of a man on a dark, unfamiliar path, doggedly pushing on, fretfully looking over his shoulder, waiting for something terrible to happen.

Eco came to visit each day. 'They're all three mad if they think that the fellow still has a chance of being elected consul,' he said, when I told him about my peculiar interview with Cicero, Caelius and Milo. 'But Cicero is right about one thing: the Clodians went too far when they burned the Senate House. They lost the sympathy of the people in the middle. Murder's an outrage, but fire scares the wits out of people.'

'Fire is a symbol of purification,' I suggested.

'Maybe at a funeral, or in a poem. But when you start burning down buildings, fire stands for indiscriminate destruction. Purifying the state may sound like a lofty idea in a speech, but not when people start getting burned. When reformers turn violent, they scare people.'

'So that anyone with anything to lose prefers things to stay as they are.'

'That's one result.'

'Then maybe Milo does stand a chance to be elected consul.'

'Never. He's tainted by Clodius's death.'

'About which we still don't have any concrete details,' I said, worriedly rubbing my chin. 'So you think the voters will make Hypsaeus and Scipio consuls? But aren't they tainted, as well? They had the support of Clodius, and now people are frightened of the Clodians.'

'Yes, but Hypsaeus and Scipio are seen as being their own men. They weren't associated with the burning of the Senate House.'

'But they're rabble-rousers nonetheless! Look at the blockade their supporters have thrown around Lepidus's house! Surely they're no more acceptable to the people in the middle than Clodius was.'

Eco looked at me thoughtfully. 'If Milo's out . . . and if Hypsaeus and Scipio are also out . . .'

'Don't say it!'

But he did. 'People will turn to Pompey.'

Pompey was much on the minds of many people in those days, including his old ally Milo.

On the fifth and final day of Lepidus's term as interrex, a trio of radical tribunes held a contio down in the Forum. Eco and I attended.

A contio is a public open-air meeting. Though it may have a feeling of informality, it is a function of the state and is governed by specific rules. Only certain people may speak at a contio, they must address a specific topic, and so on. Most importantly, only certain officials may hold a contio. The consuls may do so, for example. So may the tribunes.

Rome had no consuls for the time being. But

there were ten tribunes, as usual. Some of them were keeping very busy.

The funeral of Clodius, or rather the gathering in the Forum to hear Clodius eulogized and to burn his corpse, had been a contio, or at least had started out that way. It had been called by the tribunes Pompeius and Plancus. I had seen both of these men at Clodius's house on the night of his murder, in the anteroom where the politicians had gathered to assess the disaster. The next day these two led the procession around the Palatine and down to the Forum. It was their speeches which inflamed the mob. Pompeius and Plancus were the same tribunes who had blocked the appointment of an interrex at the beginning of the new year, and had thus pushed back the scheduling of elections at a time when Milo felt confident of victory.

Their contio on the final day of Lepidus's term as interrex was attended by a great crowd. When Eco came to my house that morning and announced his intention to attend, I declined at first to accompany him. It would be insanity to go out in public at such a time, I argued, even with bodyguards. But the pull of the Forum was too strong. For four days, except for my visit to Cicero, I had kept almost entirely to my house. I was growing restless. In times of crisis or jubilation, there is something in a Roman's blood that pulls him inexorably to join with great throngs of his fellow citizens to listen to other citizens make speeches beneath the open sky, where men and gods alike can see and hear.

Eco insisted that we push our way to the front of

the crowd. We wore our togas, as befitted the occasion; Eco's bodyguards were dressed in tunics and cloaks. Thus one can often tell at a glance, in a mixed crowd, who is a citizen and who is a slave attending a citizen.

Up on the platform, Plancus and Pompeius were joined by their fellow tribune Sallust. It was Sallust whom I heard in the house of Clodius, arguing that no one but Clodius could control the mob. He had warned of a bloodbath. But apparently he had reconciled himself to the rabble-rousing efforts of his fellow tribunes and had decided to join them. These three addressed the crowd not with formal speeches but alternating back and forth, as if having a conversation or a debate among themselves and soliciting the reactions of their fellow citizens.

The exact circumstances of the incident on the Appian Way were not discussed. I was beginning to find this paucity of details maddening, but no one else in the crowd seemed to mind or even to notice. That Milo and his men had murdered Clodius in cold blood was simply taken for granted. The issue was what to do about it. The main thing, the speakers all agreed, was to hold consular elections at once. Once Hypsaeus and Scipio were in office, Milo could be dealt with accordingly.

'But what about the rumours that Milo's raising an army?' shouted someone in the crowd.

'If his goal is insurrection,' said Sallust, 'then it's all the more important that we elect consuls at once, in order to raise a force against him for the defence of the city.'

'But what about Milo's allies here inside the city?' shouted someone else. 'They say he has secret stockpiles of all sorts of weapons. They could cut our throats while we sleep. They could set our houses on fire –'

'Ha! You Clodian arsonists shouldn't talk about fire!' said another man. There were harsh words. A scuffle broke out. Though it was some distance away, Eco's bodyguards grew tense and tightened their circle around us. The speakers on the platform ignored the interruption.

'The fact is,' said Sallust, 'Milo is back in Rome.'

This news sent a murmur through the crowd.

A man behind me, close enough for me to smell the garlic on his breath, cupped his hands around his mouth. 'The shameless pig came back to Rome the very day after he murdered Clodius!' he shouted. 'Milo must have been in his house that night when we went to pay a call with our torches. I should know, I took an arrow in my shoulder!' The man pulled his toga open at the throat to show off his bandages.

'Brave citizen!' cried Sallust. He raised his arm in salute, which prompted a round of cheering mixed with a few jeers. 'But whatever Milo's whereabouts for the last few days, we know that he was in town as of yesterday, because yesterday Milo emerged from hiding to go and pay a visit to Pompey Magnus at his villa on the Pincian Hill.'

This news set off another murmur in the crowd. In the race for consul, Pompey had given his blessing to Hypsaeus, who had served him as a

military officer in the East. But Pompey and Milo had once been allies, and Pompey and Clodius had often been enemies. Could it be that the Great One had been induced to countenance Milo's crime and to throw his support behind the murderer? Pompey's involvement could shift the balance conclusively, either for Milo or against him.

Sallust smiled, reading the crowd's anxiety and uncertainty, drawing out the suspense with his silence. 'You will be happy to learn,' he finally said, 'that Pompey Magnus, to his great credit, refused even to see the villain!'

The suspense broke with a round of cheers.

'And more than that, he sent the scoundrel a roundabout message politely asking him to refrain from calling again, so as to spare Pompey the embarrassment of refusing to see him again. Milo's perfidy is so profound that even the Great One fears it might taint him if he should brush against it.'

The tribune Plancus stepped forwards. He spoke as if engaging Sallust in conversation, but his words rang out as only those of a trained orator can. 'I should imagine that Milo was greatly offended by Pompey's rebuff.'

'I should imagine he was,' agreed Sallust. 'We know that Milo is a man who offends easily. And we have seen how deadly his grudges can be.'

Plancus mimed an expression of dismay. We were so close to the platform that I could see just how broadly he played his part. 'What are you implying, Sallust? Do you imagine that Pompey himself might be . . . in danger?'

Sallust gave a world-weary shrug, exaggerated just enough so that the gesture could be read from the back of the crowd. 'We've seen that the monster will stop at nothing to take over the state. Clodius has already fallen victim to his bloodlust. If Pompey now stands in his way –'

There were cries from the crowd:

'No!'

'Never!'

'Impossible!'

'Milo wouldn't dare!'

'Wouldn't he?' The tribune Pompeius, who had been holding back, stepped forwards. As a member of Pompey's clan, he claimed the crowd's full attention. 'I shall tell you what I think,' he said. 'It was Milo who provided a body to be cremated in the Senate House. And it's Milo who'll provide another body to be buried on the Capitoline Hill!' His meaning was clear, for who but Pompey could be worthy of a sepulchre on the hill of Rome's most sacred temples?

The crowd raised their fists and began to shout, drowning out the speakers on the platform, who seemed only too pleased to fall silent and yield to the roar of the mob. Was Milo plotting to kill Pompey? The tribunes had not offered even a shred of evidence, but the mere suggestion drove the crowd to a frenzy.

The Forum was like a great pool of sound. Individual cries were like pebbles that rippled through the crowd and echoed back from its edges. All coalesced into a deafening, indistinct roar, until

117

somewhere in the crowd someone began to chant. The chant was joined by more and more voices until it rose above the roar: 'Vote . . . now! Vote . . . now!' It was the same cry that had echoed for days around the house of the interrex Marcus Lepidus.

The crowd began to move. How this movement began, I never quite understood. I saw no signal from the tribunes on the stage. I heard no shout from the crowd, urging everyone to head for the house of Lepidus. Perhaps if I had been on my rooftop watching instead of in the thick of things, I could have seen and understood the dynamics of the mob – or perhaps not. One might as easily comprehend the uncanny unison of a swarm of bees in flight.

However it happened, the crowd became a mob, and the mob began to move as a single body towards the Palatine. Eco and I moved along with it for a while, unable to separate ourselves, like flotsam on a current. I was jostled and poked and pushed forwards against my will. I gritted my teeth and grunted. But the same experience that I found so unpleasant seemed to invigorate many of those around me, who grinned and made giddy whoops of excitement as if they had drunk too much wine.

Little by little we worked our way sideways through the press of the crowd until we reached the edge and were able to drop back. Even Eco seemed intoxicated by the excitement. 'What's wrong, Papa?' he said, smiling and catching his breath. 'Don't you want to join the march on the interrex's house?'

'Don't be funny, Eco. There's no telling what will happen. I'm going home. So should you.'

I spent that afternoon on my rooftop, anxiously looking for signs of fire or smoke. I saw none, but heard the clattering echoes of some kind of battle taking place in the direction of Lepidus's house.

A sharp wind began to gust from the north, followed by dark clouds. As the first cold raindrops pelted my face, Bethesda appeared in the garden.

'Come down from there!' she demanded, her hands on her hips.

I obeyed. But halfway down the ladder I turned to stone, as did everything around me. A bolt of lightning opened the sky. Jupiter blinked, as the augurs say. The blinding flash of bone-white light was followed by a crack of thunder so loud that the earth itself seemed to flinch. Rain swept across the garden. I hurried down the ladder, shivering, and told Belbo to light the brazier in my study.

I hardly had a chance to warm my hands over the flames before Belbo was back, announcing a visitor. 'The same as before,' he said. 'Cicero's man.'

'Tiro?'

Belbo nodded.

'Well, show him in.'

'What about his bodyguards?'

'They can stay outside in the rain.'

A moment later Tiro stepped into the room, pushing the hood back from his face. His heavy woollen cloak was wet. He covered his mouth and coughed.

'Cicero shouldn't send you out in the rain, Tiro. He should consider your health.'

'It's only a short walk. Besides, he thinks you're fond of me.'

'And that I might not come if he sent someone else to fetch me?'

Tiro smiled. 'Will you come?'

'Shouldn't you and I have a brief, polite conversation about the weather first?'

'Thunder and lightning,' said Tiro, rolling his eyes skyward. 'Omens and portents.'

'If you believe in that sort of thing.'

'Doesn't everybody?'

'Don't be disingenuous, Tiro. It doesn't suit you. Just because your master − your former master, I mean − pretends to go along with such superstitious ideas for the sake of politics . . .'

'You really despise Cicero, don't you?'

I sighed. 'No more or less than I despise all the rest of his kind, I suppose.'

'His kind?'

'Politicians.'

'No, I think you despise him more than the rest. Because once upon a time you thought he was different somehow, and then he disappointed you.'

'Perhaps.'

'Whereas you expect only the worst from the rest of them, so they've never let you down.'

I shrugged.

'But isn't it really only your own false expectations that have let you down, Gordianus? Do you think a man can cross a muddy street without

getting his feet dirty? Cicero can't walk on air. No one can.'

'Cicero doesn't just cross the muddy street, Tiro. He stoops down and flings handfuls of mud at anybody in his way. He sticks out his foot and trips people – and claps when they fall on their faces! Then he washes his hands at the nearest fountain and blithely pretends they were never dirty.'

Tiro gave me a grudging smile. 'Cicero can be a bit self-righteous.'

'Smug is more like it.'

'Yes. Well, I try to tone down those parts in his speeches. But it's a funny thing. People may say that modesty is a virtue, but they respect a man who sings his own praises. They think if he's vain, he must have a reason. And when such a bright fellow starts slinging mud, they pay attention. They figure he must have a good reason for doing that, too.'

'You don't have to convince me that Cicero knows how to manipulate an audience.'

'Gordianus, these are merely questions of style, not content. Certain things about Cicero rub you the wrong way. Don't you think I sometimes tire of his manner, spending so many hours of the day in his company? He can drive me mad! And yet I've never met a more admirable or honourable man in all my life. Fundamentally, you and Cicero are on the same side –'

'Tiro, you needn't try to convince me to come along with you. I've only been waiting for a break in our conversation to send Belbo after my cloak.

But look, here he is, already anticipating my needs.' Belbo put the cloak over my shoulders. I pulled it around me. 'The weather has turned colder.'

'Still, let's hope this rain keeps up,' said Tiro. 'It makes it harder to start fires. Keeps the flames from spreading. There, we've talked about the weather. Shall we be going?'

I found Cicero in his study, deep in conversation with Marcus Caelius.

Cicero looked up and saw me scanning the room. 'Milo isn't here,' he said. 'He's returned to his own house. A show of self-confidence. After all, what does Milo have to fear in his own home, when the people of Rome love him so?'

'Do they?'

'How can they not, after the favour he's done them, ridding the world of that appalling scoundrel — "He trapped the tyrant in iron bands —" '

' "And slew him with his own bare hands," ' I said, finishing the quotation from Ennius. 'Well, did he?'

'Did he what?'

'Did Milo slay Clodius with his own bare hands?' I remembered the marks I had seen on Clodius's throat. Something had been twisted around his neck before he died, either to restrain him, or to choke him, or to drag him.

Cicero shrugged. 'I wasn't there to see. But the image appeals to me. Like his namesake, the fabled wrestler of Croton, Milo is a strong fellow. I

suppose he could strangle a man to death. What do you think, Caelius?'

Caelius looked thoughtful. 'Strangulation? It might make people forget the blood . . . take their minds off those gaping wounds. The idea of Clodius being strangled – I like it. It's cleaner, less gory. Thinking about knives sets people's teeth on edge. Strangulation is more manly, more heroic. It suggests killing an animal barehanded. It equates Clodius with a wild beast. Best to skirt such graphic details, really, but if we must discuss the actual where and how of the murder –'

'I didn't come here to listen to two orators toss ideas in the air,' I said.

Caelius smiled. 'But how else can we see which ideas float, and which ones fall like stones?'

'You can do that after I leave.'

Tiro made a face of disapproval at my rudeness.

'Why did you agree to come, Gordianus?' said Cicero. 'I thought perhaps Tiro had converted you with his eloquence.'

'Converted me? But I thought you said we were already in the same camp, Cicero.'

'We are. You just don't realize it yet.' He laced his fingers behind his head and smiled.

'Don't be so smug, Cicero. You asked me to come. Here I am. Why did I come?' I walked to the brazier and spread my hands over the flames. 'Because it's a cold night in Rome, and dark outside. Like everyone else I'm craving warmth and light. Especially light. My reasons for coming are entirely selfish. I want more illumination on the

123

path ahead, any glimmer to show the way. Knowledge is a fire. It burns high in this house. But right now it seems to be putting out a great deal more smoke than light.'

Cicero shrugged good-naturedly. 'Well, then, perhaps you might cast some light for me, Gordianus.'

'Perhaps.'

'I believe you went down to the contio in the Forum today.'

'Yes. How did you know that?'

He waved his hand dismissively. 'One sees things, hears things.'

'How?'

'One has eyes and ears.'

'Spies, you mean.'

He shrugged. 'Let us say that very little happens here on the Palatine that escapes my notice. But there are places where my eyes and ears can't go. Not safely, anyway. Not without being noticed.'

'Such as a contio held by three radical tribunes to stir up the mob?'

'Three?'

'Pompeius, Plancus, Sallust.'

'Sallust as well? I thought he might have come to his senses by now.'

Cicero thoughtfully tapped his chin.

'Not a good sign,' said Caelius. 'Sallust is the cautious one. If he's decided to start stirring up riots with the others −'

'They didn't incite a riot,' I said. 'It ended with a march on Lepidus's house.'

'A march?' said Cicero. 'It may have begun that way, but by the time they arrived it was an all-out assault!' He stood and began to pace. He suddenly looked weary. 'You didn't witness the attack yourself, Gordianus?'

'Of course not. I went home and bolted my doors.'

'Then I'll tell you what happened. The rabble marched up the Palatine and joined their fellows at the barricade, then altogether they rushed the house of Lepidus and broke down the door. They used paving stones they'd pulled up from the street. They broke the lock and smashed the bolt into splinters. Make note of that, Gordianus, the next time you bolt your door at night and lie down to sleep, thinking you're safe: no man's house is secure if there's a mob determined to get inside. They ransacked the place. Overturned the busts of Lepidus's ancestors, smashed furniture, tore apart the ceremonial looms in the hall – so much for the patrician ladies spinning an orderly pattern for the future of Rome. The poor women ran screaming in fright.

'The mob probably intended to seize Lepidus and force him to conduct some sort of mock election right there on the spot. Not much doubt which candidates that rabble would have chosen, is there? Hypsaeus and Scipio, Clodius's old allies. As if such proceedings could carry any authority at all! The gods help Rome when the day comes that men are chosen to head the state at the whim of a raging mob!

'Fortunately, Milo was ready.' Cicero tapped his skull. 'Always thinking, ever vigilant! Milo expected that something like this might occur on the last day of Lepidus's interregnum, so he arranged to have his own men assembled in a side street, out of sight. When the attack on the house began, they rallied and mounted a counterattack from the rear. There was quite a battle, and no little amount of bloodshed. But needless to say, the Clodian rabble quickly scattered and fled. Their type is useless in a man-to-man fight. Milo's men found Lepidus locked away in an upstairs room with his wife and daughters, all ready to slash their wrists. Can you imagine? An interrex of Rome was on the verge of killing himself rather than be torn apart by a mob of slaves and freedmen, and the women of his house were preparing to die rather than be raped by such men. I tell you, even in the darkest days of the civil war, there was never such a shame on the republic! And once again it was Milo who came to the rescue. But what chance is there that his foresight and vigilance will be recognized, let alone rewarded as they should be? If ever a man deserved to be consul . . .'

Cicero seemed to speak from the heart, sincerely outraged by the attack on Lepidus, sincerely in awe of his friend's patriotic zeal. But of course, I reminded myself, it was a part of his profession to be able to speak without apparent artifice, to strike the heartfelt tone, to stir emotions in his listeners against their will.

I cleared my throat. 'Is it true, what they say about Milo and Pompey?'

Cicero frowned and looked puzzled at the sudden change of subject. Caelius raised a curious eyebrow.

'Has Pompey also become a menace to the state?' I said. 'Is that why Milo's plotting to do away with him, as Clodius was done away with – for the good of Rome? Does he intend to strangle the general 'with his own bare hands'? No wonder Pompey won't allow him into his villa.'

Cicero's frown deepened. 'Is that what was said at the contio today?'

I nodded. 'That's what really stirred up the mob. They said that Milo paid a call on Pompey, and Pompey refused to see him. It was implied that Pompey fears for his life, and with good reason.'

'What?' Cicero was aghast, or pretended to be.

'I quote the tribune Pompeius: 'It was Milo who provided a body to be cremated in the Senate House, and it's Milo who'll provide another body to be buried on the Capitoline Hill.' '

'Absurd!' There certainly seemed to be nothing theatrical or premeditated in the way Cicero spat out the word. 'Those rabble-rousers will say anything, and the idiots will believe it! The audience for the contio, Gordianus – did it seem to you that it was made up of hand-picked supporters, packed with Clodian sympathizers?'

'Not particularly. There were dissenting voices in the crowd. It was a mixed group. A great many people of all sorts were interested to hear what the tribunes had to say. I was there myself.'

'And yet the crowd was swayed by such non-sense?'

'More than swayed, Cicero, from what you've told me of the attack on Lepidus's house. It's completely false, then, what they're saying about Milo and Pompey?'

'Of course!'

'Yes, well, perhaps not completely false,' said Marcus Caelius, raising an eyebrow at me and then casting an imperturbable, catlike gaze at his agitated mentor. 'Well, Cicero, Gordianus has been candid with us. He deserves our candour in return. The fact is that Milo did attempt to pay a call on Pompey, and Pompey rebuffed him. It was a miscalculation on Milo's part, if you ask me. He felt obliged to seek the Great One's blessing. He should have known better. But our Milo is a simple man; simple in the virtuous sense, as our ancestors supposedly were. Having done Pompey so many favours in the past, Milo assumed that the Great One would feel obliged to return those favours now that Milo is in dire straits. Think again! So the radical tribunes knew about the rebuff?'

I nodded. 'How did Sallust put it? 'Pompey sent the scoundrel a roundabout message asking him to refrain from calling again, so as to spare Pompey the embarrassment of refusing to see him again.' '

'You've always had an excellent memory for words,' said Cicero quietly.

'Indeed,' said Caelius, 'you could make Tiro's shorthand obsolete!' He turned to Cicero. 'But how did Sallust and the rest find out about

Pompey's message? It was sent in secret, and to this house, not directly to Milo.'

'Perhaps Pompey wasn't as discreet as he wanted us to think,' said Cicero. 'Easy enough, to whisper the news from ear to ear until the tribunes knew about it. Pompey is like everyone else at the moment. He's testing the waters.'

Caelius turned back to me. 'And what did Sallust and the other tribunes say about the subsequent exchange of messages between Milo and Pompey?'

I shook my head. 'They only mentioned the visit and Pompey's rebuff.'

'Well then, perhaps Pompey is being discreet after all,' said Caelius. 'You see, Gordianus, Milo was quite shaken when Pompey refused his visit. When he received Pompey's message declining any further visits, Milo sent Pompey a message in return, begging him to reconsider and offering –'

'Caelius!' said Cicero.

'But we might as well tell Gordianus everything,' insisted Caelius. 'Well, then: Milo offered to quit the race for consul if Pompey wanted him to. 'A word from you, Pompey Magnus, and for the good of Rome I will abandon my ambitions to serve her.' Of course he was really fishing for some back-handed encouragement – 'No, no, dear fellow, politics prevents me from receiving your visit, but of course you must run!' But that's not what he got.'

'What did Pompey say?'

'The Great One is apparently too far above the fray to be bothered with Milo's petty ambitions. He

sent back a curt reply: 'It is not for me to say who can or cannot stand for office. I would never dream of imposing my opinion on the Roman people, who are quite capable of making their own judgment without my advice.' Cold, cold! As chilly as the rain that's coming down.'

Cicero shook his head. 'They weren't small favours, the sacrifices Milo made for Pompey over the years. But now that Milo's in trouble and Clodius is no longer a threat, Pompey can't cut his ties to Milo fast enough!'

'Pompey may yet come around, if he can be made to see that it's in his interest,' said Caelius.

'We can't count on that,' said Cicero. 'Milo will have to make his move without Pompey's support.'

Caelius nodded. 'I agree. Word will spread tonight about the rescue of Lepidus. That will count in Milo's favour; Milo stands for order and tradition against the lawless mob. And we shouldn't underestimate the resentment that decent people feel against the Clodians for burning the Senate House. I think we can count on a favourable crowd tomorrow.'

'Tomorrow?' I said.

Caelius smiled. 'Another contio, this time called by me. Be sure to come, Gordianus. We shall fight fire with fire.'

'You don't mean that literally, I hope.'

Caelius laughed.

# VIII

Eco called on me early the next morning, brimming with news.

'Papa, have you heard what happened at Lepidus's house yesterday, after the contio?'

'Yes.'

'Quite a battle, apparently. Blood all over Lepidus's house, they say. His ancestral busts ruined beyond repair. The yarn for the ceremonial looms all a tangled mess. But now he'll always be known as the interrex who held firm against the mob – he got his five days of fame!'

'We were damned lucky the violence didn't start down in the Forum, while we were still in that crowd. What if Milo's little army had shown up there, instead of waiting in ambush at Lepidus's house? I'm an old man, Eco. I can't outrun a mob.'

'No one forced you to go to the contio, Papa.'

I grunted.

'Don't you trust my new bodyguards?'

I grunted again. 'I suppose the senatorial committee will choose a new interrex today.'

'That's the word. No one knows where they're meeting – probably outside the city. They've kept the location secret, afraid of another blockade or a battle. The new interrex will have the authority to call elections, but with things so unsettled it seems unlikely that we'll actually see new consuls in the next five days. Oh, and speaking of unsettled, there's to be another contio today, this one –'

'Called by the not-so-radical tribune Marcus Caelius.'

'Yes, and they say that –'

'Milo himself may speak.'

Eco looked at me archly. 'Papa, you're remarkably well informed for a man who never sets foot in the Forum unless I drag you there. Something tells me you've been in touch with Cicero again. Tell me everything.'

I gave him the details of my visit to Cicero's house on the previous day.

Eco drew his own conclusions. 'Pompey's behaving like a bastard, isn't he?'

'Oh, I don't know.'

'What a back-stabber! Milo was his ally for years, and now –'

'Ah, but little things like murder can sour even the sincerest relationships. If Milo killed Clodius, just how far do Pompey's obligations of friendship extend?'

Eco looked at me quizzically. 'Why do you say 'if'?'

'What do you mean?'

'You said, 'If Milo killed Clodius.' '

'Oh. I suppose I did . . .'

'Well, I don't see why you defend Pompey. This 'little thing' – this murder – seems only to have strengthened Cicero's support of Milo.'

'Yes, one can't fault Cicero's loyalty.'

'I suppose it's because they're so much alike.'

'Cicero and Milo?' I thought of Cicero – frail in youth, dyspeptic in middle age, shrewd, calculating, a model of taste and refinement – and then of Milo, who seemed quite the opposite, with his robust, bullish physique, his bluff manner, and a rough edge to his character that no amount of money or education had ever managed to smooth away. 'Alike in what ways, Eco?'

'Well, they're the two brightest of the New Men, aren't they, the two shiniest new stars in the firmament? Or they would be, if Milo could ever get himself elected consul.'

Eco had a point. Cicero had been the first of his family to attain a magistracy. He had been born with money and means, to be sure, but none of his ancestors had ever held high office. With his election as a quaestor at the age of thirty, he had become, as the parlance goes, a New Man in the halls of power. This in itself was a great achievement. But Cicero's ascent had not ended with the lower magistracies; he had worked his way all the way up to consul. This was truly remarkable. As a

rule the consulship is attained only by candidates already of consular family, men whose ancestors held the consulship before them. Thus do the high nobility, by various traps and schemes, perpetuate their status and exclude newcomers. But against all odds Cicero had attained the consulship, and he was the first New Man of his generation to do so.

Milo was also a New Man. If he became consul he would be only the second New Man in living memory, after Cicero, to do so.

'I see what you mean, Eco. I suppose they see themselves as the only two members of a very exclusive club. They've risen above their birth –'

'So that they can now look down on people like you and me from a comfortable height.'

'But they're still outsiders and interlopers to the old aristocratic families who were born to privilege and great expectations.'

'Like their mutual enemy Clodius.'

'Or Pompey,' I noted. 'Or Caesar.'

'So it's all the better that they're so different on the outside,' said Eco. 'They get to play each other's alter ego.'

'Cicero and Milo, alter egos? Well, Cicero certainly seems determined to stand by Milo, no matter what he's done, whether the mob likes it or not. And whether Pompey likes it or not, for that matter.'

'But to what end?' said Eco.

For my decision to attend Caelius's contio that day, I have no one to blame but myself.

The event attracted a considerable crowd – even larger than the crowd that had attended the radical tribunes' contio the previous day. The news of the battle at Lepidus's house had made people even more restless and anxious. As I have said, in times of duress Romans gather by instinct in large groups to listen to speeches.

With Eco's bodyguards helping to clear the way, we managed to find a good spot in front of the speakers' platform, despite the crush. I peered at the sea of faces around us, trying to judge the temper of the crowd. I noticed a number of stuffy, conservative types, men of means attended by large retinues of bodyguards and retainers, dressed in immaculate togas spun from superior wool. Eco pointed to such a specimen nearby.

'Businessman,' he said.

'Banker,' I countered, merely for the sake of argument.

'Pro-Milo?'

'Anti-Clodius, more likely. And probably more outraged by the burning of the Porcian Basilica than the loss of the Senate House.'

Eco nodded. 'Probably impressed that Milo's men saved Marcus Lepidus.'

'Probably hopes there'll be someone to do the same for him if the mob ever attacks his house.'

'But is Milo the man for him?'

'Maybe that's what he's here to decide.'

More numerous than the wealthy traders and bankers in the crowd were citizens of more modest appearance, who might have been small

shopkeepers or craftsmen or free labourers. Eco nodded in the direction of such a man nearby, a glum-looking fellow attended by a single slave and dressed in a toga with a worn hem. 'That one looks to have less to lose than our banker friend.'

'And less to start with. A fire in his apartment block could wipe him out completely.'

'Well, if the worst happened, he needn't go hungry. There's always the grain dole that Clodius established.'

I shook my head. 'People like him want the state to give them order, more than they want a grain dole. He craves stability no less than our banker friend.'

'Do you think that's why he's here? Looking for law and order?'

'Why not?'

'Let's find out.' Eco took my arm and together we slid through the crowd, to the consternation of Eco's bodyguards, who were hard pressed to follow.

'Citizen,' said Eco, 'don't I know you?'

The man looked at Eco appraisingly. 'I don't think so.'

'Yes, I'm almost certain we frequent the same tavern. You know, that little place —'

'The Three Dolphins?'

'That's it! Yes, I'm sure we've spoken before.'

'Maybe.' The man's glum expression lightened a bit.

'Oh, you remember, we once had quite a laugh — you know, at that funny fellow who works there . . .'

'Gaius, you mean? Yes, he's an odd one.' The man chuckled.

'And of course . . .' Eco gestured with his hands to suggest an ample bosom.

The man flashed a crooked smile and nodded. 'Ah, the old man's daughter. The one he claims is still a virgin. Ha!'

Eco discreetly tapped his foot against mine, as if to say: The fish is hooked. Gaining the confidence of a total stranger is one of the tricks that Eco learned from me, and he likes to show off to his teacher. I saw him glance quickly at the man's hands, appraising the chapped fingertips and the red stain under the fingernails.

'Do you still work as a cloth dyer?'

'What else? Washing and dyeing, washing and dyeing. Over in the Street of the Fullers. Every day for more than twenty years now.'

'Is that right?' Eco lowered his voice to a confidential tone. 'Say, how much did they give you?'

'What?'

'This morning. You know what I mean. How much did Milo's men give you?'

The fuller looked at Eco and then glanced warily at me.

'It's all right,' said Eco. 'The fellow's with me. He's a harmless mute.'

I discreetly kicked Eco's ankle. This was a private joke – it was Eco who had once been a mute, not me. Now he had effectively prevented me from saying a word.

'So how much did they give you?' said Eco again.

'Same as everyone else, I imagine,' said the fuller.

'Yes, but how much?'

'Well, I never like to say exactly. But enough.' The man tapped at a purse tucked away in his toga and produced a muffled clink. 'And a promise for quite a bit more if I'll vote for him when the time comes. And you?'

'A hundred sesterces,' said Eco.

'What! A hundred! They gave me only half that much!'

'Ah, but the hundred was for both of us.' Eco hooked his thumb at me.

The man nodded, mollified by Eco's explanation. Then he frowned. 'But if your friend is a mute and can't even shout his support, it hardly seems fair to pay him as much as –'

'Ah, but as you can see, the two of us each have two slaves, men with strong lungs, and you appear to have only one. Even with my friend being mute, that gives us five voices to your two.'

'Yes, well, I suppose . . .'

'So, citizen, what do you make of all this?' With an expansive gesture Eco indicated the whole Forum, and by extension the crisis plaguing Rome.

The fuller shrugged. 'Same as usual, only worse. Except that now they've gone from character assassination to assassination outright. We'd be lucky if they'd all kill each other off, starting from the top down. Wipe themselves out! But you know

how it is when the big fellows start falling – they fall on top of us little fellows and crush us.'

Eco nodded sagely. 'Then you're not a particularly enthusiastic supporter of Milo?'

'Fah!' The man curled his lip in disdain. 'Oh, he's certainly better than some others, or else I wouldn't be here. You couldn't pay me enough to attend a contio held by the Clodians. That fellow Clodius was worse than a beast in rut. Screwing his own sister! And they say when he was a boy he sold himself to rich old men. You know the song – 'To get ahead, he gave them head, then took his sister to his bed.' And –'

'But what about the grain dole?'

The man was suddenly incensed. 'Just another scheme to make himself more powerful! Yes, Clodius set up the grain dole – and then who was put in charge of keeping the lists of eligible citizens? Sextus Cloelius! That's right, Clodius's number one henchman, the one who torched the Senate House. As corrupt as they come! Don't talk to me about the grain dole. It's all a racket!'

'A racket?' said Eco.

'Of course. You must know how it works.'

'Enlighten me.'

'All right: Sextus Cloelius talks a man into freeing half his household slaves. The slaves become freedmen, but where are they going to go? They still work for their old master, they still live in his house. But as freedmen they can go onto the grain dole, so their master doesn't have to feed them anymore – the state does! For his cut, Sextus

Cloelius enlists these new freedmen into the Clodian gang, to stalk the streets at night and show up at contios to terrorize the opposition. And they get to vote, as well. The grain dole! Clodius passed off the whole nasty business as a big favour he'd done for the common man in Rome, people like me, providing us with a way to feed ourselves in bad times. But it was just a way to supply himself with new voters and gang members – and to feed them at state expense! I tell you, I was born a citizen, and it makes me furious to see Clodius's gang of ex-slaves getting the same privileges as me. What a conniver that Clodius was, right up to the last – they say he was working out more new schemes to give even more power to freedmen. If he'd had his way he'd have torn down the state and put his gangs in charge of everything. Then we'd have had King Clodius, chopping off heads right and left, and a bunch of ex-slaves bullying the rest of us. We're all better off with him dead, that's for sure. Milo did a good thing. I don't mind turning up to shout a few words of encouragement for him.'

'And if it puts a little jingle in your purse . . .' said Eco.

'Why not?'

'Yes, why not? Well, I'll talk to you later, citizen. Perhaps we'll meet again at the Three Ducks.'

'The Three Dolphins?' said the fuller.

'Exactly!' Eco smiled and withdrew, taking my arm. 'Well, Papa, was I right about the fellow?'

'On the contrary, Eco, I was right. Just as I

speculated, our friend the fuller came here today to support law and order.'

'Indeed not! Papa, the man was bribed to be here, probably like three-quarters or more of the rest of this crowd. I knew I'd seen some of Milo's lieutenants passing out money when I walked through the Forum earlier this morning, on my way to your house. I suppose we should be insulted that we weren't offered anything.'

'The bribe dispensers all know us by now, Eco.'

'I suppose that's it. This little gathering is costing Milo a tidy sum.'

'Yes, but I was still right.'

'About what?'

'About why our friend the fuller is here. He's looking for the rule of law and order.'

'And a bribe,' said Eco.

'And a bribe,' I conceded.

Caelius and Milo soon arrived, surrounded by a large retinue. As they made their way through the crowd, people craned their necks to get a look at Milo, and when they saw him many began to cheer. Their excitement seemed genuine, and why not? For better or worse, Milo was the man of the hour, and this was his first appearance in public since the incident on the Appian Way. All eyes were on him. All ears were eager to hear him speak.

With or without bribery, Milo had many supporters. He had been campaigning for the consulship for a long time, and in an effort to expand his

support beyond the Best People he had spent a fortune on extravagant games and shows. Rome loves a politician who knows how to stage a spectacle. Some magistrates are required to put on shows at various annual festivals, at their own expense, as part of their official duties for the year. Other men put on shows as private citizens, in the guise of funeral games. Whatever the pretext, every politician ascending the rungs of the magistracies is obligated to outdo his rivals in producing the most memorable races and comedies and gladiatorial combats. The practice is so accepted that no one ever seems to notice that providing expensive public entertainments is just as much a kind of electoral bribery as putting coins directly into the purses of voters. Nowadays, people seem to have lost the will to object even to that.

Marcus Caelius ascended the platform and called the contio to order.

Caelius had been trained in oratory from boyhood by both Cicero and the late Marcus Crassus. He was their most brilliant pupil. He had mastered the formal challenges of constructing a speech, as well as the technical skills of modulating his voice and casting it to great distances, but more notably, over the years he had crafted a wickedly sarcastic style which set the tone for his whole generation. When older orators striving for new effects attempted to emulate this style, the result was often blatant and shrill, but it was never so when practised by Caelius himself. This was his genius, that he was able to cast over a large crowd the same charm that

he emanated in closer quarters, but without the ironical undercutting that one often felt in his immediate presence. He was able to utter the most vicious innuendoes and obscene double entendres at a public gathering without seeming vindictive or vulgar. Instead, he seemed only effortlessly clever and witty, and quite sincere. This gave him tremendous power as an orator.

Caelius was not really in his element playing the rabble-rousing tribune at a contio. He was more suited to courts of law, especially as a prosecutor, where he could pour his acid over a squirming victim before an appreciative audience of cultured jurors, educated men like himself who appreciated swift, convoluted wordplay. Still, Caelius commenced his contio displaying the self-assurance he was known for, of the sort that cannot be faked.

'Good citizens of Rome! You see beside me on the platform today a man you all know – Titus Annius Milo. His name has been on all your lips of late. You have gone to bed at night thinking about him, asking yourselves just what sort of man is this Milo? You've awakened in the morning wondering where on earth he might be. And every hour of every day you have considered the same pressing question which you must be considering even now: When will this madness be over?

'Well, we are here to get some answers. Not tomorrow, not somewhere else, but here and now. First, wonder no more where Milo is – he's standing right in front of you, his head held high, proudly showing himself in the heart of the city

he has served so long and so faithfully. You may have heard a wild rumour that Milo had left Rome for good and was never coming back. Yes, I see some of you nodding; you know the rumour. Ridiculous! Think of that which you love best in all the world. Would you ever let yourself be parted from it, or abandon it for any reason? No! Not if you had to die first. Not even' – he lowered his voice – 'if you had to kill. That is how much Milo loves Rome. He will never forsake her.

'Which brings us back to the first question: What sort of fellow is Milo, what is his character? That's something each of you may decide for yourself, when you have had a chance to hear him out. Yes, Milo himself shall speak to you today. The rules allow him to speak, since Milo is himself the subject of this contio, and I demand that he speak, since I am the tribune who called this contio. Demand him to speak, I say, because Milo did not come here willingly. Oh no! I had to drag him here today, against his will. Do you think he wanted to leave his safe house to go walking in a city where madmen run riot, crying out for his death? Milo is exceedingly brave, but he's not a fool. No, he came only because I insisted that he come, only because I, as your tribune, demanded it.

'Which brings us to the third question, which weighs like a stone on all of us, which fills our heads like the stench from the smoking ruins of the Senate House over yonder: When will this madness be over? Not until something is done about the death of Clodius, I'm afraid. Not until the whole ugly

incident is put to rest, as the shade of Clodius himself was supposedly put to rest when his friends set fire to him like a faggot in the Senate House. How did Clodius die, and why, and who killed him? The friends of Clodius claim that he was viciously attacked and killed without cause. They point the finger of blame at Milo. They call him a murderer. They insinuate that he intends to kill again, and that next time his victim will be a man far more revered, far greater than Clodius ever was.

'Then let us put Titus Annius Milo on trial. Yes! Right here, right now, let us put him on trial for murder. Not a trial such as the magistrates hold, with jurors chosen from the Senate and the higher orders. It is you, the people, citizens of Rome, who have suffered most from the chaos of the last few days, and so I bring this matter directly to you, the people, and earnestly solicit your judgment. You see, I have not come to praise Milo; I have come to try him! And if you should determine that he is a vicious murderer, that he plots more murders, then let him leave our midst. Yes! Let him be banished, let us send him into exile and make that vicious rumour real. Let us drive Milo from the heart of the city he loves into the wilderness!'

At this there were scattered cries of indignation from the crowd, as if the idea of Milo in exile outraged them. I noticed that our friend the fuller was among the first to raise his voice in protest. He was soon joined by a swelling chorus of dissent. Someone had done a thorough job of seeding the crowd. But I noticed that the man I had called a

banker was yelling in protest, too, and gesturing for those in his retinue to raise their voices; surely a man of his means had not been bought with a mere fifty sesterces.

Caelius raised his hands for silence and put on an expression of dismay. 'Citizens! Please, restrain yourselves! You love Milo, as Milo loves Rome; I understand that. Still, he must be called to account. He must be judged, and we must be sober in our verdict. No more cheering or jeering, I beg you. This is not a candidate's rally. This is a contio held in time of dire emergency, a solemn inquiry into a matter that has crippled our city with riot and fire. What we do here today will be talked about all over the seven hills and beyond the city walls. Those who cannot be here today, great and small alike, will take notice of your judgment. Remember that!'

Eco spoke in my ear: 'Another reference to Pompey?'

Caelius stepped to one side of the platform. 'Milo, come forwards!'

Proud and with head held high – that was how Caelius had described Milo. Certainly he did not have the scurrying gait or furtive look of a man haunted by guilt. He swept forwards without hesitation and with a grand, almost swaggering air of confidence. His toga was better fitted than the one he had worn at Cicero's house, draped and folded to give the best impression of his short, stocky physique. His usually beard-shadowed jaw looked so pale that I wondered if he had applied some sort of cosmetic.

At a real trial he would have been expected to put on his shabbiest toga, shamble about like an old man, wear his hair unkempt and let his beard grow stubbly; jurors expect an accused man to exploit their sympathies. Clearly, Milo was having none of that. To show himself at a trial, even a mock trial, looking more like a proud candidate than an anxious defendant, was an act of pure defiance. This partisan crowd loved it. Despite Caelius's admonitions, a loud and seemingly spontaneous cheer echoed through the Forum. Milo's lips twitched into a smirk and he lifted his chin several degrees higher.

Caelius put on a stern face and raised his arms for silence. 'Citizens, must I remind you what we are here for? Let us proceed. Let Titus Annius Milo make an accounting of his actions.'

Caelius stepped back to allow Milo full run of the platform; Milo was of the arm-swinging school of oratory which requires an expansive stage, in many ways the opposite of Caelius. His forte was not the small jest that only later in the speech blossoms into hilarity, or the elegant understatement that veils a pointed dagger. Milo represented what Cicero had once jokingly ridiculed as the hammer and yoke school of oratory: 'Pound home every point with a heavy hammer, then yoke up the metaphors and flog them all the way to market.'

But not every speaker can be a Cicero or Caelius; every orator has to find the style that suits him, and dogged earnestness bordering on stolid defiance suited Milo. That morning, striding back and forth

across the platform waving his arms, he seemed utterly blunt and candid, though I knew that his every word and gesture must have been carefully scripted and rehearsed again and again in Cicero's study.

'Fellow citizens of this beloved city! My friend Marcus Caelius is right – the madness that threatens us all will never be dispelled until the true circumstances of the death of Publius Clodius are made known. I don't know what you've heard about his death – I can only imagine the ugly rumours that have been flying and the vicious aspersions that have been cast against me, and against my loyal servants, who bravely risked their lives to save my own.

'I'm not the sort to give pretty speeches. I will be brief and to the point. I can only tell you what I know.

'Nine days ago I left Rome and set out on a short journey down the Appian Way. Some of you may know that I hold a local office back in my home town, Lanuvium. Last year my fellow Lanuvines elected me their 'dictator' – a quaint way of saying chief magistrate. The office is not demanding, but occasionally I do have to go home to fulfil my obligations. This was such an occasion. I was called upon to nominate a priest to the local cult of Juno to preside over her festival next month. Juno's patronage of Lanuvium goes back to ancient times, before the Lanuvines were conquered by Rome. Her festival is the biggest day of the year in Lanuvium. Traditionally the Roman consuls

attend. So I intend to return to Lanuvium next month, in that capacity – because there will be elections, and I will be elected consul!'

There was an outburst of cheering. Milo waited for it to subside. 'That morning I attended the regular meeting of the Senate, which broke up around the fourth hour of the day. Then I went home to change into travelling clothes. My wife was going with me. I would have preferred to start right away – the trip to Lanuvium is about eighteen miles, an easy day's journey if you get an early enough start. But with all her last-minute preparations – isn't that always the way with a wife? – we didn't leave Rome until well after midday. For her comfort, we rode in an open carriage bundled up in heavy cloaks. I should like to have travelled lighter, but my wife insisted on bringing her serving maids and boys along, so we had quite a long retinue.

'As you all know, the Appian Way heads south, straight as an arrow's flight and flat as a table. It's not until you reach the vicinity of Mount Alba that the road takes a few turns and you begin to ascend a bit. There are some grand homes in that area. Pompey has a villa in the woods not too far off the road. So did Publius Clodius. I wish I had remembered that, and been more cautious.

'Clodius must have known of my plan to go to Lanuvium that day – it was no secret. Perhaps he also knew that I would be accompanied by my wife and her servants, encumbered with a most unwarlike retinue. I'm told that Clodius had said outright

149

and in public, only a few days previously, that he intended to kill me within a matter of days. 'We can't take the consulship from Milo, but we can take his life!' That's what he said. And this was the day he intended to make good on that threat, at that lonely spot on the Appian Way.

'I found out later that Clodius had left Rome – suddenly, quietly – the previous day. To be ready for me, to lie in wait. He must have had scouts posted along the way, running ahead to let him know that I was coming. He chose a spot where the higher ground gave him the advantage. There I was, in a carriage, with all those women and servant boys, and there was Clodius with his troop of trained killers on horseback, hidden in the trees off the road, waiting and watching.

'The ambush occurred at about the eleventh hour of the day. The sun was already beginning to dip below the higher trees. And then the attack – confusion, screaming, blood. If I'd been a bird flying overhead, I might be able to tell you exactly what happened. But to me, sitting in that carriage with my wife, it all began in the blink of an eye. All at once there were men with swords standing in the road, blocking our way. My driver shouted at them. They rushed at him, pulled him from the carriage and stabbed him to death right before my eyes! I threw off my cloak. I found my sword and leaped from the vehicle. By Hercules, the screams of my wife still echo in my ears! The men who'd killed my driver came after me, but the fellows were cowards at heart. A few swings of my sword and they fled

like rabbits!' When Milo mimed the action with broad strokes through the air, it wasn't hard to imagine men fleeing from him.

'Then I realized that more men were attacking the retinue behind me. Amid the confusion I saw Clodius himself astride a horse. He turned and saw my beloved Fausta. He heard her screaming. He didn't see me – the carriage blocked his view. But he must have seen my rumpled cloak and thought that I was still in the carriage with Fausta, slumped over, dead – because he cried out to his companions, 'We've got him! Milo's dead! At last, he's dead!'

'Let me tell you, citizens, it's a strange thing, hearing a man proclaim your death in a gleeful voice. My bodyguards farther back in the retinue tried to fight their way to the carriage to help me, until they heard Clodius gloating that I was dead. Can you blame them for what happened next? They fought to defend themselves, yes, but they also fought because they were furious, because they thought that their master had been murdered and their mistress was in terrible danger. In the midst of the skirmish they came upon Clodius himself, and when the skirmish was over, Clodius was dead. I didn't order his death. It happened without my knowledge and outside my presence. Are my slaves to blame? No! They did exactly what every man here would have wanted his own slaves to do in the same situation. Am I not right?'

There was a roar of agreement from the crowd. I noticed that the banker was especially enthusiastic.

Milo seemed to draw strength from the crowd. He continued to shout above the roar. Veins bulged on neck and his face turned red. 'If Clodius had succeeded with his ambush, it's I who would be dead today!' He poked his chest repeatedly with his forefinger, hard enough to bruise himself. 'It would be Clodius that everyone would be pointing at. They'd all be accusing Clodius of murder, and saying Clodius was a threat to . . .' Milo restrained himself. It wouldn't do to say the Great One's name out loud. 'But Clodius failed! Clodius lost! He paid the price for his wickedness. He was the cause of his own death, and I won't take responsibility for it!'

This brought even louder cheers. Milo stood on tiptoe, clenching his fists at his sides and shouting to be heard. He had remarkably powerful lungs. 'I regret nothing! I apologize for nothing! And I refuse to mouth empty words of comfort to his widow or his children, and certainly not to that vile sister of his. His death was the greatest gift the gods could give to Rome. If I'd strangled him with my own hands, I wouldn't be ashamed to say so! If I'd killed him in cold blood, caught him by surprise and stabbed him in the back, still I would be proud of the act!'

Caelius hurriedly stepped forwards, his face rigid. I leaned towards Eco. 'I think Milo has gone beyond his script.'

Caelius raised his left hand for silence. With his right hand he reached for Milo's shoulder. When Milo tried to shrug him off, Caelius tightened his grip until I saw Milo wince and shoot him an angry glance.

The crowd ignored the signal for silence. They began to chant as if they were at an election rally. Several different chants started up at once. The result was deafening. The fuller joined in with those reciting an old piece of doggerel about Clodius and his sister:

> Clodius played the little girl
> While he was still a boy!
> Then Clodia made the little man
> Into her private toy!

This chant was repeated over and over, punctuated by whoops of laughter and shouted louder and louder to compete with another chant taken up by the banker and his retinue:

> Grain dole, grain dole,
> It's all just shit
> From Clodius's hole!
> Big pole, little pole,
> They all disappear
> Up Clodius's hole!

Up on the platform, Milo burst into laughter. His face turned an apoplectic shade of red. He laughed so hard he began to weep. He seemed to me like a man who has been holding a torturous pose that strains every tendon to agony for hour after hour, and suddenly cannot hold the pose any longer. He shook so convulsively that he seemed hardly able to stand up.

Caelius gave up on quieting the crowd. He wore a bemused, vaguely anxious expression, as if to say: This was not exactly what I intended, but I suppose it will do . . .

I turned to Eco, curious to see my unflappable son's reaction, but he had reverted to muteness, as confounded as I was. To ridicule the dead is to mock the gods. There was something frightening in the sudden, raging hilarity of the mob, a vertiginous sensation of teetering at the edge of a dark precipice.

The raucous chanting continued, but was suddenly joined by a noise more like screaming than laughter. An invisible, palpable tremor passed through the crowd, a quiver of anxiety. Heads turned in confusion, trying to discern the source. The ripple of apprehension was quickly followed by a wave of panic.

How had Milo described the ambush on the Appian Way? Confusion, screaming, blood – if I'd been a bird flying overhead, I might be able to tell you exactly what happened – but it all began in the blink of an eye . . .

So it was in the Forum that day, when the Clodians descended with flashing swords like a vengeful army on the contio of Caelius and Milo.

# IX

I have never been a military man, but I am not a stranger to battle. In the year that Cicero was consul, I was with my son Meto when he fought for Catilina at the battle of Pistoria. I carried a sword. I saw Romans slaughter Romans.

I have seen battle. I know what a battle looks like, sounds like, smells like. What happened in the Forum that day was nothing like a battle. It was a massacre.

During the massacre itself, there was no time to think about anything but escape. It was only afterwards that I was able to ponder exactly what happened.

Some said that the Clodians' attack was spontaneous, spurred by reports of what Milo and Caelius were saying at the contio. Infuriated at the allegation that Clodius had staged an ambush, his grieving followers decided to show the crowd at the contio just what an ambush was like. Others argued that

the attack was premeditated, just as Clodius's ambush on the Appian Way had been premediated, and that the Clodians had only been waiting for Milo's appearance and the first public gathering of his supporters to launch their assault.

Premeditated or not, the attack was well staged. The Clodians arrived heavily armed. They made no attempt to hide their weapons. They carried short swords, daggers and clubs. Some carried bags of stones. Some carried torches. They seemed to appear from all sides at once. The panicked crowd contracted into itself, so that at first there was as great a danger of being crushed or trampled underfoot by friends as there was of being cut open or clubbed to death by foes.

Of course, despite the law which forbids carrying weapons inside the city walls, many at the contio were secretly armed or had armed bodyguards, and many of them (especially those who were part of Milo's regular gang) had as much experience of street fighting as the Clodians, so the engagement was not entirely one-sided. But the Clodians had the strategic advantage of surprise and the tactical advantage of having the crowd surrounded. They may also have had a considerable advantage in numbers – that was what the bruised and battered adherents of Milo claimed afterwards, but at the time I doubt that anyone bothered to count heads.

Milo's adherents would also claim afterwards that the attacking force was made up largely of slaves. Clodius's lieutenants, they claimed, now commanded whole armies of slaves and former slaves

who owed them allegiance thanks to Clodius's radical innovations, like the grain dole. That was the true crime of what happened that day, Milo's people said: that slaves and ex-slaves had disrupted a peaceable public assembly of citizens conducting state business. What had the Republic come to when such low-born rabble ruled the streets?

But as I say, all these considerations came as afterthoughts. At the time, panic reigned.

Eco and I sensed the danger at the same moment, even though there was nothing yet to see. He reached for my arm. I reached for his. His body-guards turned outward in a ring and reached for the daggers hidden in their tunics.

Eco pressed his mouth to my ear. 'Whatever happens, Papa, stay close to me!'

More easily said than done, I thought, as bodies pressed together and were wrenched this way and that, like links of armour being tested by a smith. To be caught in such a crowd must be something like the sensation of drowning in rough waters. A sea of bodies is a solid, writhing thing that presses back against you, struggling, like you, to stay alive.

The noise became deafening – oaths, curses, screams, grunts, sudden high-pitched wails and gut-tural, choking sounds. The fuller and his slave were suddenly next to me. He was yelling, to no one in particular, 'I knew this would happen! I knew it!'

Suddenly there was a break in the crowd nearby, like a rip through a piece of cloth. The Clodians broke through. Wild-eyed men with upright daggers in their fists rushed towards me. Their lips were drawn

back, their teeth clenched. They growled like dogs.

Eco's bodyguards seemed to have vanished, along with Eco. The panicked crowd was at my back, like a solid wall; I could no more melt into it than I could melt into stone. 'That one!' cried one of the attackers, pointing with his knife. 'Get the bastard!' He rushed towards me.

I braced myself, fighting the impulse to turn away. I have always promised myself that I would not end up as one of those corpses discovered with wounds in the back. I stared at the man's face, trying to look into his eyes, but his wild gaze was fixed on something beyond me. He veered past me, his knife whistling a shrill note a finger's-width from my ear. His friends followed, shoving me out of the way. From the corner of my eye I saw flashing daggers rise into the air one after another, like long-necked birds craning skyward.

I pressed myself into the fleeing crowd, trying to merge again into its anonymity, trying not to watch. An even stronger impulse compelled me to look back.

The daggers rose and fell, rose and fell. They were met by other daggers. Streamers of blood shot upward like screams congealing in the frosty air. In the midst of the turmoil I saw the man I had taken for a banker. He was the one the Clodians had rushed to attack. His cordon of bodyguards had been breached and decimated. The slaves who fell defending him were crumpled in a mass around him, their blood-stained bodies trapping his legs so that he could not flee. The Clodians circled him like vultures, their

knives like pecking beaks. They stabbed him again and again. As he twisted and writhed, his mouth gaping in a soundless scream, greedy hands reached to snatch the silver necklace from his throat and pull a bag of coins from inside his toga.

His assailants circled him once more and then moved on, like a whirlwind. By some miracle the banker remained upright. His eyes and mouth were wide open in astonishment, his toga covered with blood. Suddenly one of his assailants rushed back and quickly, skilfuly, like a dutiful slave caring for his master's accoutrements, took the man's hand and slipped the gold signet ring from his finger.

The thief might have left it at that, but having come back to finish his business he seemed determined to strike a final blow. He slipped behind the stupefied banker and raised his dagger high, gripping it with both hands. I cringed and braced myself as if the blow were aimed at me.

But I never saw it fall. A strong hand gripped my shoulder and spun me around. I faced a hulking young man with glinting eyes and a grimly set jaw. At the bottom edge of my sight I saw flashing steel and knew he held a dagger.

I have faced the prospect of imminent death on several occasions in my near-sixty years. It always seems to provoke the same chain of thoughts in my head. You fool, I always think – because it seems that such situations could always, somehow, have been avoided or at least postponed – you fool, this is the end of you at last. The gods have lost interest in the little

story of your life. You no longer amuse them. You shall now be snuffed out like a guttering lamp . . .

It is always the same: the names of my loved ones echo in my head. I hear the sweet sound of my father's voice, which I have not heard for many, many years. And sometimes, in such moments, and this was such a moment, I see the face of my mother, who died when I was very young, and whose face I can otherwise never quite recall. I remembered it vividly in that instant, and knew that my father had been right when he had told me, as he had often done, that she was beautiful, very beautiful . . .

But of course a part of me knew that I was not yet destined to die, and understood at once when the hulking young man, in a gruff, desperate voice, said, 'Thank Jupiter I found you! The master is furious! Come on!'

The fellow was one of Eco's young bodyguards, of course. In my confusion I had not recognized him.

Eco had retreated behind a nearby temple, where a lean-to shed attached to the plain rear wall offered a degree of concealment. We could still be seen from two directions, since the shed was open at either end, but the spot was at least more defensible than standing in the open.

'Papa! Thank the gods Davus found you!'

'Never mind the gods. Thank Davus.' I smiled at the sturdy young fellow, who grinned back at me. 'What now?'

Eco peered out glumly. There was nothing and no one to be seen except blank walls which cast back the echoes of the rioting mob. 'I suppose we could stay

here. Not a bad spot to make a stand, though there's no knowing what we might come up against.'

'Should we make a run for it?'

'Maybe. To your house or mine?'

'Mine's closer,' I said. 'But we'd have to cross the Forum somehow, and I imagine there's more chance of the riot spreading up that way, towards Milo's house.' I felt a chill as I thought of my wife and daughter alone at the house, with only a barred door and Belbo to protect them.

'To my house then, Papa?'

'No. I have to get back to Bethesda and Diana.'

He nodded. The sound of the riot seemed to grow louder, though it might have been only a trick of the acoustics. Suddenly two figures appeared from around the corner of the temple. We ducked into the shadows.

From their plain tunics, the two appeared to be slaves. They rounded the corner so fast they bumped into each other and almost fell. The taller one saw the shed and pointed. 'There! We could hide there!'

The shorter, stockier one saw the shed and rushed towards it, pushing his companion out of the way. They were almost like comic slaves out of Plautus, except that in a play they would be fleeing a just beating from their master, not a bloody riot.

'Jupiter's balls!' said the taller one, hurrying to catch up. 'You needn't push me down, Milo!'

'And you needn't shout my name out loud, you idiot! Come on, before someone sees us.'

Milo was inside the shed before he realized it was occupied. The first thing he saw were four daggers

pointing towards him as Eco's bodyguards advanced. Caelius, coming up from behind, bumped into him and knocked him forwards. Milo's eyebrows shot up and he bared his teeth in a grimace as he tripped forwards and very nearly impaled himself on the nearest dagger. Caelius, glimpsing steel, skittered back and peered wide-eyed into the shed.

'Draw back!' said Eco, calling off the bodyguards. 'These two won't hurt us.'

Milo scanned the faces confronting him and stopped at mine. 'Gordianus? Is that you? Cicero's man?'

'Gordianus, yes. Cicero's man, no. And you're Milo, though who would know it to look at you? Where's your toga?'

'Are you joking? The mob is going after anybody in a toga. They're all a bunch of cut-throat slaves and thieves, killing and robbing every citizen they come to. I threw off my toga the first chance I got. Thank Jupiter I was wearing this tunic underneath.'

'You took off your ring of citizenship as well,' I said, looking at his bare finger.

'Yes, well . . .'

'I see that Marcus Caelius followed your inspiration.' I shook my head. Two of the most powerful men in Rome were deliberately posing as slaves, and behaving like slaves as well. I suddenly had to laugh.

'Stop that!' said Milo.

'Sorry. It's the tension of the moment.' But I started laughing again, and was soon joined not only by Eco but by Eco's slaves. Even Caelius, always ready to see the absurdity in any situation, barked out a laugh.

'But where's your retinue, your bodyguards?' I said.

'Slaughtered. Scattered. Who knows?' said Milo.

'I don't suppose that could be them?' I said, all laughter dying from my voice. A group of dagger-wielding men had just appeared from around the corner.

'Oh, Jupiter's balls!' Caelius groaned. He and Milo shoved their way through the shed and fled out the other side. I followed with Eco and his bodyguards bringing up the rear. Behind us I heard a clash of steel and turned to see one of the pursuers stagger and fall, clutching his chest where Davus had wounded him. At the sight of one of their own gushing blood, the brigands lost heart and fell back.

Caelius and Milo had disappeared. We found ourselves at the edge of the riot, amid the scattered bodies of the wounded and dead. The paving stones were slick with blood. Smoke belched from the entrance to the Temple of Castor and Pollux. Next door, atop the House of the Vestal Virgins, the Virgo Maxima and her priestesses had gathered on the roof and were watching the scene below with expressions of horror and outrage.

'Come! This way!' I said, pointing to the paved walkway between the two buildings. It took us to the base of the Palatine Hill and onto the Ramp. Others were ahead of us, fleeing up the long sloping path like refugees from a sacked city. I thought I glimpsed Caelius and Milo far ahead, travelling at a breakneck pace and knocking people out of their way right and left.

I was completely out of breath before I reached the top of the Ramp. Eco saw my distress and signalled to his bodyguards to help me along. They seized my arms and practically carried me the last few steps. We hurried across the street, towards my house.

Suddenly, ahead of us, from out of one of my neighbours' houses, a group of armed men burst into the street. Their leader clutched a handful of jewellery – strands of pearls and silver links dangled from his grubby fingers. In his other hand he held a dagger dripping blood. The door behind him had been knocked from its hinges.

'You there!' he shouted at us. Though he was some distance away I smelled wine and garlic on his breath. Garlic for strength, an old gladiator's trick; wine to fortify his courage. He had a red face and ice-blue eyes. 'Have you seen him?'

'Seen who?' I gestured to the bodyguards to give the party a wide berth but to keep moving forwards.

'Milo, of course! We're going from house to house searching for him. When we find him we shall crucify him for killing Clodius.'

'Searching for Milo, are you?' said Eco. He was looking at the fistful of stolen jewellery; the sarcasm in his voice made me cringe.

The thief held up his hand and shook it. 'What, these? Who ever said that justice should be free, eh? We deserve our payment, don't we? As much as these rich folk deserve their pretty things.' He made such an ugly face that I thought he was about to come after us with his dagger. Instead he threw the handful of jewellery at our feet. The silver clinked against the

paving stones and the strand of pearls burst. Pink and white baubles bounced everywhere like bits of hail. The men behind him yelled and cursed.

'Who cares?' he shouted. 'There'll be plenty more where that came from.' He turned and led his raiding party down the street away from us, towards the next house.

My heart began to pound in my chest. If they were headed in the opposite direction, that meant they had already been to my house . . .

My head felt light. I blinked at oily spots before my eyes. Confronted with the possibility of my own death, a part of me always reacted with sceptical resignation. Facing the possibility of something terrible happening to Bethesda and Diana, I felt an overwhelming dread.

Eco understood. He clutched my hand and squeezed it. As we approached the house I looked for signs of fire or smoke and saw none. Then I saw the double doors of the entrance. They were standing wide open. The lock had been broken. So had the bar, which lay across the threshold broken in two pieces.

I stepped into the foyer, which seemed very dark after the daylight outside. Rushing forwards, I tripped over something large and solid. Eco and Davus helped me up. 'Papa —' said Eco.

I hurried on. 'Bethesda! Diana!'

No one answered. I ran from room to room, only vaguely aware that Eco and his men followed after me. Couches and chairs had been knocked over. Cabinets lay on their sides with their doors open.

In my bedroom, the sleeping couch had been senselessly ripped open and the stuffing pulled out in handfuls. A pool of something dark and slick shimmered on the floor in front of Bethesda's dressing table. Blood? I shuddered, close to tears, then realized that it was only unguent from a broken jar which had fallen to the floor.

There was no one in the kitchens, no one in the sleeping quarters. Where were the slaves?

I hurried on to Diana's room. The door of her wardrobe stood open and her clothes were scattered all over the floor. The little silver box where she kept her few pieces of jewellery was gone. I called her name. There was no answer.

I came to my study. The scroll cases were empty. They had plucked every scroll from its pigeonhole, probably looking for hidden valuables. Having found none, they had at least left my scrolls and writing instruments intact. Of what use were such things to thieves? Everything lay in piles on the floor, scattered but undamaged, the scrolls still tightly rolled and tied with ribbons.

Then I caught a whiff of something foul. I wrinkled my nose and followed the smell to the corner of the room. Someone had defecated on the floor and then used a torn piece of parchment to wipe himself. I carefully picked up the scrap by a corner to see what it was and read a few lines:

Father, what wretchedness is on us now!
I mourn for you still more than for the dead.

Poor Antigone! Poor Euripides!

I stepped from my study into the garden at the centre of the house. The bronze statue of Minerva, which I had inherited from my dear friend Lucius Claudius along with the house, which had been his pride and joy and mine, which had elicited the envy of Cicero himself, had been pulled from its pedestal. Did they think to find some secret treasure chamber beneath it, or did they act out of sheer, wanton destructiveness? The bronze should have survived the fall, but there must have been some hidden flaw in its casting. The virgin goddess of wisdom lay broken in two pieces.

'Papa!'

'What, Eco? Have you found them?'

'No, Papa. Not Bethesda or Diana. But in the foyer – you should come and see for yourself . . .'

'See what?'

Before he could answer, a voice from the sky called both our names. I looked up and saw Diana peering over the edge of the roof. My throat constricted and I almost sobbed with relief.

'Diana! Oh, Diana! But what – how did you get up there?'

'The ladder, of course. Then we pulled it up after us. And then we kept out of sight and stayed quiet. The thieves never even knew we were here.'

'Your mother as well?'

'Yes. She wasn't afraid to climb the ladder at all! And the slaves, too. It was my idea.'

'And a brilliant idea it was.' Tears welled in my eyes until Diana became a blur.

'And look, Papa! I even thought to save my jewellery box.' She held it proudly before her.

'Yes, very good. Go get your mother now,' I said, impatient to see with my own eyes that Bethesda was safe. 'Tell Belbo to come, too.'

Eco spoke softly in my ear. 'Papa, come to the foyer.'

'What?'

'Come.' He took my arm and led me there.

When I first rushed into the house, I had tripped over something large and heavy. The thing I had tripped over was a body. Eco's men had rolled him onto his back and pulled him into the light.

Belbo's face, normally so bovine and amenable, was frozen in a grimace of fierce determination. In his right hand he clenched a dagger with blood on it. The front of his pale tunic was spotted with great blossoms of red.

He had died just inside the broken door, defending the breach, striving to keep them out. His dagger testified that he had inflicted at least one wound, but he had taken many more.

The tears which I had been holding back, which I had begrudgingly released in my relief at seeing Diana, now came in a blinding flood. The simple, cheerful man who had been my loyal companion for twenty-five years and the protector of my loved ones, who had saved my life more than once, who had always seemed lit from within by a steady flame which nothing could extinguish, lay lifeless at my feet. Belbo was dead.

# Part Two

## *Road*

# X

The looting and burning went on for days.

Rome was utterly without order. Fires broke out or were deliberately started all over the city. A haze of smoke settled into the valleys between the seven hills. Teams of slaves and hired freedmen, their clothes and faces smeared with soot, rushed from crisis to crisis.

I heard women screaming in the night, hoarse cries for help, the clash of steel against steel. There were wild rumours of every sort of outrage – rapes, murders, kidnappings, children trapped in houses and burned alive, men hung upside down by their feet at street corners, beaten to death with clubs and left hanging like trophies.

The day after Belbo was killed, Eco and I braved the streets to deliver his body to the necropolis outside the city walls. Two of my household slaves pulled the cart bearing his corpse. Eco's bodyguards

flanked our procession. Though we passed several gangs of looters, no one disturbed us. They were too busy plundering the living to bother with the dead.

At the grove of Libitina we entered Belbo into the registry of the dead. The cremators were very busy that day. Belbo was burned along with several others on a flaming pyre, and then his ashes were taken to a common grave. It seemed too small an end to such a robust life.

Eco and I debated whether my family should go to his house, or his family should come to my house, so as to join our defences. In the end, we decided to leave his household slaves at the house on the Esquiline, so as to guard the place, but to move Menenia and the twins into my house, which, once the door was repaired and strengthened, was arguably more defensible. The Palatine was dangerous, but there had been numerous fires and reports of atrocities on the Esquiline as well, and down in the Subura there was no semblance of order at all. Besides, my house had already been ransacked. There was no reason for the same looters to come back a second time.

As is wont to happen in such circumstances, the air of crisis actually lent a comforting solidarity to the household. Bethesda, Menenia and Diana all worked together, seeing to the repair of the damaged furniture, making lists of the things that needed to be replaced, finding ways to keep the household fed when most of the markets were shut down and the rest were open for only a few

unpredictable hours each day. The twins, Titus and Titania, sensing the gravity of the situation, were eager to help and behaved with a maturity beyond their seven years. I felt safer in the company of Davus and the other bodyguards, and it was good to have Eco beside me. But the ransacked house itself was a constant reminder of our vulnerability. Whenever I passed through the garden, I saw the Minerva lying broken on the ground. Whenever I passed through the foyer, I remembered Belbo as we had found him. I felt his absence acutely. Sometimes I called his name aloud before stopping myself. He had been at my side every day for so long that I had come to take him for granted, like the air; and like the air, once he was gone I realized just how much I had needed him.

One interrex gave way to the next, and the next, and there were still no elections or even the prospect of elections. How could there be, in such a state of chaos? Day by day and hour by hour the sentiment seemed to be growing that Rome needed a dictator. Occasionally the name of Caesar was mentioned. More often, and more vehemently, it was Pompey who was invoked, as if the Great One's name were some magical incantation that could put all wrongs to right.

Each day I thought that I might hear from Cicero again, but there were no more summons from Tiro, no hushed meetings with Milo and Caelius. I almost wished that Cicero would call for me, so

that I could get some idea of what he and his circle were up to in the midst of the disorder.

It was another who came calling for me instead.

It was a cold, bright Februarius morning. Eco had gone to check on affairs at his house, so I was alone in my study. Despite the chill, I had opened the shutters to let in some sunlight and fresh air. Perhaps the many fires all over the city had at last been quenched; I could smell only a faint tang of smoke. Davus came into my study to say that a litter accompanied by a train of slaves was camped outside my front door, and that one of the slaves had a message for me.

'A litter?'

'Yes. Quite a grand vehicle. It has –'

'Red and white stripes,' I said, with a stab of intuition.

'Why, yes.' He raised his eyebrows and I was reminded, with a pang of sadness, of Belbo. Young Davus looked nothing like him, being dark and considerably more handsome than Belbo had ever been, but he was of the same size and bovine demeanour. He wrinkled his brow. 'It looks familiar.'

'Could it be the same litter we saw arrive at the house of Clodius, on the night of his death?'

'I think it must be.'

'I see. And there's a slave with a message, you say? Show him in.'

The man was typical of Clodia's male servants, young and impeccably groomed with a striking profile and a muscular neck. I would have known

who sent him even if Davus had not told me about the litter, for there was a hint of her perfume about his clothes. I had never forgotten that scent, with its blend of spikenard and costly crocus oil. He must have been a very favoured slave to smell so strongly of his mistress.

His status was confirmed by his haughty manner. He sniffed and peered about my study as if he were thinking of buying the house, not just delivering a message. 'Well,' I finally said, 'what does Clodia want from me, young man?'

He gave me a dubious look as if to say, I can't imagine, then smiled. 'She requests the pleasure of your company in her litter.'

'In her litter? What, does she expect me to go traipsing through the streets in a litter, at a time like this, with all that's going on?'

'If it's your safety you're concerned about, don't worry. Where else could you possibly be safer?'

Certainly not here, he seemed to suggest, looking over my shoulder and through the open shutters at the broken Minerva in the garden. And he was probably right. It was the Clodians who were rioting; they all knew Clodia's litter; they would scarcely attack their idol's sister. Besides that, her retinue probably included some of the biggest and fiercest gladiators in the city. Indeed, where else could I possibly be safer than skimming across the Palatine in Clodia's litter – unless, of course, we ran into a gang of Milo's men out looking for trouble . . .

On the other hand, considering the circum-

stances – anarchy in the streets, rival gangs waging virtual civil war, a looming dictatorship, an uncertain future – it was probably not a good idea to consort with Clodia at the moment. Eco would surely have advised me against it, but Eco was not there, and I was tired of hiding in my house, playing passive spectator to a city spinning out of control. So long as Cicero had taken me into his confidence, however suspicious the circumstances, I had felt that I had access to special knowledge. The privilege of knowing more than other men reassured me; it gave me a sense of control and power, whether real or not. Now I felt cut off, adrift, more anxious than if I were deliberately courting a danger that I at least comprehended. A meeting with Clodia promised a glimmer of privileged information. I couldn't resist.

The chance to be close to Clodia again had nothing to do with it, I told myself. The opportunity to recline next to her in her litter, cocooned in the aura of her perfume, close enough to feel the heat of her body . . .

'Davus, tell your mistress that I've been called away on a small errand. I don't expect to be away long, but if I am I'll send a messenger.'

'You're going out, Master?'

'Yes.'

'I should go with you.'

'You'll hardly be needed,' said Clodia's slave, giving Davus a disparaging look. I suppose Davus looked puny to him compared to Clodia's red-haired giants.

'I suspect the fellow's right, Davus. I'd rather you stayed here to look after the house.'

I followed the slave through the foyer and out of the house. Under the cold sun the red and white canopy of the litter was dazzling. The air was almost still with only a hint of a breeze, but the fabric was so delicate that the stripes wavered and brushed against one another like trembling serpents. The red-haired gladiators surrounding the litter drew themselves to attention. One of the bearers rushed to put down a block of wood before the entrance to the litter, to serve as a step. Before I could do it myself the curtains were parted from within. The slave girl who opened them moved aside and nodded towards the place where I was to sit, next to her mistress, but all I saw were Clodia's eyes. Her famous eyes: Catullus, in one of his love poems, had said they glittered like emeralds; Cicero, in the speech which had nearly destroyed her, had said that Clodia's eyes flashed like sparks from a whetted blade. Her eyes could seduce, or scandalize; her eyes could also weep. They glittered now with tears. I wondered if she had ever stopped crying since her brother died.

She turned her face away. In any other circumstances I might have thought the movement was calculated to show off the striking profile of her forehead and the line of her nose. Her lustrous dark hair hung down, unpinned for grieving. Her gown was black, as were the cushions around her. The corner seemed to swallow her up in darkness, except for her face and throat, which were a luminous, creamy white.

I slipped into the litter beside her. She reached for my hand, still averting her eyes. 'Thank you for coming, Gordianus. I was afraid you might not.'

'Why, for fear of the streets?'

'No, for fear of your Alexandrian wife.' Her lips compressed into the barest smile.

'Where are we going?'

'To Clodius's house.' The smile grew rigid. 'Or to Fulvia's house, I suppose I should say.'

'What for?'

'You must remember, when I invited you into the house on the night he died – I had a premonition that we might need you, sooner or later. I was right. It's Fulvia who needs you.'

'Really? I seem to recall that your sister-in-law was less than pleased with my presence in the mourning room.'

'Things change. Fulvia is a pragmatist. You happen to be the man that she needs right now.'

'For what?'

'She'll explain that to you herself. But this is what I ask from you: anything that you discover about my brother's death – tell me, please.' She turned her eyes on me then, and squeezed my hand. 'I know you believe in the truth, Gordianus. I know how much it matters to you. It matters to me, as well. If only I could know for certain how Clodius died, who killed him, and why, then perhaps I could finally stop weeping.' She managed another faint smile and let go of my hand. 'We've arrived.'

'Already?' The ride had been so smooth that I had scarcely known we were moving at all.

'I'll wait here until you're ready to leave, and then take you home again.'

The slave girl pulled back the curtains for me. The block of wood awaited my step. The great forecourt of Clodius's house was empty except for several men guarding the terraces and the gate. One of Clodia's gladiators accompanied me up the steps. The massive doors opened inward as if a gust of divine wind preceded me.

A slave accompanied me through the halls and galleries and up a flight of stairs to a room I hadn't seen before. It was at a corner of the house, with open windows that commanded a view of Palatine rooftops and the great temples on the Capitoline Hill beyond. The walls were stained with a bright green wash and decorated with blue and white borders in a geometrical Greek design. It was a bright, cheerful room, airy and light.

I saw Sempronia first. She sat in a chair close by the windows, wrapped in a red blanket to ward off the chill. Her long grey hair was still worn down for mourning, but it was gathered by a pin at the nape of her neck and hung straight behind her, touching the floor. The look she gave me was almost as cold as the air from outside.

Fulvia stepped in front of the windows. The light streaming in was so bright that I saw her only as a tall, narrow silhouette. As she stepped closer the veil of shadow over her features slowly dissolved. She was as I remembered her, plainer than Clodia but striking in her own fashion, younger and with

something very shrewd about her eyes. She sat in the chair beside her mother. As there were no other chairs in the room, I remained standing.

Fulvia looked at me appraisingly. 'Clodia says you're clever. I suppose she ought to know.'

I shrugged, not sure whether to respond to the compliment or the insinuation.

'I understand that you've paid some calls on Cicero recently.' She fixed her eyes on me.

'Not in the last few days.'

'But since my husband's murder.'

'Yes, on a couple of occasions. How did you know?'

'Let's just say that I inherited my husband's eyes and ears.'

And his calculated manner as well, I thought. She was all in black, to be sure, but I saw no other signs of mourning. Had her hysterical outburst before the crowd in the forecourt that night been purely for show, or was it a genuine release of the anguish that she otherwise held in check? She certainly seemed controlled at the moment. Clodia was more like the grieving widow, I thought, and Fulvia more like the impassive heir, wasting no tears as she took on her husband's mantle.

'You're trying to figure me out,' she said. 'Don't bother. And I won't try to figure you out. Your business with Cicero is your own affair. I won't ask you to do anything that compromises whatever relationship you have with him. Or with Milo, for that matter.' I raised my hand to object, but she went on. 'Everyone knows that Milo was respon-

sible for my husband's death. That's not what I want you to find out for me.'

'What, then?'

For the first time there was a glimmer of discomfort on her face – a slight wrinkling of the forehead, a trembling of the lips. 'There's a certain man, a friend of my husband. An old friend of mine as well, actually. He's approached me, offering his services when the time comes to prosecute Milo. I could use his help, his . . . support. But . . .'

'Yes?'

'I'm not sure that I can trust him.'

'Can you tell me his name?'

'Marc Antony.' She raised an eyebrow. 'You know him?'

'No.'

'But the look on your face –'

'I know his name, yes. One of Caesar's men – oh yes, now I remember. Our paths crossed that very night. As I was leaving your house, he was on his way here. He happens to know one of my sons. We exchanged a few words.'

'Only a few?'

'Let me think. He asked me if the rumour was true. About Publius Clodius. I told him it was.'

Sempronia rustled her blanket. Would her daughter ever acquire such a hardened face?

'And how did Antony react?' said Fulvia.

'It was dark. I could hardly see his face. But his voice was rather wistful, as I recall. He said something like, 'Ah, it's all over, then. The end of

Publius, for good or ill.' Then he went on his way.'

Fulvia gazed out the window at the distant Capitoline. It was Sempronia who answered. 'He ended up here. But Fulvia was in no condition to see him, or anyone. Antony spent some time talking with the other men in the anteroom and then left. So we know that Antony was here in Rome that night.'

'Yes,' said Fulvia, keeping her eyes on something far away. 'But where was he earlier that day?'

'Are you saying that you believe he had something to do with your husband's death?'

Fulvia didn't answer. Sempronia clutched at the red blanket. 'The fellow tried to murder Clodius with his bare hands only a year ago!'

Fulvia returned from wherever her thoughts had taken her. 'My mother exaggerates.'

'Do I?'

'What's this about?' I said.

'You never heard the story?' said Fulvia. 'I should have thought it would have made the rounds, such a juicy bit of gossip. Perhaps for once the people concerned managed to keep their mouths shut. There was no cause for scandal, just a dispute between two old friends, nothing more.'

'It would have been considerably more if Antony had succeeded!' said Sempronia.

'But he didn't,' insisted Fulvia.

'Perhaps you should explain,' I said.

Fulvia nodded. 'It happened out on the Field of Mars last year, on one of the election days that

ended up being cancelled. All the candidates were present, haranguing their supporters. I'm told there was the usual milling about, some scuffling, men with moneybags offering last-minute bribes, a few minor skirmishes. You know what it's like. I mean, being a man, you must have been to elections and seen for yourself. Perhaps you were there that day.'

'No. Actually, the last time I voted in a consular election was ten years ago, when Catilina ran.'

Sempronia was suddenly interested. 'You voted for Catilina?'

'No. Actually, I voted for a fellow with no head called Nemo.'

The two women regarded me curiously.

'It's a very long story. Never mind. No, I wasn't there on the day you're talking about. But I can picture the scene. What happened?'

'Antony and my husband had words,' said Fulvia. 'As I understand it, the exchange began in a friendly manner, but it didn't end that way. Publius was always a bit vague as to who said what to whom.'

'But we know how it turned out,' said Sempronia, with equal parts of disdain and amusement in her voice, 'with Antony drawing his sword and chasing Publius from one end of the Field of Mars to the other.'

'Where were your husband's bodyguards?' I asked.

'Those particular bodyguards?' said Fulvia. 'I don't know where they were that day, but I know where they are now — off working in the mines.'

There was a glint in her eyes that made her look, for that instant, almost as hard as her mother. 'Anyway, Publius got away unscathed.'

'Except for his dignity!' said Sempronia. 'Ducking into a cabinet under a stairway in some rat-infested warehouse on the river – like a cowering slave fleeing from his master's whip in some second-rate comedy.'

'That's enough, Mother.' Fulvia turned her flinty gaze to Sempronia. The test of wills between the two of them was almost palpable, like the grating sound of steel against a whetting stone. Sempronia visibly relented, sinking back beneath her red blanket. Fulvia, protector of her dead husband's dignity, sat upright. What sort of man had Clodius been, to contend with the two of them on a daily basis, and with his sister thrown in for good measure? No wonder he had thought himself worthy to run the city, if he had learned to keep control of his own household.

'What was the nature of this quarrel between your husband and Antony?'

'I told you, I never really knew what started the incident.'

'But surely you have some idea.'

Fulvia became distant again, gazing out of the window. Was this oscillation between harsh clarity and withdrawal calculated to keep me off balance, or was it simply her nature, or a kind of malady induced by the shock of her husband's murder? 'You needn't be concerned with such specifics, Gordianus. All I want is to find out whether Marc

184

Antony played any part whatsoever in what happened to Publius on the Appian Way.'

'First, I think I would need to determine to my own satisfaction exactly what did happen on the Appian Way.'

'Does that mean you'll accept the task?'

'No. I'll have to think about it first.'

'When can you give me your answer?'

I rubbed my chin. 'Tomorrow?'

Fulvia nodded.

'In the meantime,' I said, 'I want you to tell me exactly what happened that day, so far as you know. I want to know what Clodius was doing away from Rome, who might have known of his movements, who brought his body back to Rome, and how the skirmish began.'

Fulvia drew a deep breath. 'In the first place, this talk of an ambush is complete nonsense, unless it was Milo who ambushed Clodius. It was certainly Milo's men who began the fight, without any provocation whatsoever. My husband was completely blameless. And the atrocities Milo's men committed at our country villa afterwards, terrorizing the servants . . .'

An hour later our interview came to an end.

I still had not made up my mind about helping Fulvia, though a remuneration in silver had been mentioned that was sorely tempting, especially considering the damage that had been done to my house and the fact that I needed more bodyguards. It seemed that the more prosperous I grew, the more costly it became to live — literally, to stay

alive. Simple necessity made Fulvia's offer attractive; it would also give me an excuse to go poking about into the incident that had set Rome aflame and ended in the death of a man very close to me. On the other hand, as always, there was the degree of danger to be considered. Bethesda would say I was mad. So would Eco, probably, before he insisted on sharing the danger with me.

My head was full of these thoughts as I rode home beside Clodia in her litter, but not so full that I failed to notice her perfume and the warmth of her leg where it pressed against mine.

'Did you accept my sister-in-law's commission?' she asked.

'Not yet.'

We arrived at my house. As I moved to step out of the litter, Clodia gripped my arm. 'If you do accept, Gordianus, I hope that you'll share with me whatever you may discover. It matters to me very much, to know all I can about my brother's death.'

It was the sixth hour of the day and I was hungry for the midday meal. I headed towards the kitchen, but Davus approached me in the hall and told me that Eco was waiting for me. I gathered from the look on Davus's face that someone had severely scolded him for letting me go out without him.

I found Eco in my study, and also Bethesda. 'Husband, where have you been?'

'Didn't Davus tell you? I was called away on business.'

Bethesda's nostrils twitched. She cocked her head. Self-consciously I raised my sleeve to my

nose and breathed a faint scent of spikenard and crocus oil.

'Clodia,' declared Bethesda. 'Oh, I knew already. Davus told me about seeing her litter.'

'What did she want, Papa?' Eco looked almost as disapproving as Bethesda.

'Actually,' I began, and then was interrupted by the reappearance of Davus at the door.

'Another visitor, Master.'

'Yes?'

'He says his name is Tiro . . .' It was like the old Etruscan adage, I thought. No rain for a month, and then a downpour. 'He says that you're invited to come and share a midday meal with Marcus Tullius Cicero.'

'And Eco is invited, too, of course,' said Tiro, suddenly looking over Davus's shoulder. What had become of the retiring, perfectly behaved slave who would never have thought of taking the liberty of wandering unaccompanied through a citizen's house? Tiro had become a brash freedman, it seemed, and proof of the general consensus that manners in the Republic had all gone to Hades.

'I am hungry,' Eco conceded, patting his belly.

'And I'm starving,' I said.

Bethesda crossed her arms and said nothing. Imperious she might be, but she was not Sempronia or Fulvia, after all. Thank Jupiter for that.

# XI

Armed men stood guard at the door of Cicero's house and patrolled the roof. More men were stationed inside the foyer. I felt as if I were entering a general's camp.

The shutters had been closed in the dining room to keep out the cold. Pallid winter light seeped in from the garden, warmed by the glow of hanging lamps. Cicero was already settled on a dining couch with Marcus Caelius beside him. Tiro gestured for Eco and me to take places on the couch opposite, which was long enough for all three of us to share.

Caelius was looking smug about something, as usual, which irritated me, as usual. 'Marcus Caelius, you've come up in the world since I last saw you.'

He lazily raised an eyebrow.

'I mean, you appear to be a free citizen now. When our paths last crossed in the Forum – in that

shed behind the temple – I took you and Titus Annius Milo for runaway slaves.'

Cicero and Tiro frowned. Eco glanced at me uncertainly. Caelius's face became a blank mask for a moment, then he burst out laughing. 'Oh, Gordianus, I wish I'd thought of that one myself! "Caelius has come up in the world." ' He wagged his finger. 'If one of my rival tribunes uses it against me, I shall know you've taken to writing speeches for the enemy.'

'Gordianus would never consider doing that, surely,' said Cicero, fixing his eyes on me. 'Shall we plunge straight into the meal? I can hear your stomachs growling from here. Only simple fare, I'm afraid. The cook tells me it's impossible to find provisions in the markets. But it's best for a man to keep his diet simple, anyway.' Cicero had suffered from chronic dyspepsia for as long as I had known him.

The food was superb, nonetheless. A fish soup with dumplings was followed by bits of roasted chicken wrapped in pickled grape leaves with an aromatic cumin sauce. Cicero had learned to appreciate the finer pleasures which befitted a man of his stature.

He ate cautiously, nonetheless, scrutinizing each spoonful and slice before putting it into his mouth, as if he could tell by looking which morsel might set off his indigestion. 'Speaking of coming up – or going down – in the world, Gordianus, it strikes me that accepting a ride in the litter of a certain lady these days would cause many people to think that the passenger had lowered himself considerably.'

'How could that be? A litter goes to and fro, Cicero, not up and down.'

Caelius laughed. 'It all depends who's in the litter with her.'

Cicero looked at Caelius shrewdly. 'Not a prudent comment, my friend, considering your own history with the lady in question. Or the role you played in her —'

'Comeuppance!' said Caelius, almost choking on a bite of chicken to get the word out ahead of Cicero. I gathered it was a sort of game between them, punning at the expense of their enemies, particularly the Clodii.

'I assume you're referring to a visitor I had earlier today,' I said.

'The lady who swept you away,' said Caelius.

'How is it that you know who my visitors are, Cicero? I'd hate to think that my house is being watched.'

Cicero put down his spoon. 'Now really, Gordianus! We live on the same street. I have slaves and visitors coming and going all day. They all know the lady's litter. Everyone does. She could hardly park the thing in front of your house without people noticing.' He picked up the spoon again and toyed with it. 'But the curious thing is that you should have gone off with her. I don't know where — you see, I don't have anyone watching you, or else they'd have followed.'

'But you'd like to know?'

'Only if you care to tell me.'

'As a matter of fact, it wasn't the lady in question

who – well, she does have a name, doesn't she, so why not use it? Yes, I left in Clodia's litter, but it wasn't Clodia who wanted me.'

'Pity,' said Caelius.

'Is it? I wouldn't know.' The edge in my voice surprised me. 'Clodia was only acting as go-between. She took me to her sister-in-law's house, if you must know.'

'I see.' Cicero didn't seemed surprised. Had he sent a spy to follow the litter after all? 'Would it betray a confidence to tell us what Fulvia wanted with you?'

'She wanted my help in a certain personal matter. Nothing unusual.'

'Oh, I seriously doubt that.'

'Really? I suppose you think she wanted my help in something to do with her husband's death. But we all know the story behind that already, don't we? Milo himself laid out the facts at Caelius's contio for all Rome to hear: Clodius staged a vicious ambush, the tide turned against him, one of Milo's slaves put an end to him. Ask Caelius. He was there. He heard the story just as Eco and I did, though Milo was cut off before he could quite finish.' Caelius returned my glance, unblinking and unamused. 'No, Fulvia hardly said a word about Milo, if that's what you're thinking. Nor did she have much to say about Milo's friend, Marc Antony.'

Cicero looked genuinely nonplused. 'Antony? Milo's friend? I doubt that the two of them even know each other.'

I looked at Caelius, who seemed as lost as Cicero — no telltale smirk, no twitch of secret amusement.

'Then I must be mistaken. Perhaps I mixed up the names. That happens more and more as I get older. You're only a little younger than I am, Cicero. Don't you find it's a problem, keeping names straight? A man learns so many of them over a long lifetime. Where do all the names go? It's like words on a tablet, you can only fit in so many, and then you have to write smaller and smaller until the letters become illegible and the scribbles all run together. Some people have a gift for names, I suppose, or even a slave especially trained for the task.'

Cicero nodded. 'Tiro has always had a knack for keeping names straight. He's saved me from making many a gaffe — all those small-town voters from the hinterland who take offence if you can't remember their family tree all the way back to King Numa!' It was a politician's joke. We all laughed, but Caelius practically brayed.

'But this business about Marc Antony . . .' said Cicero.

I shrugged. 'As I said, he was hardly mentioned at all. You say he's not a friend of Milo. Is he friend of yours, then, Cicero?'

He looked at me thoughtfully. 'We're not enemies, if that's what you mean.'

It was my turn to look puzzled.

'There's no ill will between Marc Antony and myself,' he said, 'at least not on my part.'

'Come, Cicero,' said Caelius, rolling his eyes. 'It's obvious that Gordianus is looking for information about Antony. Why, I can't imagine. But there's no reason to be coy. Gordianus is your guest, sharing your food. I suggest we tell him whatever he wants to know. And then, perhaps at another time, he'll return the favour and tell us something he knows.'

Cicero looked dubious for a moment, then opened his hands in a gesture of acquiescence. 'What do you already know about Marc Antony?'

'Almost nothing. I know that he's one of Caesar's lieutenants, and I understand he's back from Gaul to run for office.'

'A quaestorship,' said Caelius, 'and likely to win a spot, if and when there's a vote.'

'His politics?'

'He's allied with Caesar, of course,' said Cicero. 'Other than that, his only programme so far as I can discern is self-advancement.'

'He's an original then, unique among Roman politicians,' I said. Neither Cicero nor Caelius responded to this joke. Tiro predictably frowned, taking offence on behalf of his former master. Eco kept a straight face but shook his head almost imperceptibly, wondering at his father's impertinence.

'I understand he's very popular with his troops,' I said. 'So my son Meto tells me.'

'And why not? Antony has the common touch.' Cicero's tone was not complimentary. 'He's of noble birth, but they say he drinks and carouses

193

with the lowest soldiers from the barracks. He's always been like that. He used to hang out with his mother's household slaves and freedmen when he was growing up. Always the little boy who liked to get dirty. Always attracted to loud, vulgar pleasures. Well, he got a bad start.'

'Tell me.'

'One would have to go back to his grandfather, at least . . .' Of course, I thought; the career of any Roman of high birth could never be described beginning merely with his own birth. 'The old fellow was quite a power back when I was growing up – one of my tutors in rhetoric, as a matter of fact, and one of the best. Magnificent speeches! Words that rumbled like thunder! But he would never publish them; he said that only a fool would do that, because it just gave your enemies a way to point out your inconsistencies.' Cicero, who had made a career of publishing and disseminating his speeches, laughed ruefully.

Caelius smiled. 'Wasn't there some scandal involving Antony's grandfather and a Vestal Virgin?'

'Caelius, must you always have a scandal?'

'Yes! And if there's not one, I'll invent it!'

'Well, you happen to be right. There was a trial for despoiling a Vestal somewhere in the distant past, but he was acquitted of that and went on to a truly distinguished career. Ended up serving as consul, then censor, and was finally elected to the college of augurs for life. But his rise really began with his military service. He was one of the first to mount a campaign against the pirates in

Cilicia. Did so well, he was awarded a triumphal procession in Rome. The Senate allowed him to decorate the Rostra with the beaks of the ships he had captured, and even voted to erect a statue of him.'

'A statue?' said Eco. 'I don't recall ever seeing it.'

'That's because it was pulled down shortly after he was executed during the civil war. I remember seeing his head on a spike in the Forum; it gave me nightmares for months afterwards. Quite a shock, seeing an old tutor in that condition. Even the canniest politician was liable to make a fatal misstep back in those days.'

'Rather like these days,' murmured Caelius.

Eco, I noticed, put down a piece of chicken he had been about to eat.

'Anyway,' Cicero continued, 'Antony's grandfather had an extraordinary career, even if it did end so ingloriously. Antony never knew him, of course; the old man was killed a few years before Antony was born.

'Now Antony's father was another matter altogether. Good-looking, well liked, generous to his friends, but a terrible bungler. Like his father before him, he was sent to quell the pirates. Raised a massive war chest, gathered a formidable navy, then squandered it all in losing skirmishes from Spain to Crete. When he negotiated a humiliating peace with the pirates, that was the last straw. The Senate rejected the treaty in outrage. Antony's father died in Crete, some say of shame. Antony was only about – what, Caelius? Eleven or twelve years old?'

Caelius nodded. 'And we all know one outcome of his father's failure. The Senate looked around for someone else to put an end to the pirate problem. Pompey got the commission and came down on the pirates like a tidal wave. His own tide has been rising ever since.'

'But you're taking us astray,' said Cicero. 'Gordianus doesn't want to hear about Pompey. He wants to know about Marc Antony. Well, he's no Pompey, but Caesar seems to think he's competent. As you see, if Marc Antony has any military acumen, then it must have come from his grandfather. But there's also a strong element of his father in him. Antony's charming, affable, boisterous, and entirely too reckless. Of course, some of that may be due to the unfortunate influence of his stepfather.'

'His stepfather?' I said.

Cicero looked rueful. 'Well, it's hardly Antony's fault that his mother made that disastrous second marriage and tied her fortunes to such a loser. I suppose Julia thought she was marrying up, since Lentulus had been a consul, was a patrician like herself –'

'Lentulus? You mean Antony's stepfather was –'

'Yes, 'Legs' Lentulus,' said Cicero with loathing in his voice, 'so called for pulling up his toga to bare his legs like a schoolboy in for a strapping when his fellow senators put him on trial for embezzling public money. A man so flagrantly corrupt that he was finally expelled from the Senate – and so

persistent that he managed to worm his way back in again. Superstitious as well; some charlatan fortune-teller convinced him that he was destined to become dictator because of a few lines of doggerel in the Sibylline Books. That's how Lentulus got involved with Catilina and his traitorous clique. We all know how that ended.'

Indeed we did. It had happened in the year that Cicero was consul. The so-called conspiracy of Catilina had been ruthlessly put down; under Cicero's authority, Lentulus and a number of others had been executed without a formal trial. The Best People had lauded Cicero for his decisiveness in saving the Republic; many among the populists had condemned him as a murderous tyrant. A backlash had followed, culminating in the vengeful legislation masterminded by Clodius to send Cicero into exile. The Senate had eventually rescinded the exile; Cicero was a powerful player on the stage in Rome again; and Clodius was dead . . .

'It's ten years since Catilina,' I said quietly.

'Yes, and for ten years Marc Antony has carried a grudge against me,' said Cicero. 'He's never come to terms with the hard fact that his stepfather had to die. Antony was only twenty at the time. Passionate young men can't always be reached by reason. They can carry resentments for a long time.' Cicero sighed, whether from emotion or dyspepsia I couldn't tell. 'I've heard that he even claims that I refused to hand over the body to his mother after Lentulus was strangled, and Julia had to come begging to my wife to intercede. Nonsense! An

obscene lie! I saw to it that the bodies of all the conspirators were given proper burial.' Cicero winced and pressed his hand to his belly. He surveyed what remained of the meal before him as if to identify the guilty dish which had set off his indigestion.

Antony's grandfather, his father, his stepfather – they had all risen to glory and had all ended in ruin. The world is like a spinning disc, driving men and women to the edge and then hurling them this way and that into the void beyond its whirling rim. Most are never seen again, but some manage to grab hold of the edge and claw their way back to the centre, not once but again and again. Cicero was one of those. So was Caelius.

'You've explained his lineage,' I said. 'What about Antony himself?'

'He fell in with a bad crowd – Clodius and his gang of aristocratic young incorrigibles,' said Cicero. 'The usual formula for dissipation: high living, radical politics, mad schemes for the future. And no money to finance any of it. Antony's father left an estate so encumbered with debts that Antony refused his inheritance. Technically he started his career as a bankrupt. It was young Gaius Curio who covered his debts. He and Antony were like peas in a pod. Companions in debauchery. Inseparable. So close that their relationship gave rise to all sorts of . . . nasty rumours. Well, when Curio's father got the bill for Antony's debts, he went through the roof. Came seeking my advice. I told him to grit his teeth, hand over the silver, and forbid

his son ever to see Antony again. The next time Antony came calling on Curio the watchmen turned him away. So what did Antony do? Scaled a wall and let himself down through a hole in the roof, directly into Curio's bedroom, like a determined suitor!'

Cicero and Caelius shared a laugh, interrupted by another wince from Cicero as he gingerly clutched his belly. 'Anyway, Antony solved his money problems when he married a woman named Fadia, the daughter of a rich freedman. A freedman! The scandal of marrying that far below one's station would have ruined an aristocrat when I was young, but I suppose the incorrigibles in Antony's circle applauded him for flouting convention and landing a big dowry. At least the marriage seems to have taken Antony's mind off Curio; I'm told that Antony fathered several children before Fadia died. Meanwhile, he spent some time in Greece studying oratory, put in some military service in Judaea and Syria, helped put down a revolt against King Ptolemy in Egypt, and eventually hitched himself to Caesar and headed for Gaul. Oh, and a couple of years ago he found time to get married again – this time to his cousin Antonia.

'And now Marc Antony has become one of Julius Caesar's most trusted lieutenants. I suppose he's good at his job if Caesar deems him worthy of grooming for office and sends him back to Rome to stand for quaestor.'

While the slaves brought water and wine to refill the cups and cleared away the dishes, I mulled over

all that Cicero had told me. Sempronia said that Antony had chased after Clodius with a sword on the Field of Mars, trying to kill him. But according to Cicero, Antony had been a member of Clodius's intimate circle.

'So Antony and Clodius were good friends,' I ventured.

'They were,' said Caelius, whose age and quick-silver alliances made him more privy to the intimate affairs of the radical generation than Cicero, 'until their little misunderstanding over Fulvia.'

'Misunderstanding?'

'Apparently Antony misunderstood that Fulvia was Clodius's wife and thought she was free for the taking.' Caelius flicked his tongue to catch a drop of wine at the corner of his mouth.

'You mean –'

'Oh, the affair probably meant nothing to Antony. Between his boyhood lover Curio, his two wives, and all the whores of his youth, what was a little fling with Fulvia? But Clodius was furious when he found out. He and Fulvia were still newlyweds, more or less. And Clodius always tended to fly off the handle at the least provocation, didn't he? This was, oh, about six years ago. After that, there was a chill between Antony and Clodius. And then a whole sea between them, when Antony went off to Greece and Judaea. And then several mountain ranges, when Antony headed up to Gaul. He and Clodius never saw eye to eye again. They were never close enough.'

'Except on the Field of Mars?' I suggested.

Caelius threw back his head and laughed. 'Oh, that! How could I forget? Cicero, you must remember my telling you about it. Last year, during one of the cancelled elections, Antony and Clodius ran into each other, quite by accident, I imagine. They had words. Antony pulls out his sword – brave slayer of a thousand Gauls – and Clodius lets out a shriek and takes off like a scared rabbit. I suppose that made Antony the dog; what could he do but give chase? Of course, if he'd caught Clodius it might have been more the case of the dog and the ferret, with the mutt getting his nose bitten and howling all the way back to Gaul.'

'What started the fight? The old business about Fulvia? But you say that was six years ago . . .'

Caelius shrugged. 'Who knows? Clodius and Antony are both famous for long memories and short tempers.'

'How did we ever get started on the subject of Marc Antony, anyway?' said Cicero.

'Fulvia must have been feeling nostalgic when Gordianus visited her this morning,' said Caelius. 'Did she discuss all her former lovers with you?'

'No,' I said. 'And neither did Clodia.' The grin froze on Caelius's face. Cicero gave him an unsympathetic glance. I pulled myself upright on the couch. 'An excellent meal, Marcus Cicero. Perfect for the middle of the day – not too light, not too heavy. I might say the same for the conversation. Now I think that my son and I must be on our way.'

★     ★     ★

'Why did you bring up Marc Antony?' asked Eco on the short walk back to my house.

'Antony was the reason Fulvia wanted to see me. He's offered to help prosecute Milo. She's not sure whether to trust him. She has a suspicion that he was involved somehow in Clodius's death. Or it may be her mother who suspects Antony, and Fulvia wants to prove him innocent.'

'Did she tell you that she and Antony used to be lovers?'

'No. And just because Cicero and Caelius say so, that doesn't mean it's true.'

'But she did tell you about the chase across the Field of Mars last year?'

'Yes.'

Eco nodded. After a moment he laughed. 'That was amazing, the way you handled them.'

'Who?'

'Cicero and Caelius.'

'Was it? I'm sure they thought it was they who were handling me. I probably told them more than I should have. And now, for a few scraps of information about Antony, they'll act as if I owe them the world.'

'But the way you talk to them sometimes – practically insulting them to their faces!'

'Yes, well, it's a strange thing, but people like Cicero and Caelius like to be insulted.'

'Do they?'

'That's been my experience. I needle them, they needle me back. They know they have nothing to fear from me; nothing I might say can really hurt

them. They enjoy my needling, the way one sometimes enjoys having a mosquito bite – the itch gives them something to scratch. Not like a bee sting; not like the bloody sores I've seen Cicero inflict on his enemies with a barbed word or two.'

Davus let us in. From the look on his face I knew that something was up. Before Davus could speak, a voice rumbled behind him.

'The master of the house, home at last!'

He was a big man, probably a gladiator or a soldier, despite the richly embroidered fabric of his grey tunic and dark green cape. His nose had been broken, maybe more than once, and each of his hands was the size of a baby's head. His own head was as bald as a baby's, and almost as ugly. He had the look of a man who could walk through a dangerous place without being bothered.

'A visitor,' said Davus, unnecessarily.

'So I see. And who sent you . . . citizen?' I said, noting the iron ring on his finger. He was probably someone's freedman.

'The Great One,' he said bluntly. His voice was like gravel in a sluice.

'You mean –'

'That's all I ever call him. It's how he likes to be addressed.'

'I'm sure. And what does the Great One –'

'The honour of your presence, at your earliest convenience.'

'Now?'

'Unless you can make it earlier.'

'Davus –'

203

'Yes, Master?'

'Tell your mistress that I have yet another errand. This one will take me outside the city walls, I imagine.'

'Do you want me to go with you?'

I looked to the man I'd decided to call Baby Face, who smiled and said, 'I brought a whole troop of bodyguards with me.'

'Where are they?'

'I told them to wait across the street, down the Ramp a ways. I figured there was no need to bother your neighbours with a lot of traffic.'

'You're more discreet than some of my callers today.'

'Thank you.'

'Eco, will you come with me?'

'Of course, Papa.' Eco had never met the Great One either. I noticed that my stomach was suddenly churning. I couldn't blame Cicero's cook.

So I set out for the third time that day, thinking again of the old Etruscan proverb. But this was not a downpour. This was a deluge.

# XII

The law forbids any man with an army under his command to enter the city walls. Technically, Pompey was such a commander, though his army was off in Spain; he had seen fit to delegate its operation to lieutenants while he stayed close to Rome to keep watch on the electoral crisis. He resided at his villa on the Pincian Hill not far outside the walls. As Pompey was unable to come to Rome, Rome went to Pompey, as the mob had done when they ran to his villa to offer him the consular axes, or as Milo had done when unsuccessfully seeking an audience, or as Eco and I found ourselves doing that afternoon.

Baby Face and his troop of gladiators closed ranks around us like an armoured tortoise for the walk down the Ramp, across the Forum and through the Fontinalis Gate. We crossed the traditional boundary of the city as we stepped through the gate, but

the Flaminian Way was just as crowded with buildings outside the wall as within. Gradually the buildings became smaller and fewer until we came to an open area. The disused public voting stalls were off to our left. Up ahead to the right was a high, guarded gate that opened at our approach.

The paved path led up through terraced gardens, sometimes sloping, sometimes in steps, switching right and left as it ascended. The grounds on either side were mantled with winter greys and browns, the dreariness of the naked trees and bushes relieved here and there by statues in marble or bronze. A regal swan that might have been Jupiter courting Leda graced a small circular pool. We passed a low wall where a slave boy sat pulling a thorn from his foot, painted in such lifelike colours I might have mistaken him for flesh and blood except that he was naked under the cold sun. I saw no gods or goddesses in the garden, until we came upon the requisite Priapus, guardian and motivator of growing things, occupying a stone alcove set into a high hedge, grinning lasciviously and displaying an erection almost as large as the rest of him. The crown of his marble phallus had been rubbed shiny-smooth by passing hands.

We came at last to the villa, where more gladiators stood guard before a pair of tall wooden doors with bronze fittings. Baby Face told us to wait while he went inside.

Eco tugged at my sleeve. When I turned there was no need to ask what he wanted to show me. The view was spectacular. Tangled branches and treetops hid the path we had just ascended, as well as

the Flaminian Way and the voting stalls immediately below us, but above and beyond the treetops the whole Field of Mars lay open before us. The ancient marching grounds and equestrian training courses had all but vanished in the course of my lifetime, filled up by cheap tenements and jumbled warehouses. Dominating everything else was the great complex built by Pompey in his consulship two years back, a sprawling mass of meeting halls, galleries, fountains, gardens and the city's first permanent theatre. Farther on, like a great arm curving around the Field of Mars, was the Tiber, its course marked by a low, thick blanket of river mist that allowed only glimpses of the gardens and villas on its other bank. Clodia's garden villa, where the stylish young men of Rome used to swim nude for her amusement, was somewhere on that distant bank. The whole scene was like a painting done in muted winter hues of rust-red and grey-green, bone white and iron blue.

Eco tugged at my elbow again and nodded towards the south. The mass of the villa blocked the view of most of the city proper except for a narrow glimpse of the temples on the Capitoline Hill and a jumbled cityscape beyond. Far away, perhaps on the Aventine Hill, a plume of smoke rose like a vast marble pillar into the still air. Whatever chaos reigned at the base of that pillar, it was too far away for us to see or hear. Did a man begin to feel remote and uncaring, looking down on Rome from such a high place? Or did he become even more acutely aware of buildings burning out of control and chaos

in the streets, surveying Rome from such a godlike vantage point?

The doors behind us opened with a clank. Baby Face emerged, smiling grimly. 'The Great One will see you now.'

I must have been rather nervous as Baby Face ushered us through the foyer, into the atrium and up a curving flight of stairs, because afterwards, when Bethesda asked me, I couldn't remember a thing about the furnishings and fixtures, though I could vividly recall that my mouth was as dry as vellum and my heart seemed to have swollen to twice its normal size.

We were led to a room of many windows at the southwest corner of the house. Curtains and shutters had been pulled back to allow an expansive view of the city. The column of smoke off to the south which we had glimpsed from the doorstep was at the centre of this view, and was joined by two more pillars of smoke, closer and off to the left, probably made by fires on the Esquiline Hill or down in the Subura. Pompey stood at the windows, his back to us. He was only a silhouette at first, a crown of unkempt curls above powerful shoulders and a robust, well-padded torso. As my eyes adapted to the light I saw that he wore a long, voluminous woollen robe of emerald green. His hands were joined together behind his back, his fingers tapping nervously against each other. He heard us enter and slowly turned around. Baby Face moved inconspicuously into a corner. I glimpsed

the shadow of another guard on the balcony outside the windows.

Pompey was the same age as Cicero, which meant that he was a few years younger than me. I could have wished for as few wrinkles, though not for as many chins. It occurred to me that Pompey might be the sort of man who turns to food in a crisis. Commanding armies on the march kept him busy and fit. Holed up in his Pincian villa, he had taken on the weight of the world.

But there were no puns in my mind at that moment. This was not Fulvia or Clodia, mysterious and grimly determined but made vulnerable by their sex. Nor was it Cicero or Caelius, a known quantity with whom I could exchange careless banter. This was Pompey.

When he was young, poets had swooned for his beauty. With his luxuriant, wind-tossed locks of hair, his smooth brow and chiselled nose, people had called the boy general another Alexander even before his military prowess proved them right. Young Pompey's typical expression had been a placid, dreamy half smile, as if the contemplation of his own future greatness kept him perpetually cheerful but also a bit aloof. If his face had a flaw, it was a tendency to roundness and a fullness in his lips and cheeks that appeared either ripely sensual or pleasantly plump, depending on the angle and the light.

As he grew older his face seemed to flatten a bit and to grow even rounder. The chiselled nose became fleshy. The wild locks were shorn in deference to maturity. The smile became less sensual, more

complacent. As his prestige and power grew, it was as if Pompey had less need of physical beauty, and so put aside the comely garment of his youth.

All this I had seen from a distance as Pompey built his career, orating in the courts of law, campaigning for office on the Field of Mars, cutting a great swathe through the Forum attended by his vast retinue of military and political lieutenants, each of those lieutenants in turn attended by his own coterie of followers seeking favours at second hand from the Great One. But what cannot be seen from a distance are a man's eyes, as I now saw Pompey's eyes staring into mine with a disconcerting intensity. For some reason I recalled a famous quote from his youth. When he was sent to drive the dictator Sulla's enemies out of Sicily, the people of the liberated city of Messana had complained that Pompey had no jurisdiction over them because of ancient agreements between themselves and Rome. Pompey had replied, 'Stop quoting laws to us. We carry swords.'

'Gordianus the Finder,' he said, 'and your adopted son Eco.' He smiled to himself and nodded, as if pleased that he could remember such insignificant details without a slave to remind him. 'We haven't met before, have we?'

'No, Great One.'

'I didn't think so.'

The silence that followed was uncomfortable for me, but apparently not for Pompey, who paced slowly before us, his hands still clasped behind his back. 'You've had a busy day,' he finally said.

'Pardon, Great One?'

'Clodia comes by to carry you off in her litter. You pay a call on Fulvia. I suppose Sempronia was there, as well. No sooner are you home than Cicero's freedman comes calling, and you and your son are off to confer with Cicero and Caelius. Milo wasn't there today, was he?'

I started to answer, then realized that Pompey was looking not at me but at Baby Face, who shook his head and answered, 'No, Great One. Milo hasn't left his house all day.'

Pompey nodded and returned his gaze to me. 'But you've met with Milo before, under Cicero's roof.'

It was not a question, but it seemed to require a response – an admission, rather than an answer. 'Yes.'

'It's been quite a while since I saw Titus Annius Milo. How is he looking these days?'

'Looking, Great One?'

'He's always been so proud of his powerful physique, naming himself after Milo, the legendary wrestler of Croton, and all that. Is he holding up?'

'He appears fit enough.'

'And his state of mind?'

'I'm not privy to that, Great One.'

'No? But you're a reader of signs, are you not? Surely you read something from his face, his voice.'

'Milo is anxious, angry, uncertain. But you hardly need me to tell you that.'

'No, I do not.' His smile seemed without irony, merely a gesture of appreciation for not wasting his time. 'What did Clodia want with you this

morning?' When I hesitated, Pompey frowned. 'Don't tell me it's none of my business. It is. Everything that happens in Rome nowadays is my business. What did Clodia want with you?'

'To take me to Fulvia. Only that.'

'And what did Fulvia want?'

'Great One, surely words spoken in confidence by a grieving widow –'

'Finder, you make me impatient.'

I considered how to answer. 'A certain man has approached her. She's uncertain whether to trust him.'

'Surely suitors haven't started knocking on her door already!'

'Not a suitor, exactly,' I said, though in fact Antony had once been Fulvia's lover, if Caelius was to be believed.

Pompey looked profoundly uninterested. 'Well, I won't press you for details; Fulvia's personal affairs are of no immediate importance to me. Did you agree to help her?'

'I haven't yet decided.'

'Perhaps I could help. Who knows? I might possess whatever information you're seeking.'

It seemed unlikely. Marc Antony was Caesar's man, not Pompey's. 'Are you offering to help me, Great One?'

'Perhaps. I'm a reasonable man. If I can give something of value to you, then I imagine you'll be more willing to give me what I want.'

'And what is it that you want from me, Great One?'

'I'll come to that in a moment. Do you have any questions for me?'

I thought carefully and saw no danger in asking. 'What can you tell me about Marc Antony?'

'Caesar's lieutenant? I know that his father made a mess of clearing out the pirates before the Senate finally gave me the job. And that his stepfather got himself executed for treason at Cicero's behest. And I recall that young Antony went off soldiering in my old stamping grounds out east for a few years before he signed up with Caesar. What else is there to know?'

'Perhaps nothing.'

'By Hercules, he's not the one courting Fulvia, is he? I don't see how. He's already married to his cousin Antonia, and that's not the sort of marriage it's easy to step out of. But if he is a suitor, Fulvia would do well to avoid him; that's my advice. Clodius may have been an extortionist and a rabble-rouser, but at least he knew how to bring home the silver; look at that house they ended up in. Young Antony's another matter. Like Caesar and the rest of that circle, always more and more in debt, always selling themselves for the next loan to see them through. They'll come to a bad end, the lot of them. I only hope they don't bankrupt the Republic along with them.'

He fell silent and raised an eyebrow in mild surprise — at himself, I realized, for saying more than he meant to.

'And what did Cicero make of your visit to Fulvia?' said Pompey, pressing on.

I cleared my throat. 'He was curious — like yourself, Great One.'

'He wasn't somehow behind your visit to Fulvia, was he? No? I thought perhaps he'd set you up to be his spy. That would be so very like Cicero. Covert networks, unsigned letters, messages sent in some secret code invented by Tiro, paid informers, one lurker keeping watch on the next. Like a spider casting webs in all directions. He'd have turned out differently if he'd had any talent as a military man. More action, fewer words. Are you Cicero's spy, Finder?' He disconcerted me again with his gaze.

'No, Great One.'

'Perhaps you are and you simply don't know it.'

The suggestion surprised me, then made me uneasy. 'I think I know all of Cicero's tricks by now.'

Pompey raised an eyebrow. 'Really? Even I wouldn't make that claim! What do you make of Caelius's behaviour? Why is he standing up for Milo? What's in it for him?'

'Caelius has cast his lot with Cicero; Cicero has cast his lot with Milo.'

'So by extension, Caelius is Milo's man?'

'I'm not sure that Caelius is anybody's man.'

'You speak the truth there, Finder. And what do you make of Milo himself?'

'As I said before, Great One —'

'Yes, I know: 'anxious, angry, uncertain'. But what do you make of him?'

'I met him for the first time only recently — since the death of Clodius.'

'Really? No previous connection?'

'None.'

'But you do have some old connection with Clodius.'

'No. I did a bit of work for Clodius's sister a few years ago –'

He nodded. 'When she helped prosecute Caelius for murder. I spoke in Caelius's defence, you may recall.'

'Yes. I'm afraid I missed your speech.'

'It wasn't a very good one. Just as well; a good speech would have been wasted. No one would have remembered it, not after the speech Cicero made that day for Caelius – or against Clodia, should I say? So, Finder, were you ever in Clodius's camp?'

'I was not and I am not.'

'And you're not in Milo's camp, either?'

'No.'

He appraised me for a long moment, then turned to Eco. 'What about you? Like father, like son?'

Eco cleared his throat. 'I helped my father when he worked for Clodia, but I never met her brother. I went with my father to Cicero's house today, but I have yet to meet Milo face to face.'

'And your loyalties?'

'I'm my father's man.'

Pompey smiled. 'A loyal son makes the best partisan of all, eh, Finder? But what about your other son, the one who's off in Gaul? Has he not pulled the rest of the Gordiani into Caesar's orbit along with him?'

'My son Meto is a loyal soldier, but my family has no special allegiance to Caesar.'

Pompey regarded me curiously. 'How is it that you manage to navigate such an independent course, Finder, without being smashed on the rocks?'

'It seems to me, Great One, that if I let another man navigate for me, I would have been smashed on the rocks long before now.'

'Do you always steer your own course, Finder? But how? Do you have some special knowledge of the stars? Or do you sail blindly into the future?'

'As blindly as every other man, I suppose. Perhaps it's the stars that are steering us.'

'Ah, yes, I know that feeling. You believe you have a destiny, then?'

'A very small one, perhaps.'

'Better than none at all, I suppose.' The Great One shook his head, as if the idea of having no destiny, or only a small one, was too difficult for him to imagine. 'Destiny is a strange thing. Look at Clodius, ending as a bloody corpse on the great road his ancestor built; it's almost too appropriate, like a Greek tragedy. Look at Milo. I suppose the appropriate end for him would be to get caught in a trap of some sort and eaten alive by his enemies.'

'I don't follow you, Great One.'

'You know, like the legendary Milo of Croton.'

'Is there a story attached to his death? Famous athletes have never been my particular interest.'

'No? But you can't really understand our Milo unless you know about his namesake. What a man

216

calls himself tells you what he thinks of himself, and sometimes where he's headed. Surely I needn't point that out to a man who calls himself 'Finder'.'

'I understand . . . 'Great One'.'

Pompey didn't even blink. 'I shall tell you about Milo of Croton, then,' he said. 'Come, it's warmer on the balcony. We can sit in the sun. I'll have some heated wine brought. Alban or Falernian? I prefer Alban myself – a drier aftertaste . . .'

So we sat on the south-west balcony of Pompey's Pincian villa, sipping ten-year-old wine and looking out over the city. The fire on the Aventine Hill had apparently been extinguished. The great column of smoke had been cut off at the base and seemed to float above the rooftops like something from a nightmare. A new pillar of smoke, thicker and jet black, had appeared in the vicinity of the Colline Gate, far away to our left.

Pompey swirled the wine in his cup. 'When our Milo was young, he was quite an athlete. Or so he says; after the third cup of wine he starts bragging about his athletic glory days the way a soldier brags about old battles. He won many competitions, especially as a wrestler. I don't know what sort of competition a boy has growing up in a village like Lanuvium, but Milo was always the strongest, the fastest, the most determined. Powerful as an ox. Stubborn as an ox, too – that's our Milo.

'He's still as vain as a Greek about his physique, you know. Not exactly the Greek ideal – too short and stocky – but he's certainly kept himself fit. I've seen him naked at the baths. Belly like a brick wall,

shoulders like catapult stones. He could crack a nut between those buttocks!' Pompey let out a coarse laugh that was quietly echoed by the guard at the end of the balcony, who could hardly help over-hearing. I realized that Eco and I had been admitted to a certain intimacy with the Great One. He was sharing with us the sort of manly talk a commander shares at ease with his subordinates.

'So when Titus Annius was casting about for a name to give himself, he settled on Milo. Do you remember the old schoolboy exercise about Milo of Croton?'

When I showed a blank expression, Eco, whose spotty education had nonetheless been more formal than mine, ventured to answer. ' "Compose a recitation on the following theme and show how it might instruct us through life: Milo of Croton, having accustomed himself to carrying a calf every day for exercise, kept on carrying it until it was grown to a bull." '

Pompey and Eco shared a nostalgic laugh. 'The moral of the theme: as a boy grows into a man, so grow his burdens,' said Pompey, 'and if you're a fellow like Milo of Croton, you won't shrug them off, but just keep smiling through clenched teeth as you lug them forwards, grunting and groaning. I'm sure that our Milo had to write on the same theme. The lesson seems to have stuck with him.'

He took a sip of wine, frowned and called for the steward. 'Is this really the best Alban we have? It's gone off. It won't do. Bring the Falernian. Now, where was I? Oh, yes. Feats of strength. Milo of

Croton could hold a ripe pomegranate in his fist, they say, so firmly that no one could wrest his fingers apart, and yet so carefully that the pomegranate wouldn't bleed. He could stand on a discus covered with grease and maintain such perfect balance that no one could push him off. He could tie a cord around his head, hold his breath, and make the veins on his forehead bulge out until the cord broke – now that's something I should like to see!

'But Milo of Croton wasn't always graceful. Once at the games at Olympia when he was on his way to accept the laurel leaf crown for wrestling, he slipped and fell flat on his back. As he was scrambling to get up, some of the wags in the crowd started saying he shouldn't be crowned, having displayed such clumsiness. Milo said, 'That wasn't the third fall! I fell only once. Let's see one of you throw me two more times!' That shut them up in a hurry.

'He won twelve crowns altogether, six at Olympia and six at Delphi. When Croton went to war with the Sybarites, for a helmet Milo wore all his laurel leaf crowns at once – enough to cushion a blow – and dressed like his hero Hercules in a lion's skin, carrying a club. He led the people of Croton to victory. And when, in gratitude, they decided to erect a statue of him, Milo himself carried his own statue through the square and placed it on the pedestal.

'When Pythagoras the philosopher was living in Croton, he and Milo became great friends. Opposites attract: the thinker and the strongman. Lucky

for Pythagoras, since Milo saved his life. There was an earthquake, and in the dining hall at the philosophers' school a pillar gave way. Milo held up the collapsing ceiling while Pythagoras and his students cleared out, then slipped out from under it and managed to save himself as well.

'Do you begin to see, Finder, how these legendary feats might bear some allegorical relation to the way in which our Milo conducts himself and sees his destiny? The legendary hero whose clenched fist cannot be opened against his will; who will not be shoved aside, no matter how slippery his footing; who carries a great burden, but does not complain; who can hold his breath until the veins in his forehead pop out; who is best friends with a famous wise man; who is willing to throw himself into the lurch to save his friends; who goes into battle wearing the mantle, or in this case, the name of his boyhood hero; who would gladly put his own statue upon a pedestal; who cannot be thrown down by anyone . . . but who might, all on his own and in full sight of the watching world, fall flat on his back.'

I considered this as I sipped freshly poured Falernian from my cup. A late afternoon breeze had begun to stir the sky high above Rome, slanting the pillars of smoke and tattering their upper reaches.

'But what of the death of Milo of Croton, Great One?'

'How does the adage go? 'To possess great strength counts for nothing unless a man knows

220

how to use it.' That was the undoing of Milo of Croton. He set out on a journey one day, on foot, and lost his way in a deep forest. Far from the road he came to a cleared place where some woodsmen had been working, but the day was late and the woodsmen were gone. He saw a huge log. There was a long crack along the whole length of the log, with several iron wedges driven into the gap. Apparently the woodsmen had intended to split the log in two, but the job was too big for them and they left it for another day. Milo thought, I shall split the log myself. Think how surprised they'll be to find that one man has done the job for them, using only his bare hands! How clever they'll think me! How grateful they'll be! Another famous feat of strength for Milo of Croton! So he pushed his fingers into the narrow breach until his palms were flat against the two sides. He pushed them apart with all his might. The iron wedges loosened and fell out – and instantly the crack snapped shut. Milo's hands were trapped. His arms were bent. The log was too heavy for him to shift. He couldn't move.

'Darkness fell. There was a howling in the woods. Wild beasts crept out of the forest into the clearing. They could smell his fear, sense his helplessness. They only nipped at him at first, but when they saw that he couldn't defend himself, they clambered onto him, fangs flashing. They tore him apart. They devoured him alive.

'The next morning, the horrified woodsmen found what was left of Milo of Croton.' Pompey

sipped his wine. 'Need I belabour certain obvious parallels to the peril in which our Milo finds himself?'

'No, Great One. You seem to know a great deal about both Milos.'

'My father used to tell me stories about Milo of Croton when I was a boy. As for Titus Annius Milo, he and I have been allies now and then.'

'But not any longer?'

'Clodius and I were allies once, too,' he said, deflecting the question, 'just as Caesar and I were once allies, and still are, for all I know.'

'I don't understand, Great One.'

'Some things only the Fates seem to fathom. No matter. What about you, Finder? Who are your allies? Whom do you serve? You seem to be a man who moves through every camp but belongs to none.'

'It would seem that way, Great One.'

'That makes you a rather unusual fellow, Finder. A valuable man to know.'

'I'm not sure how, Great One.'

'I want you to do a bit of work for me.'

I felt several things at once – excitement, wariness, a sinking sensation. 'Perhaps, Great One. If I can.'

'I want you to take a trip down the Appian Way, to the place where Clodius was killed. Take along your son, if you like. Have a look at the site. Talk to the local people. See what you can find out. If you're as good as your name, perhaps you'll discover a few things that others have overlooked.'

'Why me, Great One? Surely there are other men you could send.'

'There's no one who could move as freely as you seem to move between Fulvia's house and Cicero's. As I said, you're an unusual fellow.'

'The Fates seem to have landed me in a curious spot.'

'You're not the only one. We must all submit to the Fates.' He drained his wine slowly, never taking his eyes off me. 'Finder, let me explain something to you. As a general, I have been very nearly infallible. I've moved from triumph to triumph without a misstep, with hardly even a moment's hesitation. I have the instinct for it, you see. A peculiar genius, all my own. I could do it with my eyes shut. But politics — politics is another matter. I approach the Forum the same way I approach a battlefield. I marshal my forces, I lay out a plan — but things never seem to go exactly as I want. I'll think I'm headed straight for the prize, and suddenly I find that I don't know where in Hades I am, or how I got there. I lose all sense of direction.

'Julia always said I had bad advisors. Probably right. On a battlefield, your troops are here, the enemy is there, and a man either gives you the right information or else he'll be dead the next day. But in this hazy murk, a dagger can be aimed at your heart and you never know it, and so-called advisors have a habit of telling you what they think you want to hear, never mind the facts. I wouldn't care to tell you how many times I've charged down a

path using a map that led me straight into a brick wall. That mustn't happen now – not now! No false advice, no fawning lies, no blind spots. I must know the lay of the land, the disposition of the enemy, the precise movements of all the forces around me. First of all, and above all else, I want to know exactly what happened on the Appian Way. Do you understand?'

'I think so, Great One.'

'Can I trust you, Finder?'

I looked at him for a long moment, wondering if I could trust Pompey.

'No need to answer,' he finally said. 'My general's instinct senses no deceit in you. So: will you do what I ask?'

Fulvia had already asked me to investigate the circumstances of her husband's death. Now Pompey was doing the same. I felt Eco's eyes on me. I took a deep breath.

'I'll go down the Appian Way. I'll find out whatever I can about Clodius's death.'

Pompey nodded. 'Good. I'm sure we can agree on terms; I've never asked a man to march for me without proper payment. As for lodging, you can stay at my villa while you're down there. It's not far from Clodius's place. Probably just a stone's throw from the spot where he was killed.'

He took a sip of Falernian and gazed down at the city. 'I shall be leaving Rome myself in a day or two. When I come back, I shall put an end to all this nonsense.'

'Nonsense, Great One?'

224

By a wave of his hand he indicated the pillars of smoke. 'This infernal disorder.'

'But how, Great One?'

Pompey looked at me shrewdly. 'I suppose there's no harm in telling you. Tomorrow, the Senate will convene in the portico at my theatre, out on the Field of Mars.'

'Outside the city walls?'

'Yes. That way I can attend – legally attend – the proceedings. Let no man say that Pompey thinks himself above the law! A lot of business has piled up, as you can imagine. A number of proposals shall be put forth. One of them is to rebuild the Senate House. No controversy there. I shall suggest that Milo's brother-in-law Faustus Sulla be given the contract. Let no man say that Pompey is unfair to the relatives of Milo! Besides, such a commission seems only proper, since it was Sulla, Faustus's father, who remodelled the old Senate House. Thus the Senate shall pay homage to the memory of the dictator Sulla and his achievements. Many Romans flinch at that word, dictator. They forget how important it is to have some mechanism whereby supreme power can be placed in the hands of a single man, when circumstances demand it.'

He took another sip of wine and stared at the pillars of smoke as if he could disperse them by sheer will power. 'And there will be another, more important proposal – that the Senate declare a state of emergency and issue the Ultimate Decree. Do you know what that means, Finder?'

'Yes,' I said, remembering the last time such a

decree had been issued, when Cicero was consul and had demanded extraordinary powers to deal with Catilina and his circle. 'The Ultimate Decree instructs the consuls to do 'whatever may be necessary to save the state.' '

'Martial law,' said Pompey, bluntly.

'But there are no consuls.'

'Yes, that's a problem. How can troops be levied from the countryside if there are no consuls to levy them? Well, it's only a technicality, really. Someone other than a consul will have to do the job, of course. Fortunately, as a man who has twice been elected consul and as the current commander of the Roman troops in Spain, I have both the necessary expertise to raise a militia here in Italy, and the skill to deploy it in the most efficient manner to bring order to the city.'

'The Senate will agree to this?'

'I'm certain they will. It's all a matter of counting the votes ahead of time. Oh, some of Caesar's supporters will make a fuss, as may some of the more hidebound conservatives, like Cato. A terrible precedent, they shall say, but what other solution have they to offer? They won't protest too vehemently. I shall find ways to mollify them. The important thing is that order be restored. If we must resort to certain innovations to achieve that end, if the law must be slightly bent, then so be it.'

He at last turned his gaze from the pillars of smoke, which, for the moment at least, had refused to disperse. 'Well then, shall we discuss your fee, Finder?'

# XIII

A man commences a journey on the Appian Way with the smell of fish in his nostrils and the sound of dripping water in his ears.

The smell comes from the fish markets just outside the Capena Gate, at the southern end of the city. Fishermen from the Tiber and as far away as Ostia string up their catches on lines, presenting row upon row of fish hung up by their gaping jaws, with here and there a basket full of molluscs, octopi or squid. On a normal day, at a normal hour, the place resounds with the jabber of kitchen slaves, housewives and marketers. We set out in the grey hour before dawn, before the markets would normally be open, but even so the place was unnaturally quiet and deserted. According to Bethesda, there had been no market outside the Capena Gate for days. Like startled minnows, the fishermen had all been scared away. Still, there was

a strong odour of fish about the place, as if the sea had penetrated the very stones beneath our feet.

The sound of dripping water comes from a leak in the Appian aqueduct. It was built by the same Appius Claudius Caecus who built the Appian Way, two hundred and sixty years ago. When the aqueduct reaches the city it merges with the wall and for a considerable distance flows inside it, a river within a wall, a marvel of design and engineering spoiled by only one defect: at the Capena Gate, the aqueduct leaks. In warm months the great arching blocks of stone overhead are covered with dripping moss, like the ceiling of a grotto. In the dead of winter the moss dies back and sometimes the water freezes into a dully gleaming sheet of ice. On this morning it was not that cold. The water seeped, slowly but freely. As we stepped through the gate, one drop in particular, an especially large, especially frigid drop, struck the back of my neck and wriggled down my spine. I gave a jerk and must have made a curious noise, for Eco gripped my arm and Davus looked at me with alarm.

I knew what Davus must be thinking: it's an ill omen to begin the first step of a journey with a shudder and a curse from the master. Eco, less superstitious, probably feared that I was having a seizure. Then a drop glanced off the tip of Eco's nose, making him blink in confusion. When Davus tilted his head back and opened his mouth to laugh, another drop struck him square between the eyes.

'There, now we've all been anointed by the Capena Gate. A very good omen,' I declared for the benefit of Davus.

Eco raised a dubious eyebrow. 'Where is this stable that Pompey mentioned? I've never noticed it before.'

I looked around. Towards the left, just beyond the market, stood the dense grove of trees that surrounded the shrine of Egeria with its limestone springs. It could hardly be in that direction. I looked towards the right. 'That must be the place, over there. It looks like a stable, doesn't it? Usually all the hanging fish would hide it from view. I see an open door and a light inside. Someone must be up already.'

A narrow path flanked by cypress trees led to the long, low building in the shadow of the city wall. I took a step inside the open door and was met by an odour of horse dung and hay that was a welcome relief to the stink of fish, then by a pitchfork aimed at my throat.

'Who are you? What do you want?' The man held a lamp in his other hand. The glow lit up his gaunt, wary face.

'We come from your master,' I said. 'I thought you'd be expecting us.'

'Maybe. What are you called?'

'Finder.'

'All right, then.' The man lowered his pitchfork. 'I have to be careful. There's been a lot of trouble lately. Desperate men, damned good horses, and me in between – me the one who'll pay if there's any stolen. Understand? And I'll tell you, the master keeps some fine ones here. Fine horses! Takes a military man to really appreciate what a horse is

worth. Keeps them here for convenience, for when he wants to take a ride to his villa down south. Come along and see. Careful, follow the lamp. He said you could have your pick. How many are you? Three? Here, I happen to have three blacks, not a spot of white on them. Those are the ones I'd take if I were you.'

I saw the three he meant and reached towards the nearest. The beast had a long, powerful neck and bright eyes. 'Why? Are these the fastest?'

He shrugged. 'Maybe, maybe not. But they'd for sure be the hardest to see if you do any riding after dark. Something to think about, these days, making yourself hard to see if you're out in the open at night.'

The three horses looked fit and strong enough, and were very black indeed; even in the glow of the man's lamp they tended to vanish into the shadowy stalls. I took his advice.

Davus had some trouble mounting his horse. It turned out he had never ridden a horse before.

Eco looked thoroughly disgusted – not angry at Davus but at himself for not thinking of such an elementary detail before we set out. What use was a bodyguard on horseback if he couldn't control his mount? Davus was now my personal bodyguard; I should have been the one to ask if he could ride, but I was so used to Belbo that I took it for granted. 'You've never even been on a horse?' I asked.

'No, Master.'

'You know nothing about riding?'

'Nothing, Master.' Davus peered uncertainly at the ground on either side, like a man atop a rickety table.

'Then today you shall learn how to ride,' I said. And tomorrow you will hardly be able to stand upright, I thought. What good would a bodyguard be, with saddle sores and wooden limbs?

The horse snorted. Davus gave a start and gripped the reins tightly. The stableman was greatly amused. 'Don't worry! I tell you, these horses are the best. Trained to do all the thinking. Battle horses — keep their wits no matter what. Smarter than your average slave, that's for sure. The Great One even lets women ride them!'

Davus took this as a challenge. He wrinkled his brow, forced the queasy look from his face and sat upright.

We ambled away from the stables, letting the mounts get a feel for us. Eco was fretful, but not about Davus. 'Do you think it was a good idea, bringing strangers into the house?'

'They're Pompey's men. Don't you think we can trust them?'

'I suppose so . . .'

'It was the only way. Well, perhaps not the only way . . .' In fact, for the time that Eco and I would be away, Pompey had offered to allow Bethesda, Menenia and Diana and whatever attendants they needed to take up residence in his old family house inside the city wall, in the Carinae district, on the western slope of the Esquiline. It made sense; they would certainly have been safe there, and the place

231

was situated midway between Eco's house and mine. But I didn't want to slip quite so far, quite so quickly into Pompey's camp. Putting my family completely in his care would mean putting them completely in his power, and in a way that outsiders would surely notice. On the other hand, it was out of the question for me to leave Rome even for a few days without doing something to safeguard the family households, especially if Eco went with me, which he insisted on doing. The solution was to borrow a troop of bodyguards from Pompey as part of my fee, sufficient to protect both the house on the Esquiline and the house on the Palatine in our absence. Pompey was agreeable. His men had arrived at my house early that morning before Eco and I departed.

'I didn't like the looks of some of those fellows,' brooded Eco.

'I think that's the point. They're frightening.'

'But can we trust them?'

'Pompey says so. I doubt that there's a man on earth better at keeping discipline in his own ranks than Pompey.'

'Bethesda wasn't pleased.'

'Bethesda wasn't pleased about any of this. Her household is in chaos, her husband is traipsing off into danger again, and another man's gladiators are tracking mud into her house. But I suspect she was secretly glad to have the protection. Those men who ransacked the house and killed Belbo – that shook her more than she'll admit. And mark my words, by the time we get back, she'll have every

one of Pompey's brutes trained to take off his shoes before he steps on the carpets and to ask permission before he goes to the privy.'

Eco laughed. 'Perhaps Pompey will take her on as a drill sergeant!' We rode on a bit. 'Menenia was reasonable enough about the whole thing,' he noted. The wistfulness in his voice made me suspect they had come to more than a mental understanding during the night.

'Menenia is the soul of reason,' I said.

'And Diana —'

'Don't say it. I saw the way she was looking at some of those fellows. I'd rather not think about it.'

Davus shifted uneasily and cleared his throat, but Eco pressed on. 'She's seventeen, Papa. She should get married soon.'

'Perhaps, but how? A decent marriage means negotiations between the families, planning, announcements to friends — all the things we went through when you married Menenia. Can you imagine managing all that, with things as they are now?'

'The riots will pass, Papa. Things will get back to normal soon enough.'

'Will they?'

'Life goes on, Papa. Things are bound to get better.'

'Are they? This time I'm not so sure . . .'

There was not a person to be seen along the road, at least not any living person. Lining the way, as always along the major thoroughfares outside any city, were a succession of tombs and sepulchres,

large and small. Burial within city walls is illegal, so the neighbourhoods of the dead begin just outside the walls. Crooked cenotaphs with inscriptions worn smooth by time stood alongside newly sculpted family portraits in marble and limestone. Among the grandest tombs were those of the Scipios, the family whose glory had dominated Rome in the age before my father's birth. They conquered Carthage and began the work of empire; now they were dust.

Equally grand were the tombs of the Claudii. The Appian Way was their road, or so they considered it, since it had been built by their ancestor. The dead Claudii in their ornate stone tombs were clustered thickly along the way, like jostling spectators at a parade. The Claudii continued to make their mark on Rome; Publius Clodius, affecting the plebeian variant of the name, had been the latest to hold sway. As Pompey had noted, his murder on the road of his ancestors had been a twist of fate of the sort so beloved by melodramatic playwrights and sentimental rhetoricians. The irony might some day provide a theme for schoolboy compositions: Appius Claudius Caecus built the Appian Way. Two hundred and sixty years later his descendant Publius Clodius was murdered there. Compare and contrast the achievements of these two men.

Beyond the tombs were great drifts and piles of rubbish and debris, bits of broken pottery and worn-out shoes, shards of glass and bits of metal and plaster. A city as vast as Rome produces a great deal of trash, and it all has to go somewhere. Better

to cart it outside the walls and dump it in the city of the dead than to let it pile up among the living.

At the farthest edge of the city, where the tombs and trash heaps grew fewer and farther between and the countryside began in earnest, we passed the Monument of Basilius. I've never known who Basilius was or why his tomb, built like a miniature Greek temple atop a little hill, should be as grand as those of the Claudii or Scipios. The inscriptions are so old they can no longer be read. But the monument's prominence and location make it a landmark of sorts. The Monument of Basilius marks the farthest reach of the city's vices, or the farthest incursion of the countryside's menace, depending on your point of view. Bad types of all sorts congregate there. The vicinity is notorious for robberies and rapes. Thus the commonplace warning to a friend setting out on the Appian Way: 'Be careful passing the Monument of Basilius!' That morning, those had been Bethesda's next to last words to me. At the moment, the only vagrants to be seen were a few wretched figures huddled under coarse blankets against the monument's base, surrounded by empty wine vessels. They were probably as harmless and miserable as they looked; on the other hand, bandits are notorious for feigning such disguises.

I spurred my mount to a trot, eager to put the place behind us. But as we hurried on, all my inner senses told me I was getting closer to danger, not farther away. When I had insisted that Pompey supply guards for my family in my absence, he had

offered to send more guards along with Eco and me. I had refused. His men were likely to be recognized. What was the point of sending me to find out what Pompey's men could not, if people could tell at a glance that I came from Pompey? Besides, I had reasoned, three healthy, armed men on horseback, offering offence to no one, should have little to worry about.

Bethesda's very last words to me that morning – with what glimmered suspiciously like a tear in her eye – had been 'You are a fool.' I hoped she was wrong.

Past the Monument of Basilius, the Appian Way stretches like a long, straight ribbon towards Mount Alba on the horizon. The land on either side is as flat as a table, dotted here and there with distant trees and houses. A man can see for miles. There was no one but us travelling on the road that morning, no slaves at work in the fallow fields. Except for a few plumes of smoke from hearth fires in scattered houses, there were no signs of life at all. This is one of the safest stretches on the whole Appian Way, since the topography affords no places for ambush. The fresh air, the smell of earth, the vast emptiness, the sun rising over the long ridge of hills to the west, all these things made me feel exhilarated, glad to be leaving the city and its madness behind me for a while. But one of us did not look happy at all.

'Is something wrong, Davus? You seem to be getting the hang of riding.'

'Master? No, the horse is fine.' Even as he spoke

236

he tightened his grip on the reins, as if the beast might overhear and rear up just to spite him.

'Is it something else, then?'

'Nothing, Master. Only . . .' He scanned the empty fields on either side with such a disconcerted look that I followed his gaze, thinking there must be some menace lurking in the clumps of frigid earth and brown grass.

'For Jupiter's sake, what do you see, Davus?'

'Nothing, Master.'

'Don't keep saying that! You must see something.'

'No, Master, that's exactly it. I'm seeing nothing. Nothing at all. And it seems to go on forever.'

'Are you going blind?'

'No! I can see everything. Except that there's nothing to see!'

I suddenly understood. I couldn't help but laugh at the absurdity of it. Eco frowned and drew his mount closer. 'What going on, Papa?'

'Davus has never been outside the city in his life,' I said. 'Isn't that right, Davus?'

'Yes, Master.'

'How old are you, Davus?'

'Nineteen, Master.'

'Davus is nineteen years old, Eco, and he has never been on a horse, and he has never stepped foot outside Rome.'

Eco cursed and rolled his eyes and rode on ahead.

'He's angry at me, Master.'

'No he isn't, Davus. He misses his wife and he's worried about her.'

'Then you're angry at me.'

'No, Davus. Forget that I laughed. Don't give it another thought. You'll need all your thinking to stay upright on that horse and to keep track of all the nothing that's going by.'

We rode on for a while, the stillness broken only by the clop of hooves against the road. Tufts of steam rose from the horses' nostrils. I took a deep breath, hungry to feel the bite of cold air in my lungs. The empty azure bowl of the morning sky was like crystal. The brown winter earth was like a slumbering giant across whom we made our tiny progress. I was unspeakably glad to be away from Rome.

'He was a very good slave, wasn't he?' said Davus, with a frown so heavy it pulled his chin to his chest.

'Who?'

'The bodyguard you had before me. The one who was killed.'

I sighed. 'His name was Belbo. Yes, he was a good slave. A good man.'

'I suppose he was stronger than me. Smarter than me, too.'

I looked at Davus's hulking arms and shoulders and saw the unhappy befuddlement on his face. 'Probably not,' I said.

'But I'll wager he knew how to ride a horse. I'll bet he wasn't afraid of an empty field.'

'Don't worry about it,' I said, as gently as I could. None of this was his fault, after all.

# XIV

'The sun is up, Eco. The air is cold and clear. There is not another person on the road, not another person in sight. Ah – can you hear that?'

'I don't hear a thing, Papa.'

'Exactly. Not even a bird or a cricket. Silence. I believe my faculties are beginning to return. I may actually be able to think again!'

Eco laughed. 'Did you ever lose the ability?'

'It's not a joke. Can't you feel it? With every step the horses take us farther from the city, the clearer my head becomes. It's as if I've been in fog, and now it's lifting.'

'The haze we left behind in the city was smoke, Papa.'

'The haze that's visible, yes. But there's another haze that's settled over Rome. Panic, confusion, deception – no one can think straight. People are behaving like madmen, rushing wildly about,

hiding in holes, running from their shadows. It's like a bad dream that won't end. But now I feel like I'm waking up. Don't you feel it, too?'

He looked about, took a deep breath and laughed. 'Yes!'

'Good! Perhaps together we can begin to make sense of things.'

'Where shall we start, Papa?'

'On this very spot – but let's go back in time twenty-one days.'

'Why?'

'Because it was exactly twenty-one days ago that Clodius set out on the Appian Way. I figured it out last night.'

'And Milo?'

'Milo set out the next day, the day of their fatal encounter – but we'll come to that. Let's begin with Clodius and reconstruct the events as they happened, so far as we know from both Milo and Fulvia.' I had not yet shared with Eco all the details of my interview with Fulvia the previous day. 'To begin: Fulvia told me that Clodius left their house on the Palatine at about the third hour. Not as early as we did – we set out even before sunrise, before the first hour. But the third hour would have been an early start for a man like Clodius.'

'Why, because he was as dissolute as Cicero claims?'

'No, because whenever a man as powerful as Clodius leaves town, even on a short trip, there are always a great many loose ends and last-minute details to be dealt with. I gathered from Fulvia that

such was the case with Clodius that morning – hastily scribbled notes, messengers dispatched, and so forth. Finally, Clodius set out. On his way, before he'd even left the Palatine Hill, he paused to look in on a friend who had fallen deathly ill: Cyrus the architect.'

'The name's familiar. Will we be questioning him?'

'I'm afraid not. Cyrus died later that very day, not long after Clodius left him. He was an architect to the rich and famous, much sought after. He seemed to have been above politics. Cicero hired him to rebuild his house on the Palatine after it was burned down by the mob. Clodius hired him when he bought that monstrosity of a house from Scaurus, to design all the changes. I gather that Cyrus had been spending a great deal of time at Clodius's house in recent months, overseeing workers, dining with the family.'

'So Cyrus worked for both Cicero and Clodius?'

'I gather that he had an artist's temperament – the type that's too talented to take sides. Not only did both Clodius and Cicero use his services, they both gave him legal advice. It seems that Cyrus consulted both of them, separately, when he fell ill and drew up his will – and named both of them among his heirs. After Clodius's farewell visit that morning, Cicero went to see Cyrus, and was with him when he died.'

'An architect with a sense of symmetry,' noted Eco. 'You say he was above politics, but I wonder.

All the time he was spending at Clodius's house, dining with the family, able to wander about at will – what a splendid eavesdropper he'd have made for Cicero.'

'I thought of that. Even if he wasn't a deliberate spy, even in normal conversations Cyrus could have inadvertently given Cicero a great deal of information about Clodius's household and dealings. And Cicero would know just how to extract the information he wanted. But this is merely supposition. We've no cause to think that Cyrus was in any sense a spy. Cyrus merely constitutes a curious link between Cicero and Clodius – just another example of what a small town Rome really is. Cyrus's name comes up again later, which is why I mention him now, but his part in the story is probably insignificant.'

'Understood.' Eco looked at me shrewdly. 'All the same, I'm suspicious of this Cyrus fellow. I shall be keeping a close watch on him – dead or alive.'

'That's the spirit!'

'Ugh! Papa, it's not like you to pun.'

'None intended. To continue: Clodius paid a last visit to the ailing Cyrus and then set out on the Appian Way. The reason for his trip was some business in the town of Aricia, about fifteen miles from Rome. It's an easy day's journey on horseback, the traditional first night's stop on a trip south, a place with inns and taverns for travellers.'

'Clodius had business there?'

'He was slated to address the town senate the next morning. Fulvia didn't seem to know what the

occasion was or why Clodius's presence was required. Perhaps it was time for an annual pig festival in Aricia, or a celebration of some local deity. Politicians are always taking trips to outlying towns to court the voters. Clodius happened to be a major property owner in the vicinity; he and Fulvia owned a villa just this side of Aricia. Something to note: Fulvia didn't go with him. That's a little odd. From all I've heard, Fulvia was very much the politician's dutiful wife, and wives generally go along on this sort of trip. While the politician makes friendly jabber with the local magistrates, the politician's wife radiates matronly virtue and shares recipes with the magistrates' wives, or something like that. But Fulvia stayed at home.'

'Did you ask her why?'

'She told me she was concerned about Cyrus's condition.'

'Was she that close to Cyrus?'

'You've seen her house — imagine having your architect die on you in the middle of redoing that monstrosity!'

'I see what you mean. But does it really matter that Fulvia didn't go with Clodius?'

'Maybe, maybe not. Consider this: if a man was plotting to ambush his enemy — as Milo contends that Clodius was — he'd leave his wife at home, don't you think? But here's something curious: Clodius did take his young son along with him. The boy is only a child — eight years old. That seems to negate the idea that Clodius left Fulvia behind because he was plotting violence. You'd

think he would have left his son safely at home, too.'

'Did Fulvia say why he took the boy with him?'

'She says Clodius wanted to introduce his son to the city leaders in Aricia. Now that sounds like a typical Roman politician – never too soon to start cultivating the heir! And of course, absent his wife, what better way to show himself off as a good family man than to bring along his little boy? Clodius's enemies –'

'Meaning Cicero and Milo.'

'– have spent years painting him as an incestuous, whoremongering former male prostitute who lives to seduce other men's wives and sons – which may or may not have touched on the truth. That sort of talk doesn't necessarily ruin a man's reputation in jaded, sophisticated Rome, but it's poison out in the countryside, where people still take old-fash-ioned virtues seriously. So when Clodius shows up to speak to the citizens of Aricia, he wants to present himself as an upstanding husband and father. How better to do that than to deliver his speech with eight-year-old Publius junior by his side?'

Eco frowned. 'But the boy wasn't there when Clodius and Milo had their skirmish on the Appian Way the next day, was he?'

'No. But we shall come to that. One more thing to consider, while we still have Clodius setting out for Aricia: a large contio was held in the Forum that morning, called by the same radical tribunes who've been instigating riots since Clodius died.

Normally, Clodius would have made a point of attending such a contio, to make sure things went according to plan. Instead, he headed off for Aricia.'

Eco shrugged. 'A man can't be in two places at once.'

'No, so he has to make a choice. Some would say that it's hard to imagine Clodius missing a rabble-rousing contio just to curry favour with the town fathers at a rest stop on the Appian Way – unless he had an ulterior motive.'

'Such as an ambush on his mortal enemy?'

'So his enemies might suggest. Simply another point to keep in mind.'

'What sort of entourage did Clodius take with him?'

'Three friends and a number of slaves – Fulvia says twenty-five or thirty – most of them on foot and all of them armed.'

'So many?'

'A large bodyguard, granted, but hardly unreasonable. How else could a man like Clodius travel safely in the countryside? As it was, the bodyguard wasn't adequate to save him in the end. But there will be those who'll suggest that such a formidable group must have been intended for attack rather than defence. Another detail to be noted.'

'So at last we have Clodius on his way.'

'Yes. He deals with last-minute business at home, gives Fulvia a kiss, stops in to see the dying architect. He and his thirty or so men stride through the Capena Gate – perhaps a cold drop of water falls on

his neck just as it did on mine, and gives him a start. It's mid-morning – the market is jammed with shoppers and stinks of fish. Slaves and humble citizens recognize him, hail him. Those who despise him only scowl and bite their tongues – they'd be outnumbered in a crowd like that. He and his friends get horses from somewhere – Pompey's can't be the only stable in the area – and they're off on the Appian Way, with their entourage walking behind them. Clodius probably pauses to pay homage at the tombs of his illustrious ancestors – his son is with him, and what patrician father would pass up the opportunity to impress his birthright on a boy?

'They pass the notorious Monument of Basilius and Clodius doesn't give it a thought – the place is dangerous only at night, and there's a troop of armed men marching behind him. The road is wide, so Clodius and his three friends ride abreast, with his son at his right hand listening to the grown-ups converse. The little fellow must be quite impressed with his father – all those men at Papa's beck and call, the huge crowds that gather when Papa speaks, such a grand house to grow up in. To think, it will all be in ruins the next day.

'Now Clodius and his company have come to the same long, dull stretch of road where we find ourselves. Clodius has his friends along to keep the conversation lively, and of course his son, to whom he can point out the various shrines and tombs that continue to dot the way now and again. When that fails, he can brag about the road itself, as every

Claudian has done since it was built. It is a remarkably fine road, isn't it? The blocks so perfectly cut and fitted, the surface so level and smooth, the way so remarkably wide – ox carts going in opposite directions can pass without even pausing. You'd think the gods themselves had made such a road, but no, it was Appius Claudius Caecus, many-times great-grandfather of our own Publius Clodius. One more thing for that little boy to be proud of.

'Aricia lies ahead at the end of the journey, about four hours away. A horseman in a hurry could make it sooner, but since the bodyguards are walking, Clodius and his friends on horseback are obliged to keep a slow but steady pace. On the way to Aricia, what will they pass?'

'A lot of nothing!' said Davus, asserting his presence after a long silence. He seemed in control of his horse and in better spirits, ready to laugh at himself.

'A lot of empty farmland, to be more precise, interspersed with woods here and there and some marshes in the low spots, all very flat and not particularly scenic. To the left, distant mountains on the horizon. To the right, a gentle, gradual slope towards the sea. And up ahead, growing steadily larger as they draw nearer, Mount Alba. What do you think of it, Davus?'

He peered at the low, peaked mass on the horizon. 'It must be enormous!'

I smiled. 'Not really. Only a small mountain, as mountains go, but a major landmark in these flatlands. There are several small towns among the

ridges and foothills. Aricia is one of them. But the first one we'll come to, just as the ground begins to rise, is Bovillae. You've taken this road plenty of times on your way down to Neapolis, Eco – how far is Bovillae from Rome?'

'A little past the eleventh milestone.'

'And what's there, at Bovillae?'

'I've been through the place, Papa. I'm not sure I've ever stopped.'

'Think!'

He stared through narrowed eyes at the foothills ahead as if by squinting he could make out the details at such a distance. 'I seem to remember an inn along the road. And a stable.'

'Yes, the stable has probably been there in one form or another for well over two hundred years, since the first stretch of the Appian Way from Rome to Bovillae was paved. Appius Claudius Caecus built the road as a military route for the legions to use, that's why it's so wide and so straight. Bovillae was the first post-station for military messengers, a place to change horses. And where there's a stable, of course there's an inn. What does the inn at Bovillae look like?'

'A stone building. Two storeys.'

'Yes, there's probably a communal sleeping room upstairs, a tavern downstairs, and a cookhouse at the back. A stable and an inn; what else?'

Eco shrugged. 'A few houses here and there, away from the road. Oh, and an altar to Jupiter, built under a circle of old oak trees with a little creek nearby. A very pretty spot.'

'Oak trees, yes; once the road starts ascending to higher ground at Bovillae, the trees get thicker. The top of the mountain is a veritable forest. I don't suppose you've ever seen a forest, Davus?'

'I've seen what they call groves, growing around temples in the city.'

'Not quite the same thing. Well, so much for Bovillae. Not much to it, is there? Not a very special place to breathe your last breath, but that's where Clodius died the next day. The skirmish started farther up the road, but apparently Milo's men chased Clodius to the inn, where he made his last stand. According to Fulvia, it was a senator named Sextus Tedius who came along later and found the body lying in the road. He had his slaves put the corpse into his litter and sent it on to Rome. You and I saw the condition it was in when it reached Fulvia – stabbed and strangled. And after Bovillae, Eco? What's next on the road?'

'The land begins to rise, as you said. Wooded slopes with rich people's estates – pylons set on either side of private roads leading up to big houses that you can barely glimpse as you go by.' He cocked his head and squinted. 'Something new, closer to the road – a temple of some sort . . .'

'Not a temple, but a residence: the House of the Vestal Virgins. You're right, it's new, built only in the last few years. Before that, the Vestals lived somewhere higher up the mountain. There's a temple of Vesta somewhere up there. Not a place we men are likely to set foot in. Press on, imaginary rider. What's next along the road?'

'On the opposite side of the road . . . something else religious . . . having to do with women. A shrine, not a temple . . . a shrine to Fauna, the Good Goddess!'

'Excellent! A place for Fauna's female worshippers to leave offerings and make prayers, and another place where we wouldn't be particularly welcome. But according to Fulvia, it was on the stretch of road directly in front of the shrine of the Good Goddess that the skirmish between Clodius and Milo began. We'll want to take a careful look at the lay of the land and see whether it looks like a suitable place for an ambush. But let's return to Clodius on the day before his death, on his way from Rome to Aricia. He'll have passed all these places, perhaps without stopping, wanting to press on now that he's so close to his destination. What comes next, Eco?'

'Hmm. I seem to remember some impressive pylons on the left and a road heading up to a villa on the ridge above.'

'Yes. If my assumption is correct, that's where we'll be spending the night.'

'Pompey's villa?'

'From the directions Baby Face gave me, I think that must be the place.'

Eco whistled. 'The view must be extraordinary.'

'Yes. Pompey seems to like living in places where he's able to look down on the world around him. But don't stop yet. What's next along the road?'

'More private estates. One of them must belong to Clodius.'

'Yes, his is that enormous thing that seems to perch on the side of the hill.'

'The place where they cut down all those trees and did all that excavating?'

'Yes. Apparently a great deal of the interior space is underground, like a vault – defensible as a fortress, Fulvia told me. From what she said, I gathered that Clodius was especially proud of the place, even happier with it than that palace of a house on the Palatine. We'll get the chance to take a closer look at it. That's where Clodius's journey ended for the day, just a mile or so this side of Aricia. There must have been a few hours of sunlight left. Clodius probably inspected the grounds, talked to the foreman, saw to whatever it is that estate owners see to when they arrive at one of their estates. His cook prepared a dinner that night to which some of the local elite were invited. It all sounds very respectable, very boring. After all that riding, little Publius junior probably fell asleep on his dining couch. The next morning, Clodius delivered his address to the town senate of Aricia, followed by a brief reception. Then back to his estate by shortly after midday or early afternoon. Fulvia says that he intended to spend at least another night there.'

'Did he have more business in the area?'

'I don't know. Let's be sentimental and assume that he wanted to spend some fatherly time with his son, strolling through the wooded grounds around his villa. But then a messenger arrived.'

'A messenger?'

'The one that Fulvia dispatched that morning, to give her husband the sad news about Cyrus the architect. She asked Clodius to return to Rome at once.'

'Was it really necessary for Clodius to hurry home?'

'Fulvia seemed to think so. Cyrus was close enough to have named Clodius among his heirs, and Fulvia was depending on the man to finish their Palatine house. She felt overwhelmed by his death. She wanted her husband to come home.'

'And Clodius dropped everything to come running at her call?'

'You don't find that credible, Eco?'

'I don't know, Papa. You've had more contact with the woman than I have.'

'Yes, well, I'll venture to say that when Fulvia tells a man to do something, the chances are good that the man will do what Fulvia says.'

'Even Clodius?'

'Even Clodius. Which is to say that I find what Fulvia told me credible if not necessarily convincing: that Clodius intended to spend another night at his country villa, but instead found himself unexpectedly back on the Appian Way headed towards Rome, because of that message from Fulvia. If that was the case, then there was no premeditated ambush, was there? When Milo and his entourage passed by, Clodius should have been off strolling in the woods with his son; instead, Clodius was on the Appian Way, but only by chance.'

'But where was his son, if the boy wasn't with him when the skirmish occurred?'

'Fulvia says that Clodius had promised the boy a stay in the country, and left him at the villa with his tutor.'

'Does it strike you as credible that he would leave the boy behind, Papa?'

'Perhaps. You might think Fulvia would have wanted her son brought back to her, but the rich see these things differently. I suppose, if I owned a huge villa in the country with a full staff of slaves to run the place, I might feel comfortable leaving my eight-year-old son in their keeping. Or perhaps the boy is an insufferable brat and a terrible traveller. Perhaps he'd been a complete pest all the previous day and Clodius couldn't abide another long trip with the monster and wanted to be rid of him.'

Eco laughed. 'That's better! Forget the sentimentality.'

'Of course, to some it might look suspicious that Clodius just happened to set out from his villa with an armed company just as Milo was approaching on the Appian Way, and just happened to leave his young son behind, out of harm's way. Another detail to be noted.'

'So we finally come to Milo. What was he doing on the Appian Way?'

'You heard his speech in the Forum the other day. He was expected for a religious ceremony in Lanuvium, which is the next town you come to after Aricia, a couple of miles farther south. From what I've been able to tell, the bare facts of the

account Milo gave at Caelius's contio are true: he attended a meeting of the Senate in Rome that morning and later he set out at the head of a large retinue, riding with his wife in a carriage. Milo claims they got a late start and didn't pass Bovillae until about the eleventh hour, the last hour of daylight. If that's true, it would seem to contradict Fulvia's story about Clodius heading home, because the eleventh hour of a winter day is too late for anyone with a scrap of sense to set out on a journey of several hours with a troop of men on foot. It would have been long after dark before Clodius got to Rome, and travelling by night is a dangerous business, if only because of the chance that a man or beast will trip in the dark and break a leg. So did the incident really occur that late? Fulvia says that Clodius's body, carried in a litter, arrived at her house on the Palatine at the first hour of the night – only an hour or two after Milo claims the skirmish began, which is impossible.'

'So there's a discrepancy about when the incident occurred. Fulvia says it happened earlier in the afternoon; Milo says it happened not long before sunset. Is that important, Papa?'

'It means that one of them has to be mistaken – or deliberately lying.'

'I shall try to contain my surprise!'

'Yes, but why lie about the time, Eco? And if Fulvia or Milo has lied about that, then what else might one or the other be lying about?'

'Do you think we're likely to find out, simply by going to these places and asking some questions?'

'We can try,' I said.

Mount Alba loomed straight ahead of us, steadily growing larger. Clouds had gathered at its summit, casting a shadow over the higher slopes, so that the mountain seemed to erupt from the surrounding sunlit plains like a brooding mass of doubt. Davus frowned, viewing the prospect with misgivings. He was not the only one.

# XV

Though we arrived at Bovillae before the fourth hour, the midday meal was already being prepared. Smoke rose from the cookhouse behind the inn, carrying smells of baking bread and roasting meat.

'I'm starving!' said Eco. Davus's stomach growled in sympathy.

'Good,' I said. 'We won't have to invent any pretences for why we're stopping at the tavern.'

It was a two-storey building made of much-weathered stone. The land all around was cleared and trammelled by the passage of many feet over many years. It was to this place, according to Fulvia, that Clodius had fled when Milo's men overwhelmed him. He had taken refuge in the tavern. Milo's men had stormed the place. Fulvia knew no details of the battle, only that eventually a passing senator on his way to Rome had come upon

Clodius's body lying in the road outside the tavern, and had sent it on to Rome in his litter.

Davus walked the horses to a hitching post beneath a nearby stand of trees. There was a trough with water for the horses and a bench for Davus to sit on while he watched them.

Before we went inside, Eco and I took a quick look at all four sides of the building, to see how defensible it looked. There were large, shuttered windows in the upper storey, inaccessible as there was no way to climb up to them. The shuttered windows in the rear and side walls of the lower storey were small and set high up. A man might have been able to wriggle through one, but only if given a boost and if there was no one inside to stop him. The back door, made of solid wood, opened onto a covered walkway to the cookhouse. The front door, which at the moment stood open, was also made of solid wood. The doorway was so narrow that Eco and I had to turn sideways and step inside one at a time. The windows on either side of the front door were slightly larger and situated a little lower than the other windows on the ground floor, but a man would still have had a difficult time scrambling in or out of them.

All in all, the inn appeared to be a reasonably defensible building. Still, I saw the signs of a recent, losing battle.

So did Eco. 'Did you notice the difference in the shutters, Papa?'

'Yes.'

'The ones on the upstairs windows are all made of old, grey wood —'

'– while the shutters on every one of the downstairs windows are conspicuously new, as are both the front and back doors. There's a lot of new plaster around the doorway, as well. You and I know all too well how doors can be broken and need replacing.'

'Where do you suppose everyone is, Papa?'

'Who would you expect to be here? There were no other travellers on the road this morning. We're probably early for the regular midday clientele.' As my eyes adjusted to the dim light I saw a plain, rustic room with a few tables and benches. A steeply angled stairway to the upper floor began at the far left corner. Underneath the stairway a counter blocked off the back portion of the room. In the wall behind the counter there was a little archway with a cloth curtain tied back to show a shadowy storage room that led through to the rear door. After a moment the door rattled and opened to show the silhouette of a large woman outlined by bright sunlight. She closed the door behind her and waddled up to the bar, wiping her hands on the front of her coarse gown. She smelled of baking bread and roasting meat.

'I thought I saw someone come in.' She peered at us with a squint that I took to be almost hostile until I realized she was waiting for her eyes to adjust to the dimness. She was a strong-looking woman with meaty arms and a round, open face surrounded by a tangle of greying red hair. 'That's your fellow with the horses over by the trough?'

'Yes,' I said.

'Three altogether, are you?'

'Yes, travellers.'

'Hungry travellers,' added Eco, leaning against the bar.

She showed the hint of a smile. 'We can take care of that, as long as you have something that jingles.'

Eco produced his coin purse.

She nodded. 'I've got a couple of rabbits roasting. It'll be a little while before they're done, but I can bring you some bread and cheese in the meantime.' She reached under the bar and produced two cups, then went back to the storage room and returned with a pitcher of wine and a pitcher of water.

'Could you take some food out to the fellow under the trees, too?' I said. 'I can hear his stomach growling from here.'

'Certainly. I'll send one of my boys to take care of him. They're out in the cookhouse watching the fire. With my husband,' she added, as if making of point of letting us know that she was not a woman alone. 'Travellers, you say. Headed north or south?'

'South.'

'You've come from Rome, then?' She poured out generous portions of wine, then added splashes of water.

'We left early this morning.'

'What's it like up in the city?'

'An awful mess. We're glad to be away from it.'

'Well, it's been an awful mess around here, too,

let me tell you. Ever since that accursed day . . .'
She sighed and shook her head.

'Ah, yes, we must be close to where it happened –
the skirmish up the road.'

She snorted. 'Call it a skirmish if you like, but I'd
call it an all-out battle, to judge from the damage
that was done and the dead bodies lying all about.
And it may have started up the road, but right here's
where it ended.' She slapped the top of the counter.

'What do you mean?'

'Aren't we talking about the same thing? Milo
and Clodius and all the blood that was spilled?'

I nodded. 'No one in Rome talks about anything
else these days. But everything is so confused and
jumbled. Every new version contradicts the last
one. Something happened on the Appian Way
and Clodius ended up dead – that's about the only
thing all the stories agree on. Where, when and
how, nobody knows for sure.'

She rolled her eyes. 'So much suffering and
destruction, you'd think people would at least
bother to find out what really happened, if only
to be glad it didn't happen to them. But you said
you were hungry. I'll get you some bread, hot from
the oven.'

Eco opened his mouth to call her back, but I
squeezed his arm and shook my head. 'The woman
is eager enough to tell us what she knows,' I said in
a low voice. 'Let her do it at her own pace.'

She returned with a steaming loaf of bread in a
basket and a piece of cheese the size of a brick, then
went back to the storeroom and returned with a

heaped bowl of black and green olives. She put her elbows on the bar, leaned towards us and resumed her tale without any prompting. 'It was my brother-in-law who owned this tavern, my little sister's husband. A hard-working fellow, from a long line of hard workers. Inherited the place from his father; the family's owned this inn for generations. He wept with joy the day my sister gave him a son to leave it to.' She sighed. 'Who could have known how soon he'd be passing the place along? The boy's still a baby, and now that his papa is dead there's not another grown man on either side of the family to run the place. So we've taken it over, my husband and I, with our boys helping us, while my poor widowed sister stays with her baby. Ah, poor Marcus! That was her husband's name. There's always some danger when you run a place like this on the road, always the risk of being raided by bandits or runaway slaves who'd slash your throat without a thought. But Marcus was a big, stout fellow, not afraid of anything, and this inn was his whole life. Always had been, since he was a child. I think he didn't realize the danger that day when Clodius's men came running in, all bloody and out of breath. He didn't turn them away, he just asked them what he could do to help. Clodius staggered inside, wounded and bleeding, and told him to bolt the doors. Then they laid Clodius right here, flat on his back.' She slapped the counter, hard enough to cause ripples in our cups. By the dim light I studied the mottled, stained surface of the old wood. A lot of wine must have been spilled on that counter over

the years, I told myself, but there were stains which might have been something else.

'Marcus should have sent them all right back out into the road, that's what my husband says. But what does he know? He wasn't here. But my poor sister was. She told me all about it. She'd left her baby with me that day. Oh, how she loved working in this tavern, as much as Marcus did; nothing could keep her away. When Clodius and his men showed up, she was upstairs, shaking out blankets and sweeping the floors. If only her little boy had been sick; if only something, anything, had kept her at home that day. The shock of what happened to Marcus was bad enough, but for her to have been here, to have seen and heard – it's broken something inside her. Ah, well, that's why we have to do everything we can to keep the place going until little Marcus is big enough to take his father's place.'

I nodded. 'So the skirmish – the battle – began up the road, but Clodius ended up here. Had he ever been in the tavern before? Did he know your brother-in-law, Marcus?'

'Oh, certainly. Publius Clodius stopped in here plenty of times, on his way to that villa of his up on the mountain. I met him myself a few times over the years. So charming – you could tell right away that he was highborn, there was no hiding that. Just a certain way he had of carrying himself, and always such fine clothes and fine horses, and how his hair and fingernails were always so nicely groomed. You don't often see a man who keeps his fingernails so well cared for. But he was never aloof. He always

remembered Marcus's name, always asked him how little Marcus was coming along. He had a young son himself.'

'So I've heard.'

'Of course, not everybody liked Publius Clodius. He stirred up some hard feelings around here, back when he started building his villa.'

'Hard feelings?'

'Well, there were some who said that the way he got hold of the surrounding land wasn't completely honest, and others who complained that some of the trees he cut down were part of the sacred grove of Jupiter. And the Vestals had to move out of their old house. But Clodius gave them money to build their new house, which is only a little farther from the Temple of Vesta than their old one, so I could never see what all their complaining was about.' She shook her head. 'But I'll speak no ill of the dead, especially when the poor man's lemur left his body within the sound of my voice.'

'So your brother-in-law was friendly with Clodius, despite any hard feelings that some of your neighbours might have had?'

'Oh, yes. I suppose that's why Clodius ran to this place when he found himself in trouble. If only he hadn't brought the trouble with him! But I don't blame the dead. I blame the other.'

'The other?'

She picked up a rag from behind the bar and began twisting it, clenching her fists until the knuckles turned white. 'The one whose men were

after Clodius that day. He's the bastard to blame for what happened here.'

'Titus Annius Milo, you mean.'

She made a noise in her throat as if she might spit. 'If you want to call him that. Milo! He chose that name for himself, didn't he? What a vain fellow, thinking he takes after some great Olympic hero. Well, no one is overawed by your so-called Milo in these parts. He's just another fellow from the far side of the mountain who went off to Rome to make his fortune. He comes from Lanuvium, did you know that?'

'Yes, I think I'd heard that.'

'Titus Annius Milo, you call him. He wasn't born with that name either. He wasn't even born with the name Titus! The fellow was born plain Gaius Papius, like his father before him, and let me assure you that the Papii of Lanuvium never did a single thing of importance that anyone can remember. By birth he's as common as dirt. But when his father died, his grandfather adopted him. That was his mother's father, Titus Annius, the one with the noble ancestors. So Milo took the old man's names and added a name of his own, and Gaius Papius turned into Titus Annius Milo. Now everyone's heard of him. He inherited his grandfather's money, too, when the old man died, but they say he's squandered it all on those fancy funeral games he put on to impress the voters in Rome. The things a man will do to get himself elected to high office! Well, no man among my relatives would ever vote for the fellow. Always pretending and putting on

airs, as fake as all three of his names. No, we never had any use for Milo.'

She paused for breath and began to wipe the counter with her rag, as if she could rub away the bloodstains. 'Oh, Milo would stop in here from time to time on his way home to Lanuvium, buy a round of wine for everybody, say a few pretty words, make sure everyone noticed him. The local boy who'd become such a powerful fellow in Rome, friend of Cicero, ally of Pompey, sure to become consul one of these days! But if you ask me, Milo hasn't got a speck of Clodius's charm. Clodius would come into this room and it would be as if someone had lit candles all around – everything suddenly had a glow to it. Milo would come in, blustering and grinning, and it was like someone blowing bad breath in your face. His charm was all for show. You could practically see him gritting his teeth at having to mix with the common folk he'd left behind. As for that wife of his, what's her name –'

'Fausta, I believe,' said Eco.

'Ah, yes, Fausta Cornelia – well, there's a case of a man marrying upward if ever there was one! Now how did the old dictator Sulla's daughter ever end up hitched to Gaius Papius from Lanuvium? All a game of money and politics, I suppose. Marriage between people like that always comes down to a cold calculation, doesn't it? They say it hasn't stopped her from having all the lovers she wants. They say Fausta's more of a slut now than she was with her first husband. For all that, let me tell you,

she never pretended to have the common touch. When she and Milo would come parading up the Appian Way and he'd stop in here to buy drinks for everyone, the great Fausta Cornelia would stay most firmly ensconced in that fancy carriage of hers, rigid as a statue, staring straight ahead, as if it might give her a gas pain just to look at a person like myself. Well, I could understand her staying out of the tavern, a lady like that – Clodius's wife, Fulvia, was the same, she and her women would always keep to themselves when Clodius stopped in, but you'd see her on the grass under the trees, playing with her little boy or nursing the little girl, behaving like a normal person. Not like Fausta Cornelia, too good to even exchange a glance with the likes of myself. But there was one time, one time –'

The woman suddenly shook and choked with laughter. 'Nature gets the better of everybody in the end, eh?' she managed to say, regaining herself. 'I remember the time – oh, she must have needed to relieve herself very badly, because she actually sent a slave to ask me where the toilets were. So I sent a girl to show her the way to the little building over by the stream, past the stables. And the girl came back, saying that Fausta Cornelia hadn't found the toilets to her liking and that she'd refused to use them. You can bet that Milo left the tavern and set out pretty soon after that. I suppose she held it in all the way to Lanuvium! But how? Even the Appian Way has a few bumps in it. We all talked about it afterwards, wondering whether she'd had

an accident in the carriage, and how Milo would react. Oh, can you imagine the look on the man's face –'

She burst out laughing again, until tears flowed down her cheeks. Finally she recovered and stood wiping away the tears with the backs of her hands. 'Ah! The rabbit! It'll be done by now, surely.'

And with that she disappeared again through the back door.

Eco raised an eyebrow. 'It seems that Clodius and Milo were both rather well known in these parts.'

'Yes, the ambitious local boy, and the aristocratic outsider with money and charm. Two types bound to excite strong reactions in people. Admiration, respect –'

'Envy, hatred . . .'

'Yes,' I said, 'and both of them politicians, not shy about putting themselves forwards. We know how skilful Clodius was at laying on the common touch; he made an art of it. Milo, who really did have common roots, seems to have been rather clumsy at it.'

'So our hostess says, Papa, but she's obviously biased. And what's this about Clodius cutting down sacred trees, displacing the local Vestal Virgins –'

Kicking open the back door, out hostess returned bearing a steaming platter. A tall, hulking figure came in after her, carrying a steaming bowl. The fellow was so large that I felt a little apprehensive until I realized who it was.

'Davus! What are you doing? You're supposed to

be watching the horses. A fine thing if we were to finish our meal and find them gone. I don't care to walk the twelve miles back to Rome.'

'Don't worry,' said the woman. 'I sent one of my boys to take his place. Your horses will be safe, you have my word for it. Isn't it all right for your slave to come inside? The clouds are starting to creep down from the mountaintop, and a fellow can catch a chill, sitting out in the open air. Let him warm up a bit.' She cast a look at Davus such as women, alas, have all too rarely cast at me. Just because a fellow happens to be nineteen, has wavy black hair, oxlike shoulders and a profile like a Greek statue . . .

'She's brought him inside so that she can look at him!' said Eco from the corner of his mouth.

'Obviously,' I agreed. 'This is the woman who preferred Clodius to Milo, remember.'

The woman put plates and utensils before the three of us and filled our cups. The steaming platter turned out to be the roasted rabbit. Rabbit is not my favourite flesh – too greasy and bony – but it was well cooked and I was too hungry to quibble. The steaming bowl was full of glazed turnips. I complimented our hostess on the sauce.

'Oh, it's simple enough. A bit of cumin, a little garlic, some honey and vinegar and olive oil, a pinch of rue. A root vegetable calls for a spicy sauce, my mother always said.'

'It's really quite excellent,' I said, and meant it. But it was time to bring her back to the death of Clodius. 'Did you do much of the cooking here at the tavern before that unfortunate day?'

'Oh, every now and again, especially after my sister had her boy.'

'But you weren't here that day?'

'No, as I said, there was only my sister, working upstairs, and Marcus.'

'Had Clodius come through Bovillae the previous day?'

'So my sister told me, but he didn't stop in. She saw his entourage come marching through, but they passed so quickly that she only caught a glimpse of Clodius, riding at the head with his little boy beside him and a couple of friends.'

'And on the day of the incident, Milo must have passed through here not long before the battle.'

'Oh, yes, my sister remembers that vividly – remembers everything that happened that day, like a bad dream you can't forget. Milo did stop for a while, to water his horses, but none of his men came into the tavern. Still, she says you couldn't miss his entourage. It went on and on, like one of those triumphal processions in the city. That's how he usually travelled, at least when she was with him.'

'Fausta Cornelia, you mean.'

'Yes. You'd think she couldn't leave the house without ten slaves to make up her face in the morning and ten slaves to tuck her into bed at night. And I suppose Gaius Papius – Milo, if you must – simply liked showing off all those slaves and bodyguards to his friends and family back in Lanuvium. 'Look at me! I just can't seem to leave the house without having a hundred minions trailing behind me!' '

'A hundred? Were there that many people in his entourage that day?'

She shrugged. 'Oh, I don't know the number. As I say, I didn't see it myself, my sister did. But she says that while Milo was watering his horses at the stable, with his people milling about, they filled up the road, like a crowd in the Forum in Rome, and when they finally got going again, the procession just seemed to go on and on. Marcus made a joke of it, she said. If only Milo had watered his slaves as well as his horses, they could have sold every drop of wine in stock and paid for a new roof!'

'So Milo's party was bigger than the group that Clodius passed through with on the previous day?'

'Are you a simpleton, or are you just not listening? Yes, definitely. Much, much bigger.'

'But Clodius's party was made up entirely of armed men – so I've heard – whereas you make it sound as though Milo travelled with hairdressers and cosmeticians.'

'Fausta's slaves were in the party, yes, but Milo always travelled with plenty of gladiators, some of them pretty famous. Ever heard of Eudamus and Birria?'

'Of course. They were in Milo's party?'

'He owned the two of them. Isn't that just like him – to buy a pair of famous gladiators just so he could show them off? Even I've heard of Eudamus and Birria, and I have about as much interest in seeing men kill each other in an arena as I do in watching a beetle roll a piece of dung across the road. Though some of those gladiators aren't hard

270

to look at . . .' She cast a glance at Davus, who busied himself with tearing a bit of rabbit flesh off the bone. 'Eudamus and Birria, on the other hand – now those two are about as pretty as a donkey's hind end, and about as hard to miss. They always brought up the rear of Milo's entourage. Huge, like walking trees. You never see one without the other. My husband says they used to fight as a team in the arena.'

'Yes, two against two, sometimes two against four,' said Davus, pulling a rabbit bone from his mouth. Eco and I both looked at him in surprise.

'Go on, Davus,' I said.

He cleared his throat. 'It's just that when I was a boy my old master used to take us all to watch the fights,' he explained. 'He owned a few gladiators himself. Thought about training me for the arena, but finally decided I was too small and he could make a better deal selling me as a bodyguard. He always said that no man ever lost money betting on Eudamus and Birria. It didn't matter what sort of weapon they used, or in what combination – trident and net, short sword, axe, with shields or without. They could paralyse a man with fear, just by staring at him. The two scariest men who ever lived, that's what my old master used to call them.'

I speared a turnip with my fork and dabbed it in the sauce. 'And these gladiators were with Milo when he passed through that day?'

The woman nodded. 'Of that I'm certain, because they were the first of the men who came

271

running after Clodius. My sister saw them from an upstairs window.'

'Is that where she stayed during the attack, upstairs?'

'This is how she tells it: she heard the noise when Clodius and his men rushed in, and she started to come down. She just caught a glimpse of them, then Marcus yelled at her to go back upstairs.'

'How many men did she see?'

'Not very many. Five or six, she said, and Clodius lying on this counter, gripping his shoulder and gnashing his teeth, giving orders to the rest.'

'Giving orders?'

'Yes, telling them to close the shutters and so forth.'

'Then he was wounded but still conscious.'

'Very much so. Determined, my sister said. All his men were looking to him for directions. But the looks on those men's faces . . .'

'What sort of look?'

'Like men with death on their heels, bracing themselves to turn and look it in the face. That's just how she put it. Panic-stricken, gasping for breath. When they heard her on the stairs, they all gave a start and looked up at her like startled rabbits. All except Clodius, she said. He smiled at her. Smiled! Then Marcus yelled for her to go back, and she ran up the stairs.'

'Then what?'

'She ran to a window to see what they were running from. Just a little up the road a man had fallen. Two men stood over him, hacking at him

with swords – blood flying all over the place. The fallen man must have been with Clodius. The other two were Eudamus and Birria. She recognized them right away – like demons from Hades, she said, like monsters from an old story. Farther up the road she could see more fallen men, and what looked like a whole army of gladiators heading for the tavern. Imagine how she felt! Eudamus and Birria finished hacking at the fallen man and came lumbering towards the tavern. The others came rushing up behind them. Oh, it makes me sick to think of it. My baby sister . . .' She shook her head and patted her hand against her breast.

Eco pushed his plate away, looking slightly queasy. Davus stared intently at the woman and used his teeth to tear a shred of rabbit flesh off a bone.

'And then what?' I said.

'Marcus had barred the doors and the shutters downstairs. The attackers got closer and closer, and then they were at the door. Bang, bang, bang! Beating at the door, at the shutters, with their fists, with the pommels of their swords. The racket was terrifying. She covered her ears and still she could hear it. It went on and on – men crying out, the crack of splintered wood and broken hinges, screams and yells, clanging steel.' The woman rolled her eyes up. 'Sometimes I can't sleep at night, imagining what she must have gone through, trapped up there, alone and helpless. She finally gathered up all the blankets, crouched in a corner and piled the blankets on top of her. She says she

can't even remember doing it, but she must have, because finally she realized that all the noise was over and there she was, sweating under all those blankets but shivering as if she were naked.'

'How much time had passed?'

'Who knows? A few moments, an hour? She couldn't say. Finally she got up the courage to peek through the blankets. She was still all alone upstairs, and there was only silence from down below. She went to a window and looked out. She saw bodies scattered here and there along the road, and the strangest thing – right in front of the tavern, a litter with a group of people standing around it.'

'A litter?'

'Yes, not a carriage or a wagon, but a litter, the kind that's carried by a team of slaves, with curtains for privacy. The litter had been put down, the bearers were standing by. An old man in a senator's toga and a woman were standing over one of the fallen men in the road with their heads together, talking.'

'Did your sister recognize the senator?'

'No, but she knew the litter. We've seen it for years, heading up to Rome and coming back again. It belongs to an old senator who owns one of the villas on the mountain, Sextus Tedius. I've never seen his face. He's not the sort to come into a place like this.'

'And the man they were leaning over?'

'Clodius.'

'Your sister was able to recognize him, even at a distance?'

'I suppose so. That's what she said, that it was Clodius.'

'How did he get from the tavern into the road?'

'Who knows? Probably Eudamus and Birria dragged him out there, like dogs with a rabbit.' I thought of the marks around Clodius's throat. Perhaps he had been literally dragged by the neck.

The woman looked at our plates. 'Why, you two haven't finished your meat! On a chilly day like this, a man needs plenty of hot food in his belly, to keep up his strength. This one knows how to eat!' She cast a toothy grin at Davus, who finished sucking the last bit of marrow from a bone and cast a lingering glance at the uneaten meat on our plates. 'Wasn't it good?'

'Excellent,' I assured her. 'Roasted to perfection. I'm afraid we stuffed ourselves with too much of your fine bread and cheese beforehand.' I slid my plate and Eco's towards Davus. 'You say your sister saw bodies scattered along the road and Senator Tedius and his wife —'

'Not his wife. Senator Tedius is a widower. The woman would have been his daughter, I imagine. His only child; she's never married and is very devoted to him.'

'I see. Then she saw Senator Tedius and his daughter with their litter out front, discussing what to do with Clodius. Where were Milo's men?'

'Vanished. They'd won the battle, hadn't they? What reason did they have to stay? My poor sister finally found the courage to creep down the stairs. I know what she saw, because I saw it myself later —

275

everything overturned and broken, the door off its hinges, all the shutters smashed. It was as if the Furies themselves had been unleashed in this room. And worst of all, right at the foot of the stairs, poor Marcus, pierced all over with wounds and not a breath left in his body. At the foot of the stairs, don't you see – defending her. She must have lost her senses for a while, because the next thing she remembers is arriving at my house up the hill. She could barely talk for weeping. Oh, how she wept!'

'And the people outside the tavern,' I said quietly. 'Senator Tedius and his retinue?'

She shrugged. 'They were all gone by the time my husband and I got here. So was Clodius, or whatever was left of him. Later we heard that Tedius had sent the body on to Rome in his litter, and hundreds of people gathered at Clodius's house in Rome that night and lit bonfires. His poor widow! But Fulvia's grief couldn't have been any greater than my sister's. There were no gatherings here, no bonfires, just a great mess to be cleaned up. The next day my husband saw that all the bodies were gathered up and laid out in rows over by the stable. A man from Clodius's villa came with a wagon and claimed them. But they didn't clean the blood from the Appian Way – you can still see great patches of it between here and the shrine of the Good Goddess. And nobody's offered to pay a single sesterce towards the repairs we had to make to this place. I told my husband that he should take Milo to court for damages, but he says we should wait and see how things go up in Rome before we get ourselves into

more trouble. How do you like that? Honest men suffer in silence while a man like Milo can still put himself forward for consul. It's an outrage!'

I nodded sympathetically. 'So you and your husband arrived after everyone else had scattered?'

'Yes. All we saw were dead bodies.'

'At what time of day did all this happen?'

'The battle? Well, considering when we arrived, and from all my sister said, I think it must have been about the middle of the afternoon. I'd say Milo arrived in Bovillae at the ninth hour, watered his horses, rounded up his entourage and moved on, and then his gladiators chased Clodius here at the tenth hour.'

'Not later? Not closer to sunset?'

She shook her head. 'Why do you ask?'

I shrugged. 'One hears so many different versions of the story up in Rome . . .'

There was a noise from the open doorway behind us. I stiffened, but the woman smiled at the men who entered. 'Roasted rabbit today, if I can trust my nose,' said one of them.

'And turnips with our hostess's special sauce!' said one of his companions, sniffing the air. They settled themselves on some benches in a corner.

'What do we owe you?' I asked the woman. As I counted coins from Eco's purse I leaned towards her over the bar. 'Your sister — how is she now?'

She shook her head. 'A broken woman, as I told you. I don't know if she'll ever get over it.'

'Is there any chance that she could receive a visitor?'

'A visitor?' The woman frowned.

I lowered my voice even further. 'Forgive me: I haven't been entirely forthcoming with you, I'm afraid. But now that I've heard you speak, I know I can trust you. I didn't just happen to pass by today.'

'No?' The woman looked at me suspiciously, but with growing interest.

'No. I'm here on behalf of Fulvia.'

'Clodius's widow?' She raised her eyebrows.

'Yes – please, keep your voice down. I wasn't sure I could trust you before, but now that I've heard your feelings about Clodius, and about Milo and his wife . . .'

'Roasted rabbit! Roasted rabbit!' The newcomers began to chant and beat their fists against the tables, laughing good-naturedly.

'Just wait your turn!' shouted our hostess, with a glare that they took for a joke. They laughed and began another chant that quickly disintegrated into laughter: 'Tur-nips! Tur-nips! Tur –'

She leaned closer and spoke just above a whisper. 'I see! So you're here to help wreck Milo's schemes.'

I pursed my lips. 'I can't say that's my purpose for being here, exactly, but I can say that Fulvia has asked me to find out what I can about her husband's death.'

'Ah!' She nodded knowingly.

'So you can see why I would like to speak to your sister, if I could.'

'Of course.' She nodded sagely, then frowned. 'But it's not possible.'

'I realize her fragile condition –'

'But it's not only that. She's not here.'

'No?'

'She's gone off with her son to stay with our aunt down in Rhegium. Everyone thought it would be best, for her to get as far from this place as possible for a while.'

I nodded. One couldn't get much farther away than Rhegium, at the very tip of the Italian peninsula.

'Roasted rabbit and turnips and sauce! Roasted rabbit and turnips and sauce!'

The woman shrugged. 'I really must see to the others now. But good luck! Anything that helps to bring Milo down a peg or two . . .'

'Oh, but one more question –'

'Roasted rabbit and turnips and sauce –'

'Yes?'

'Marc Antony – does that name mean anything to you?'

She thought for a moment, then shook her head.

'Are you sure?'

'Never heard of him. He must not be from around here.'

'Roasted rabbit and turnips and sauce –'

Our hostess groaned. 'I'd better feed this lot quickly, before we have another riot in this place!' She rolled her eyes and cast a final grin at Davus, then hurried away.

# XVI

'Where to now?' said Eco as we stepped out of the inn. 'I could use a nap after that meal.'

Davus yawned and stretched in agreement.

'Nonsense! The day is early and we have a lot more to do. Davus, fetch the horses.'

We set out on the Appian Way and soon passed the stable and the outbuilding where the toilets had failed to meet with Fausta Cornelia's approval.

Eco laughed. 'Do you think that Milo's wife can be half as disagreeable as our hostess seemed to think?'

'I've never had the pleasure of meeting the lady myself, but she's certainly been the subject of more than her share of gossip. Not that I ever seek out such tales; Bethesda tells them to Diana, you know, and I can hardly help overhearing.'

'Of course, Papa, I understand. It's the same with Menenia, always subjecting me to distasteful gossip.

But it would be rude to plug my ears, wouldn't it? So – tell me what you've heard, and I'll tell you what I've heard!'

I laughed. Davus, immune to the irony, looked at us as if we were crazy. 'Mostly to do with her sexual habits,' I said. 'When her previous husband, Gaius Memmius, was off governing some province, she chose to stay in Rome, and carried on so scandalously that when Memmius got home he divorced her. Then she married Milo.'

'Children?'

'Not yet. They've been married only a couple of years. But from what one hears, she's been too busy with her lovers to do much procreating with her husband.'

'Poor Milo!'

'Save your sympathy. I suspect it's as our hostess said – the two of them married each other for politics and profit. Whatever else she may be, Fausta is the dictator Sulla's daughter, and that means a great deal, especially to the so-called Best People with whom Milo has been trying to ingratiate himself most of his life.'

'What could it have been like, to have been Sulla's child?'

'I doubt whether you or I can even begin to imagine, Eco. She and her twin brother Faustus were born late in the dictator's life, and he was apparently quite pleased with himself – imagine cursing a child with a name meaning Lucky Omen. If Fausta's a spoiled brat, blame her doting monster of a father.'

'Marrying her was a step up for Milo, I can see that. But what was in the marriage for Fausta?'

'She may not have had many choices. Memmius had divorced her and left her with a tarnished reputation. Milo looked to be a rising star, didn't he? He'd just inherited a lot of money from his grandfather; never mind that he proceeded to squander it all on the old man's funeral games. Apparently she didn't marry Milo for his lovemaking, since she seems to look elsewhere for that.'

Eco nodded. 'I suppose you've heard the story about Milo catching the radical tribune Sallust in bed with her – the day after their wedding! He had his slaves beat Sallust black and blue and confiscated his moneybag for a fine.'

'Yes. Which makes me wonder how much of Sallust's alliance with the Clodians these days is from political sincerity and how much is from a desire to get revenge on Milo. Then of course there's the tale of how Milo caught his old friend Sextus Villius in bed with Fausta. Milo flew into a rage and dragged Villius screaming from the room. But in fact Fausta had been entertaining two lovers, and the other one had managed to hide in a wardrobe. While Milo was thrashing Villius out in the hall, the second lover sneaked back into bed with Fausta and gave her the ride of her life!'

'The lady seems to have a penchant for getting caught,' observed Eco.

'Or maybe she has a taste for cruelty and likes to see her lovers thrashed.'

Davus looked at us and made a face. I suspect he

had never heard two men speculate about other people's behaviour in such a prurient fashion.

Eco shook his head. 'I'll say it again: poor Milo. He married Fausta for prestige, and all he's gotten is embarrassment. Even her twin brother makes jokes about her.'

'Yes, I know the story. While her first husband was gone from Rome she was stringing along two lovers at once, one a fuller who owned a wool-washing operation, and the other a fellow called Macula, on account of a birthmark on his cheek that looked like a stain. So Faustus observed, 'I don't see why my sister doesn't get rid of that Stain – after all, she has the personal services of a fuller!' '

Even Davus laughed.

I pointed at a circle of oak trees a little off the road. 'Your memory was perfect, Eco. There's the altar of Jupiter that you mentioned.'

'Perhaps we should stop and do something pious, to make up for all this gossipmongering.' Eco, the complete sceptic, likes to taunt me for what little religious sensibility I possess.

'It wouldn't hurt to leave a few coins and say a prayer, my son. We've had a safe journey and good fortune so far.' As we dismounted under the shade of the oaks, a man in a scrappy white robe appeared from behind the stone altar. His jaw was covered with stubble and he smelled of wine. He introduced himself as Felix, and explained that he was the priest of the place and offered to recite an invocation to Jupiter on our behalf, for a small fee. Eco rolled his eyes, but I gestured for him to

open his purse. The prayer was a simple formula, mumbled so quickly that I scarcely heard it. Instead I looked into the shadowy recesses of the trees around us and listened to the nearby babbling of the stream and the rustling of the branches. So close to the normally busy, altogether civilized expanse of the Appian Way, this ancient spot possessed a powerful sense of the ineffable and unseen. There is good reason why the altars and temples of the gods are erected in some places and not in others. The places chose the altars, so to speak, and not the other way around. This was such a place, and no matter what sort of priest maintained it, its special-ness was as palpable yet elusive as the mist of a breath in cold air.

When the prayer was done we turned to leave, but the priest reached for my arm. 'You're passing through?' Felix said. He had the narrow face of a ferret, and his teeth were yellow.

'On our way from here to there.'

'You know what happened just up on the road, don't you?'

'Quite a few things over the years, I should imagine.'

'No, I mean the business with Milo and Clodius.'

'Oh, that. Are we close?'

'Close? Can't you hear the lemures of the dead, shaking the leaves around us? The battle ended just down the road, at the old inn.'

'Yes, we just ate there. The proprietress told us something about it.'

Felix looked disappointed, then brightened. 'Ah,

but she couldn't have shown you where the battle started.'

'No. Is it interesting to see?'

'Interesting? When you go back to Rome, you can tell all your drinking friends that you saw the very spot where the bloodshed began.'

'What makes you think we're from Rome?'

He raised an eyebrow as if to say that our origins were all too obvious to a country dweller like himself. 'So, do you want to see the place or not?'

'Are you offering to be our guide?'

'Why not? I've been the priest at this altar for twenty years, and I know everything there is to know about these parts. Of course, I would require a small gratuity, for the upkeep of the altar . . .'

I narrowed my eyes and looked at Eco. 'What do you think?'

Eco stroked his chin. 'I suppose it might be interesting. We're not in too much of a hurry.'

'Oh, it will only take a moment,' said Felix. 'I can't leave the altar for long.'

I pretended to consider, then finally nodded. 'Very well. Come along with us.'

Davus, Eco and I kept our horses to a slow walk, so that the priest, on foot, could keep up. Past Bovillae the road began a steady ascent. The wooded hillside rose on our left and sloped downward on our right. Despite the increasingly jumbled landscape, the road that Appius Claudius had built continued steady on its course, as smooth and broad as ever.

'So you saw the inn already,' said our guide. 'Did you notice the new doors and shutters? You should've seen the place right after the battle – like a crone with her eyes and teeth plucked out. And all those bodies lying about!'

'Did you see the battle yourself?'

'I heard the fighting when it started up the hill, and knew that something was up. Then I saw them come running past – you can see a bit of the road from the altar – that fellow Clodius stumbling and tripping, practically carried along by his men, five or six of them, and then a little later those two monsters lumbering after them – Eudamus and Birria.'

'You recognized them?'

'Who wouldn't? I never miss a gladiator show when I get the chance to see one. For religious purposes, you understand. The games started as funeral rites, you know. They're still a sacred institution.'

I didn't care to argue the point with a priest. 'Were Eudamus and Birria the only ones who came after Clodius and his men?'

Felix snorted. 'Now wouldn't that make a legend – the two gladiators who laid siege to the inn at Bovillae and conquered it all by themselves! No, they weren't the only ones. A whole army came down behind them.'

'An army?'

'Perhaps I exaggerate.'

'How many men, then? Ten, twenty?'

'Maybe more than that.'

'Then Clodius was greatly outnumbered?'

'You could say that.'

'And the siege at the inn – did you see that as well?'

'Well, not exactly. Not while it was happening. I stayed at the altar, of course, to protect it.'

'Of course.'

'But everyone knows how it turned out. Marcus the innkeeper slaughtered, and that scoundrel Clodius and his men lying dead in the road.'

'Scoundrel?'

The priest looked up at me sidelong and clicked his teeth. 'I mean no offence, citizen. You were a partisan of the fellow?'

'No. Our hostess at the inn had a different opinion of Clodius, that's all. Say what you please about him.'

'Then I'll go ahead and call him a scoundrel, if you don't object.'

'You preferred Milo?'

Felix raised an eyebrow. 'I'm a priest of great Jupiter. I keep my thoughts on higher things than the squabbling of petty politicians up in Rome. But when a man commits sacrilege as blatantly as Clodius did, the gods are bound to strike him down sooner or later.'

'Sacrilege? You mean the time he disguised himself as a woman to sneak into the rites of the Good Goddess in Rome, with the objective of making love to Caesar's wife even as the rites were being performed?' This had been one of Clodius's most infamous escapades.

287

'That was indeed a terrible sacrilege,' said the priest. 'Clodius should have been stoned for that, but he managed to bribe the jury.'

'A failure of earthly justice,' said Eco, nodding in agreement but with a mischievous twinkle in his eye. 'And a lapse of heavenly justice, too. When I was a boy, everyone told me that any man who dared to violate the rites of the Good Goddess would be struck deaf, dumb and blind. But Clodius was the same after he sneaked into the rites as he was before. I wonder why the Good Goddess spared him. Did his gown and makeup fool her? Or was she as charmed by Clodius as Caesar's wife was?'

The priest refused to be nettled. 'Of course she spared him – so that he could meet a more horrible fate these ten years later, here at Bovillae! Do you think it's only a coincidence that the battle began right in front of the Good Goddess's shrine on the Appian Way? Fauna had a hand in his fate, you can be sure.' The priest nodded gravely, daring Eco to refute his logic. 'But that wasn't the man's only sacrilege, or even the worst. Up in Rome I don't suppose you've heard much about what Clodius did to the grove of Jupiter here on Mount Alba, or the way he treated the local Vestal Virgins.'

'Our hostess at the inn mentioned something about it,' I said, 'but the story's new to me.'

Felix shook his head. 'You'd think such crimes would be brought to light when a man runs for public office, but I suppose people were ready to elect Clodius praetor without giving a thought to

his religious offences in these parts. I'll tell you, then. It all had to do with that gigantic villa of his up on the hill. It was a simple enough place to start with, but that wouldn't do. He had to keep expanding it, turning it into his private fortress. His property came right up against some of the most sacred parts of the mountain – the grove of Jupiter, the Temple of Vesta, the House of the Vestal Virgins. When he needed more land, Clodius somehow got the property lines redrawn. He claimed a large part of the sacred grove – which he then proceeded to chop down for lumber! And he had the Vestals evicted from their house, which he then dismantled stone by stone to add a wing to his own villa – using the old mosaics and statuary for decorations! Look, there's the new house of the Vestals over there, on the left; you can just glimpse it through the trees. At least he left the Temple of Vesta alone, but that's small recompense for what he did to the grove. To my mind there's no more impious act than doing harm to a sacred tree, and Clodius ordered them cut down by tens and twenties!'

'But how did he manage to lay claim to these sacred properties?'

'How should I know? I'm only a simple priest, assigned to a single altar. Who knows what sort of threats and bribes he made? Men like that will stop at nothing to get what they want.' He looked at Eco. 'Do you doubt me now, young man, when I say that the gods were at work when Clodius was struck down?'

'The gods are at work in all things,' I said, to mollify him, 'even in our chance meeting, and this conversation. So, you saw the flight to the inn, but not the battle itself.'

'But I could hear it from the altar. Cracking and crashing and screaming!'

'How long did this go on?'

'Hard to say. Not too long. Then a lot of yelling, and things fell quiet for a while. Then the old senator and his daughter came down the hill in their litter.'

'You mean, after Eudamus and Birria and Milo's men had gone back up the hill,' I said.

'No. The senator went by, and it wasn't until quite a bit later that Milo's men started back up the hill with the prisoners.'

'Prisoners?' I frowned.

'Five or six of them, I'd say.'

'How could you tell they were prisoners?'

'Because their hands were bound! They were all huddled together, looking scared out of their wits, with Milo's men surrounding them and Eudamus and Birria prodding them on with an occasional jab to their behinds.'

'But who were these prisoners? Clodius's men?'

Felix shrugged. 'Who else?'

'But I thought that the five or six men defending Clodius at the inn were all killed.'

'Yes, I suppose they were. Maybe these were some of his men rounded up from the woods.'

'Were these prisoners wounded? Were they bloody?'

He looked puzzled. 'Now that you ask me, no, I don't think they were.'

I shook my head. According to Fulvia, at least half of Clodius's men had scattered and fled into the woods early in the battle – these were the few survivors who had eventually come back to her with fragmentary reports of the disaster – and all the rest had died, either along the road or protecting Clodius at the inn. According to her, no one in Clodius's entourage was missing or unaccounted for. Who then were these prisoners the priest spoke of? And if Senator Tedius had come along in his litter before Milo's men departed, not after, how was it that when the innkeeper's wife ventured to look out of the window after the battle, she saw only Senator Tedius and his daughter standing over Clodius with their retinue, and no sign of Milo's men? The precise sequence of events was suddenly muddled in my mind. What exactly had the innkeeper's wife seen with her own eyes? Her sister-in-law was only a secondhand witness, and might have inadvertently changed some detail or left something out. If only the woman was not so far away, in Rhegium . . .

'Well, this is the spot!' announced the priest, a little out of breath from the uphill climb. 'There's the shrine of the Good Goddess, up ahead on the right.' He pointed to a miniature temple with a round roof just off the road, ringed by oak trees. 'This is where the battle started. Clodius and his men were coming down the hill, and Milo and his men were heading up.'

Was that how it had happened – two parties simply happened to pass on the road and somehow came to blows? Or had there in fact been an ambush, no matter how ill conceived on the part of Clodius and his smaller force? The spot was perfect for it; the trees were dense enough on either side to provide hiding places and the slope of the land would have favoured an attacker coming from above.

But who, excepting the parties involved, had actually witnessed the event?

'Felicia!' cried the priest to a tall, lithe figure in a white gown who had stepped out of the woods surrounding the shrine of the Good Goddess. As she approached us she raised her hand in greeting and smiled, and I saw that she was older than I had first thought. There was a luminous quality about her pale face and a gracefulness in her step that at a distance projected the illusion of youth. Clearly, she had once been a stunningly beautiful woman. She was still very pleasing to look at.

The priest stepped towards her and put his hands on his hips. 'Kindly wait your turn, Felicia. I am escorting these men for the moment.'

'Of course, of course!' She mocked him by making a pretence of being intimidated, fluttering her eyelashes and wringing her hands. 'I know the rules. You get first chance at the travellers from the north, I get first chance at the ones from the south.'

'Besides, Felicia, no one here can go into your shrine. All men!'

'So I see!' She appraised each of us in turn,

smiling at Eco, letting her eyes linger on Davus, looking at me last.

'Oh, all right, Felicia, they're yours. I have to get back to the altar anyway.' The priest looked up at me and unabashedly stuck out his empty palm.

'Ah, yes,' I said. 'The gratuity – for the upkeep of Jupiter's altar.' I nodded to Eco, who produced a sum from his purse that was as usual a little too stingy. I frowned, and he tipped out another coin. I nodded, took the money and dropped it into the priest's open palm, where it vanished from sight with almost magical speed.

The priest, without another word, did the same.

# XVII

'So, Felicia,' I said, finding it impossible not to return the woman's beaming smile, 'you must be the attendant at the shrine of the Good Goddess.'

'I see to the needs of the female travellers who wish to stop and worship here, yes.'

'For a gratuity.'

'Only an impious mortal expects to get something from the gods in return for nothing.'

I nodded. 'You and your brother seem to have made quite a business of showing the local sights to visitors.'

'People want to know what happened here on the Appian Way.'

'Indeed they do.'

'But how did you know that the two of us are brother and sister? Did Felix tell you?'

I had referred to the priest as her brother in a religious sense, not suspecting they were actually

kin. It was a family business, then, attending to the shrines and profiting from the tourists on this stretch of the Appian Way. There seemed to be a bit of sibling rivalry as well.

'I suppose my brother also told you that I used to be a temple prostitute in the service of Isis in my younger days,' Felicia said. Not waiting for an answer, she raised her chin, adding even more height to her tall, narrow figure. 'Yes, it's true. I was a temple prostitute. But today I serve only Fauna, the Good Goddess.' She seemed quite proud of both facts.

'Fascinating,' I said. 'And did you happen to be on duty here that day?'

'The day of the battle? Oh, yes.'

'And did you see what happened?'

'Oh, yes!' It seemed to me that she kept her eyes unnaturally wide open, as people do when fighting off sleep or trying to frighten small children. She pointed towards Bovillae. 'Milo's party came up the hill from Bovillae — such a lot of them!'

I raised an eyebrow. 'All hairdressers and cosmeticians, from what I've heard.'

'Not at all. Well, yes, there did seem to be a number of bath and bedchamber slaves — you should have heard the way they squealed when the fighting began! But there were plenty of armed men as well. In front, behind, all up and down the sides. Like a little army marching off to battle.'

'Where was Milo?'

'Near the front of the procession, in a carriage with his wife.'

'Did they stop here?'

'At the shrine? No. Fausta Cornelia never stopped here.'

'Really? I would assume that Sulla's daughter, a woman of such high standing, must play a leading role in the cult of the Good Goddess.'

'In Rome, perhaps. But I find that most of the women who stop at this shrine are from smaller towns and more humble circumstances. Many of the women from the city seem to consider themselves a bit above stopping at such a humble place to pay their respects to the goddess. They had rather attend to her in more lavish surroundings, I suppose.'

'That hardly seems pious of them.'

'I make no judgment.' Her smile never wavered. Her eyes never narrowed. 'But you wanted to know about the skirmish. Well, it began right there, directly in front of the shrine. I was sitting on the steps, warming myself in a bit of sunshine. I saw the whole thing.'

'What hour was this?'

'About the ninth hour.'

So far, every witness had confirmed Fulvia's account and refuted Milo, who placed the skirmish two hours later. 'You're certain?'

'Yes. There's a sundial in the glade behind the shrine. I'd looked at it not long before.'

'How did the skirmish begin?'

'Milo and his company were coming up the hill, Clodius and his men were coming down the hill.'

'Clodius was out on the open road, then? He didn't suddenly appear out of the woods?'

'No.'

'He didn't lay an ambush?'

'Not at all.'

'Was he on horseback?'

'Yes. So were a couple of his companions. The rest were on foot.'

'Were there any women or children with him?'

'No. All grown men.'

'How many?'

'About twenty or twenty-five.'

'Armed?'

'They looked like a group of trained fighters, if that's what you mean. You seem to be more curious about such details than most of the travellers I've talked to.'

'Do I?' I studied the empty stretch of road. 'So, when the two parties met, did they simply begin fighting?'

'No, it wasn't like that.'

'Did they exchange insults?'

'No, not at first. Quite the opposite, in fact. As soon as the two parties caught sight of each other, everyone fell silent. They all stiffened a bit. I could see the reaction as it moved through the two groups, like twin ripples from the meeting point. Necks stiff, jaws clenched, eyes set straight ahead – posturing, the way men do around each other. There was a bit of confusion as they passed. The road is wide, but both parties had to draw in and stretch out a bit to make room. Clodius's men became more spread out than Milo's. There was some jostling even so, and some grumbling. There

was a tension in the air that set my teeth on edge – how can I explain it? – like raking your fingernails across a slate tile. I remember gasping suddenly and realizing that I'd been holding my breath, watching and waiting for something dreadful to happen.

'While the two groups were still passing each other, Clodius and his friends on horseback drew away from the road, just in front of where I was sitting, letting their men go ahead of them. Milo and his wife proceeded up the hill in their carriage, getting farther and farther away. Finally the last of Milo's party and the last of Clodius's party passed one another, right in front of me. Clodius tugged at his reins and fell in behind his men. I drew a breath of relief. I whispered a prayer to the Good Goddess, thankful that nothing had happened after all. But Clodius couldn't leave well enough alone. Some demon must have poked at him. He looked back and shouted something over his shoulder at the two gladiators at the rear of Milo's train.'

'Two gladiators?'

'Yes, acting as a rearguard, I suppose. They're famous, or so my brother says . . .'

'Eudamus and Birria?'

'Yes, those two.'

'And what did Clodius say to them?'

She blinked. 'If I were still a temple prostitute and not an attendant of the Good Goddess, I would quote his exact words.'

'A modest approximation, then?'

'It was something like, 'Why so glum–looking,

Birria? Hasn't Eudamus been letting you clean his sword often enough?' '

'I see. Then what happened?'

'The one called Birria spun around – lightning quick, like snapping your fingers – and threw his spear at Clodius. It happened so fast that I'd never have seen it if I hadn't been looking straight at him. Clodius was still looking back, laughing at his own joke. The spear struck him very hard.'

'Where?'

She reached up to her shoulder. 'Here, I think. I barely saw it strike – the spear flew faster than I could follow it, and struck so hard it knocked Clodius clear off his horse. Then there was a moment of total confusion – men shouting, turning about, bumping into each other. I got up from the steps and ran into the shrine, but I kept watching as best I could from the shadows. It all happened very quickly. I'd never seen a battle before. I suppose all battles must look like that – a bunch of men running around swinging their weapons at each other, shouting at the top of their lungs. It all looked rather ridiculous, to tell you the truth, and yet at the same time rather awesome. The only thing I could think of was when I was very young and I used to watch strangers copulating in the shadows of the Temple of Isis. It was hard not to laugh, but at the same time there was something frightening about it. Fascinating, revolting and absurd all at once.'

'What happened to Clodius?'

'Someone pulled the spear from his shoulder and

he managed to get to his feet. Some of Milo's men made a charge —'

'Where was Milo?'

She thought for a moment. 'Nowhere to be seen, at least not yet.'

'Then from what you say, the battle began spontaneously and without Milo's knowledge, while he was away at the head of the entourage. The parties met by chance and passed each other in silence, without incident until Clodius hurled a parting insult and Birria hurled a spear back at him on an impulse.'

Felicia nodded agreement, with the same imperturbable smile and the same glassy look in her eyes. Was that all there was to the incident?

'Still, Papa, a citizen is responsible for his slaves' behaviour,' Eco reminded me. 'Milo might not have countenanced Birria's crime, but he was to some degree legally culpable.'

'And a man is also responsible for any false tales he puts forwards,' I said, thinking of the very different but no less vivid account of the same incident that Milo had delivered at Caelius's contio. So far, everything Felicia had told me agreed with Fulvia's version of the incident, gleaned from the survivors among Clodius's party, except that Fulvia had omitted Clodius's parting insult; without that detail, Birria's attack appeared entirely unprovoked, perhaps even premeditated. But the detail of the insult seemed genuine enough, and it was hard to imagine that Felicia was mistaken or lying. It was understandable that Fulvia might have omitted a

fact that impugned her husband's memory. Her sources might have withheld it from her, or perhaps might not have heard the insult themselves. But Milo's elaborate tale of a cold-blooded ambush appeared to be a complete fabrication. 'How did the battle proceed?'

'Badly, for Clodius and his men,' said Felicia. 'They were greatly outnumbered, of course. A few of them were killed right away. A number of them ran off into the woods, with Milo's men chasing after them. One of Clodius's friends on horseback shouted that he would go for help and headed up the hill, trying to gallop through Milo's ranks. Headed back to Clodius's villa, I suppose.'

'Did he make it through?'

'I don't know. I didn't see.'

'And Clodius's other friend on horseback?'

'I think he must have been knocked off his horse, because the next time I looked, all of Clodius's men – those who were still with him and standing – were on foot. The horses were gone.'

'Which explains why Clodius made his retreat on foot.'

'And why he headed down to Bovillae for safety,' said Eco. 'Milo's men blocked the way back to his villa. It was either retreat to the inn or make a stand in the road.'

'And Clodius was already badly wounded,' I said. 'Your brother says he was stumbling and had to be helped. Yet he reached the inn well ahead of his pursuers. How did he get such a head start, I wonder?'

'Milo's men didn't chase after him right away,' said Felicia. 'They seemed uncertain whether or not to follow. They looked like hounds, running back and forth, unable to pick up a scent. Until Milo arrived.'

'And then?'

'Milo was furious. He stamped his feet, shook his fists, stood right in Birria's face and screamed at him – like some fool taunting a wild bear. I cringed to see it. But then Milo calmed down and held a sort of council, conferring with some of his men in a circle. They seemed to come to a decision, and Milo dispatched Birria and Eudamus and a large party of men in the direction of Bovillae. The rest closed ranks around Milo. He drew his sword and kept peering into the woods.

'I grew frightened myself. Some of Clodius's men had fled into the woods, with Milo's men after them; I worried that they might emerge in the glade behind the shrine, or try to take refuge in the shrine itself. So I stayed quiet and hid among the shadows. No one noticed me.'

'When did Senator Tedius pass by?' I said.

'That was the next thing that happened. A fancy litter came down the hill with a little retinue. I knew who it was, because Senator Tedius's daughter often stops here at the shrine.'

'Unlike Fausta Cornelia?'

'Tedia is a very old-fashioned woman. Very pious, very virtuous. Not proud or vain, in the way that so many younger women of high birth are these days. But she didn't come into the shrine that

302

day. When Milo's men stopped the litter, she stayed inside. Tedius got out and talked to Milo for a while. From the way he gestured, I assumed that Milo was trying to persuade him to turn back. But the senator is a stubborn man. He insisted on proceeding, got back into the litter and set off again down the hill towards Bovillae. More time passed, I don't know how long. Milo paced and fretted. Fausta Cornelia finally got out of the carriage and began to dog his steps. They had some sort of argument, but kept their voices low. Finally Eudamus and Birria came back, bringing the prisoners with them.'

'Prisoners . . .' I shook my head. 'Your brother mentioned them. But who could they have been?'

'Some of Clodius's men?'

I shook my head. 'I don't think so.'

'Why not?'

Because, I thought, Fulvia told me specifically that none of her husband's men had been missing. Felicia looked at me shrewdly, or as shrewdly as anyone could with those glassy eyes and that unwavering smile. 'You seem to know a lot already about what happened that day.'

'And you seem to have already told this story a number of times before.'

She shrugged. 'The Appian Way is a busy road, even in these troubled times. And people are naturally curious.'

'Do you tell what you saw to anyone who happens to pass by?'

'So long as they donate something to the shrine.

I've never been one to withhold favours, either in my old profession or my new one.'

I looked at her and shook my head. I found little to admire in her, but I saw nothing to despise either. When I considered the danger into which she had unwittingly, even stupidly placed herself, merely for the sake of taking in a few coins from strangers, my blood ran cold. 'Felicia, have you any idea of the risk you've taken? I'm amazed that you're still alive, you and your brother both.'

Her smile wavered. Her eyes flickered, as if just beginning to focus. 'What do you mean?'

'Do you have no idea of the magnitude of what you saw that day? You act as if it were merely a curiosity, an amusing story to tell to travellers for profit. But at this very moment, up in Rome, a very powerful, very ruthless man is struggling for his survival. Milo is telling everyone that he was ambushed by Clodius that day.'

She shrugged. 'Well, I don't care what the man says. I know what I saw, and the things I told you –'

'If produced in a court of law, could send Milo into exile, discredit his followers and cause enormous embarrassment to some of the most powerful men in Rome. Men who have spies everywhere, and assassins, and whole stables full of fellows like Eudamus and Birria. Milo's agents may have been here already, snooping about. If they managed to pass by you and your brother, it can only be because the gods made them look the other way. Or have you already spoken to them, as freely as you've

spoken to me? They may already know who you are and what you've been telling. In that case only their incompetence can explain that fact that you're still alive to tell the tale to me. Or is it your lemur I'm speaking to?'

Her lips tightened. Her eyes narrowed. After a moment she rallied and managed a semblance of her previous bland serenity, but could not quite control the quaver in her voice. 'I serve the Good Goddess –'

'Do you think that will protect you? That it will mean anything to such men, any more than your brother's priesthood will mean something to them?'

'Then you believe . . .'

'That you are in great danger, or soon will be.'

Her smile at last faded and her eyes for the first time seemed to truly see me. 'Who are you?'

'A man who was glad to hear the truth and wishes you no harm.'

She stared at me for a long moment. 'What would you suggest that I do?'

'At the very least, stop telling what you know to every traveller who passes by, and tell your brother to do the same. Keep your mouths shut! Better than that, I'd suggest that both of you take a lesson from the birds.'

'What?'

'Fly south for the rest of the winter.' Like the innkeeper's widow, I thought. Perhaps it wasn't grief that had sent her to Rhegium, but common sense. 'Fly south, or else go to Rome with your brother and seek the widow Fulvia's protection.

She'll expect something in return, especially if there's a trial, and you could be placing your fortunes with a losing side. But whatever you do, leave this place.'

'But who would attend to the shrine? How would I make a living?'

'I suspect you still have sufficient attributes to support yourself, one way or another.'

Her smile flickered. 'I'll think about it. In the meantime, I'll take your advice and say no more.' Just as boldly as her brother, she held out her empty palm. When Eco looked into his purse with a parsimonious frown, I took the bag from him and pulled out one of the larger coins.

The sight of it in her hand prompted the return of her former glassy-eyed state. 'You're generous, stranger, with your advice and with your money.'

'Use it for lodgings when you leave.'

'Perhaps. But you've paid for more than I've given, I think. Shall I tell you something else? Something I haven't told to every curious traveller passing by?' She saw my reaction and laughed. 'I love that expression on a man's face – so eager and attentive. Well, then: do you remember passing the House of the Vestals on your way here from Bovillae?'

'Yes. Your brother pointed it out.'

'But you didn't stop to speak to any of the Vestals?'

'No.'

'Since you seem so anxious to know everything that happened that day, it might profit you to speak

to the Virgo Maxima. Ask her about the visitor who came to her after the battle. Ask about the offering that was made and refused.'

'Can't you tell me?'

'The virgins of the goddess Vesta do not tread on my authority, and I do not tread on theirs. Ask the Virgo Maxima, if you can manage to penetrate her haughtiness. Whatever you do, don't let her know that I sent you. Whether she confides in you or not is her affair. There, now I've given you full value for your coin.' She began to walk back to the shrine.

'Felicia . . .'

She turned back. 'Yes?'

'One last question. I meant to ask your brother and forgot. A name: Marc Antony. Does it mean anything to you?'

She shook her head, turned away and resumed walking.

'And Felicia . . .'

'Yes?'

'May the Good Goddess protect you from harm.'

# XVIII

Following Felicia's advice, we turned around and made our way back to the House of the Vestals.

From the Appian Way a narrow, winding lane led up to the forecourt and main entrance. Both the lane and the building were clearly of recent construction; broken earth and tree stumps lined the lanes and the sharp edges and stained walls of the house were not yet softened by the wear of time. It was a humble dwelling compared to the great House of the Vestals in Rome, but hardly a hovel; many a dweller on the Palatine would have been proud to claim it. Or so it appeared from the outside.

It is not true, as many people think, that all men are forbidden at all times to enter any part of a sanctified building where Vestals dwell. I myself had once penetrated into the very sleeping cubicles of the House of the Vestals in Rome, when I was

called upon to investigate the scandal that led to the trials of Catilina and Crassus for desecrating the purity of certain of the Vestals. The penalty for such a crime is death for the man, and for the Vestal something far worse: she is buried alive.

That incident was now twenty years in the past, and the circumstances had been highly unusual. But it occurred to me, as I recalled it, that Clodius had been involved in that affair as well. It had been one of his earliest escapades. The general consensus finally held that Clodius had tried to falsely incriminate the accused parties for his own obscure motives, and the reaction against him had been so hostile that for a while he had dropped from sight. Early on, Clodius had set a pattern of attacking powerful men and revered institutions, and had occasionally paid a price for his impudence.

I had no expectation of being allowed into the sleeping chambers of the House of the Vestals on Mount Alba, but if the rules of the dwelling followed those of the one in Rome, during daylight hours the foyer and perhaps one or two public rooms would be open to male visitors. Vestals are not entirely shut off from the world of men, after all, and must have practical means of meeting and dealing with the tradesmen who serve their needs and the state priests who oversee their activities.

Still, the wizened slave woman who answered the door peered at Eco and me as if she had never seen a man before, or so I thought until I realized that her squinting was due to her poor eyesight. Her hearing also seemed to be impaired. I found

myself repeating my request to see the Virgo
Maxima in a louder and louder voice, until at last
a stout woman wearing the simple white woollen
gown of a Vestal appeared behind the slave and
gently told her to move aside.

The Vestal wore the traditional headdress of her
order, an oblong, purple-bordered scarf wound
around her close-cropped hair and secured with
a metal clasp at her forehead. Her plain, round face
was untouched by cosmetics, but her skin had the
smooth creaminess of women who have spent their
lives indoors and have never had to labour. I judged
her to be well into her sixties, which meant that she
had long ago completed her original thirty-year
term of service to the goddess and had voluntarily
elected to stay on as a virgin for life.

'You'll have to excuse the slave,' she said. 'She's a
little deaf.'

'So I noticed, except that she didn't seem to have
any trouble understanding you, even though her
back was turned to you.'

'She only has difficulty hearing a lower range of
tones – men's voices. She can understand most of the
women here with no trouble. Her deafness is not a
disability under this roof. Now, you say you wish to
see the Virgo Maxima. What is your business?'

'It's a matter of some delicacy. I would rather
speak of it only to the Virgo Maxima.'

She gave me a brittle smile at odds with the
softness of her face. 'You'll have to do better than
that, I'm afraid. To begin with, who are you and
where do you come from?'

'My name is Gordianus. This is my son Eco. There's also a slave with us, looking after our horses in the court. We come from Rome.'

'What business brought you here?'

'Once again, I'd rather speak of that only to –'

'You must understand, Gordianus of Rome, that there recently has been a great deal of violence and disruption in these parts. Men have been killed in broad daylight only a few steps from our door. The local innkeeper was horribly murdered, his young wife made a widow. And the troubles of this house started well before the recent violence. Driven from our home, forced to look on helplessly while sacred groves were desecrated – I won't go into those matters, except to say that at the best of times the women of this house are accustomed to being suspicious of men from the outside world, if only for the sake of preserving their purity. Given our recent experiences, we have even greater reason to be cautious. And I must say, just to look at you, Gordianus of Rome, I can't imagine what possible business you could have with the Virgo Maxima.'

It is unusual to encounter a woman used to dealing with men strictly on her own terms. The Vestal clearly had no intention of admitting me to the Virgo Maxima's presence without good cause, and just as clearly she was not the sort to let slip any confidences behind her superior's back. How, then, to gain her trust? It was Felicia who had pointed me here, but she had also forbidden me to invoke her name. There was another name I could invoke, and

though I was wary of revealing my commission from Pompey even within these walls, it began to seem the only way. Then the Vestal spoke my name again, under her breath.

'Gordianus . . .' She wrinkled her fleshy brow and gazed pensively into space. 'Gordianus of Rome . . . the name is unusual.'

'There are not a great many of us.'

'I suppose not. And even fewer who would be about your age.' She eyed me carefully. 'Was it you who came to Licinia's assistance those many years ago?'

'If you mean, am I the Gordianus who assisted the Virgo Maxima in Rome to get to the truth of a certain impropriety, the answer is yes.'

'A 'certain impropriety'? I would call the discovery of a dead man in the sleeping chamber of a young Vestal something more than that.'

'I didn't wish to mention the details myself.'

'Good; you are discreet. And modest, perhaps. Not a typical man at all.'

'How is it that you know of that incident? The trials of Catilina and Crassus and the Vestals were public knowledge, of course, but the dead body was kept secret.'

'Not from me. I know everything, including the fact that it was Clodius who arranged the murder, in a vain attempt to implicate Catilina. That odious scoundrel was making trouble for us even then, and getting away with it.'

'Were you there at the time, serving the goddess in Rome?'

'No. I have always served here, at Vesta's temple on Mount Alba.'

'And yet you know the most intimate secrets of the mother house in Rome?'

'The mother house?' She flared her nostrils.

'The headquarters of your order, I mean –'

'Headquarters? If you are implying that the House of the Vestals in Rome is somehow the superior of this House, you are sorely mistaken, even if you are Gordianus the so-called Finder. The order of the Vestal Virgins was founded here, on Mount Alba, in the most ancient of days; Silvia the mother of Romulus was a member of the local sisterhood and helped preserve the eternal flame in Vesta's temple. The order in Rome was not established until much later, in the days of King Numa, and the eternal flame in the Temple of Vesta in Rome was lit from the original flame here on Mount Alba. Oh, yes, Rome takes pre-eminence nowadays; great men leave their wills in the keeping of the Roman Vestals, and the Roman Vestals have the honour of protecting the sacred relics that Aeneas brought from Troy. But we of Mount Alba are the original sisterhood. "Mother house", indeed!'

'I meant no offence, Virgo Maxima.'

She looked at me shrewdly. 'Why do you call me that?'

'Because you are the Virgo Maxima here, are you not?'

She tilted her head back, and though she was too short to look down her nose at me, she did her best.

'Of course I am.' She smiled faintly. 'Which is why I know certain secrets of the Virgo Maxima in Rome, and why I honour the name of Gordianus the Finder, who once helped in secret to save the honour of the sisterhood, not to mention the life of an innocent young Vestal. So, you wished to speak with me in private? Come, and bring your son. We can talk in the room outside my chamber. The door slave will act as chaperone. If I pitch my voice low enough, she won't hear a word that either of us says.'

What struck me most about what little I saw of the interior of the House of the Vestals that day was how shoddy the construction appeared to be. From a distance, the facade of brick and wood appeared to be at least sound if not distinguished, but all the craftsmanship that had gone into the building had been put on the outside, for show. The foyer, the hallway down which the Virgo Maxima led me, and the anteroom where she allowed me an audience were all marked by a carelessness on the part of the carpenters that was painfully obvious. Corners met at the wrong angles with crude patchwork to make up the difference, the floors were uneven, and gobs of plaster seemed to have been laid on with all the skill of a bored child. The Virgo Maxima followed my gaze and read my thoughts.

'It's nothing at all like our old house. What a grand place that was, so full of memories. It wasn't the original house where Silvia served, of course, not nearly that old. But a very old house,

314

nonetheless, full of history. Generations of Vestals had lived and died there. The place had a sacred character such as only accrues with time. Ah, but how could the ancient sisters who chose the location of that house have known that one day long after they were dead, along would come a fellow like Clodius who couldn't be satisfied until he'd got his greedy hands on the land and the house itself.'

'I've heard a bit about this from some of the local people,' I said.

'Everyone on Mount Alba knows what Clodius did – driving us from our home, cutting down forests that had been sacred to Jupiter since the beginning of time. The shameful thing is that so many of the local people enthusiastically supported him, not just rich and powerful men from Rome who have country homes along the road, but even some of the local farmers who serve in the municipal senates. The religious objections meant nothing to them; it was all a matter of politics and greed. Clodius handed out money and promises to the right people, and in the end there was nothing we could do about it. Even our sisters in Rome, from the 'mother house' as you call it, were unable to help us. Or unwilling! Who knows what sort of influence Clodius's wife and mother-in-law exercise over the Vestals in the city. Ah, but I'm talking more than I should. It fills me with such anger and shame to have a visitor see the situation in which we find ourselves.'

'Clodius built this house for you, as a replacement for the property he seized?'

'Yes, and after all his smooth words of reassurance I almost came to trust him. We had no choice in the matter, so why not look to the future with hope and try to be optimistic? 'The old house is hardly livable in any more, it's falling down around your ears,' he told me. 'Full of character and charm, to be sure, but just an old, dingy house if you look at it in the sunlight – stains on the floors, nicks in the walls, creaky old stairs. Think how much more comfortable you'll be in a new house, with everything clean and bright. And all at my expense, to make up for the inconvenience.' He didn't mention that the place would be built by slaves more used to shovelling dung than trowelling mortar, and designed by an architect who wouldn't know a plinth from a portico. This place is a disaster! And our old house . . .' She sighed. 'Our old house, for all its shabby quaintness, was built of solid stone and had a roof that never leaked once in all the years since I became a Vestal. Stained or not, some of the floors had the most beautiful black and white mosaic tiles, pictures and patterns that would take your breath away – now I suppose they're decorating the lavatories in that sprawling villa of his up on the hill.'

'I still can't imagine how he ever got the legal right to seize the property.'

'It all went back to documents from the time the Appian Way was built. Appius Claudius Caecus managed to obtain a great deal of property for himself and his family all along the road. Clodius's villa, or the core of it, had been in his family for

generations, going back to the time the road was built. Because the old House of the Vestals was within a certain distance of that property he was able to declare a special necessity when he decided to expand his villa and to make a claim on our house as well as parts of the grove of Jupiter. Clodius was quite expert at producing documents out of thin air. In the end he got his way, legally and without violence, and there was nothing we could do about it.'

'But there were hard feelings?'

She gave me a withering look. 'Gordianus, do not insult me with polite understatement, and I will endeavour to treat you with the same courtesy. But I've gone on about matters which are no doubt of more interest to myself than to you. Forgive me if I don't offer you food or wine; it would not be proper for me to entertain two male visitors in such a fashion. We shall also remain standing, of course, except for our chaperone.' She nodded to the old slave, who sat on a backless chair in the corner. 'You said you had some business with me, Gordianus.'

'Yes. Thank you, Virgo Maxima, for favouring me –'

'Let us deal with the matter quickly. The briefer your stay under this roof, the better. I'm sure you understand.'

'I'll be as forthright as I can. I understand that a visitor came to this house, shortly after Clodius was killed down in Bovillae.'

She looked at me intently but did not answer.

'I understand that this visitor made some sort of offering.'

'Who told you this?'

'I have been asked not to say.'

'You keep a secret, yet you think that I should reveal to you the business of this house?'

'Virgo Maxima, I would never ask you to betray a confidence. If what I ask is improper, forgive me.'

She regarded me for a long moment. 'Because you once helped the Vestals in Rome, I shall tell you what you want to know. Yes, a woman came here that day.'

'At what time?'

'Very late in the afternoon. Shadows were gathering.'

'Who was she?'

'I can't tell you that, not because I wish to keep a secret from you, but because I don't know. The day was cold; she wore a robe with a hood and kept her face hidden, and as I say, the daylight was failing.'

'But you heard her voice?'

'She spoke in a low, husky voice hardly above a whisper.'

'As if she were concealing her voice as well as her face?'

'That thought occurred to me at the time.'

'What did she want?'

'She came bearing news. She said there had been a battle between Clodius's men and Milo's men out on the road, and that it had ended down in Bovillae. She told me that Milo was unwounded but that Clodius was dead.'

'So she merely came to give you this news?'

'No, she gave me an offering – a rather generous offering – and requested that we make a prayer to Vesta on her behalf.'

'A prayer?'

'Yes. A prayer of thanksgiving.'

'Giving thanks that Milo was safe?'

'That was not how she put it.' The Virgo Maxima lowered her eyes. 'She asked for a prayer of thanksgiving that Clodius was dead.'

'Isn't that unusual, giving thanks to the goddess for a man's death?'

'Unusual but not entirely unheard of. There are some deaths at which the gods themselves rejoice.'

'You accepted her offering?'

'Yes.'

'You made the prayer of thanksgiving?'

'The goddess received it as warmly as any other prayer.'

I tried to remember exactly what Felicia had said to me. Ask her about the offering that was made and refused . . . 'You say that she made a generous offering and that you accepted it.'

'Of course I accepted it. If the sisterhood here on Mount Alba were wealthy enough to wave aside offerings, we should have paid to build a new house ourselves when Clodius evicted us.'

'But wasn't there something she offered which you refused?'

The Virgo Maxima eyed me warily. 'If you already know so much, why do you ask?'

'To find out what I don't know.'

She considered for a long moment before she answered. 'Yes, she offered something which I didn't take. She offered it as proof that Clodius was dead, and also as payment for the prayer. It was Clodius's gold signet ring, taken from his dead finger. The proof I accepted. But the ring was hardly appropriate for payment. I told her that coins would please the goddess more.'

'Where is the ring now?'

'The woman still has it, for all I know. And now, Gordianus, I think it is time —'

'Only two more questions, please, Virgo Maxima.'

'Very well. The first?'

'Milo's wife, Fausta Cornelia — would you know her by sight, or by the sound of her voice?'

She smiled at so obvious a question. 'Perhaps, perhaps not. I've met many senators' and magistrates' wives at one time or another. If you asked me to pick her out of a crowd, I couldn't, but I suspect she would look familiar. Would I recognize her if a hood hid her face, and she spoke in a whisper? Almost certainly not. And your last question for me, Gordianus?'

'Can you tell me anything interesting about Marc Antony?'

She laughed. 'One question so transparent, the other so peculiar. Have we moved on to a different subject entirely, Gordianus?'

'I have a reason for asking.'

She shook her head. 'Marc Antony? The son of Antonius who failed against the pirates?'

'Yes.'

'Off fighting Gauls, isn't he? Really, I know nothing about the young man.'

'Neither does anyone else, apparently. Virgo Maxima, I thank you for your indulgence.'

She regarded me kindly. 'People should remember the past, and past favours.'

'They should; and would more often, I imagine, if they could spend less time fretting about the future.'

# XIX

'A mystery woman!' said Eco, when we were back on our horses.

'The Virgo Maxima?'

'No, Papa! The woman who came to her with Clodius's ring.'

'Not too mysterious, from the look of things.'

'You think it was Fausta Cornelia?'

'Who else? Rather vulgar of Milo, to send his wife off to the nearest religious establishment to brag about what he'd done. Unless it was Fausta's idea, which I suppose is more likely. Women of her social standing have a certain sense of how to mark the auspiciousness of an occasion. She probably wanted to offer sincere thanks to Vesta for looking after her household, and incidentally to indulge in a little blasphemous gloating.'

'But why conceal her identity? She never seems to bother about hiding anything else.'

'You mean her affairs?'

'I said it before: the woman has a penchant for getting caught. Not the secretive sort by nature.'

'Perhaps she hid her identity thinking to conceal her husband's role in the incident.'

'Is that credible? The next day the whole world would be talking about Milo's part.'

'Ah, but this was only shortly after the battle, Eco. Everything must have still seemed very much up in the air. Something awesome had occurred, overwhelming yet also exhilarating. Clodius, dead at last! Cause for jubilation – but also for fear. How will the world react? Will there be some terrible retribution? Can the crime still be concealed? Discretion is advised, but for something so extraordinary, there must be an act of pious thanksgiving. So while her husband regroups, Fausta slips away to the nearby House of the Vestals. She gloats over Clodius's death – but in disguise. Where is the mystery?'

'I suppose you're right, Papa . . .'

'I only wonder where Clodius's ring ended up. The decent thing would be to return it to his widow by an anonymous courier. Somehow I imagine it on a shelf with Milo's old wrestling trophies, where he can take it down to fondle and gloat over whenever he's had a bit too much wine.'

'Possession of the ring would make for a damning piece of evidence.'

'As would the Virgo Maxima's tale, if she could say that it was Fausta who came to her. But the ring

323

is missing, and all the Virgo Maxima can tell us with certainty is that an unknown woman came to the House of the Vestals – a mystery woman, as you say. I think Fausta Cornelia may be cleverer than her husband.'

'Didn't we know that already? She keeps fooling him over and over.'

'Or making a fool of him, anyway. And here we are, back at the shrine of the Good Goddess. I don't see Felicia about, do you? Perhaps she took my advice and headed south already.'

'More likely she's gone home for the day. The sun's getting low, Papa. What next?'

'I'd hoped to make it to Clodius's villa today, but we probably don't have time.'

'I think we've accomplished quite a lot for one day, Papa.'

'We found out more than I expected to. Yes, I think it's time to find Pompey's villa and come to rest.'

The way to Pompey's place was easy to find. A pair of stone pylons chiselled with the letter M (for Magnus) marked the turnoff. A long, winding road led up to the ridgetop. It was not paved but was excellently graded and maintained, and shaded by a canopy of towering oaks. Here and there statues of woodland beasts adorned the route or could be glimpsed in open meadows. I had the feeling not so much of entering the woods as of passing through a park.

The villa itself was a long, two-storey building

that sprawled along the ridge, the red tiles of its roof making it visible from a great distance amid the stony grey-green and umber winter landscape around it. As we entered the forecourt a slave appeared almost at once to help us dismount and to take our horses. Another slave must have run to alert the foreman, for even before Davus's mount had disappeared into the stable, the door of the main entrance opened and a tall, sturdy-looking man with greying hair and a look of authority stepped out to greet us. When I produced the letter of commission which Pompey had given me, the man hardly glanced at it.

'Yes, we've been expecting you,' he said.

'How can that be?'

'The master sent a messenger a couple of days ago saying we should look for you.'

'But I met your master only last night.'

The man gave me a wry look. 'The master has a way of knowing what a man will do before the man himself knows.'

'Your master was very confident of my co-operation.'

'I suppose he was,' said the foreman, with a look that implied and why not? 'These are your companions?'

'My son and my bodyguard.'

'No one else? This is your entire party?' He peered at the road behind us.

'I prefer to travel discreetly.'

'There's safety in numbers.'

'Not always,' I said, thinking of Clodius.

'Ah, well, I prepared the villa for a larger party,' sighed the foreman, evidently disappointed that his master's foresight had fallen down at details. He clapped his hands. 'Well, then, your stay shall be all the more comfortable. Feel free to sleep in a different room every night and eat several meals a day. The idea seems to please this one.' He raised an eyebrow at Davus, who returned a crooked smile as he reached back to rub his saddle-weary rump.

In the city, Pompey was known for his lack of ostentation, as a man who cared little for the gaudy ornaments of wealth, but there was nothing spartan about his villa on Mount Alba. Perhaps, like many politicians, he maintained a stern, sober guise in the city but allowed himself to put on a more festive and pleasure-loving face in the seclusion of the countryside. Or perhaps the luxurious amenities to be found at every turn were put there solely for visitors, such as myself. Many a rich man keeps his country villas not as private retreats but for the entertainment and lodging of others.

The bathing rooms in our wing were lit by skylights above and by a row of tiny windows at eye level, through which I caught glimpses of the twilit sea on the far horizon; we had risen high enough on the mountain to see the coast. The walls and floors were decorated with ornately patterned tiles whose subtle grey-blues and moss greens duplicated the colours of the distant, darkening sea. The three pools were kept at perfect tempera-

tures for taking the cold, warm and hot plunges; I went through all three several times, feeling my saddlesore body grow more and more relaxed. As the natural light began to fade, lamps were brought; the reflection of their orange flames danced upon the water. A wizened, toothless old slave with remarkably strong hands gave us massages. I insisted that Davus be given a thorough massage as well, considering that he was likely to be even stiffer than myself the next day. Even the towels we were given were inordinately thick and luxurious. No day could have had a sweeter ending.

Our dinner was served in a heated room near the baths, where the same furnaces which heated the water also sent warmed air through vents in the floor. The quality and variety of the meal was remarkable, especially a course of little pies filled with wild game and onions.

Our sleeping chambers were located above the baths, yet another clever way of making the most of the heat generated by the furnaces and the steam. The furniture was mostly of Eastern design and manufacture; the gold-painted chairs with tasselled red pillows were a bit elaborate for my simple tastes, as were the madly patterned hangings which covered the doorways. Pompey had spent many years in the East and had apparently developed an appreciation for the florid styles and delicate craftsmanship to be found in those lands he had conquered or pacified, where such booty was his for the taking.

The bed was a beautiful thing carved from some dark, exotic wood, strewn with plump silk pillows

and soft woollen blankets, and covered with a gauzy canopy. Bethesda would have deemed it too fine to sleep on. Diana would have adored it. Though I had planned to stay up for a while to sort out with Eco all that we had seen and learned that day, and intended only to test the bed to see how soft or hard it was, I must have fallen asleep only moments after putting my head on a pillow and closing my eyes. When I next opened them, the room was bright with the cold light of morning.

I rose, sinking my toes into the plush wool rug, stretched myself, smiled at the surprising lack of soreness in my buttocks and legs, drank from a ewer of cold spring water, relieved myself into the pot by the bed, pulled on my cloak and my shoes and finally stepped towards the light. It streamed through shutters drawn over a wide doorway on the southern side of the room. I pulled them back, stepped onto the spacious balcony, and stood astonished at the view. Of all the luxuries at Pompey's villa, surely this was the most unusual and offered the most enduring delight.

Towards the west I was able to look down on the wooded hillside above the Appian Way, catching glimpses of the wide ribbon of road below. Beyond the road were the foothills, where shreds of mist still clung to treetops, and beyond the foothills a wide expanse of open plains and farmland extended to the distant blue-green sea. Above all was the deep blue bowl of the cloudless sky. If the day remained clear, the sunset from this vantage point would be extraordinary.

I turned and walked to the opposite side of the balcony with the morning light on my face and looked down onto a wood-encircled lake hidden from the lower world. Its placid surface, as smooth as polished silver, reflected the forested cone of Mount Alba. The sun had just risen from behind the mountain and for the moment seemed to be balanced on its highest peak.

'What a view!' said Eco, joining me on the balcony. When I gave a start, he laughed. 'Relax, Papa! If we aren't safe in this house, we aren't safe anywhere. What a view,' he repeated, turning his head from side to side to take it in. 'Pompey seems to have a penchant for houses with a view, just as Fausta Cornelia has a penchant for getting caught . . .'

I took up the theme. 'Just as Clodius had a penchant for making trouble and for acquiring real estate —'

'Often both at the same time.'

'And as Milo has a penchant for social climbing,' I went on, 'and Cicero for winning impossible cases. Every man acts out of his own nature, and moves on a singular path towards his destiny.'

'What's your penchant, Papa?'

'Trying to figure out the others! Not always a rewarding pursuit, or a pleasant one.'

Eco sighed. 'Things could hardly get more pleasant than this.'

'Yes, men like Pompey do know how to live.'

'I could get used to it.'

'Best not to, Eco. We'll be out of here as quickly

329

as possible. Aren't you missing Menenia and little Titus and Titania?'

He looked wistful. 'Menenia never served me a meal like the cook made last night. Or gave me a massage like that shrivelled old bath attendant!'

'Men like Pompey own all the best slaves.'

'Speaking of which, Papa, I had to rouse Davus from his bed before I came here. He's practically paralysed.'

'The more muscles a man has, the more there are to ache.'

'Did a wise old Etruscan say that?'

'I doubt there was ever a wise old Etruscan who didn't know how to ride a horse. But Davus is young and supple. We'll see that he gets another good dose of riding today to work out the stiffness.'

'Papa, you've never been one to torture a slave.'

'Consider it the revenge of the old on the young. But it's time to start moving. First, we eat. Shall we see what the cook has come up with this morning to help you stop missing Menenia?'

Our bellies were warmed by freshly baked bread sprinkled with sesame seeds, a porridge of oats and honey, and a warmed compote of spiced apples. Davus joined us. Though the simple act of walking and sitting seemed to cause him considerable agony (manifested by grunts and grimaces), this did nothing to impair his appetite. He consumed as much as Eco and I combined.

I intended to take our horses and head out again on the Appian Way, but when the foreman

discovered our destination he suggested that we walk instead. It seemed there was an ancient footpath that ran along the ridge that would take us directly to Clodius's villa. 'It's considerably shorter,' he explained, 'and of course more discreet than being on the open road. Besides, it's much warmer today, thanks to all this sunshine, and the walk is quite beautiful. It will take you through the grove.'

'The grove?'

'The sacred grove dedicated to Jupiter . . . or what's left of it.'

'Yes, I think I should like to see that. Come, Eco. Well, Davus, it looks as if you're to be spared the agony of mounting a horse again, at least for the moment.'

His smile of gratitude turned into a wince as he rose to his feet.

As Pompey's foreman had promised, the walk offered splendid views, especially on a day when the sky was cloudless and the visibility unlimited. The mountain peak brooded above us and the plain shimmered below, both equally remote. The hidden lake showed nothing of itself, only a perfect reflection of the sky. The sea was too distant to be heard, even as a whisper. The taciturn woods, as we passed into their shadow, blocked off all sight of the rest of the world except for fleeting sunlit glimpses.

I found myself bemused by the shade-dappled boulders strewn along the path, by the rustle of last autumn's leaves beneath our feet, by the canopy of gnarled branches above. I have always delighted in

the beauty of the countryside, even though my one attempt at living there, on my farm in Etruria, had failed so utterly. That chapter of my life, like so many of those who participated in it, belonged now to the dead past.

As the path continued to descend, we came to a cleared place and the foundation of a house. The outline of the various rooms could be seen amid the scattered debris of stone and old wood. There was little of any decorative value remaining, except for a few fragments of mosaic floors that had been damaged in removal and left where they were. There was also a marble statue of a female form, its head missing, that lay broken in pieces on the ground. I was reminded with a shiver of the fallen bronze Minerva in my own house. This goddess, I suspected, had been knocked over by careless workmen rather than angry looters, though the man to whom workers and looters alike had owed their allegiance was almost certainly the same. Living and dead, Clodius had left destruction in his wake.

I took time to wander through the ruins for a while, tracing the demarcations of halls and cubicles where my presence would never have been allowed when the house stood, trying to imagine the sounds, smells and shadows of the place. The Virgo Maxima had mourned for its rustic charm, gone now forever. I felt her presence in that place, her brittle humour and forthright bitterness, far more than I felt the presence of the goddess, who no doubt had

abandoned the desecrated place as surely as the missing head of her broken statue.

Farther up the hill, through the trees, I could see the white columns and round roof of the circular Temple of Vesta – her original temple, as the Virgo Maxima had sternly reminded me. Even in daylight and at such a distance, the flame that burned eternally within could be seen by the lurid glow it cast on the smooth inner curves of the surrounding columns. The temple was unharmed and the land around it untouched. Even Clodius had not been impious enough to disturb the sacred flame.

We returned to the path and moved on.

The character of the woods began to change in some subtle way. Even my irreligious son sensed it, and mentioned it before I did. It may be as Eco suggested, that the trees outside a sacred grove, having been felled and allowed to grow back many times over many generations, establish a character somehow different from the trees within the sacred precinct, which have never been brought down by any mortal, and have never been scarred by any flame except fire sent from heaven by Jupiter himself. Such sacred woods are different in many small ways – the distance between the trees and the quality of the light that enters between them, their relative ages, the kind and amount of foliage at their feet. However it may be, after a time it was clear to us all, even to city-bound Davus, that we had entered a place that was special to the god.

All the more shocking, then, was the sudden

devastation we encountered in the very heart of those woods. We rounded a bend in the path, ducked beneath a low branch, and found ourselves in a clearing where only stumps remained. It was not a small clearing, but a whole hillside that had been denuded, as if some rapacious devourer of trees had gorged itself at this place.

'This must be what the priest Felix was talking about,' I said.

' 'They cut them down by tens and twenties,' he said. But it looks even worse than that to me.' Eco shook his head. 'What sort of woodsmen would inflict such a scar on a sacred grove?'

'What sort of workers would carelessly knock over a statue of Vesta and leave the broken pieces where they lay? Clodius was known to recruit many of his free labourers from among the hungry rabble in Rome. Not a very skilled bunch, I imagine, but loyal.'

'And not very pious, from the way they desecrated these holy places.'

'Ah, but these places weren't holy once Clodius was through with them. I'm sure he attended to all the legal formalities to see that the House of the Vestals and this section of the grove were duly desanctified before he plundered them.'

'Surely a place either is holy or it isn't, Papa.'

I had to smile at my son's sudden passion for things sacred. 'Eco, you know better than that. A place is sacred or not depending on the judgment of the proper authorities. Some of those authorities no doubt are very sensitive to the mysterious signs of

the gods, and as pious as men come. Others are not quite so pious, and more likely to see auspices in the glitter of a coin than in a flash of lightning. It is the Roman way, Eco, or at least it has been in my lifetime, and one of the reasons, I suppose, that so many men of your generation tend to have so little religious sentiment.' We kept walking steadily as we spoke, for I felt no desire to stop and contemplate the devastation.

We came at last to the end of the clearing. The path took us into a dense stand of trees, where for a brief moment the sacred nature of the grove seemed to reassert itself amid the hushed shadows. But we had reached the farthest edge of the woods, and after only a few more steps we found ourselves again in bright sunlight. The band of woods we had just passed through had merely been left as a screen to hide the devastated hillside. We had arrived at Clodius's Alban villa, the destination of the lumber from all those felled trees.

Like his house in the city, Clodius's villa still had an unfinished look – the decorative stonework in some places was only partly done, scaffolding clung to sections of the facade, and the landscaping was interrupted here and there by piles of crushed stone and stacks of brick and lumber. But the villa was built on such a massive scale that even in its rough-hewn state it was impressive. The grove of Jupiter awed a man in one way; a building such as this was awesome in its own right.

The hillside on which it was situated was so steep that I would have thought it unsuitable for building.

Clodius had given the architect Cyrus a difficult site on which to do his work, and Cyrus had responded with a building of daring innovation. No doubt the structure was fixed into the earth by some sort of stilts, but any such supports were concealed behind solid walls. Viewed from the side, the villa appeared to perch precariously on the hillside. On the downhill side, a long covered gallery ran the entire length of the topmost floor. Its seaward views must have rivalled those of Pompey's villa. It was surely no coincidence that there were no windows or other means of ingress on the lower floors, which made the building practically impregnable to anyone approaching from below. The long gallery would not only afford spectacular views, but could be used to defend against attackers, like the parapet of a fortress.

The entrance to the villa was located on the opposite side of the topmost floor, which was the only part of the building visible from the eastern, uphill side of the building. A great mass of earth had been removed from the hillside to make a level courtyard in front of the entrance. Materials for constructing a wall were stacked around the courtyard's perimeter, but the wall had not yet been erected. Clodius and his architect must have realized the vulnerable nature of the villa's entrance, and had intended to do something about it. Neither of them would finish the job now.

We came to the entrance, a double door made of solid oak, ornately carved and darkened by age. I wondered if it had come from the House of the

Vestals. I rapped on it politely with my foot. When there was no answer, I rapped again.

'I wonder what sort of reception we should expect,' said Eco, casting a wary eye at the nearby stable and the silent courtyard. There was not a person or animal in sight. 'Where is everyone?'

'Fulvia told me she's shut the villa for the time being.'

'You mean there's no one here?'

'A place as big as this can hardly have been abandoned entirely; there must be some staff in residence. No, I took her to mean that she's cancelled construction, closed the kitchen and shut off the visitors' quarters. I'm sure we'll find someone here.'

I had no sooner spoken than the door to the stable opened and a boy stepped out, carrying a heavy basket with both arms. He saw us, let out a scream and ran back into the stable, dropping his burden behind him. The basket tipped over, spilling its contents. I tried to make out whether it was millet or oats . . .

Then a giant wasp buzzed by my head. That was what it seemed like, at least, for a brief, paralysing instant: a sudden, malicious whirring in front of my face, so close it tickled my nose with the wind of its passing and left a sharp rushing sound in my ears. Then there was a thud of collision and the music of vibrating wood, and the sight of a shuddering spear in front of my face, impaled in the door.

Which happened that politely with me four. When there was no answer, I raised erom.

"I wonder what sort of response we should expect?" said Eco, that he stay of strike nicely polite and the storm would be. I now mean not a present or a table in right. "What is it?" evident of Positive and one and a time the rest for the one ... was"

"For your more examiner than the ....

As promising exist of .... ... henely had even abundant ejectile and evening he come will at runanee. but, I what but to ... ... the ... ... ... ... you normal, crowd the saffind and and and the ... ... ... ... as if it nothing

Which surprised me more — the spear from an unknown quarter that barely missed my nose, or the blinding speed with which Davus reacted?

However stiff-muscled and slow-witted he might appear, Davus had the reflexes of a chasing hound. He was across the courtyard and scrambling over a pile of bricks before I had time to blink. Even Eco, as quick and nimble as I was in my prime, was left looking after him like a dazed runner left at the starting block.

Davus reached the top of the brick pile and leaped open-armed into space. An instant later there was a sound of two bodies colliding and a sharp exhalation that turned into a yelp of pain. Then Davus called out, 'Master! Come quick, I can't hold him!'

Eco raced across the courtyard. I followed behind. He went one way around the brick pile, I

went the other. I heard another collision, a grunt, a spray of flying gravel. I came upon Davus on the far side of the pile, just getting to his feet. Together we ran to find Eco, who stood clutching his middle, the breath knocked out of him. Lying flat on his back in front of Eco, his eyelids flickering, was a boy who could hardly have been more than ten years old.

'I didn't touch him,' said Eco, catching his breath. 'He ran straight into me, almost knocked me down. He fell back and must have hit his head . . .'

The boy was dazed but not seriously hurt. He gradually came to his senses and gave a start when he saw the three of us peering down at him. His first reaction was an attempt to scramble to his feet, rendered impossible by the fact that Davus stood with a foot on each sleeve of the boy's tunic, pinning him down.

'You needn't struggle, young man,' said Eco. 'It doesn't look like you're going anywhere.'

The boy stuck out his jaw and narrowed his eyes, but his mask of defiance was all too easy to see through. His chin quivered and his eyes shifted constantly from face to face.

'We have no desire to hurt you,' I said, in a gentler tone than Eco had used. 'What's your name?'

The boy squinted up at me. From his point of view on the ground, we must have looked like giants, especially Davus. The squint was clearly for show, another way of masking his fear; his eyesight had to be perfect to have thrown a spear with such

accuracy. 'My name is Mopsus,' he finally said. His voice shook.

'And your friend? The boy in the stable, the one who screamed when he saw us. That's why you threw the spear, wasn't it, because he screamed and you thought he was in danger?'

The boy's squint relaxed a bit. 'My little brother, Androcles.'

'Ah, your brother. No wonder you were worried for him.' I looked towards the stable. The door, which was barely ajar, gave a little jerk. 'Androcles must be quite worried for you right now. But he needn't be. As I said, we have no desire to harm either of you.'

'Then what are you here for?' His gruff voice rose to a squeak. Davus laughed. The boy turned red with anger. He thrashed helplessly on the ground, which made Davus laugh again.

'Tell this big elephant to get off me!' Anger finally drove out fear and lent a surprising authority to his voice.

'Certainly, as soon as you've answered a few questions. Why does no one come to the door? Where is everyone?'

The boy shifted and wriggled, straining against his confinement. There was no way for him to escape from his long-sleeved tunic as long as Davus stood on the sleeves. Nor could he kick high enough to strike Davus.

'You really are stuck, I'm afraid,' I said.

'We could string him up, Papa. Perhaps start a fire under him, roast him like a pig —'

'Eco, don't joke! He'll take you seriously. Something tells me this young fellow has seen awful things done to helpless men. That's why he's so afraid of us. Am I right, Mopsus?'

The boy said nothing, but the look in his eyes answered for him.

'My name is Gordianus. This is my son, Eco. And that elephant, as you call him, is my bodyguard, Davus. We come to this house in peace, just the three of us. We did nothing to your brother. He saw us from the stable door, screamed and ran back in.'

Mopsus wriggled in a paroxysm of disgust. 'Stupid Androcles! He always was a little screamer, afraid of his shadow!'

'I am not!' squeaked a voice from the breach of the stable door.

'Androcles, you fool! Get out of there! Run to the mill! Wake them up, tell them –' Mopsus bit his tongue.

Davus and Eco looked to me. I put a finger to my lips. I walked in a circle around the brick pile, retracing my earlier steps to the courtyard, then approached the stable door from a direction that couldn't be seen from the breach. I yanked the door open, thrust out my arm and put my hand gently but firmly on the shoulder of a little boy who looked up at me with eyes like moons.

'Don't be afraid, Androcles. You're not a screamer, like your brother says, are you?'

The child looked at me solemnly and shook his head.

'I thought not. Here, take my hand. Good. Now, let us go and talk some sense into your silly older brother.'

Mopsus writhed in disgust. 'Androcles, you idiot! Now they've captured you, too.'

Androcles looked up at me solemnly, then at Eco and Davus in turn. 'I think they may be all right, Mopsus. Not bad, like the others.'

'The others probably sent them, you stupid ass, to ambush us and finish us off!' Mopsus's voice squeaked out of control again, making Davus laugh.

'The big elephant is funny.' Androcles gazed up at Davus with a look of awe.

'You won't think it's very funny when they flay us alive, like they did to Halicor!' said Mopsus.

Androcles shuddered at the idea, but when I squeezed his hand he seemed reassured. 'Halicor was the tutor of young Publius Clodius, wasn't he?' I said.

'How would you know that, unless they sent you?' Mopsus practically spat the words. Having his little brother for an audience gave him the courage to keep up a pretence of toughness.

'By they, you mean the men who killed Halicor?'

'Who else? Milo's men! Maybe Milo himself sent you –'

'No!' The sternness in my voice silenced him. 'Look at me, Mopsus. And you, Androcles. I swear to you, by the shade of my own father, that Milo did not send me here and I have not come on his behalf.'

'Who did send you, then?' said Mopsus warily.

'The day before I left Rome, I had a long talk with your mistress. Fulvia asked me to do some work for her.' It was true, after all, if not the entire truth. I saw no need to complicate matters by mentioning the Great One.

Mopsus softened a bit. 'The mistress sent you?'

'Fulvia asked me to investigate a certain aspect of your late master's death. I'm called the Finder. I have experience in such matters.'

'Maybe he can find the men who killed Halicor!' suggested Androcles, looking at his brother with wide eyes.

'Don't be ridiculous, screamer, we know who killed him. We saw them do it with our own eyes.'

'Did you, indeed? Your mistress didn't tell me that, only that Halicor had been killed, along with the foreman and two other slaves. She mentioned no witnesses.'

'That's because no one knows that we saw,' said Mopsus.

'Until now!' Little Androcles put his hands on his hips and looked accusingly at his older brother, as if to ask which of them was the stupid screamer now.

'I shall want to hear all about it,' I said, 'but first I want to know what you meant when you told Androcles to run to the mill and wake the others. What others?'

Mopsus looked up at me, biting his lip and debating whether to cooperate. I could almost see his thoughts at work. His little brother seemed to be in no harm, and no real threats had been made

against them; his captors had disavowed any allegiance to Milo and instead had invoked the name of his mistress in Rome, a lady probably as remote and exotic to such a boy as a goddess from Olympus. Perhaps most importantly, he was beginning to get very tired of being pinned to the ground.

'Let me up and I'll tell you,' he said.

'You won't run away? Because if you do, Davus will run after you – I can hardly stop him, he's like a dog without a leash – and when he catches you, he'll never stop laughing.'

Androcles covered his mouth and giggled at the thought. Mopsus turned red. 'I won't run. Just get the elephant off me!'

'Davus, step back.'

Davus did so, but remained poised to chase after the boy, his long muscular legs ready to spring. He looked like one of those magnificent giant cats one sees at exotic animal shows in the arena, except for his grin, for such beasts never smile. Where had the crippling stiffness of the morning gone to? Ah, to be that young again, invulnerable like Achilles.

Mopsus got to his feet and dusted himself off. He made a sour face at Davus, who showed the good sense to suppress his laughter. 'What were you saying?'

'The others you mentioned – down at the mill . . .'

'Asleep, probably. Like they usually are at this time of the morning after they've been drinking the night before, which they have been ever since they

344

broke into the little house where the master stored his wine.'

'Mopsus!' His little brother frowned at him and shook his head.

'What do I care? It's only the truth. It's their job to guard the house, our job to take care of the stable. They should get into trouble!'

'Then there's no one in the house at all?' I said.

'No. It's all locked up. After what happened, the mistress called all the servants back to Rome, except for the men to guard the building.'

'And us, to look after the animals,' added his brother. 'Tell her we're doing our job.'

'I shall do that,' I promised.

'But don't tell on the others,' said Androcles, suddenly very earnest. 'Not if it means they'll be punished.' He suddenly began to cry.

'Oh, shut up,' said Mopsus. 'He's remembering what Milo's men did to Halicor and the foreman. That's not how the mistress would punish drunken guards, stupid. She'd have them whipped a bit. She wouldn't cut their limbs off.'

'How do you know?' The child sniffed.

'Because I'm not stupid like you.'

'Androcles doesn't seem stupid to me,' said Eco, putting his hands on his hips. 'He's not the one who threw a spear at three perfectly peaceable strangers.' How like him to take the underdog's side, I thought; was this how he kept peace between the twins at home? But it occurred to me that the boys' squabbling was also a way of skirting the ugly subject of Halicor and his fate, even as they

kept bringing it up. What exactly had they wit-
nessed?

'You were here on the day of the battle, then?
You remember it well?'

'Of course we were here, tending the stable as
always,' said Mopsus. 'It turned into a busy day,
what with the master and his men getting packed
and ready to go.'

'What time of day was that, when your master set
out for Rome?'

'In the afternoon.'

'What hour?'

The boy shrugged.

'Closer to the ninth hour, or later, around the
eleventh hour?'

Androcles tugged at my hand. 'The ninth hour.'

'You're sure of that?'

'There's a sundial behind the stable. After the
master set out, I went to look at it because I was
hungry and I wondered how long until dinner.'

'And when your master set out, did it seem that
he had planned to leave at that time?'

'Not at all,' said Mopsus, before his brother
could answer ahead of him. 'He was going to stay
another day or two. He left because the messenger
came.'

'And what was the messenger's news?'

'About the old architect, Cyrus. He was dead,
and the mistress wanted the master back in Rome.'

'You seem to know a lot about your master's
business for a stableboy,' said Eco, who seemed
determined to needle him.

346

'I've got eyes and ears. Besides, who do you think is the first person a messenger on horseback sees when he arrives at the villa? Me, because I'm the one who takes his horse.'

Eco looked sceptical. 'And this messenger felt compelled to share his news with you, even before he'd delivered it to Clodius?'

'He said, 'Better get the horses ready for your master and his friends,' and I said, 'Why?' And he said, 'Because the mistress wants him back in Rome,' and I said –'

'Yes, I think we understand,' said Eco.

'So your master received the message,' I said, 'decided to head back to Rome and rounded up his retinue. But wasn't his son with him, the boy, Publius Clodius? I suppose he must be about your age, Androcles.'

'Of course Publius was here,' said Androcles. 'With his tutor, Halicor. Halicor kept him busy most of the time, but sometimes Publius would slip away and come to find Mopsus and me. We told him we had work to do, but he said as long as he was with us, it was all right to go off with him. So we'd go to play in the woods, or over at the ruins of the witches' house.'

'Witches?'

'I think he means the Vestals, Eco. That day, after the messenger came, did Publius set out with his father?'

'No, he stayed behind with Halicor. Mopsus and I were glad, because that meant he'd be wanting to play with us and we wouldn't have to work so

347

much, and the foreman and Halicor might get angry, but so what, because Publius was always getting into trouble and then getting out of it again.'

'Taking after his father,' said Eco under his breath.

'And as soon as the master and his men rode off, Publius came and found us in the stable –'

'We had a lot of work to do,' said Mopsus, 'cleaning up after they were gone. Quite a few of the men had slept in the stable, and men make more of a mess than beasts.'

'But Publius came and wanted to play. Mopsus told him we had work to do, but Publius said he was hiding from Halicor and we had to help him hide. So Mopsus and I went to a corner and had a talk, and we decided to show him the secret passage. Can you imagine, even Publius didn't know about it, the master's own son!'

'A secret passage?' said Eco. 'I think these boys are telling us stories, Papa.'

'No, it's true!' insisted Androcles.

'Yes, it's true,' said Mopsus, crossing his arms and sounding very adult. 'We're probably the only two people alive who know about it, except Publius, now that both the master and Cyrus are gone, because they were the only ones who were supposed to know, except of course for the slaves who did the actual building, but who knows where they are now? Not even Halicor or the foreman knew about it. I'll bet that even the mistress doesn't know.'

His brother scoffed, but I thought young Mopsus might be right. Fulvia had said nothing of a secret passage to me, nor had she mentioned these two boys; she had only said that her son somehow managed to elude Milo's men when they came to the villa and terrorized the slaves. Possibly her son had been unforthcoming with details, and she had not wanted to press him; or perhaps young Publius was as good at keeping secrets as his father.

'So you took Publius off to the secret passage, to hide from Halicor. I wish that you could show me. Of course, if the house is locked –'

'Oh, but that's the wonderful thing about the secret passage,' said Androcles. 'You don't have to go into the house to use it. You can enter the passage from outside the house. Come, I'll show you.' He took my hand. His older brother looked dubious, and shot a wary glance at Eco, but followed along, persuaded by a newfound trust, or else by his fear of being chased down and tackled again by a laughing Davus.

Androcles led us around the corner of the house and down the steep hill into the woods at the base of the house. From a distance, this side of the house appeared almost featureless except for the long portico along the top. Closer at hand, I could see numerous openings set in rows, not so much windows as apertures for ventilation and light, set too high in the wall to be reached and too small for even a child to climb through. The foundation was largely hidden by trees and dense thickets. It was amid this growth that Androcles showed us a path,

and at the path's end, in what appeared at first sight to be a featureless wall, was a hidden entrance. A section between two upright posts appeared to be immovable but in fact was a sliding panel that could be opened just enough to allow a man to slip inside. I have seen several examples of hidden doors in my life, especially in my early travels, but seldom had I seen one as well concealed. Most so-called secret entrances are not really hidden, but are daunting because the means of opening them is secret. This door was simple to open, but would have been almost impossible to detect unless one knew of its existence.

The opening led to an ascending stairway, and then through a very narrow, dark hall that seemed to run through the very heart of the lower floors of the villa, those subterranean sections which had been constructed in the excavated hillside. The way was lit only by tiny openings which served as spyholes into the various rooms we passed. The rooms themselves were mostly undecorated and empty except for a few crates and odd pieces of furniture. Some were pitch black. Some had not yet been properly finished by the carpenters. Like Clodius's house in the city, the villa had been in a state of expansion at the time of its master's death, full of the promise of his grandiose schemes for the future.

'All these gloomy underground chambers – what did Clodius need them for?' said Eco.

'This was obviously to be more than a simple country villa,' I said. 'More of a stronghold, I

imagine – a place to store treasure, stockpile weapons, house a private army of gladiators . . .'

'Or keep prisoners?'

'I hadn't thought of that. Yes, it's not hard to imagine these rooms as cells or torture chambers.'

'Perhaps his city house has secret passageways in the walls as well.'

'It wouldn't surprise me. More work for Cyrus the architect!'

We ascended more stairs, which were lit by tiny openings with direct sunshine, indicating that the stairwells were located at one end of the building. We walked down more narrow corridors, looked into more cavernous, gloomy, unfinished chambers. At last there was a change in the pattern and we found ourselves in a labyrinthine passage that snaked this way and that. We were somewhere in the upper, older part of the villa now, where the addition of a hidden passage between the existing walls had required the architect Cyrus to exercise considerable ingenuity. The rooms now revealed by the spyholes were adorned with opulent decorations and furnishings, full of all the things that make a home – except people to live there. The rooms were silent and still. Even on a sunshiny day such as this, with the first hint of an early spring in the air, all the shutters were closed, casting the whole house in a deep-shadowed gloom.

At last Mopsus gestured for us to stop. 'Here – this is where we were when it happened.'

'Who was here?'

'Androcles and I. And Publius, of course, hiding

from Halicor. Publius thought it would be great fun to spy on the grown-ups. He could hardly stop giggling whenever he looked through the hole.'

The nearest spyhole was at eye level for a boy, closer to waist high on a man, so that I had to stoop to look through it. The floor of the secret passage was substantially higher than that of the adjacent rooms, so that I actually found myself looking down into the room beyond. It appeared to be an office for transacting business and keeping records. Pigeonhole scroll cases lined one wall, but were mostly empty, their contents scattered on the floor along with various writing materials – wax tablets, styluses, jars of ink and sheets of papyrus spattered and smeared with something that looked more like blood than ink. The room reminded me of my own ransacked study.

'So the three of you were here,' I said. 'What did you see?'

'Halicor and the foreman, talking about Publius,' said Mopsus.

'And not too nicely, either!' added Androcles.

'What did they say?'

'A lot of things,' said Mopsus. 'They talked about how impossible it was going to be to control Publius, especially with his father gone. They argued. The foreman said it was Halicor's fault for letting Publius out of his sight. Halicor said that he was a tutor, not a bodyguard, and it wasn't his job to keep Publius safe, and that was what the master really cared about. That sort of thing. Lots of yelling. Grown-up talk.'

'And then?'

In the deep shadows of the corridor I saw Androcles's eyes glitter with tears as he stepped behind his older brother, holding on to him like a shield. Mopsus straightened his back and put on a hard face. 'Then there was yelling from somewhere else in the house. I don't think Halicor and the foreman heard it at first, because they were yelling at each other. Then the door flew open, so hard it banged against a shelf and knocked some things off. Men ran in. They carried swords —'

'And there was already blood on the swords!' said Androcles, peering around his brother's shoulder.

Mopsus wrinkled his brow. 'And then Milo came in —'

'How did you know it was Milo?'

'Because that's what Halicor called him. 'Milo!' He shouted the name as if Hades himself had come up through the floor. I whispered to Publius, 'Who is Milo?' and he whispered back, 'The worst man in the world, except for Cicero!' '

'Clodius was already teaching the boy to know his enemies,' observed Eco.

I nodded. 'And then what happened?'

'Milo and his men swarmed into the room like bees. They pushed Halicor and the foreman against the wall and poked their swords at them. Milo was angry. 'Where is he?' he shouted. 'Where is Publius Clodius?' And the foreman said, 'He's not here, we don't know where he is,' but that just made Milo angrier. 'You!' he said to Halicor. 'Who are you?'

353

And Halicor said, 'I'm just a tutor, the boy's tutor, but the boy has run off, he's hiding from me.' And Milo shouted at him to shut up and knocked him down and kept yelling, 'Where is Publius Clodius?' And then they were stabbing the foreman, and cutting off pieces of Halicor's fingers –'

'It was awful,' said Androcles. 'I thought I was going to throw up, but my belly was empty. I was glad when they dragged Halicor and the foreman into the hall. At least we couldn't see what they were doing.'

'But we could hear the screaming,' said Mopsus. 'We all covered our ears. Poor Publius. He could have spoken up, you see, shouted out, 'Here I am!' Maybe he could have saved Halicor.'

I shook my head. 'If the men came for Publius and found him, they'd have had no reason to leave Halicor alive.'

'What would they have done to Publius?' said Androcles.

'Taken for him for a hostage, probably,' said Eco grimly. 'Or else finished him as they finished his father.'

'Two of the men were so big,' said Mopsus, shivering as he remembered. 'Even bigger than the elephant here. They were the ones who did most of the cutting.'

Eco looked at me. 'Eudamus . . .'

'. . . and Birria. Never one without the other.'

'Halicor screamed and screamed,' said Mopsus. 'I bet he would have told them where Publius was, if

354

he'd known! But he didn't, so they just kept cutting off pieces.'

His little brother began to weep. I put my arm around him.

'We couldn't even run away, or else they might have heard us,' said Mopsus. 'We just had to stay very still. Finally, the screaming stopped.' Mopsus shivered. 'The three of us just stayed here, afraid to even whisper. Every now and then I looked through the spyhole, thinking that maybe Halicor or the foreman would come back, but they didn't. Androcles started whining, saying he had to take a piss –'

'No I didn't! It was Publius who had to go!'

'Whatever. Yes, maybe it was Publius. But I told him he would be crazy to go outside, because Milo and his men were probably looking for him all over the place. And then I think we all started to wonder about the master, because how was it that Milo had dared to come breaking into the house, and why hadn't the master come back to stop him? I think we all started to realize that something really terrible must have happened, but I didn't want to say anything, and neither did Publius, I guess, because he was very quiet. It was dark by that time, and there didn't seem to be anyone in the house at all. We got very hungry. Finally I sent Androcles to sneak into the kitchen to get us some food –'

'Because you were afraid to go yourself!'

'No, because I had to stay and protect Publius. And finally Androcles came back and said that some

355

of the slaves were hiding in the stable, and at least two of them had been killed besides Halicor and the foreman, and some of the bodyguards who left with the master that afternoon had come back and they were wounded because there had been a terrible battle with Milo, and they said that they didn't know where the master was, but that he'd been hurt and gone to Bovillae but wasn't there any longer, and all the men who had been with him were dead . . .'

'I think Publius was very brave,' said Androcles quietly. 'He didn't even cry. And he wouldn't eat anything. He said Mopsus and I could eat all the food I'd brought back.'

'So we spent the night hiding in the secret passageways, even though it was awfully cold and dark. And the next day, the mistress sent some men from Rome for Publius, and then later she shut down the house. Everyone left except for us.'

'And those lazy guards,' said Androcles. 'They're probably awake by now. They'll be wondering where we are.'

'Let them wonder,' said his brother. 'Maybe they'll think the witches came and got us. Imagine if that happened, and it was their fault, sleeping when they should be keeping watch. They'll be worried sick.'

'Tell me,' I said, 'do you know of any prisoners who were taken by Milo?'

'Prisoners?' said Mopsus. He shook his head. 'Not that we ever heard about. Milo killed quite a few of the master's men, but everyone who wasn't

killed came back sooner or later, at least the men from this villa.'

The cramped, dark passageway had begun to close in around me. I was ready to be outside again. The boys led the way back through the winding corridors and down the stairways. When we finally stepped through the hidden door and emerged into bright sunlight, I heard distant voices calling out from up the hill: 'Mopsus! Androcles!'

'You see, I told you they'd be worried,' said Mopsus.

'These so-called guards – were they here the day that Milo came?' I said.

'No. They're all new, all from the city. They hate it here. They're always complaining, saying they're bored and there are no women about except the witches in the house down the hill, and they won't have anything to do with men.'

'Then I've no need to talk to them. Will you and your brother be all right? They won't be angry at you?'

'Afraid of that bunch of drunks and cowards?' said Mopsus. He had regained his former bravado. 'I'll tell them we heard a funny noise in the woods and went to take a look, and they'll all go scurrying back to the mill.'

'Very well. Then I have a request: tell them nothing of our visit –'

'I certainly wouldn't tell them about the secret entrance!'

'Exactly. And when I get back to Rome, I shall make sure that your mistress knows what a clever

and valuable pair of boys she has serving her, here at her Alban villa.'

We left Mopsus and Androcles and returned up the hill, skirting the courtyard in front of the villa's entrance to avoid the guards. As we made our way around a pile of stones and rubble, I stubbed my toe against something and looked down in some surprise to see the face of a goddess staring back at me.

It was the marble head of Vesta, separated from the headless statue we had seen at the remains of the House of Vestals. Her expression was warm and serene, as befits the protector of the family hearth, but as I looked at her more closely I could not help thinking that there was the faintest glimmer of malevolence in her lapis lazuli eyes, and in the set of her mouth a hint of satisfaction at the way Fate had dealt with the mortal who had treated her and her attendants so shabbily.

# XXI

We returned to Pompey's villa the way we had come. After a midday meal we mounted our horses to pay a call on Senator Sextus Tedius, the man who had found Clodius and sent his body back to Rome in his litter.

'Well, Davus,' I said, 'it looks as though you shall get in some riding today after all.'

'This morning's walk worked out all the stiffness, Master.' Davus smiled, but when his bottom made contact with his horse I heard a stifled groan.

To reach the villa of Senator Tedius, we passed through Aricia, where Clodius had addressed the local magistrates on the day of his death. Though the town is larger and more hospitable than Bovillae, being the traditional first night's stop for many southbound travellers from Rome, a man could still pass through and hardly know he had been there.

Pompey's foreman had given us directions to our destination, which turned out to be a much more rustic and humble dwelling that those of Clodius or the Great One. Sextus Tedius was clearly a man of wealth, as the extent of the property surrounding his house testified, but his dwelling was altogether lacking in ostentation. It looked large enough to serve the purpose of a country villa, with room for guests and gatherings, but no statuary lined the road, no mosaics decorated the porch, no elaborate lamps hung above the door. Judging from his house, I suspected that Tedius's money was very old, his taste in literature and art austere, and his politics staunchly conservative.

Pompey's foreman, when he had given me directions, had informed me that the senator had long been a supporter and admirer of the Great One. Considering the personality suggested by his house, and the fact that he was partial to Pompey, I decided that a candid and formal approach would be best. When the doorkeeper inquired after my business, I handed him my letter of commission from Pompey and told him I wished to speak to his master.

After a short interval the slave summoned Eco and me to the senator's private study, where the shutters had been thrown open to admit a view of the town of Aricia below. The view was sunlit, but the air was bracing. Our host sat in an old-fashioned backless chair, holding himself very upright for a man of his years. The only concession to comfort was a blanket thrown across his lap to keep his legs

warm. His hair was white, tinged with just enough yellow to suggest that he had once been blond. His face and hands were darkened and leathery, suggesting that he had spent much of his life outdoors, and the lines around his mouth were deeply etched; even so, it occurred to me that he might still be a handsome man if he would only relax the severity of his countenance.

'You're one of Pompey's men?' he said.

'My name is Gordianus. I come on the Great One's behalf.'

'In this house, we call my good neighbour the general by the name he was born with,' said Tedius, not harshly but firmly. 'A man's greatness, or his smallness for that matter, is best left for posterity to determine. While he lives, a man's acts speak for themselves.' He looked at me shrewdly and allowed something like a smile to bend his lips. 'But the man who sent you knows my sentiments well enough; Gnaeus Pompey and I have often discussed such matters over a cup of wine in this very room. He knows that I am a Republican through and through, and that I believe in the great institution of the Senate, not in great men. If I did not believe that he was ultimately loyal to the Senate himself, I should be very disturbed by the way he elevates himself above the rest of us by the use of that name, Magnus. Tell me, have you just come from Rome?'

'We set out before daylight yesterday morning.'

'Then you left before the Senate was to meet at Pompey's Theatre. I hoped to attend myself, but

my leg won't allow it.' He frowned at his left leg, as if to communicate his disappointment with it. 'I understand that a proposal to rebuild the Senate House was to be put forth, with the contract going to Sulla's boy, Faustus.'

'I believe that is correct,' I said, remembering what Pompey had told me.

'And I hear there was also to be a proposal to issue the Ultimate Decree, empowering Pompey to raise troops to quell the disorder in the city.'

'Perhaps. As I said, I left before dawn.'

'You have no news for me, then? Yet you say that Pompey sent you.'

'I come on behalf of Pompey, yes, but not as a messenger. I come to seek information, not to convey it.'

Tedius raised an eyebrow. 'I see.'

'The Great One – Gnaeus Pompey – has commissioned me privately to discover everything I can about the death of Publius Clodius.'

'Surely Rome has talked of nothing else for days.'

'Yes, but talk and truth can be far apart. Pompey would know the truth.'

'Does he intend to administer justice himself?' Tedius still seemed intent on drawing information from me.

'I think he wishes to see clearly. No general can proceed through a landscape obscured by mist. Is it true that you and your daughter found Clodius lying in the Appian Way?'

'Who does not already know this? I sent his body on to Rome in my litter.'

'Let me understand the sequence of events clearly. When did you depart from this house?'

The senator gazed at me for a long moment, his face as unreadable as a leather mask. I think he was unused to being questioned by anyone, let alone a man so far beneath his rank, but at last he spoke. 'My daughter and I and our retinue left this house at about the ninth hour of the day. I had planned to be in Rome by nightfall.'

'When did you first realize that something was amiss on the Appian Way?'

'As we approached the shrine of the Good Goddess. My daughter is a pious woman; on the way to Rome she customarily makes an offering at the shrine. But we came upon a large entourage in great disarray, with agitated slaves and bodyguards shouting and running about. Clearly, there was something amiss, as you put it. I first realized that Milo must be in the vicinity when I saw that wife of his, Fausta Cornelia. She was in a carriage by the side of the road with her cloak pulled tight about her. Her face was as white as the moon – not due to cosmetics, either – and a cadre of slaves was fussing over her, fanning her and cooing at her. While I was watching, she seemed suddenly to have had enough of them and began flailing at them. The simpering slaves scattered like pigeons.'

'And Milo?'

'I came upon him surrounded by some of his men, all standing about with drawn swords. Some of the swords had blood on them. I saw there were also a few bodies lying about. I told my daughter to

sit back, draw the curtains on her side of the litter, and not to show herself. Milo's men raised their swords as my party approached, but when I announced myself he called them to order.'

'Are you a friend of Milo's?'

Senator Tedius made an expression between a wince and a sneer. 'The man has his uses, I suppose. I would hardly call him a friend. What sort of man countenances such embarrassing conduct from his wife? I don't care if she is the dictator's daughter. And I don't care for fellows who give themselves names which are more heroic than they are — calling himself another Milo of Croton, indeed! I asked him what the trouble was. He said he had been set upon by bandits.'

'Bandits?'

'I suppose he wasn't prepared to say what had really happened, and that was the first lie that popped into his head. Bandits had attacked him, he said, and some of his men had chased the brigands in the direction of Bovillae. He suggested that I turn back, for my own safety. 'How many bandits?' I asked. 'Oh, a great many, and all heavily armed,' he said. But I suspected he was exaggerating, and when he repeated his warning I told him not to be ridiculous, that I had business in the city the next morning and I intended to press on. 'Then wait here with me,' he said, 'until my men return, and we're sure the danger's over.' That seemed reasonable; but then I saw Fausta Cornelia approaching, with her entourage of slaves all fluttering around her like pigeons. I did not intend to spend

even a moment in the company of that harlot. I told Milo that I felt perfectly safe under the protection of my own bodyguards. I proceeded on my way.'

'Down the hill towards Bovillae?'

'Yes. I remember, my daughter –'

'Yes?'

'The detail has nothing to do with the incident.'

'Please, give me any detail that you remember.'

Sextus Tedius tilted his head back and parted his lips. He studied me for a long moment through narrowed eyes. I could not read his expression at all. 'Very well,' he finally said. 'My daughter suddenly realized that she had failed to make an offering to the Good Goddess. Tedia is very pious, as I told you. It seemed to her a bad omen to begin our journey without stopping at the shrine, especially when we had been warned of danger. She wanted to turn back, but I was determined to press on. I was curious, I suppose; I could tell that Milo was lying about something. But Tedia was apprehensive. When we passed the House of the Vestals – their new residence – she pleaded with me to take refuge there until we were sure there was no danger. My daughter is as pious towards Vesta as she is towards the Good Goddess. I told her I had no intention of hiding myself among virgins, but that if she insisted I would leave her with the Vestals and return for her presently, once I saw that all was well in Bovillae. But Tedia refused to be left behind. She said that it was not her own safety which concerned her, but mine. Tedia is my only child;

she is very loyal to me. Since I was determined to press on, she remained with me in the litter.

'As we came down into Bovillae, we passed a dead body lying by the road. The corpse was very bloody, with many wounds. I forbade Tedia to look at it, but still she became frightened and urged me to turn back. I paid no heed; I called to the litter bearers to hurry on. As we approached the inn, I saw that a battle had taken place. The front door and the window shutters were all broken and ajar, and there were more dead men lying about. I must admit that I began to feel a bit of trepidation, and I whispered a prayer to Mercury. Milo had spoken of bandits, and now it appeared that these bandits had come down to Bovillae, ransacked the inn and murdered the customers! Where were Milo's men, who supposedly had pursued these bandits? Had they all been killed, or had they fled into the woods? And where were the bandits? I told the bearers to stop. Tedia assisted me from the litter. We went among the fallen men, hoping to find one of them alive. And the first one we came to – was Publius Clodius!'

'You recognized him at once?' The senator had not been expecting to find Clodius, I reasoned, and the face of a dead man, its features robbed of animation, is not always easy to recognize.

'How could I not know him?' said Tedius. 'If you had suffered through as many of the man's ranting speeches in the Senate as I have –' He shook his head. 'Yet another fellow who gave himself a new name, changing his proud patrician Claudius

to the plebeian Clodius just to curry favour with the masses! And actually enrolling himself among the plebeians, giving up his patrician status! His ancestors must have cursed him from Hades. How fitting that he should die on the road named for one of those whose name he mocked.' The senator's jaw pulled into a frown. He turned his gaze to the window and seemed lost in thought.

'But you didn't leave him there, in the road,' I prompted.

Tedius sighed. 'Publius Clodius was a menace to the state. His death was a blessing to Rome, and an even greater blessing to this mountain, which he had done so much to despoil and defile. But he was a fellow senator, after all, a colleague. And a Claudian by blood, no matter what spelling or legal fiction he affected. And once a man is dead, what use is there in despising him? No, it would not do to leave him in the road, like a dead dog. I sent his body on to Rome in my litter, instructing the bearers to deliver it with the greatest respect into the care of his wife.'

'But Clodius's Alban villa was nearby. Why did you not have his body taken there?'

'It seemed more fitting to send him to the city.'

'And you and your daughter turned back?'

'I certainly had no intention of sitting in a litter beside a bloody corpse for three hours!' Tedius snapped. 'Besides, Tedia was by that time quite distraught, and I had begun to fear for our safety. Don't you see, I believed that Clodius and his fellows had been attacked by the same bandits of

367

whom Milo had spoken. It seems silly now, that I hadn't yet figured it out – that it was Milo and Clodius who'd had the battle. But there you have it: I took Milo at his word that he'd encountered bandits on the Appian Way, and it appeared to me that the same bandits had also attacked Clodius and his men at the inn in Bovillae, either before meeting Milo or after. Clearly, the road was not safe for myself or my daughter. Tedia and I and my bodyguards returned home on foot.'

'You walked all the way?'

'There were no horses to be had. The stable in Bovillae was locked, and all the stable slaves had fled. And me with my bad left leg! That day seems to have ruined it for good.' He sighed and smoothed his hands over the blanket which covered his legs. 'We made slow progress, as you might imagine. After a while we were overtaken by a troop of armed men coming up from the direction of Bovillae, led by Milo's famous gladiators, Eudamus and Birria. In the midst of them were five or six men with bound hands.'

The same prisoners of whom Felix and Felicia had spoken, I thought. 'Who were these bound men?'

Tedius raised an eyebrow. 'That remains a bit of a puzzle, doesn't it? At the time I thought they must be the fictitious bandits of whom Milo had spoken, captured at last by his gladiators. I even gave Eudamus and Birria a salute as they passed.'

'Did you speak to them?'

'Are such creatures able to speak? To be candid, I

was too out of breath to converse, and my leg had begun to ache. I had stopped for a rest, at a spot just below the House of the Vestals. After a while, Tedia and I pressed on. By the time we got back to the shrine of the Good Goddess, Eudamus and Birria had apparently rejoined Milo, and his entourage had moved on.'

Milo and the gladiators had gone on to Clodius's villa on the mountainside, I thought, where they proceeded to kill Halicor and strangle the foreman and to search for young Publius while the hapless boy watched. And Fausta . . .

'Tell me, Senator, did you not pass Milo's wife on the road, heading back towards Bovillae, on her way to the House of the Vestals?'

'Fausta? No, I didn't see her again that day. And what business would that impious woman have had at the House of the Vestals? I doubt that she herself can remember a time when she was a virgin!'

I saw no reason to mention the Virgo Maxima's visitor, Eco's 'mystery woman'. Had Fausta gone to the House of the Vestals before Tedius passed it on his way home? No, that was impossible, since it was the triumphant Eudamus and Birria who would have brought Clodius's ring to Fausta as a trophy, and the gladiators had passed Tedius while he took a rest below the House of the Vestals; if Fausta had then gone back to the house to make her offering, she would certainly have passed Sextus Tedius. And what was I to make of the maddening detail of the unknown prisoners? After all the different accounts I had heard of the day's events, and all the details I

had collected, it seemed to me that not all the parts of the puzzle fitted together, and that a vital piece must still be missing.

My thoughts were interrupted by a woman's voice calling from the hall. 'Papa, are you warm enough?' A moment later she appeared in the doorway. At the sight of Eco and me she stiffened and lowered her eyes. 'Papa, I didn't realize . . .'

'Two visitors from the city, daughter,' explained Sextus Tedius. 'They come from Pompey. It's nothing that concerns you.'

Tedia was a tall, strong-looking woman of middle years, as plain and unadorned as the house in which she lived. She wore no jewellery or makeup. Over her head she wore a white linen mantle tied at the back with a blue ribbon. Why had she never married? She was hardly beautiful, but among her class, marriages are made for money and politics. Perhaps her father had never made the right alliances; or perhaps, because she was an only child and her father a widower, it had been decided that she should stay with him as his caretaker. The role of the dutiful daughter evidently suited her; Tedius had made much of her piety and her devotion to him.

'I came to make sure you were comfortable, Father,' she said, keeping her eyes averted.

'I require nothing, daughter. Run along, then.' She left the room.

'Any other questions?' said Tedius. 'My leg's begun to ache and I wish to be alone now.'

I thought for a moment. 'Only one more ques-

tion. Did you happen to see Marc Antony that day?'

Tedius raised an eyebrow. 'Young Antony? I'm not sure that I would know him if I saw him. Wouldn't he have been up in Gaul, with Caesar? Ah no, he's back in Rome, isn't he, campaigning for something – a quaestorship? Comes from a good family, but far too radical for my tastes. He wasn't with Clodius that day, was he? Antony used to be part of that circle of degenerates, before he found his military career. At any rate, no, I didn't see or hear of him that day. Now, I trust that you'll report back to the general that I gave you my full co-operation. Give Gnaeus Pompey my regards when you deliver your reconnaissance.'

A slave showed us out. In the foyer, Tedia suddenly joined us. She looked as stern as her father, but kept rubbing her hands together nervously.

'You had no right to come here and pester my father.'

'Your father agreed to see us. I came on behalf of –'

'I know who sent you. I overheard everything.'

'Everything?'

'My father and I have no secrets from one another.'

'Is your father aware of that fact?'

My needling stiffened her resolve. She stopped wringing her hand and made them into fists at her sides. Drawn up to her full height, she was a formidable woman. 'If Pompey intends to call

my father to Rome to be a witness against Milo, it's out of the question. His health is far more delicate than he lets the world know. His leg –'

'There's no talk of a trial and witnesses – not yet, anyway. Are you saying your father would refuse to appear at a trial?'

'I'm saying that you should leave us alone. That's all we want, you know, the people in these parts. To be left alone. Why you people from the city must continually come here, making trouble . . .'

'Your father looks like a man who can take care of himself.'

'Do you judge everything by its appearance?' said Tedia, ushering us out the door and closing it behind us.

When we returned to Pompey's villa that afternoon, it seemed to me that our work in the vicinity of Mount Alba was done. The essential truth of what had happened that day on the Appian Way appeared evident, and though some questions remained unanswered, those riddles could best be solved in Rome, if at all. I suggested to Eco that we head back to the city the next morning.

He disagreed. 'But Papa, didn't you tell me you can't think straight in the city? That your head is clearer here in the countryside? Let's stay on a while longer.'

'But Bethesda and Diana, and Menenia and the twins –'

'They're all perfectly safe with Pompey looking

after them, probably safer than they will be after we return and Pompey takes back his guards. We haven't yet talked to anyone in Aricia, where Clodius addressed the town senate, or to anyone in Lanuvium, where Milo was supposedly heading to instal a priest. Pompey's a military man; he'll expect a very thorough report.'

'Eco, if I didn't know better I'd suspect that you want to stay here at Pompey's villa for as long as you can, simply to enjoy the food and the baths and the massages.'

'And the fabulous view, Papa. Don't forget the view.'

'Eco!'

'Well, why shouldn't we take advantage of the Great One's hospitality while we can? You need some relaxation, Papa; the turmoil of the city has tied you into knots. And there's always the chance that if we keep digging for a while longer we'll uncover something completely unexpected . . .'

So I allowed Eco to persuade me to stay on for a few more days at Pompey's Alban villa. The meals were sumptuous, the baths steaming, the beds luxurious, the servants obsequious. And the views – of the hidden lake mirroring the stars at night, of the peak of Mount Alba haloed by the rising sun, of morning mist moving like smoke through the woods, of the sun sinking like a blood red disk into the distant sea – offered unending fascination. But in the end our time seemed ill spent, for though we made numerous inquiries of numerous people, making forays to Aricia and

Lanuvium and back to Bovillae, we discovered nothing new about the circumstances of Clodius's death, and nothing that contradicted or filled the gaps in what we had already learned.

I noticed, in our trips up and down the Appian Way, that Felicia seemed to have abandoned her shrine, and her brother Felix his altar. They had simply disappeared. Either they had taken my advice, I thought, or else I had given it too late.

I tired of the luxury of Pompey's villa. I grew impatient to return to Rome. I missed my family and worried about them. I wanted to know what had become of Pompey's plan to have the Senate invoke the Ultimate Decree and to give him authority to restore order. Travellers and messengers brought news to Mount Alba, but it was hard to trust their stories, especially since they often contradicted one another. Had Pompey been granted military control of Italy, and left the city to levy troops? Had elections at last been scheduled? Had there been more riots? Had formal charges of murder been lodged against Milo? I heard all these things, which were credible enough, but what was I to make of the tale that Caesar had been seen in the Forum, thinly disguised, or that Milo had killed himself, or that Pompey had been assassinated by a group of radical senators at a meeting in his theatre? I had complained that a man could not think in the city, but after a while the confusion and ignorance in the countryside were even more maddening.

And so Eco, Davus and I set out on a morning that was decidedly more springlike than wintry, so

mild in fact that we rode without our cloaks. We should have arrived in the city not long after midday, but a sudden gathering of thunderclouds opened over our heads, forcing us to take refuge in the inn at Bovillae until late in the afternoon. We set out again as the day was waning. Shadows were long, verging into twilight when we at last approached the outskirts of the city.

Be careful passing the Monument of Basilius, goes the commonplace warning. We were not careful enough.

Vigilance alone may not save a man, but it may at least show him the faces of his adversaries. That would have counted for much, in the days that followed; or it might have meant the end of me for good, if I had got a better look at them.

As we passed the monument, I noticed a few dozing drunkards slouched against the wall, broad-brimmed hats pulled down to cover their eyes. By the turn of his head, I saw that Eco took note of them as well. Without a word, we both dismissed them as harmless. But they must have been waiting to spring. There must have been a scout on the road, alerting them that we were coming. They may have been watching and waiting for hours, or days.

I heard a shuffle of footsteps behind us, and then a cry from Davus. As I turned to look, something heavy but soft, like a club wrapped in padding, struck the back of my head. I lost my balance and clutched at the reins. Something gripped my leg and pulled. I fell. Earth and sky changed places. In

the confusion I caught a glimpse of Davus flying upward from his horse, his arms outstretched and flailing as if he was climbing an invisible ladder. In one hand he held his dagger. He must have realized what was happening and had time to draw it before we were attacked. But his horse had reared wildly, out of his control. If he had been a better horseman . . .

As I struck the hard, stone surface of the Appian Way, I heard Eco call out 'Papa!' Where was he? I rolled upright, raising my hands to cover my face. Eco was still on his horse, but several men in dark cloaks seemed to be clambering up him, as if horse and man were a tower to be scaled. From the corner of my eye I saw a dark shape approach. I rolled away and collided with something warm and immovable. It was Davus, flat on his back on the paving stones, his eyes closed, his face pale, as still as death. He still held his dagger clutched in his hand. An image of Belbo's lifeless body flashed in my mind –

'Papa!' Eco cried again. Then he made another, muffled noise, as if his mouth had been covered.

I reached for the dagger in Davus's hand. What enormous hands he had! I pried at his fingers until the dagger slipped free. I almost had it –

Then darkness descended all at once as the sack was pulled over my head. It swallowed my shoulders, then my arms. A rope slithered snakelike around my chest. Another rope bit into my ankles. The inside of the sack tasted of onions and dirt. I coughed and spat. Another coil of rope slipped

around my throat and began to tighten. What an end – strangled to death inside a filthy sack on the Appian Way!

Someone cursed. 'You've got it around his neck, you idiot!'

The rope loosened, then tightened again around my jaw, working its way between my lips, gagging me.

'Not too tight. We don't want to strangle him.'

'Why not? Say it was an accident – say he died of fright. Save us a lot of trouble.'

'Just shut up and follow orders! How about the other one, tied up tight? Good.'

'And the slave?'

'Looks dead to me.'

'Me, too.' I heard the sound of a vicious kick.

'Then leave him. We weren't meant to take him anyway. Strong-looking fellow – a good thing his horse threw him, or we'd have had our hands full. Enough talk! Bring out the wagon.'

Hooves clopped and wheels rumbled on the paving stones. I was lifted aloft and dumped onto something firm but forgiving. The voice that had ordered the others spoke close to my ear. 'As for you, it's time to be very quiet and very still. You're a sack full of onions, do you understand? Lying in the bed of a wagon with a lot of other sacks full of onions. You're going on a long trip, so wriggle about and make yourself comfortable if you need to. If you have to empty your bladder or your bowels, go ahead and do it, if you can stand to lie in your own stink. Then don't move. Understand? Or

else this!' Something sharp poked into the small of my back.

I grunted. The dagger poked me harder.

'Not even that much noise, or next time I'll push it in to the hilt! Now we're off.'

The driver called out. An ass brayed. The wagon began to roll. The ruts and potholes of any lesser road would have caused it to jostle and pitch, but on the smooth, broad Appian Way, the wagon hardly swayed at all. I tried to lie very, very still.

# Part Three

## *Rex?*

# XXII

'Forty,' announced Eco. Then he counted again, wagging his finger at each scraped mark on the earth wall in turn, moving his lips as he pronounced the numbers. Towards the end he counted aloud. 'Thirty-seven, thirty-eight, thirty-nine, forty. Forty days, exactly.'

'Perhaps. You're assuming that it took them four days to bring us here,' I complained. 'How can you know that? It was all so miserable and confused. They gave us almost no food or water, and kept us blindfolded so that I never knew day from night. It might have been three days, or five, or six.'

'Might have been, but wasn't,' said Eco matter-of-factly. 'The trip from the Monument of Basilius to this place, wherever in Hades it is, took four days.'

'How can you be so sure, when I'm not?'

'They hit you on the head, remember, Papa? I think you were more dazed than you realized.'

'I was awake enough to know when we passed through Rome. We should have made a noise then and there, and taken our chances.'

'Chances? Papa, we've been over this a thousand times. We had no chance at all. I had a dagger poking into me the whole time, and so did you, until we were through the city and well out the other side.'

'You're sure it was the Fontinalis Gate that we passed through?'

'Certain. I overheard –'

'Yes, I know: you overheard someone asking directions to the Street of the Silversmiths, and someone else telling them to go straight ahead and turn right.'

'Exactly. So at that moment we had to be passing through the Fontinalis Gate, heading north out of town on the Flaminian Way.'

'Past the Field of Mars,' I mused, 'and the voting stalls. They must be overgrown with weeds by now.'

'Right past Pompey's villa up on the Pincian Hill,' said Eco ruefully. 'Maybe the Great One himself looked down from his garden and thought, 'I wonder where that wagon with all those lumpy sacks of onions is headed? And when will I hear back from that Finder fellow and his son?' '

'If Pompey has spared a thought for us at all. If it wasn't Pompey himself who's put us here!' I paced, as much as I could in the cramped space of the pit.

'And then on we rolled, into the countryside, heading north and west for a miserable eternity.'

'Only it wasn't an eternity, Papa. It was four days. I clearly remember.'

'Nonetheless, I insist we draw brackets around those first four marks of yours, since we can't be certain of them.'

'Since you can't be certain. If you draw those brackets again, I'll only rub them out again.'

The two of us were play-acting, in a way, since we had already engaged in this same argument a hundred times. There was only so much to talk about, stuck in a pit with bars across the top for forty days – or was it closer to thirty-seven? I sometimes wondered if we both had gone mad already. How would we be able to tell? I picked up the little stick that Eco used to make his daily marks and etched brackets around the first three marks. 'Now, if we count the marks remaining, the undisputed number of days will be –'

'Damned rats!' One of the creatures had sneaked into the cell again and was sniffing at the bit of bread we had put aside the previous day. Our keepers usually brought us fresh bread every morning, but not always; sometimes they skipped whole days, so we had learned to save a portion of food for the lean days. The rats were a new phenomenon, and had appeared only in the last few days. Eco ran across the small cell and stamped his foot at the creature, which squeaked and scurried away into a rocky crevice we hadn't managed to fill with dirt. 'Can you believe it,

Papa? The little monsters are coming out in broad daylight now!'

'Not exactly broad daylight.' I rolled my eyes up, looking beyond the iron bars overhead to the ceiling far above, where gaps in the slats admitted a few beams of sunlight. The pit had been dug in the earth floor of a disused building. The irregular walls around us were made of packed earth and stones. Covering the pit (and extending an unknown distance all around it, for we had tried to dig at the edges without success) was a grate made of iron bars. If we jumped, we could reach the bars; this at least allowed us a way to exercise our arms every day. I had been able to poke my head between the bars, but there was little to see; the building appeared to be a disused stable. Far above the grate was the ceiling, which badly needed repair. The place was dim and draughty, but our keepers had given us plenty of smelly blankets to huddle under at night.

'Better the rats should come out in daylight than during the night,' I said ruefully. Nights in the pit were as black as pitch, except for a few stars which occasionally glimmered through the holes in the ceiling. In such utter darkness, the scurrying and squeaking of the rats was almost more than I could stand.

'The rats aren't the only ones who're hungry,' said Eco.

'I know. I hear your stomach growling, son. Perhaps you should eat that crust of stale bread, before the rats get to it.'

'I don't know. What time do you think it is?'

'Hard to say. Noon, perhaps, judging from the light. Maybe they're not coming to feed us today.' Maybe they won't come back at all, I thought, but didn't say it aloud, though the same morbid thought must have occurred to Eco from time to time. Abandoned entirely, we would have a chance to try to dig our way out without being stopped; but without food and water, would our strength last that long? We were at the mercy of men we never saw, who had never revealed their intentions. They looked after us in a desultory fashion, feeding us on most days, occasionally hauling up and emptying the bucket we used to relieve ourselves and supplying us with enough fresh water to drink and clean ourselves. Why had they not killed us and left us on the Appian Way, as they had done with Davus? Why had we been taken so far from Rome – or were we indeed such a great distance from the city? Perhaps the four days of travel which Eco claimed to remember so clearly had been spent going in circles to confuse us. Why were they bothering to keep us alive at all, and for how much longer would they do so? What did they ultimately plan to do with us? Who were they?

'Forty days!' I said. 'You know the story Bethesda tells –' My voice caught in my throat, saying her name aloud. What had become of Bethesda and Diana in my absence? After a certain point I had tried simply not to think about them, for it was too unbearable. And yet what else was there to think of that could offer me any comfort? 'She tells that old

Hebrew tale she learned from her father, about the virtuous man and the great flood. He built a huge boat and loaded specimens of every creature on it, and then it rained for forty days and nights without stopping. Imagine having to endure that – forty days in a cramped boat stinking of every sort of animal, sodden and seasick with the rain coming down.'

'At least he didn't have to go hungry,' said Eco, whose stomach growled. 'He had all those animals he could eat.'

'I think the point was to save the animals,' I said. 'Anyway, be glad it's hardly rained at all.' During the one significant storm that had occurred since our captivity began, rain had poured in through the leaky roof above and collected in a pool on the floor of the pit. 'We're very lucky that one of us hasn't become seriously ill.'

'Not necessarily, Papa.'

'What do you mean?'

'If they've kept us alive this long, it must be because they've been ordered to do so. Maybe if one of us fell ill, they'd let us go, or at least move us out of this horrible place.'

'I suppose they might . . .'

'Oh, this is maddening!' Eco suddenly spun about and pounded his fist against the earth wall, striking a spot already pummelled by many previous blows. At least twice every day, and sometimes in the middle of the night, he would be seized by a sudden fury that could only be relieved by hitting something.

I envied the release this action gave him. Our captivity was indeed maddening, and the hardest thing I had ever had to endure. There is something in the spirit of a Roman that cannot acquiesce to such an unnatural condition. In other lands, where kings rule, imprisonment is a common punishment. This is because a king wishes to see his enemies suffer. What better way than to lock them in a cage or throw them into a pit where he can watch their inevitable physical and mental decline, tell them about the suffering of their loved ones outside, listen to their pleas for mercy and taunt them with false promises of release? But in our Republic, punishment is not designed to bring pleasure to a given ruler; it is meant to permanently remove an offender from the community, either by killing him (sometimes, admittedly, with rather gruesome punishments involved, especially for religious crimes), or by allowing him to choose exile instead of death. The notion that anyone should be indefinitely locked away, even for the most horrible crime, is too cruel even for Roman tastes.

I remembered the debate which took place in the Senate when Cicero was consul and announced he had uncovered a conspiracy by Catilina's circle to bring down the state. Cicero wanted them executed on the spot. Others disagreed, and it was Caesar who had suggested that those involved be rounded up and placed under permanent arrest. Against this novel idea was the practical problem of where such alleged criminals were to be incarcerated, since Rome has no prison to speak of, only a

few small holding cells where malefactors are kept for a short while to await execution. There was also the danger of establishing a precedent for lengthy imprisonment, for once the state was allowed to take away a citizen's freedom of movement, where would such a course lead? Surely implicit in the very concept of citizenship was an individual's right to come and go as he wished, unlike a slave; if an individual had done something so terrible that he should no longer have the most basic right of a citizen, then surely he deserved either exile or death.

In the end, of course, Cicero had prevailed. The alleged conspirators (including Marc Antony's step-father) had been rounded up and strangled to death without a trial. Many disagreed, later if not at the time, and their anger, harnessed by Clodius, eventually led to Cicero's exile for sixteen months. But even his worst enemies had never proposed that Cicero should be put into a prison, like a slavish courtier who had offended a monarch.

Such repetitious, circular meditations were my means of dealing with the madness of our situation. They wore a groove into my mind, just as surely as Eco's fist had impressed its shape into the earth wall that held us prisoner.

Eco stopped his pounding. From the unseen world above we heard the familiar sound of a wide, rickety door swing open and shut. I smelled the aroma of fresh bread, so faint I might have only imagined it. Eco's belly growled louder than ever, and I began to salivate, as dogs do when they know

they're about to be fed. How ruthlessly imprison-
ment strips away a man's dignity. How swiftly it
reduces him to the status of an animal.

The next day was the forty-first of our captivity,
according to Eco's reckoning. I decided to calculate
the exact date, but the imposition of the leap-
month of Intercalarius complicated the matter. I
knew that Februarius was past – we had been
captured two days after the Ides, which in Februar-
ius fell on the thirteenth – and I knew that all of
Intercalarius had come and gone, so we were
somewhere in early Martius.

'Of course, the leap-month of Intercalarius
doesn't always have the same number of days,' I
said. 'It's only inserted into the calendar every other
year, and even then not always, and each time the
priests adjust it according to however many days are
needed to fill out the year properly.'

Eco frowned. 'So how many days are in the leap-
month this year?'

'Twenty-seven, I think.'

Eco shook his head dubiously. 'That just doesn't
sound right to me. I thought Intercalarius always
had the same number of days as Februarius.'

'No.'

'But –'

'Besides, this year Februarius had only twenty-
four days.'

'Not twenty-eight?'

'No. This year Januarius had twenty-nine days, as
always, Februarius had twenty-four, Intercalarius

had twenty-seven, and Martius will have the cus-
tomary thirty-one. Eco, this information has only
been posted on scrolls in the Forum every day since
the new year began. How can you not have seen
it?'

'I never pay attention to such things, Papa. I have
enough garbage in my head already.'

'But how do you keep up with which days the
Senate is meeting, and when the holidays fall, and
when the banks are open?'

'I ask Menenia. Women always know these
things. They have an instinct for it. They know
which markets are open on which days, and which
are closed, and when you have to buy extra food
because there's to be a holiday, and so on.'

'Do you always ask Menenia when you need to
know the date?'

'Yes.'

'Say you're writing an important letter, and you
need to know the day of the month –'

'I ask Menenia.'

'And she knows?'

'Always. Doesn't Bethesda always know the
date?'

'Now that you mention it . . .'

'Try it. Next time you need to know, ask her.'

'You mean, instead of following the postings in
the Forum, and making my own calculations –'

'Just ask Bethesda.'

'It can't be that simple. When I think of all the
hours and the days I've wasted over the years –'

We both laughed.

I regrouped my thoughts. 'So, if this is indeed day forty-one –'

'How on earth do the priests calculate how many days to put into Intercalarius, anyway? And why don't they leave Februarius alone?'

'Not 'how on earth', Eco, but 'how in the heavens?' It all has to do with the movement of the stars and the phases of the moon and the length of the seasons and so on. The years go round and round, each pretty much like the last, but not exactly. Some cycles have more days in them than others, and there's no perfect system to account for the discrepancy. So the calendar has to be adjusted every two years.'

'Except when it's not.'

'Other people have other sorts of calendars, you know –'

'Just as other countries have kings.'

'Which Rome shall never have again –'

'Unless it does.'

'Be quiet! The Roman calendar is the most perfect yet devised. It has twelve months.'

'Except when it has thirteen, as this year.'

'And all of these months have either thirty-one or twenty-nine days.'

'Except for Februarius, which has twenty-eight. Only this year, according to you, it has only twenty-four.'

'It works out in the end.'

'Or does it? I mean, the calendar is so permanently out of joint now that sometimes the seasons don't match the traditional holidays.'

'Yes, and I've seen it get progressively worse in my lifetime. I suppose it would be even worse without snipping away at Februarius and inserting Intercalarius as needed.'

'That's another thing, Papa – 'as needed'. The priests always seem to decide to insert the leap-month at the last moment. Can't they tell a year in advance whether they'll need it?'

'Apparently not.'

'I'd say the Roman calendar needs serious re-forming.'

'It's interesting that you say that. Your brother recently mentioned in a letter that Caesar thinks the same thing. It's one of his pet projects. When he has time, in between slaughtering Gauls and dictating his memoirs on horseback, the general likes to fiddle with ways of fixing the calendar.'

'A new calendar for Rome? It would take a king to force a change like that.'

He meant for me to laugh, but I frowned instead. 'You shouldn't talk that way, Eco. You shouldn't even joke about it.'

'Sorry, Papa.'

'Anyway,' I said, 'if Caesar can fix the calendar, surely you and I can at least figure out what day this is.'

'Without Menenia and Bethesda to tell us?'

'Entirely on our own! Now, if it's been –'

I sucked in a breath as I heard the familiar rattle of the door swing open and shut in the room above. I let out a low moan and slumped down against the wall, bowing my head and clutching my stomach.

The hatch in the grate creaked open. A rope slithered and I knew that a basket of fresh bread was being lowered to us. Eco unhooked it and attached the empty basket from yesterday.

I moaned again, trying to make it sound as if I were stifling the sound instead of forcing it. A proud citizen does not like to show weakness to the slave of his enemy.

'What's wrong with him?' asked a voice from above.

'What do you care?' said Eco.

I kept my head lowered, resisting an urge to look up. I could never make out much of our captors' faces, anyway. Due to the dim light and the distance, they were nothing more than hulking silhouettes.

'Would you empty the bucket?' said Eco.

'Again? I emptied it just yesterday.'

'Please?'

The man made a grunt of disgust. 'Oh, all right. Here's the rope.'

Eco attached the bucket. There was a faint sloshing noise as the man pulled it up, fist over fist. As he walked away, I heard him mumble, 'What's this?' There was a pause, and I imagined him squinting, grinding his jaw, wrinkling his nose as he studied the watery contents. Then he resumed his walk to the door and pulled it open. From somewhere farther away I heard the ghost of a hushed conversation and then a distant splash as they emptied the contents.

A little later the man returned and lowered the bucket back into the pit. 'Is he all right?' he said.

I stifled a moan and pulled my hands from my stomach.

'Just go away,' said Eco coldly.

Footsteps departed. The door opened and shut.

After a while I said to Eco, 'How do you think it went?'

'You seemed convincing to me.'

I nodded. We both looked towards the little mound of earth which covered the body of the rat Eco had killed that morning, whose blood we had copiously added to our own urine in the bucket.

'Do you think we'll be able to catch another rat as easily?' I said.

'In broad daylight if we have to,' Eco assured me.

# XXIII

I opened my eyes to pitch darkness. The air was cold and clammy, stale and foul-smelling.

Where was I? The pit, of course. Now I remembered. Where every day was like the last, where nothing ever changed — except that something was different. We were not alone.

I felt it, sensed it. How? Not with my eyes, certainly. Was it a noise? The sound of another breath, besides Eco's? Or a faint movement? Or a smell . . . ?

Yes: the smell of garlic, sweated from pores, exhaled on the breath. Another stench added to the miasma that settled in the pit at night, pressed down by the dank evening air. My head reeled from it.

Who eats garlic? Gladiators. They claim it gives them stamina. Lets them knock down an opponent with a single breath, runs the tired joke. I broke into

a sweat, despite the chill. Perspiration poured off my forehead in such a torrent that I had to wipe it away with my sleeve, the filthy sleeve of a tunic worn for forty-odd days in a row. I could hear them breathing now, even above the sudden booming of my heart. Who, or what, was in the pit with us?

Surely no one could have entered through the grille above without waking us. The hatch was too small for a man to pass through; for that there was a trapdoor, which was locked with a heavy chain. The chain would have clanged and clattered. The hinge of the trapdoor (never used once since Eco and I passed through it) would have squealed and groaned. I suddenly had a horrible intuition of how the intruders had entered, and where they had come from . . .

Deep in the earth a flame leaped up, and a red glow illuminated the jagged fissure that had opened in the side of the pit. The earth itself had gaped up. The glow showed the two of them in silhouette – huge, hulking, monstrous, looming larger as they lumbered closer. They must have come straight from Hades.

Eco stirred and woke. 'Papa . . . what –?'

I touched his lips for silence, but the two intruders had already seen us. I saw them clearly as well, for the fiery glow had seeped into every corner of the pit. It glinted off the blood-encrusted swords they carried. It lit up their hideous faces. What do men look like who have killed hundreds of men without regret, who take pleasure in cruelty, who feed from the savage pleasure of

extinguishing the lives of others? Such men look like Eudamus and Birria, of course. The two of them stood over us, looking almost comic the way they leered and smirked and flared their nostrils. What a despicable fate, I thought, that these should be the last two faces I should ever see this side of Hades.

Or . . .

No, don't even think it! But why not? Hope until the last possible moment! Seize hope, wrap your arms tight around it, strangle it! The gods have been amused by your small life for fifty-odd years. Why should they give up on you now? Think: among your fellow mortals, who knows any more which ones are friends and which ones are foes? Maybe . . . just maybe . . . Eudamus and Birria are here not to slaughter you, but to save you, yes, to rescue you from this wretched place!

Gordianus! You have no weapons, but you still have your dignity. Stand up! Don't cower like a victim. Stiffen your spine. You are a Roman citizen. They are another man's slaves. Give them the barest nod of acknowledgment. Try not to look at their swords. Show no fear. Look them in the eye. Stare them down. Never mind that they tower over you, and the stench of garlic withers you like a leaf in autumn. Never mind that glint of metal you glimpse from the corner of your eye as they swing their swords aloft – don't flinch!

What is it like to be beheaded?

You shake like a leaf! You try to stop, and yet you shake and shake and shake until . . .

I opened my eyes to the soft light that passed for morning in the pit. Eco leaned over me, looking concerned, gently shaking me.

'Papa! Are you all right?'

'What?'

'First you seemed to be having a horrible nightmare. Then you seemed to relax. Then you let out such a horrible noise that I had to wake you.'

'A dream. Just another bad dream . . .'

'The one about Eudamus and Birria?'

'Yes.' I tried to swallow. My mouth was as dry as parchment. 'Do we have any water left from yesterday?'

'A little. Here.' He dipped his cupped hand into the bucket and put it to my lips.

I sucked it up greedily. 'Sometimes I wish the dream would come true, for better or worse. If only someone would come, to put an end to this misery one way or another.'

'Hush, Papa. You'll feel better after you've got up and stretched a bit.'

So began, by Eco's calculation, our forty-second day of captivity, the fifth day of the month of Martius, nine days before the Ides, in the year without consuls.

'What do you think is happening in Rome right now, Papa?' said Eco, with a wistful note in his voice.

I cleared my throat. 'Who knows? We heard all sorts of wild rumours on Mount Alba, before we were captured. Some made more sense than others.

I can't believe that Milo would kill himself, for instance. He's too stubborn. He may have caught himself in a trap that he can't get out of, like his namesake from Croton, but he'll see it through to the end, kicking and screaming. Of course, anything may have happened – by Hercules, forty-two days is an eternity!'

'Long enough for the Hebrew god to flood the whole world,' said Eco wryly.

'And long enough for the Roman state to be drowned in blood, I suppose. But if I had to place a wager, I'd bet on order rather than chaos, in the short run, anyway. We know that Pompey intended to get the Senate's authority to raise troops to quell the lawlessness in the city. I'd bet he got his way on that. Pompey at the head of an army is a pretty unstoppable force.'

Eco was sceptical. 'Good for conquering foreign troops in the field, maybe, but what about people throwing rocks in Roman alleys?'

'I can't see the Clodian rabble standing up to Pompey's troops.'

'Soldiers can't be everywhere at once. Little riots and fires can pop up anywhere at any time.'

'Yes, there could still be disorder, even with Pompey's troops in charge, but only on a minor scale. The Forum will be safe.'

'Safe enough for elections?'

I shook my head. 'This business with Milo and Clodius will have to be dealt with first. Can you imagine, if they held the elections and Milo were to win? It's still possible, I suppose, but the inevitable

result would be another round of riots, and that would mean open warfare with Pompey's troops in the streets — I can't see the Senate allowing that to happen.'

'Then who's running the state? Do you think they've appointed Pompey dictator?'

'Surely not, with Caesar up in Gaul at the head of his own army. Caesar might feel he had no choice but to march on Rome himself.' I quailed at the thought of Meto being swept into civil war.

'Surely not.'

'It sounds unthinkable, I know, but who would ever have imagined that the Senate House would be burned down in broad daylight?' I shook my head. We had already had this conversation a score of times. Sometimes Eco assumed the voice of reason, sometimes I was the insidious doubter. It was impossible not to speculate on what was happening in our absence, just as it was impossible to know.

After a long pause, Eco said quietly, 'That wasn't what I meant, you know.'

'What do you mean?'

'When I said, 'What do you think is happening in Rome, right now?' I didn't mean politics or elections or any of that. I meant —'

'I knew what you meant. I could tell from the tone of your voice.'

'Why did you change the subject, then? Don't you want to talk about it? About home . . .'

'Thinking about them makes me feel warm at first, comforted. But then something cold creeps

in, and makes a knot in my gut, as cold and hard as ice.'

'I know, Papa. I'm frightened for them too.'

'We've been gone so very long now. They must think we're dead. Can you imagine Bethesda grieving? I can hardly bear it.'

'I know what you mean. I imagine Menenia weeping, and it tears my heart. Women grieving – remember Fulvia and Clodia, that night we saw Clodius's body? He was really quite an awful fellow, wasn't he, Papa?'

I shrugged. 'It all depends whom you ask. He was ruthless to his enemies, that's for sure. He caused more than his share of suffering in this world. But he also gave a great deal of hope and some real power to a great many people who had neither, not to mention the guarantee of enough bread in their bellies. To those people he's a hero.'

'But still a vain, power-mad, greedy man. You can see that just by looking at the houses he built.'

'I suppose.'

'And yet, when he died, his sister wept. And Fulvia – do you remember the way she tried to show nothing when we were in the room? But afterwards, in front of that crowd, the way she shrieked and wailed. I thought it was an act at the time, but now I think she was truly suffering, lost, hopeless. I think of Menenia and Bethesda, grieving for us, frightened of the future, and I think of Clodia and Fulvia, and I feel a great sadness for them all.' He wrinkled his brow and turned his eyes upward to the patches of sunlight that

showed through the bars and the roof. 'But we're still not talking about the real worry, are we? We're talking about them grieving for us. What I really meant is —'

'What if something has happened to them?'

'Yes.'

I sighed. 'It all comes back to Pompey. He promised he would see that they were kept safe while we were gone. Pompey is a man of his word.'

'But we've been gone far longer than he could have expected. He probably thinks we're dead, too.'

'Yes, probably. If he thinks about us at all.'

'And what if Pompey isn't in control of the city? What if he's been assassinated? Or what if something totally mad has happened, a civil war with Caesar, and Pompey's gone off to Spain to rally his army there?'

'We have no way of knowing, Eco. No way of knowing . . .' I put my face in my hands.

The stable door rattled and opened. Eco took a deep breath.

The basket for bread was raised and lowered, along with a bucket of fresh water.

'What's wrong with that one?'

'My father, you mean. Why can't you say, 'What's wrong with your father?' ' Eco sounded genuinely angry. I kept my head lowered and clutched myself. Despair was what I felt; it was simple enough to feign distress.

'All right, what's wrong with your father?'

'He's not feeling well.'

'Seems to be eating the same.'

'He's hardly eating at all.'

'Then what happened to all the bread I brought yesterday? Did you eat it all yourself? Taking food from your sick father's mouth?'

'I ate what I needed. The rats took the rest of it last night, if you have to know.'

The man grunted. 'So, do you need the bucket emptied again today?'

'No.'

'Are you sure?'

'Just go away now, if you don't mind. I think you're only making my father feel worse.'

'Why don't you let me empty it anyway? Get rid of the smell for you.'

'Just go away!'

Eco bent over me, much as he had bent over me when he woke me from my dream that morning. There was a long pause, then footsteps retreated and the door swung open and shut. I strained to listen and thought I could hear a murmur of discussion outside the stable.

We had not been able to catch another rat that day, after all.

The next day, however, Fortune smiled on us, and not on a certain especially plump, especially curious and (most important for us) especially slow fellow-inhabitant of the pit. This was good, since our keeper insisted on emptying the bucket that afternoon. Eco assured me that his face showed great displeasure at seeing so much blood amid the urine.

403

Once again there was a discussion outside the stable. The voices were raised noticeably louder than before, and both carried a distinct tone of recrimination. The keeper's seldom-seen companion came in and had a look at me himself. 'Where do you hurt?' he asked gruffly.

I grunted.

'His belly, you fool,' said Eco, managing to sound as if he were both angry and anxious and trying hard to show neither.

Our keepers withdrew in silence, but there was another heated discussion outside the door, receding into the unseen, unknown distance.

'Since we'll be getting out of here soon . . .' I began.

Why not be madly optimistic? It was the forty-fourth day of our captivity, seven days before the Ides of Martius, the fourth day of my feigned malady. Eco had again succeeded in capturing, killing and bleeding a rat. 'His craving for a bit of bread outweighed his better judgment,' to quote the solemn eulogy which Eco delivered as we buried the creature in a corner out of sight, and hopefully out of smell.

'Yes?' prompted Eco.

'Since we'll soon be out of here, I think we should try to figure out as best we can who had a reason to put us here.'

'Perhaps we'll be able to find out from our keepers.'

'If all goes well, either we will be running from our keepers or they will be running from us. I doubt that there will be much conversation. Anyway, going over the known facts of our dilemma will give us something to puzzle over for an hour or two.'

'Again?'

'Humour me. Unless you have an appointment to be somewhere at a certain time? I thought not. Well then, what did we discover on the Appian Way? Or more to the point, what did we not discover?'

'That's a question fit to give Aristotle a headache, Papa! You might as well ask me to prove a negative.'

'You're right. Step by step, then. If we believe the account of the priestess Felicia, Milo and Clodius met on the Appian Way by accident. There was no ambush. The two parties passed without incident until they were nearly clear of each other. Clodius uttered a parting insult to Birria. Birria, on impulse, turned and hurled his spear at Clodius. It was no more premeditated than a brawl in a tavern.'

'But it's possible, Papa, that Birria intended to throw the spear all along, on his master's orders. Perhaps Birria hurled an insult at Clodius first and Felicia didn't hear it; Clodius responded and Birria used that as a pretext to begin the attack. It could have been premeditated, or perhaps Milo issued an order to Birria on the spur of the moment, when the two parties met. Milo had the superior force.

Perhaps he saw his chance to kill Clodius and seized it.'

'A good point, Eco. At any rate, we've seen no evidence whatsoever that Clodius planned or instigated the skirmish in any way, except by hurling an insult at Birria. The conflict probably occurred spontaneously, or possibly at Milo's instigation. What ensues? Clodius's outnumbered men are quickly overwhelmed. Some are killed on the spot, others flee into the woods. The wounded Clodius, without his horse and cut off from his villa by Milo's entourage, is assisted by some five or six of his men downhill towards Bovillae. He takes refuge at the inn, where the innkeeper knows and likes him.'

I rubbed my hands together to warm them. The pit seemed especially dank that day. 'Milo's men do not follow immediately. Felicia says they ran about like hounds who'd lost a scent, until Milo came up. He was furious at first, especially at Birria.'

'Because Birria had attacked Clodius on his own – or because he had failed to finish the job?' said Eco.

'I suspect the first. Once Milo calmed down he held a sort of conference, and only then did he dispatch Eudamus and Birria and several others to pursue Clodius. This seems highly significant to me; had Milo planned all along to assassinate Clodius, I think his men would have been prepared to pursue Clodius at once and would have done so, especially since he was wounded and moving slowly on foot. Why did they wait? I think it must be that they

needed instructions from their master, who was completely taken aback by what had happened. Why did he upbraid Birria? Because the gladiator had acted rashly and stupidly and without his consent. True, Milo might have been mad at his men for failing to make a clean killing of Clodius, but I favour the idea that the incident was spontaneous and unplanned, and that when Clodius made off on foot, no one was quite sure what to do next.'

'But they did eventually pursue him.'

'Yes, because Milo made a decision to finish what his men had already started, without his consent. Which was more dangerous to him, Clodius wounded, or Clodius dead? Wounded, Clodius could return to Rome, rally his forces, bring legal proceedings against Milo for attempted murder, end Milo's bid for the consulship. If Clodius was dead, Milo would be liable for murder, but at least Clodius's followers might be paralysed with confusion, and Clodius himself wouldn't be around to accuse him. Either way, Milo was facing the ruin of everything he'd worked for. That's another reason I can't believe that the incident was premeditated. To have murdered Clodius by poison or stealth would have been one thing, but to have done so in such a clumsy fashion could only hurt Milo in the end. I wonder if he thought of his namesake Milo of Croton in the forest, trying to split that giant log and getting his hands hopelessly trapped? Did he hear the howling of hungry wolves as he paced there on the Appian Way, fretting over what to do next? It should have been an occasion of

triumph for Milo – the end of Clodius, once and for all, within his grasp – but I think it must have been a very miserable moment for him.'

'But he finally decided to send his men after Clodius,' said Eco.

'Once you've wounded a dangerous beast, it's always best to kill it. No doubt it's what Milo of Croton would have done.'

'So he dispatched his men, then waited for news. Rather cowardly of him, not to join the battle himself.'

'If you asked him, I imagine he'd say he hung back to stand guard over his wife and household.'

Eco snorted derisively, then his face became shadowed. I had said the words sarcastically, but as soon as they were out of my mouth, it was hard not to think of our own loved ones and how vulnerable they were without us.

'Anyway,' I said, 'not too much later, along comes Senator Tedius and his daughter in their litter, with their own retinue of household slaves and bodyguards. Tedius and Milo recognize one another. Milo tells an outright lie – that he was set upon by bandits – and advises Tedius to turn back. The stubborn old senator instead presses on, despite some demurral on the part of his pious daughter.

'Meanwhile, down in Bovillae, the battle is joined. The innkeeper's wife – whose evidence we have secondhand from her sister – actually sees Eudamus and Birria kill one of Clodius's men on their approach to the inn. There's a terrific assault which destroys all the shutters and doors on the

lower floor. The innkeeper is killed, along with Clodius's defenders. Clodius somehow ends up out in the road. We presume that Eudamus and Birria take his gold ring as a trophy, and to deliver proof of his death to their master. And then, for some reason, Eudamus and Birria and their men vanish, for when Tedius arrives a little later, the battle is over and the victors are gone. Tedius finds the inn a shambles. He sees blood and bodies scattered all about, including that of Clodius. The innkeeper's wife emerges from hiding on the upper floor. She looks out the window to see Tedius and his daughter leaning over Clodius. She goes downstairs, discovers her dead husband and loses her senses.

'Tedius, despite his dislike of the man and his politics, does the honourable thing and loads Clodius into his litter, then sends the body on to Rome. He still thinks all the killing is the work of bandits, and decides to return to Aricia on foot. He turns about and trudges up the hill. While he stops to rest close to the House of the Vestals, Eudamus and Birria appear on the road and pass him, returning to Milo. How was it that he didn't see them before? Eudamus and Birria have prisoners. Felicia, peering out from the shrine of the Good Goddess, also sees these prisoners. Who are they? Not any of Clodius's men; the ones who fled with Clodius were all killed, and Fulvia told me that none of her husband's men were unaccounted for. So where did Eudamus and Birria come from and who were their prisoners?

'The gladiators return to Milo and deliver Clodius's ring, proof that he's dead. Milo then hands it over to Fausta, who proceeds down the road to make her offering at the House of the Vestals. But somehow Sextus Tedius never sees her. And when Tedius finishes his rest and moves on, by the time he reaches the shrine of the Good Goddess, Milo and all his company are gone.

'We know that Milo and the gladiators headed for the villa, where they killed the foreman and Halicor the tutor when they weren't able to find young Publius Clodius. Why was Milo seeking the boy? Is he really so spiteful and bloodthirsty that he wanted to murder Clodius's son? Or did he intend to somehow use the boy as a hostage? And how did he know that young Publius was staying at the villa?

'These are the questions, then, for which we have no answers.' I picked up Eco's marking stick and for each question scraped a numeral in the wall.

'One: Where were Eudamus and Birria when Sextus Tedius arrived at the inn?

'Two: Who were the prisoners Eudamus and Birria herded up the road?

'Three: How did Fausta return down the road to make her offering at the House of the Vestals without passing Sextus Tedius?

'Four: When Milo forced his way into Clodius's villa, he demanded of Halicor and the foreman, 'Where is Publius Clodius?' – but how did he know the boy was at the villa, and what did he intend to do with him?'

I stood back and studied the marks – I, II, III, IV.

They elucidated nothing. The longer I looked at them, the more they began to appear to be only an assemblage of upright and slanted lines signifying nothing, not even the numbers in my head. They were random lines etched by an idiot. For one brief, shuddering instant I thought I must truly have gone mad. The captivity, the darkness, the stench, the nightmares and the rats all coalesced like a black fog around my head. Nothing made sense; nothing was real. The whole drama of the murder on the Appian Way was only an elaborate fantasy I had contrived to amuse myself, a madman's epic. Milo and Clodius were figments of my imagination. Nothing existed but the pit.

'Papa? Are you all right?'

'What?'

'Your hand's shaking. You dropped the stick.' Eco stooped and retrieved it for me.

His voice returned me to the moment. I clutched the stick in my hand, more firmly than I needed to. I reached out and slowly scraped another numeral into the wall, keeping my hand and my voice as steady as I could. 'And now the more immediate questions, which surely must be related in some way to the first four.

'Five: Who waylaid us upon our return to Rome? We can be sure, I think, that they were not common kidnappers, looking for a ransom. They'd have wanted me to write something on a scrap of parchment, to prove I was alive. And they'd have figured out by now that there's no ransom to be had. We'd already be dead.' The numerals on

the wall began to lose their meaning again and I looked away, at the dank mound where Eco had buried the newest rat that morning. 'Unless we're dead already.'

'Of course they're not common kidnappers,' Eco said, pretending not to hear my muttering. 'They acted for someone who didn't like what we were up to on the Appian Way.'

'More precisely, someone who was afraid of the information we might be bringing back to Rome. Therefore, six: To whom did we make ourselves dangerous with our investigation on the Appian Way?'

'But isn't it obvious, Papa? Milo, of course. We know he lied outrageously at Caelius's contio, with that tale about an ambush, and we know how to prove it. It's as you said to Felicia when you advised her to fly south – Milo is in a desperate situation, willing to commit desperate acts.'

'Which leads us to the final question.' I scraped the numeral VII into the wall. 'Why were we kidnapped, not killed? If Milo – or whoever – merely wanted to dispose of us, why did his henchmen not murder us and steal our valuables, to make the incident look like another robbery by nameless bandits by the Monument of Basilius? If he wanted to ascertain what we had uncovered first, why were we not questioned, and then killed? Why did Milo not finish us off, as he finished off Clodius? Does he have some future use for us? I can't imagine what. It makes me wonder whether it was Milo who put us here after all.'

'Who else? The only other person you kept asking questions about was —'

'Marc Antony,' I said.

The stable door rattled open.

'Perhaps this is the day we'll find out,' whispered Eco. I dropped to the floor of the pit, hugging myself.

The inspection of the bloody urine proceeded like a ritual, with our keepers — both of them had come in together — peering into the bucket like augurs studying some poor chicken's entrails.

'Your father doesn't look well,' said the one who usually stayed outside.

'What, have you just figured that out?' Eco sounded outraged, frightened, frustrated. There was a quaver in his voice. Some of this was acting, but I could tell that the quaver came not from desperation, but from its opposite, a sudden exhilaration so acute it made him tremble like the plucked string of an instrument. Had the moment come at last? Yes! I sensed it, too. A frightful, wonderful rage welled up inside us both, a joyous fury that had been suppressed for long days in the dark but finally, finally, at that very instant, was ready to be released.

'Your father had better come with us,' said the one who usually stayed outside. He bent to unlock the chain that held the trapdoor shut. The two of them pulled up on the heavy iron door and let it drop back onto the grille with a clang.

The door of the cage was open.

'I don't think he can stand.' Eco's voice

413

broke like a boy's as he fussed over me, acting helpless.

'How in Hades are we going to get him out?' complained our usual keeper.

'Get your father onto his feet somehow,' said the other. 'That's it. Get him to raise his arms. If he can't raise them himself, raise them for him! By Hercules, is the fellow still alive or not? There, now we'll each grab a forearm. Be careful leaning over, you fool!'

The greatest mistake a general can make, as Caesar and Pompey would agree, is to underestimate the strength of your enemy. I had convinced them that I was weak, in pain and very ill. They took hold of my forearms to haul me up, expecting a frail body that offered no resistance. The instant before they heaved together, I pulled downward with all my strength. Eco joined in, jumping up to grab their arms above the elbows.

All could have been lost in that instant. They could have kept their balance and pulled themselves free, leaving me to fall onto my backside, looking like an utter fool. The door would have hurriedly clanged shut, our keepers would have cursed us and then laughed at us, and we would have been left alone in the pit once more, to follow the same maddening thoughts in the same dogged circles, to sleep amid rats, to despair for our loved ones, to lie in anguish and wonder how much longer we could bear it.

But that was not what happened.

First, their heads collided with a loud knock. The sound had a lower pitch than two stones struck

together, but higher than two hollow gourds. It was one of the sweetest sounds I ever heard.

What followed happened very quickly.

One of them, the one who usually stayed outside, tumbled headfirst into the pit. I fell upon him at once. Eco's marking stick was still in my hand. In the past few days we had managed to sharpen it to a fine point by whetting it against some of the stones in the pit. I stabbed him at least once before I realized there was no need. The fall had broken his neck.

I turned and saw that I was alone with his lifeless body in the pit. Eco had already scrambled up and out. I heard the sound of a struggle taking place in the stable above.

I put the makeshift dagger between my teeth, tasting blood, and leaped for the opening. I grabbed one of the iron bars and pulled myself up. We had practised this movement every day, leaping and pulling ourselves up, strengthening our arms. Still, I thought that pulling myself through the opening would be a greater challenge than it was. Instead I seemed almost to fly upward, as if an unseen hand pushed me from below. Cold fury propelled me, and the certain knowledge that Fortune had turned in our direction.

Eco and the keeper were rolling on the floor, thrashing at each other. Eco was by far the smaller of the two, but he was driven by the same fury that drove me, and he was managing to hold his own. I ran towards them, raising the crude wooden dagger. There was already a patch of blood on the

man's forehead. There was more blood, and a loud scream, when I brought the dagger down on his neck. He escaped from Eco's clutches and ran for the door, blood spurting between the fingers that clutched his neck.

We followed him outside, dazed by the full light of day. I girded myself for more fighting, but there was no one to be seen. We were alone on a patch of weedy ground in front of a disused stable, surrounded by trees and overgrown farmland.

'The other one is still in the pit!' said Eco. He ran back inside, lifted the trapdoor single-handed and dropped it shut with a great clang. 'Ha! See how you like that! Now you'll tell us where we are and who you work for, you son of a sow!'

I followed Eco inside, still exhilarated but suddenly weary. 'Come, Eco. We'd better hurry. Who knows where the other one went, or if he has more friends close by? We're not out of danger yet.'

'But, Papa —'

'Eco, the fellow is dead.'

'No!' Eco peered down into the dim pit. The man had landed in a convoluted heap that no living person could contrive. Still, Eco was unconvinced until a large rat went scurrying over the fellow's head.

'Papa, you killed him?'

'No. The fall broke his neck. It happened in the blink of an eye.'

'Too bad. He should have suffered!'

I shook my head, unable to agree. The fellow had never shown us any cruelty, as many men

would have, given such power over others. He had been our servant, in fact, bringing us food and disposing of our wastes. Our argument was not with him.

The fact that I was able to think so calmly was a dangerous sign. The cold fury had begun to leak out of me. The bloody stick in my hand revolted me. The moment of escape towards which all had been building had come and passed. If more adversaries were to arrive, they would find me with my edge for violence blunted. The truly dangerous part of our escape was just beginning.

# XXIV

We were alone and friendless in unknown territory. We had no money. We did have a day's ration of bread – the food that our keepers had brought for us that morning.

We were somewhere in the countryside. That was unfortunate. In a city, we could have stolen what we needed – new clothes to replace our filthy rags, enough small coins to visit the local baths and a barber to make ourselves look respectable – and then proceeded to ask questions of strangers and move about without attracting undue notice. In a city, we might have found someone we knew, or who knew a mutual friend, and so might agree to loan us money or arrange for our return to Rome. But the countryside was another matter. Walking on country roads, we could not help but be conspicuous. Enemies searching for us would have a great advantage. Given our wretched appearance,

strangers might take us for runaway slaves, despite our citizen's rings. It is easier to skulk through a crowded alley than across an empty field.

Where were we? From the surrounding hills and farms, there was no way to tell. I could determine directions by the sun, but was Rome north, south, east or west? Near or far? There was no way to begin the journey home except to begin walking, keeping out of sight as much as possible. I tried to keep track of our route, so that we could find our way back later, but I was dazed and exhausted and every field looked the same.

We slept that night under the open sky. We were cold, and snuggled together for warmth, and I woke before dawn with a gnawing in my belly and my feet like ice. But for the first night in many nights I did not dream of Eudamus and Birria, and the sight of the open sky above when I opened my eyes was very sweet indeed.

We came upon a paved road that was clearly a major highway, but which? All roads lead to Rome, but only if you go in the right direction.

'North or south?' I said.

Eco scrutinized the road for a long moment. 'South.'

'I agree. Do you think we might be like dogs, and find our way home purely by instinct?'

'No,' he said bluntly. He was beginning to feel hungry. So was I.

We proceeded south, avoiding other travellers as best we could.

<p style="text-align:center">★    ★    ★</p>

'When Fortune smiles, the Fates may yet play a joke.' So goes the old Etruscan aphorism.

Stomachs growling, feet aching, we walked for hour after hour, thinking that sooner or later the road must lead to some place where we could at least determine where we were. We came to a region where the road traversed a series of low, rolling hills, so that we were able to see, intermittently, what was coming our way a considerable distance ahead. We first saw the approaching entourage three hilltops away, then two. Someone in their party had probably seen us first, since there were so many of them and some of them had the higher vantage point of riding on horseback. It would almost be more suspicious to attempt to hide beside the road than to simply pass by with heads lowered. They could hardly be a search party, since they were coming towards us, and not from behind. Still . . .

We reached the next hilltop. There they were, cresting the hill just opposite us, with a small valley between.

'If any of them should question us,' I said to Eco, 'allow them no liberties. We are citizens, after all. We have every right to be on this road . . . wherever it is. And –'

'Papa . . .'

'And if they do speak first, then we might as well ask how close the next town is, and what it's call –'

'Papa!'

'What is it, Eco?'

'Can you not see with your own eyes?'

I stopped and stared at the approaching group of

men. They looked like serious travellers on serious business, sober-faced and dusty from hard riding. Some were obviously bodyguards. Others . . .

'By Jupiter, Eco! Can it be?'

Eco nodded and raised his hand in a gesture of greeting. After a final moment of disbelief, I did the same. Even so, the riders hardly glanced at us. No doubt they took us for a pair of bearded derelicts. It was Tiro who gave a start, muttered an exclamation of surprise and reached for his old master's sleeve. The entourage came to a halt.

'By all the gods!' Cicero leaned forwards and peered at me as if I were some freakish curiosity being shown off in the arena. 'Can it be Gordianus, beneath all that hair and filth? And Eco?'

'You're alive! Both of you, alive!' Tiro's voice caught in his throat. He leaped from his mount and rushed to embrace us both, weeping with joy.

Cicero managed to restrain any such feelings and remained on his horse. He caught our scent and made a face. He stared at me and slowly shook his head. 'Gordianus, you look frightful! What on earth have you been up to?'

'Your disappearance has been much talked about in Rome,' said Cicero that night, as we dined in a private room at an inn outside the town of Ariminum.

'I'm surprised anyone noticed I was gone.'

'Oh, quite the contrary. You're better known than you might think. There's been no end of speculation. Even vendors in the fish markets talk

about the inexplicable disappearance of the Finder and his son; so my slaves tell me, anyway. Of course, Rome has been full of all sorts of strange happenings and curious rumours in the last month. Your vanishing was just one more.'

'But my family is well?' I had already asked this question more than once.

Tiro patiently reassured me. 'Quite well. Just before we left Rome, I paid a visit to see if there was any news of you. They were all in good health – your wife and daughter, your son's wife and children. They were quite worried about the two of you, of course . . .'

Eco shook his head. 'We should be hurrying back to Rome right now, Papa, instead of sitting here stuffing our faces!'

'Nonsense,' said Cicero. He gestured to a slave to refill my cup of watered wine and bring more food. 'I think you have no idea just how wretched you both looked when I came upon you this afternoon. Fortunately, the town of Ariminum has good baths, so we were able to get you decently washed and barbered. And this inn has decent food, so hopefully we can begin to fatten you up a bit, as well. You've almost begun to look like human beings again. As for the idea that you should go riding breakneck back to Rome, I advise against it. You need rest and recuperation, good food, country air and sunshine, and above all the safety of travelling in an armed company. Oh no, I insist that you stay with me, at least until we reach Ravenna tomorrow.'

Cicero had explained that he was on a journey to see Julius Caesar at the commander's winter head-quarters in Ravenna. I had not yet discovered why. He and Tiro had left Rome four days previously – a bit of information which Eco had seized upon with a good deal of gloating, citing it as proof that his memory of a four-day journey at the beginning of our captivity was accurate. Indeed, his reckoning of the days and my calculation of the date proved to be exactly right: it was six days before the Ides of March, seventy-two days since the death of Publius Clodius. We had been held prisoners for forty-four days somewhere in the vicinity of Ariminum, where the northernmost spur of the Flaminian Way ends and the newer Popillian Way continues northward towards Ravenna.

'What else are they talking about in Rome?' I said. 'The vendors in the fish markets, I mean. I take that as a good sign, that the markets are open.'

'Yes, things have calmed down considerably in Rome since your . . . misfortune. The Senate authorized Pompey to raise troops to maintain order, and they've done a reasonably good job. There have been some clashes between soldiers and civilians, and a few minor incidents of arson, but for the most part order has been restored.'

'And elections?'

Cicero winced. Dyspepsia, or politics? 'The question of elections became increasingly . . . pro-blematic. Untenable, ultimately. Can you imagine, thirteen interrexes since Lepidus, and no elections? That's over now. Only a few days before Tiro and I

left Rome, the Senate voted to make Pompey sole consul for the rest of the year.' His voice trailed away to a dry whisper. He coughed and reached for his cup of wine. The cancellation of the consular elections had to signify a great personal and political defeat for him. What would become of his champion Milo now? Would the electoral process ever return to normal?

Cicero cleared his throat and went on. 'There has been a great deal of wrangling and manoeuvring in the Senate, as you can imagine.' He made this comment without his usual relish. Cicero had made much of my wretched appearance, but I began to see that he looked rather tired and drawn himself. 'First the Clodians tried to force Milo to hand over his slaves for questioning. Milo forestalled them there, eh, Tiro? He made the slaves in question freedmen ahead of time so that even the Senate couldn't round them up and torture them for evidence. We countered with a demand that Fulvia deliver Clodius's slaves for a bit of torture and interrogation. She and her family didn't care very much for that idea.' Cicero smiled wanly at this minor triumph. 'Since Pompey became consul, the Clodians have been trying to force a special inquest into Clodius's death. A show trial with Milo being crucified like a slave is what they'd like, something overblown and dramatic. Then they'll claim that Milo's offence was so spectacular that the Senate had to pass a special law just to deal with it. They proposed such an inquest, and we countered by attaching additional legislation which specifically

condemned the burning of the Senate House and the attack on the house of the interrex Lepidus. That way, all three incidents would have been condemned equally in the eyes of the law, and all the malefactors would have been liable for equal penalties. Oh, the Clodians don't like the sound of that! No, no, no! They expect someone to be destroyed for the death of their precious leader, but they think they can burn down half the Forum and not pay for the crime! Well, we shall see, we shall see . . .' Cicero threw back his head and narrowed his eyes. It occurred to me that he had had too much to drink. I had never, ever before seen Cicero inebriated.

He wrinkled his nose. 'Meanwhile, Pompey has his own ideas of how to straighten things out. He's come up with a package of new laws; these will speed up the courts and put down sedition, he says. Pompey's idea of law and order is to make it easier to convict a man and to inflict harsher penalties on him, never mind whether he's guilty or not! Some of his so-called reforms are positively ludicrous. Shorter trials, he says; that's the answer. We can't afford the luxury of letting an orator take the time he needs to build an irrefutable argument. No more of this nonsense of the prosecution and defence each taking a whole day to deliver their speeches! Instead, the prosecution will be allowed two hours, and the defence will be allowed three hours. I suppose if an advocate is in the middle of a speech when the time runs out, they'll clamp his jaw shut. And witnesses! Witnesses will come first, not last,

before the speeches instead of after. That makes the witnesses the main focus of the trial, and the speeches a mere addendum! Pompey's never been much of an orator himself. He distrusts oratory, so he wants to demote it, dismiss it. But to give such prominence to witnesses is pure folly – anyone with sense knows that most witnesses are deluded, or unreliable, or bribed. And no character witnesses! Pompey has forbidden character witnesses. Never mind that a man can arrange for half the Senate to speak up for his good character, such testimony is now irrelevant. Juries will now be drawn from a list of eligible names hand-picked by Pompey himself. Hand-picked by a single man, not even by two, because we have only one consul, and that one not even elected by the citizens!'

Tiro laid a restraining hand on his old master's elbow, but Cicero shook it off. 'I know what I'm saying. And I'm not drunk. I'm just tired, very tired. Travelling disagrees with me. Besides, Gordianus appreciates candour. Don't you, Gordianus? Ah, but I forget, you're one of Pompey's men now, aren't you?'

'What do you mean?'

'One could hardly help but notice all those guards keeping watch at your house for the last month. They do come from Pompey, don't they?'

'Perhaps,' I said, uneasy at Cicero's scrutiny but for the most part glad to learn that Pompey had kept his word. 'It doesn't mean I'm Pompey's man.'

Cicero stared into his cup and blinked. 'Gordianus, I have never pretended to understand your

desultory allegiances. For all I know, you're spying on Pompey and not for him, and somehow managed to talk him into guarding your family while you do it.'

'You were talking about Pompey's reforms,' I said, wanting to change the subject.

Cicero laughed aloud. How much wine had he drunk? 'So I was. You know, my very favourite is the Great One's brilliant new innovation for rooting out bribery. If a man's convicted of bribery, he can arrange for a pardon, provided he can turn around and convict two other men of bribery! Soon everyone in Rome will be standing in a circle pointing the finger of blame at the man next to him. That's one way to keep everyone busy while the Republic slips away from us. It's ludicrous, it makes a mockery of the law. But Pompey's never understood the law, never had any real respect for it, any more than he respects oratory. He respects institutions, like the Senate, but only in some vague, abstract, sentimental way. He has no regard for the law at all. He doesn't see how beautiful it is, how awesome, how it circles and binds us all together, like a golden thread. He rips his way through it like a man getting rid of cobwebs. He has the vulgar, pragmatic mind of an autocrat.'

Cicero pressed his stomach and winced. 'Thank the gods that Caelius is a tribune this year and has the power to veto any legislation that infringes on individual rights. Caelius has warned Pompey that he'll use his veto on the new laws. Do you know what Pompey replied? He said, quite calmly, 'Do as

427

you must, but I shall do whatever is necessary to defend the state.' So typical! Why doesn't he just pull out a sword and brandish it in Caelius's face? In the end there'll be a compromise, of course; there always is. We shall have to let Pompey have his way, or else he'll complain that he doesn't have enough power to keep order and demand even more. And where will that lead?' Cicero made an elabourate shrug of disgust. 'Ah, but Gordianus, you've hardly spoken at all about your travails.'

'You've hardly asked.'

'How awful for you! Kidnapped, trundled off to some place far from Rome, kept in a pit. Who could have perpetrated such an atrocity?'

'I have wondered about that a great deal. I had much time to consider it.'

'I'm sure you did! And did you come to any conclusions?' Did he look at me shrewdly, or had his eyelids simply grown heavy from fatigue and too much drink?

'Not yet.'

'Ah, Gordianus, always the one to bide his time, sift every shred of evidence, seek for further revelations, postpone the final judgment. You'd have made a terrible advocate. You don't have the gift for making things up. So you have no idea who kidnapped you, or why?'

'We never properly saw our captors, and they never gave us any clue about who employed them, or why we were kept alive, for that matter.'

'Ah, a mystery, then! But here you are, free again at last and safe.'

'Yes, safe. But of course it matters to me a great deal to know who treated my son and myself with such contempt. We're both alive and well –'

'Amazingly well, considering!'

'But it might easily have been otherwise. If one of us had been wounded in the attack, or fallen ill in that terrible place . . .'

Cicero nodded vaguely. Tiro shuddered.

'But I will discover who was behind it. I suppose the prudent course, now, would be to retrace our steps to find the stable where we were kept. But I doubt we could find it again. What do you think, Eco?'

'I think we were trying too hard not to be seen to memorize an unfamiliar landscape. Besides, Papa, a disused stable on a derelict piece of farmland might belong to anyone. Finding the place wouldn't necessarily lead us to the men who captured us. They'll be long gone.'

'We might make the search anyway,' I said. 'We would need bodyguards, of course.' I turned back to Cicero, who looked uneasy for an instant and then smiled blandly.

'I would love to accommodate you, of course, Gordianus, but I really have no men to spare. I probably haven't enough protection as it is – your example has illustrated all too well the lamentable danger of the roads in these dreadful days.'

'You might turn aside from your own journey for a day or two, Cicero. Join with us to search for that stable and the men who kept us.'

'Impossible, Gordianus. My own mission is too

important and cannot wait. Tomorrow I press on to Ravenna.'

'Ah, yes, your mission, Cicero. What is it you're seeking from Julius Caesar? Or is it a secret of state?'

'There's no secret. It's Marcus Caelius again. Such a busy tribune! Caesar wants to be able to run for consul next year, but that's not possible so long as he's commanding his troops and can't come to the city. So his supporters have fashioned a special exemption allowing Caesar to run for consul in absentia. It would set a bad precedent, of course, but if Pompey can be made sole consul, Caesar's supporters think it's only fair that he should be able to run while he's still up in Gaul. It becomes an issue of preserving the peace – I mean to say, the balance – between the Great One and Caesar. But Caelius has threatened to block the special exemption, just as he's threatened to block Pompey's reforms.'

'And your part, Cicero?'

He shrugged. 'Certain parties have prevailed upon me to use my influence with Caelius to dissuade him from baiting Caesar. Caelius is willing to back down, but both he and I would like to make sure we have a complete understanding of Caesar's goals and attitudes. So I'm headed for Ravenna to have a friendly discussion with Caesar. To clear the air, so to speak.'

'Wheels within wheels,' muttered Eco.

'Better than one great wheel driving the whole engine of the world, which is what some people would like to see,' said Cicero. 'But I'm pressed for

time. Caesar will be leaving Ravenna any day now, heading back into the field. There are rumours of a new uprising led by some Gaul with a typically unpronounceable name. What is it, Tiro?'

'Vercingetorix,' said Tiro crisply. He was clearly not inebriated.

'Whatever,' agreed Cicero. 'So you see, I have no time to go off looking for – what did you call it, Eco? 'A disused stable in a derelict field.' And neither should you, Gordianus. Don't tempt the Fates. You're safe in my company. I'll provide all your needs. Accompany me to Ravenna tomorrow, and then accompany me back to Rome.'

'We should head back to Rome at once,' said Eco glumly. 'For Bethesda and Menenia to suffer even one more day than they should, not knowing what's become of us –'

'Ah, but don't you have a brother who's likely to be with Caesar in Ravenna?' said Cicero. 'Yes, your son, Gordianus – the one called Meto. Your family will have written to him about your disappearance, I'm sure. He'll be as distraught as they are. This is your chance to see him before he heads back north with Caesar. You see, you must come with me to Ravenna. But now, I think it's time for everyone to retire. You look weary, Gordianus, and Eco is yawning. Tonight, you'll have the best accommodations our host has to offer, with a soft bed in a private room. I arranged it for you myself. I predict that you will sleep like stones.'

And we did.

# XXV

Caesar's residence in Ravenna was a large villa on the outskirts of the city, with numerous tents, stables and makeshift buildings set up around it. Like all military camps, it resembled a small city, where the needs of a vigorous, mostly young male population with strong appetites could be accommodated on a daily basis. One invariably encounters three things in such places: the sight of prostitutes, the constant smell of cooking, and the sounds of the crudest language imaginable.

We arrived shortly after midday. Cicero and Tiro went to seek an audience with Caesar. Eco and I went in search of Meto. He was not hard to find. A foot soldier pointed the way to a tent filled with young officers. As we stepped inside, there was a sudden hush which had nothing to do with us, followed by a rattling noise, then an outburst of raucous laughter and cursing. They were playing dice.

The four dice being used were an old-fashioned set made of bones, pointed at two ends with the numerals painted on the four flat sides. A young man stepped out of the crowd and leaned forwards to scoop them up, and I saw with a catch in my throat that it was Meto.

Since he had begun his career with Caesar, we had seen each other only a few times a year at most, and never for long enough. Each time I saw my younger son I braced myself for an unpleasant surprise – a limp, a digit missing, a fresh scar across his face to add to the faded one he received in his first battle. So far he had kept himself intact, if not unmarked. Each time I saw him I was struck anew by how young he still looked. He was twenty-six now, very much a man by every measure, with a few grey hairs at his temples already and a ruggedness to his features that comes from years of hot sun and cold wind, but when he smiled as he scooped up the dice I could not help but see the child I had redeemed from slavery and adopted twenty years ago. He had always been a good-natured boy, affectionate, laughing, mischievous but even-tempered. It was hard to imagine him killing strangers for a living.

Meto became a soldier at the age of sixteen when he ran off to fight for Catilina. In the battle of Pistoria he gained the scar across his face that he was still so proud of. I had thought – hoped – that would be the end of a youthful folly, but Meto still sought the thing he had found with Catilina. He found it again in Caesar. And Caesar, fortunately,

had found Meto, discovering his talent for words and taking him into his private service as a sort of literary adjutant. (Caesar the politician was always busy writing and publishing the memoirs of Caesar the general, and commanded his own private troop of wordsmiths.) In recent years Meto had also found service as a translator, having shown an aptitude for learning the Gaulish dialects. In addition to these sedentary pursuits, he still saw plenty of battle and danger, often at the side of the great general himself. I could never stop worrying about him.

He had not yet seen us across the crowded tent. As he rattled the four dice in a cup, he narrowed his eyes and seemed to mutter an invocation – to a god, to a lover? Who were his gods these days? Who were his lovers? We never talked of such things any more. He gave the cup a final shake and let fly the dice.

A hush, the rattle of bones, then more laughter and curses. Meto himself was loudest of all, raising his arms triumphantly in the air as he laughingly announced, 'The Venus Throw! One of each number – the Venus Throw beats all! Pay up, pay up!' The long sleeves of his tunic slid down his upraised arms and I noticed a new scar, red and gnarled, which cut across the biceps of his left arm. It was ugly, but seemed to cause him no awkwardness or pain. He reached into his tunic for a little bag and opened it wide for the others to throw coins into.

Then he saw Eco and me.

I think I knew then how my own face must have looked, on those occasions when I had been separated from him by great distances, and had worried for him, not knowing if he was alive or dead, and then at last had seen him again, often by surprise when he appeared in Rome without announcement. It was the look of a man whose eyes discern in an instant what his heart has spent long hours desiring.

'Doesn't your commander object to your gambling?' I said.

'Not as long as we wager only with coins that have his image on them.' Meto laughed at his own joke. Roman coins do not bear the images of living men, only dead ones. Not even Caesar dared to mint a coin with his own portrait.

We had retired to a quieter place, a tiny room in the villa that was crammed with scrolls, parchments and maps. There was barely room for the three of us. This was the place where Meto did much of his work for Caesar, reading and emending his latest volume of memoirs. Deciding on a consistent spelling of Gaulish names was an ongoing crisis, I gathered.

I asked him how he knew that Eco and I had been missing.

'Diana sent a letter. It's a good thing you taught her to write, you see? Though her syntax is atrocious. You really should spend more time drilling her, Papa, or else hire a decent tutor. I could tell she was very upset. Her hand shook. Here, I'll show

435

you.' He shuffled among a pile of documents and retrieved a slender, folded wooden tablet. I untied the ribbon that held it shut. The letters etched into the wax coating on the inner surface were indeed uncertain and wavering.

Brother,

We are in great worry and sadness here. Papa left on a journey of a few days and on the way back they were attacked and carried off, him and Eco.

There is maybe cause for hope. There was a note give to the guard outside the door early this morning, by a man who hid his face. The note was addressed to Mother, but of course I had to read it for her. It says: 'Do not fear for Gordianus and his son. They have not been harmed. They will be returned to you in time.' But who knows who the note is from? Or whether to believe it? It makes me more worried than before, almost.

The city is not as wild as it was, but still dangerous, especially at night. Mother and me, and Menenia and Titus and Titania are all safe. We have plenty of the great man's guards to keep us safe. Don't worry for us. But I long for Papa and Eco to come home! Oh, Cybele, let them come back soon!

I will write again when that happens. Or Papa will write himself to you! Take care of yourself, my brother.

I closed the letter.

'My sister's grammar is poor, Papa, but not so atrocious that you should be moved to tears,' said Meto archly.

I cleared my throat. 'I can hardly stand to think of them, waiting for us, worrying –'

'I arrived in Ravenna only a couple of days ago, from up north. Diana's letter was waiting for me. You can imagine what a fright it gave me. I petitioned Caesar for leave at once, to head home to try to sort things out. I was planning to leave tomorrow. And now here you are! The gods seem to like our family, don't they?'

'It's because we have a family like none other,' said Eco, laughing. 'One of everything! Like the Venus Throw. I think we keep them amused.'

'Well, I'm glad they finally grew bored of watching you and me in that pit,' I said.

Meto frowned. 'In her letter, Diana mentions guards. 'We have plenty of the great man's guards to keep us safe.' What is that about? And where in Hades have you been all this time?'

So we told him the tale, or most of it, as briefly as we could. The sun was fading before we finished.

I opened Diana's letter and read it again, more calmly. Who had sent the note addressed to Bethesda, advising her not to worry? What a peculiar sort of kidnapping!

My wits still must have been dulled by our captivity, for it was only as I reread the letter a third time that an equally obvious question occurred to me. How had Diana known that Eco and

437

I were attacked and abducted on our way home? 'On the way back they were attacked and carried off,' she wrote. Who had seen it happen, and who had told her about it?

Meto found accommodations for us in the villa, in a tiny room even smaller than his office. It reminded me uneasily of the pit. When it came time to sleep I tossed and turned for a while. When Eco began to snore, I realized that I was so sick of being cooped up with him that I might strangle him. So I gathered up a blanket and found Meto, who was still awake and talking with his tentmates. He found a spare cot for me and I pulled it outside, to a spot where I could fall asleep looking at the stars. I wanted to gaze at them for hours, and breathe in the clear, cold air, but I fell into a dreamless sleep almost at once.

The next morning, Meto took us to see Caesar.

A guard escorted us to a courtyard inside the villa. He and Meto seemed to know each other quite well. We sat on a bench to wait. A few moments later, Cicero and Tiro appeared, formally attired in togas and escorted by the same guard. 'I must warn you, he's very busy today,' said the guard to Cicero. 'But I'll do my best to make sure that you see him.'

Cicero and Tiro sat on the bench across from us. Cicero looked rather peeved, I thought.

'Did you not see Caesar yesterday?' I said.

'No. We arrived in the afternoon, of course, when he was at his busiest. You know how it is

with these generals. Pompey is the same. Sometimes one has to wait days to see them. You'd think, since I'm here to smooth the way for his next campaign for consul, that he'd see me at once. But of course a man like Caesar has much important business. Every hour is taken.'

I nodded.

A few moments later the guard appeared. Cicero quickly stood and began straightening the folds of his toga. The guard ignored him and nodded to us. 'He'll see you now.'

As we walked past Cicero, I found it hard not to grin. The look on his face was priceless.

Meto had first introduced me to Gaius Julius Caesar some years ago. On subsequent occasions, I never expected him to remember me, but he always did. Caesar's mind was like a fisherman's net. No fact or face, once apprehended, ever slipped away from him.

His study was a spacious room with tall windows thrown open to admit the morning light. One wall was covered by an enormous map made of sheepskins stitched together and dyed in various colours to show the various tribes of the Gauls, with pictures to show their cities and strongholds. What sort of place could Lutetia be? Or Alesia? Or Cenabum, which for some reason was circled in red? Was the island of Britannia really as huge as the maps showed it to be? Meto had been to all these places, even to Britannia, where the barbarians paint themselves blue. He had learned the language

of the Bituriges and the Helvetii, whose very names I could hardly pronounce. I had travelled much in the East, but never in Gaul. Meto had entered a world and an existence I could only wonder at.

And he had fallen into the orbit of a man whose force of personality I could only wonder at, as well. Gaius Julius Caesar was unique among men. I have never met anyone else whose intellectual and physical vigour were so keenly evident even in a glance or the exchange of a few brief words. I had never had serious dealings with Caesar, as I had with Crassus and Catilina, and now Pompey, but I could see that he abundantly possessed an element in his personality which they too possessed, a drive for power and for what men call greatness. But Caesar seemed somehow accessible in a way the others were not; he was not as frighteningly single-minded as Crassus, or as elusively seductive as Catilina, or as intimidating as Pompey. He seemed at once more than human, and yet vulnerable, a man who could both divinely inspire his men and make them feel protective of him. He was quite human in his vanity, at least; he had begun to bald at an early age (he was now in his late forties), and according to Meto was still self-conscious about his lack of hair.

He was dictating to a secretary as we entered, but stood and opened his arms when he saw Meto. He gave him a warm embrace and kissed him on the lips. 'So, Meto, you shall not be deserting me after all?'

'I shall not be leaving for Rome, if that's what you mean. My father and brother are safe and sound, as you can see.'

'Ah, Gordianus! And . . .' Caesar hesitated for only a heartbeat. 'And Eco. The three of you look so little alike. That always confuses me for a moment, when I see you all together. But of course the sons were chosen and adopted by their father, and thus are like him in spirit, not in flesh. It was a false alarm then, the rumour that they had been kidnapped?'

'Not false at all,' said Meto. 'They made their escape only a few days ago, and only a few miles from here.'

'That must be quite a tale. You must tell me all about it.' Caesar indicated that we should sit.

'But you must be very busy, General,' I said, thinking of Cicero waiting in the courtyard.

'Not particularly. I shall be heading back to Gaul in a few days, but preparations proceed without me. I'm filling the time by dictating a new chapter of my memoirs. That little skirmish with the Eburones last year – you must remember it well, Meto.' He reached out to touch Meto's face. Meto returned his smile. The moment seemed disconcertingly intimate, until I realized that Caesar had brushed his fingers against a very slight scar on Meto's cheek.

'My father and brother were waylaid on the Appian Way,' said Meto. 'He was doing some work for Pompey, looking into the murder of Publius Clodius.'

'Really? Now that is interesting. What did you discover, Gordianus?'

I looked at Meto, chagrined that he should bring my affairs so blatantly to Caesar's attention. But I

kept no secrets from Meto, and Meto evidently kept no secrets from Caesar. 'I was merely able to confirm what everyone in Rome already seemed to know — that Clodius was killed by Milo's slaves after an altercation on the Appian Way.'

'As simple as that? I presume you'll be giving Pompey a somewhat more comprehensive report. But I've made you uncomfortable, Gordianus. I have no intention of interrogating you. Settling the matter of Milo's guilt and punishment falls to Pompey, not to me, and quite properly so. Milo was his man, after all, until Milo became Cicero's man. Let Pompey have the headache of disposing of Milo and restoring order in the city. I have a greater task ahead of me: restoring order in Gaul. The chaos begun by the murder of Publius Clodius has reached even there. Remarkable, isn't it, the repercussions that can follow upon a single death?'

'Please explain,' I said.

'Certain rebellious elements among the tribes, hearing of the strife in Rome, concluded that I would be detained in Ravenna indefinitely, unable to rejoin my troops. They seized the opportunity to instigate a revolt, which has spread rapidly. The first blow was struck at Cenabum — you can see it on the map there. The man I personally appointed to run the Roman trading post was murdered and his property plundered. A young Avernian named Vercingetorix seems to think the time is right to make himself king of the Gauls. He's already managed to unite a great many tribes under him. Worst of all, he's cut me off

from the main body of my troops. It poses something of a puzzle, how I shall reach my men.' Caesar studied the map and suddenly seemed very distant from us. 'So you see, a simple murder on the Appian Way has already had profound consequences far beyond the death of a single man. Publius Clodius in death has caused even more havoc than he caused in life, and Milo has wielded his greatest influence on the course of the world as a killer instead of a consul.' Caesar looked away from the map. 'But you haven't yet told me the story of your misfortune, Gordianus.'

'There's not much to tell. We were waylaid in the vicinity of the Monument of Basilius by men whose faces we never properly saw, bound inside sacks and transported to a place which turned out to be somewhere near Ariminum. We weren't too badly treated. When we made our escape, one of our keepers was killed and the other escaped. Unfortunately, I doubt that we could find the place again.'

'Was there a request for ransom?'

'Apparently not, though someone did send my wife an anonymous note saying that we would not be harmed and would eventually be released.'

'How curious. Do you think this episode was connected with your investigations for Pompey?'

'Perhaps.'

Caesar laughed. 'You're a reticent fellow, Gordianus. I respect a man who's able to say no more than he should – that's rare. It's obvious you were never trained as an orator! I should like to think I

might call on you myself some day, if I ever need a man of your talents and discretion.'

'That would be an honour, Caesar.'

He smiled for a moment, then gazed at the map again with an abstracted look. The recounting of my misadventures had distracted him for a moment, but now his attention had returned to the consuming problems of Gaul.

'Shall we leave you now, Caesar?' said Meto.

'I do need to return to my work now, yes. I'm glad to learn that you shall remain beside me, Meto, especially in the days to come. It was good to see you again, Gordianus, and you, too, Eco. I wish you both a safe and uneventful journey back to Rome. And Gordianus . . .'

'Yes, Caesar?'

'When you report to Gnaeus Pompey, say that you spoke to me and tell him, if you would, that I send him my warmest regards. He was my son-in-law, you know, and still would be if ill fortune had not intervened. He should have had a son from Julia, and I a grandson. But the Fates deemed otherwise and robbed us both.'

'I'll do as you ask, Caesar.'

The secretary called for the guard, who came to escort us out. The man paused. 'Shall I show the others in now, Caesar?'

'What others?'

'Cicero and his man. They're waiting in the courtyard. He insists that he has business of the greatest importance.'

Caesar pressed his fingers together and studied

the map of Gaul. 'No, not yet. I shall finish dictating this chapter first. Perhaps, after I take my midday meal, I shall have time to receive Marcus Tullius Cicero.'

The guard escorted us down a hallway and back to the courtyard. At our approach, Cicero rose to his feet. Before he could say a word, the guard cut him off with a shake of his head. Cicero crossed his arms and sat down again. He did not look at us as we passed by, but instead pretended to find some grim fascination in the fountain in the centre of the courtyard. I tried very hard not to smile.

# XXVI

We ate with Meto in a large tent filled with soldiers. Under normal circumstances, I would have judged the food barely passable and the company just tolerable. After long days of captivity, however, and the deprivation of any variety in my tablemates, the simple meal and the loud, vulgar conversation made me feel that I was at a feast fit for King Numa.

In the midst of the talk someone mentioned Marc Antony.

Meto saw my reaction, noticed the same reaction from Eco, and raised an eyebrow. 'Do you know him, Papa? Ah, but that's right, I introduced you to Marc Antony last year. Here in Ravenna, wasn't it?'

'Yes.'

'He's looking very sleek,' said one of the men. 'All that lolling about down in Rome agrees with him.'

'I should think that Rome is considered a hazardous posting these days!' said another.

'He keeps himself fit doing daily drills –'

'At the widow Fulvia's house!'

There was a round of suggestive grunts and laughter.

I turned to Meto. 'Do I take it that Antony is here in Ravenna?'

'Yes. He's been in the camp for several days, conferring with Caesar about the situation in Rome. He's heading back tomorrow, I think. What's that look on your face, Papa?'

'Oh, nothing.' When this did not satisfy him, I indicated that we should move outside where we could talk more discreetly.

'Well, Papa?' he said, as the three of us strolled between the tents.

'It's probably nothing at all, but when I told you yesterday about our investigations on the Appian Way, I forgot to mention Marc Antony.'

'Antony? What possible connection –'

'He threatened Clodius's life last year on the Field of Mars – chased him to a warehouse on the river, where Clodius hid in a cupboard under a stairway.'

Meto laughed. 'Oh, that story!'

'You know it?'

'Of course. Antony loves to tell it, especially when he's a little drunk. He claims he had no intention of killing Clodius. He just wanted to turn him into a eunuch.'

'What did they fight about?'

'Who knows? Papa, their relationship went back a very long way. They'd been in love with the same woman, Fulvia. They may have been in love with each other at some time or other, for all I know. They probably met on the Field of Mars, exchanged a few friendly insults, Clodius said something that tugged a bit too hard on Antony's balls, and Antony whipped out his sword. But no one was hurt in the end.'

Eco groaned. 'Meto, the puns!'

Meto smiled and shrugged. 'I can keep it up all day. But what has this to do with –'

I had told Meto the day before about my commission from Pompey, but had not mentioned Fulvia. My meeting with her had come to seem incidental. 'Fulvia asked me to find out if Antony was involved in her husband's death.'

'But he's one of the people working to bring Milo to trial.'

'That proves nothing.'

'Did you find any evidence to implicate him?'

I considered this carefully. 'No one who witnessed the event or the aftermath had anything at all to say about Antony.'

'Well, there you have it.'

'Perhaps.'

'Really, Papa, Antony is a good soldier and a friend of mine. I can't stand by and hear him called a murderer.'

'No one has called him a murderer, Meto.'

'But you seem to think he might be.'

What had Cicero said about me? Always the

448

one to bide his time, sift every shred of evidence, seek for further revelations, postpone the final judgment. 'If Fulvia were here with us now, I couldn't in good conscience say that I had proved otherwise.'

'Then let's go and ask him.'

'What?'

'We'll ask him.'

'As simple as that?'

'Why not? Antony isn't exactly simple, but he's as clear and plain to read as Caesar's Latin. Come with me.'

'Come with you where?'

'To Antony's quarters. They're on the far side of the villa. This way.'

Eco and I followed after him. 'But Meto, this is mad! What do you expect me to do? Say, 'Hello, do you remember me, Meto's father, and by the way, did you help murder Publius Clodius?' '

'I imagine you can be more subtle than that, Papa.'

'And if he should decided to whip out his sword and give chase, like he did with Clodius on the Field of Mars?'

'You heard the fellows in the tent – Antony's got a bit plump, attending all those dinner parties in Rome. Maybe you can outrun him. Here, we enter through this door.'

As with Caesar, we had to apply to a guard before reaching the man himself. My hope was that Antony would be too busy to see us, but at the sound of Meto's voice a head poked through the

449

curtains to his office, wearing a broad grin. 'Meto! Have you eaten yet?'

'I've swallowed my ration of swill for the day, if that's what you mean.'

'Join me anyway. I managed to salvage a few edible things out of the pot. Who are your friends? Ah – it's your brother, isn't it, and your father, the famous Finder.'

'Famous?' I said, as we stepped through the curtains.

'Or infamous. Whatever. Come in. Sit. Manius, find something else to do.' Antony gestured to a secretary, who promptly scooped up his tablet and stylus and left the room. 'Wine? Well, that goes without saying. I know how you take yours, Meto: neat. Meto's like me, has a terrible allergy to water. Do you take yours watered, Gordianus? And you, Eco?'

'More water than wine for me,' I said. 'I've been away from wine for a while. I'm having to get used to it again. Besides,' I added under my breath, 'I may have to do some running soon.'

'And the same for me,' said Eco, raising an eyebrow.

Physically, Antony had the potential to be intimidating. He had a wrestler's build, with a muscular neck and shoulders and a broad barrel chest – rather like a younger, taller version of Milo, I thought. He was only a few years older than Meto, probably thirty or thirty-one. In profile, his jutting brows and chin and his dented boxer's nose gave him a rather brutish appearance, but when he

looked at me straight on this impression was melted away by the gentleness of his eyes and mouth and the fulness of his cheeks. Antony was handsome in a homely sort of way, to use one of Bethesda's phrases. He had a sort of look that many women find irresistible and that many men trust instinctively, as Meto certainly seemed to do.

'When did you arrive, Gordianus?' Antony looked at me with an expression that hardly seemed that of a guileful killer, or a kidnapper, for that matter.

'Just yesterday.'

'Oh?' He nodded, then frowned. 'Don't tell me you came with Cicero?'

'We arrived together, yes. But I only joined him on the last leg of the journey, quite by chance.'

'That's good to hear. Then you're not a part of his little mission to Caesar?'

'Most definitely not.'

'Papa and Eco are here on their own business,' said Meto.

'Really? What's that?' said Antony.

'They're here to investigate you.'

'Meto!' This was really too much.

Antony narrowed his eyes. 'Me? This isn't related to that old business about King Ptolemy's daughter back in Egypt, is it? I swear, I never touched the child!' Antony and Meto both laughed at what was apparently an old joke.

'No,' said Meto, 'it's something to do with —'

'With a nasty rumour that someone started down in Rome,' I said. 'My son seems determined to

make light of the situation, but it's deadly serious.'
Meto had controlled the conversation long enough. Since he insisted on forcing the matter, I decided to make the best of it. 'I'll begin by telling you what I told Caesar earlier today: at the request of Gnaeus Pompey, Eco and I did a little snooping into the circumstances of the death of Publius Clodius. Outrageous as it may seem, we encountered a rumour – and I tell you this, Marc Antony, because you're my son's friend and I think you should know that such a thing was said about you – we encountered a rumour that you were somehow involved.'

'Ridiculous!' said Antony, who did not look amused.

I shrugged. 'An outrageous rumour, as I said. I'm sure that no one of good sense would credit it for an instant.'

'But who would say such a thing about me?' Antony was suddenly on his feet, pacing across the small space. 'What utter nonsense, that I could have any hand at all in what happened to Clodius! There's no bottom to people's vileness, is there? No lie so vicious that someone won't stoop to utter it. Cicero! You heard this from Cicero, didn't you, on the ride up?'

'No.'

'Tell me the truth, Gordianus. Oh, it sounds just like him, telling a lie so crazy that people begin to think there must be something to it! I'll tell you, this is the last time, and I mean the very last time, that the old coot is going to take a piss on my head.

452

I'll snatch him in the middle of his snivelling petition to Caesar and throw him down a well. I'll twist his throat until his head snaps off! He'll never spread another lie about me again!' At that moment, Antony looked quite capable of carrying out such threats.

'Marc Antony, I swear to you, the rumour didn't come from Cicero.'

'Then where did you hear it? Who's saying these thing about me?' Antony's anger was palpable and seemed to heat the whole room like a brazier. But I sensed that none of his fury was directed at me. It was because I was Meto's father, I realized, and therefore to be trusted and respected. Antony was not a simple man, Meto had said, but clear and plain. He had cause to be angry, but was disciplined enough to hold his anger in check while he sought for the party that had truly offended against him.

'It was a fish vendor, wasn't it, Papa?' said Eco suddenly.

'What?'

'It was a fish vendor who told us about the rumour, as I recall.' My elder son was not so clear and plain as Antony.

'Ah, was it?' I said.

'By Hercules, you mean they're spreading such a lie even in the marketplaces?' Antony looked ready to smash something, but refilled his wine cup instead.

'Yes, I remember now,' I said. 'But it was only one person who mentioned the idea to me – no, actually it was two people – and it may be that they

453

were simply confused, because at the same time they brought up a story from last year, about an altercation between yourself and Publius Clodius . . .'

'What, that bit of silliness on the Field of Mars?'

'These people seemed to think you meant Clodius actual harm.'

'If I'd caught him, you know what I would have done? I'd have used the flat of my sword to spank him! That would have been humiliation enough.'

'What was his offence?' said Meto.

'The usual one, not knowing when to keep his mouth shut. Nothing political. Something personal dredged up from the past.' Antony hesitated. 'Since you've been so candid with me, Gordianus, I'll tell you. Clodius made a rude suggestion involving my friendship with Gaius Curio. Curio was off in Asia, serving as quaestor, and his father had just died. Well, it's no secret how the elder Curio did everything he could to come between Gaius and me when we were young – following Cicero's advice, I might add! So there were we, out on the Field of Mars, and Clodius said something like, 'Now that his old man's dead and out of the way, I suppose you and Gaius Curio can finally get married. Which one of you will be the bride?' Normally I might have laughed it off, but he caught me on a day when I was in no mood for his needling, so I pulled out my sword. I suppose I looked angrier than I was – it's a problem I have – and Clodius simply panicked. He shrieked and ran!' Antony laughed at

the memory. 'And I chased after him! I couldn't help myself!' Antony clutched himself, laughing. 'If I'd caught him, I swear, I'd have pulled off his toga and spanked his bare bottom – sent him back to the Field of Mars stark naked with his red cheeks glowing. That would have shut him up! Can you imagine? The mob would have deserted him. He'd have had to retire from public life. But he'd still be alive today!'

The laughter caught in Antony's throat. He sighed and made a face that was hard to read. He poured himself more wine, drained his cup and looked at me steadily. 'Gordianus, I swear to you by the shade of my father, I had nothing to do with Clodius's death. So I hope that you'll go back and find whoever these rumourmongers were, and set them straight.'

I tried to return his gaze with one as steady. It's not often that I find myself the less honest of two parties in a conversation. 'I intend to do that, Marc Antony.'

'Good! Such a rumour should be nipped in the bud, before some scoundrel like Cicero puts it to his own use. Oh, Mercury and Minerva!' He slapped his forehead.

'What's wrong?' said Meto.

'What if this awful rumour should reach all the way to Fulvia? Since Clodius died, I've worked so hard to be strong for her, to give her someone to lean on, someone she can trust absolutely. I couldn't stand it, if anything should poison that. But what am I saying? Fulvia would never believe

such a rumour, not for a moment. She knows me better than that.'

I shrugged and made a sympathetic smile.

That night we learned from Tiro that after waiting in Caesar's courtyard all day, Cicero had once more failed to gain an audience with the general. He would have to seek an audience again the next day, and so would not be heading back to Rome again until at least the day after that, at the earliest. To Eco and me, eager to return to our families, this seemed an eternity.

'But Papa, Antony's leaving for Rome early tomorrow morning,' said Meto. 'Why don't you travel with him?'

'We could hardly presume –'

'It would be no imposition, Papa. Come, I'll ask him myself if you want.'

'Stay where you are, Meto! You've already put me on the spot with Antony once today.'

'Papa, you need to go home, and you need a safe escort. You don't want to travel with Cicero, anyway, do you? He'd drive you mad. And he'll travel slower. Go with Antony. He likes you, couldn't you tell? He'll be glad to have your company. And you can get to know him better and make up your mind about him, if you haven't already. It's so perfect, the gods themselves must have arranged it.'

'What do you think, Eco?' I said.

'I think I want to get back to Rome as soon as possible, and that Caesar seems determined to keep Cicero waiting as long as he can.'

'Then, if you really think Antony would be amenable, Meto . . .'

'We'll ask him right now.'

This, I gathered, was how things were done in Caesar's army. Having lived so long in devious Rome, I found it hard to get used to such forthrightness.

We departed for Rome before dawn.

The journey lasted for four days and passed without incident. Antony seemed to be as transparent as Meto had indicated. He drank more than he should, and when he drank he showed his emotions more plainly than most men. I could imagine him killing out of pain or rage, or professionally, as a soldier, but it was difficult to see him as a conspirator in some devious plot. He was equally outspoken about those whom he hated (Cicero, chiefly) and those whom he loved (Curio, Fulvia, Caesar and his wife and cousin Antonia, in that order so far as I could tell). His lack of charm was in itself charming, just as his homeliness made him oddly handsome. I became very relaxed in his company, and began to see why Meto was so fond of him.

On the last day we talked a little about his military service in Egypt. Four years had passed since Antony had helped the Roman governor of Syria to restore King Ptolemy Auletes to the throne that had been usurped by his daughter Berenice. 'I loved Alexandria,' Antony told me, 'and the Alexandrians loved me. Do you know the city?'

'Oh, yes. I met my wife there.' I remembered something he had said back in Ravenna. 'Antony, what did you mean when you referred to 'that old business about King Ptolemy's daughter'?'

'When was that? Jog my memory, Gordianus.'

'You said, 'I swear, I never touched the child!' It was some sort of joke. You and Meto both laughed, anyway.'

'Ah, that wasn't about Berenice. I was referring to Ptolemy's other daughter.'

'And?' Eco raised a suggestive eyebrow.

'Nothing happened! She was only fourteen, entirely too young for my tastes.' This rang true; Fulvia was older than Antony. 'Oh, some of my officers claimed I was moonstruck for the girl, in a daze after I'd met her. I still take some needling about it. All nonsense! Though I have to admit, she was quite impressive, child or not.'

'Remarkably beautiful?' I thought of my own Diana, only a few hours away.

'Beautiful? No, not at all. Plenty of women are beautiful, and so are quite a few boys, but not her. Beauty is common, compared to what she possessed. A certain quality; I can't explain it. She was unlike anyone else I've ever met, except maybe Caesar.'

Eco laughed. 'A fourteen-year-old girl reminded you of Caesar?'

'It sounds absurd, I know. If she'd been just a little older . . .'

'If this was four years ago,' I said, 'she'd be eighteen now.'

458

The idea cast a strange look across Antony's face. Dazed, his officers had said. Moonstruck. 'Maybe some day I shall return to Egypt to see what's become of her.'

'What do they call this unusual female?'

Antony smiled. 'Cleopatra.'

# XXVII

We crossed the Tiber as the light of day began to soften and approached the city. The Field of Mars opened on our right. To our left, the old city walls skirted hills covered with buildings. The Flaminian Way ran straight ahead towards the Capitoline Hill, with its temples clustered crownlike at the summit. I had never been so glad to see a place in all my life.

Outside the Fontinalis Gate we dismounted from our horses and took our leave of Antony. I hardly noticed the armed soldiers who flanked the gateway. I had grown used to seeing soldiers at Caesar's camp, and travelling with Antony.

Eco and I hurried through the narrow streets and cut across the Forum, not far from the charred, ruined mass of the Senate House. Here we saw more soldiers, publicly bearing arms in the Forum as if they were an occupying army. Rome had seen civil war and armed soldiers inside her gates, but

never had an army been used to police the population by the consent of the Senate. People seemed to be going about their business in a normal manner, but everything seemed strange to me. We saw a crowd in front of the Rostra, gathered for what appeared to be a contio of some sort. We made a wide detour to avoid it.

We slipped behind the Temple of Castor and Pollux to reach the Ramp, which was guarded by yet more soldiers. My heart was racing as we neared the top, not from exertion but from excitement. I crossed the street and rapped on the door of my house.

The door opened. An ugly, unfamiliar face peered out at me. For an instant I was confused. This was not my house. My family didn't live here. We were not even in Rome, or at least not in the Rome I knew. I felt as the lemures of the dead must feel when they walk the earth, reduced to shadows and finding nothing as they remember it.

But it was my house, of course. The ugly face of the guard was unfamiliar because he came from Pompey's household. He didn't recognize me either, and looked ready to break me in two if I tried to slip past him. The family must be safe, after all, I thought. I felt a giddy urge to hug him, but didn't dare.

'Who are you and what do you want?' he snarled.

'You stupid oaf,' said Eco. 'This is Gordianus, the owner of this house, and I'm his son, Eco. Now run tell the —'

He was interrupted by a cry of pure joy. The guard understood at once and drew aside, with a sudden smile that changed the whole nature of his face. Diana was suddenly before me, and then pressed close to me with my arms around her. Bethesda and Menenia appeared, and the laughing twins, but I saw them only uncertainly, like images in water, their ecstatic, beaming, impossibly beautiful faces glimmering through a veil of tears.

Then I saw another familiar face. He hung back from the rest so that I only glimpsed him between barrages of hugs and kisses. The look on his face was not so much of joy as of intense relief, clouded by embarrassment.

Davus was alive after all.

'I thought Davus must be alive. I hoped it was so,' I said, reclining on my favourite couch with my right arm holding Bethesda beside me. We had eaten inside, then pulled chairs and couches for everyone into the garden to enjoy the last of the day. The weather was mild for the Ides of March, which was of course more like April, figuring in the leap-month. Butterflies flitted amid the columns of the peristyle. The plants all around were beginning to quicken and stir with the spring. The statue of Minerva, I noted ruefully, remained broken and prostrate where she had fallen.

'But I thought he was surely dead,' said Eco, peering at Davus as if still unsure of the evidence of his eyes. Davus blushed under his scrutiny.

'Until a few days ago, I thought the same thing,' I

said. 'My last glimpse of Davus on the Appian Way was of a dead man, or so I believed. Our captors thought so, too, and left him for dead.'

'I hit my head,' said Davus quietly, lowering his eyes. 'They must have dragged me off the road, behind a tomb. I woke up hours later with a nasty bump on my head.'

'And when did you realize the truth?' asked Bethesda, lazily tracing her fingertips over my earlobe and neck.

'When I reread Diana's letter to Meto. She made no mention of Davus, but she knew that we had been attacked and abducted on our way back to the city. How? It was possible that some passerby witnessed the attack, happened to recognize Eco or me, and felt obliged to inform the family. Possible, but not likely. It was also possible that whoever came upon Davus's corpse, if indeed our abductors had left it in the road, just happened to recognize him as my slave and returned him to the family, and that from his condition and the place where he was found, and the fact that we were missing, Diana could have inferred that we had been attacked and abducted. That chain of possibilities seemed unlikely. The simplest thing is often the true thing. Davus must have survived, I reasoned, and brought home the tale of the attack. That seemed unlikely, too, but I wanted to believe it, and so I quietly did. I am more pleased than I can say to discover that I was right. To have first lost Belbo, and then you . . .'

Davus continued to blush, and would not look me in the eye.

'But we are all well, all together,' I said, pulling Bethesda closer to me. The warmth and firmness of her body – the simple, solid reality of it – felt incredibly good to me. With my other hand I reached out to Diana, who sat on a low chair to my left. She smiled and lifted her chin as I stroked her black, shimmering hair. Surely there was no finer or more beautiful thing in all creation, I thought, than Diana's hair. Yet even as she smiled, there seemed to be an anxiety that clouded her face and would not disperse. Perhaps she could not quite trust that all was well again, after so many long days of worry.

Eco reclined on a couch across from me, with Menenia beside him and Titus and Titania at his left hand. We talked for a while longer, about our captivity, about the state of things in Rome, about Bethesda's success in bending Pompey's guards to her will. The sky darkened and stars began to appear. After a while, Eco and Menenia sent the twins to bed and retired to their room for the night. Davus withdrew, and a few moments later Diana left the garden as well, still looking uneasy. Bethesda and I were alone.

She brought her face close to mine. 'I missed you,' she whispered.

'Oh, Bethesda, I worried for you so much.'

'I worried for you, too, husband, but that's not what I said. I said I missed you.' She smoothed her hand over my chest and down towards my legs, ending in a place that made her meaning unmistakably clear.

'Bethesda!'

'But husband, you must be voracious after so long.'

It was a curious thing, but during our time in the pit I had experienced hardly any amorous impulses or fantasies at all. A few times, purely for physical relief, I had tended to myself while Eco slept. I assumed he had done the same, though probably more often. And on a few occasions, I had resorted to a certain fantasy involving a certain highborn lady and her red and white striped litter. But for the most part I had retreated from my body as much as I could. Denying pleasure was perhaps a way of also denying the more imminent prospects of pain and death. It was as if I had been buried alive – which was not far from the truth.

Now I was free and back in Rome at last, safe and fed and surrounded by my loved ones. But I was also tired, exhausted by four days of riding and still not fully recuperated from the debilitating effects of our captivity. Much, much too tired for what Bethesda wanted, I thought . . . and yet the movements of her hand began to stir me, and her warmth seemed to pour a kind of vitality into my body, bringing me fully to life again. I felt myself sinking into a state beyond words or caring, like a stone dissolving into water.

'But not here,' I whispered. 'We should go . . . inside . . .'

'Why?'

'Bethesda . . . !'

So we did it there in the garden like young

465

lovers, not once but twice, with the moon for a lamp. The night air grew chilly, but that only made the places where our flesh touched burn all the warmer.

Only once did I have the sensation that we were being watched, but when I looked around it was only the head of Minerva that looked back at me, lying sideways in the grass. I ignored her until we were finished the second time. When I looked again, she still seemed to be watching me, with a look of hurt in her lapis lazuli eyes. And when will you tend to my needs? her expression seemed to say – as if single-handedly I could put the goddess of wisdom together again and return her to her pedestal.

Bethesda and I eventually retired to the bedroom, but at some point in the night I got up to relieve myself. The hulking shadow I saw across the garden alarmed me at first, until I realized who it was.

'Davus!' I whispered. 'Why are you up? Pompey's guards take the night watch.'

'I couldn't sleep.'

'But you should. I'll need you fresh and alert tomorrow.'

'I know. I'll try to sleep now.' He began to walk off, slump-shouldered. I touched his arm.

'Davus, I meant what I said tonight. I thought we had lost you for good. I'm glad it wasn't so.'

'Thank you, Master.' He cleared his throat and looked away. What was wrong with him? Why did he feel so guilty?

'Davus, no one blames you for what happened.'

'But if I'd known how to ride a horse –'

'I've ridden horses all my life, and they pulled me off my mount with no trouble at all.'

'But nobody pulled me off my horse. I was thrown! If I'd stayed on, I could have ridden for help.'

'Nonsense. You'd have stayed and fought, and they'd have killed you for certain. You did your best, Davus.'

'And it wasn't good enough.'

Where had he come by such a conscientious nature, having been a slave all his life? 'Davus, Fortune smiled on you. The horse threw you, you were left for dead, and you're alive today. Fortune smiled on all of us. We're still here, aren't we? You should let that be enough.'

He finally looked me in the eye. 'Master, there's something I have to say. You said you were glad to find out I was still alive, but you can't know how glad I was today, when you showed up at the door! Because – well, I can't explain it. I wish I could, but I can't. May I go now?'

'Of course, Davus. Get some sleep.' He lumbered away, tongue-tied and close to tears. I thought I understood. Minerva, who could see everything from the place where she had fallen, must have had quite a laugh at me that night.

The next morning I asked Diana to show me the note she had mentioned in her letter to Meto, the one that had arrived by anonymous courier

addressed to her mother. It was just as she had transcribed it:

Do not fear for Gordianus and his son. They have not been harmed. They will be returned to you in time.

I showed it to Eco. 'Does the handwriting look familiar to you?'

'No.'

'Nor to me. Still, it tells us something. The parchment is of good quality, as is the ink; it didn't come from a poor household. Moreover, the spelling is correct, and the letters are properly made, so we may assume that the writer is educated.'

'Probably a slave, taking dictation.'

'Do you think so? To send a message such as this, I imagine a man might actually write the note himself. I think it might profit us to look among my records and correspondence, to see if we can find another example of this handwriting.'

'I don't have many such specimens, and neither do you, Papa. Most letters come on wax tablets, so that you can write over them and send them back.'

'Yes, but we may find something – a bill, a receipt, anything. Do you see how he's made the letter G in my name? That's rather distinctive. If we could find the man who makes his Gs that way . . .'

'We'd find a man who must know something about our captivity.'

'Exactly.'

468

Eco smiled. 'I need to clean my study and sort through my correspondence, anyway. Shall we start here, or at my house on the Esquiline?'

'Here, I think. Unless of course you want to drop by your house just to have a look at it, since you've been away so long. Of course, we should report to the Great One, sooner or later –'

As if responding to a cue in a play, Davus appeared in the doorway.

'A caller, Master.'

'Anyone I know?'

'I think you gave him a nickname. Something silly . . .' Davus looked thoughtful. 'Oh, I remember: Baby Face!'

I turned to Eco. 'It looks like we shall be seeing the Great One sooner then, not later. Should we take cloaks, Davus?'

'No, it's mild this morning, Master, and the sky is clear. Shall I . . . shall I come with you?'

'I doubt if there's any need, Davus, with Baby Face and his men to look after us. Stay here. You've done such a good job of looking after the women in our absence.'

I thought this would cheer him up, but my words of praise only seemed to plunge Davus into a deeper gloom.

# XXVIII

As consul, despite the fact that he retained command of his legions in Spain, Pompey was now legally able to enter the city and might have taken up residence in his old family house in the Carinae district. Instead he chose to remain in his villa out on the Pincian Hill, probably because it was more defensible, I thought, as we ascended through the terraced gardens ringed with soldiers keeping watch among the statuary. Was this how a king would live, if Rome had a king?

The Great One received us in the same room as before. He sat in a corner with a pile of documents on his lap, dictating to a secretary, but as we entered he put the documents aside and dismissed the secretary. He showed us onto the terrace, which was bright with morning sunlight. No columns of smoke marred the skyline of the city. Pompey had vowed to restore order, and so he had.

'You've been gone for a very long time, Finder. I must confess, I had almost given up on you. It was a pleasant surprise when I received news of your return yesterday. You both look well enough, if a bit thinner than when I last saw you. I managed to keep myself informed of your circumstances, thanks to your wife. You were waylaid down by the Monument of Basilius, I understand. And not too many days ago she received some sort of note advising her not to worry, promising that you would eventually be freed. And here you are.'

'Except that our captors didn't free us, Great One. We escaped.'

'Really?' Pompey raised an appreciative eyebrow. 'You've had an adventure, then. Here, sit. I could use a good story to distract me from my own affairs for a while. Begin at the beginning.'

If Pompey preferred to call it a story rather than a report, I had no objection, though it was clear from his frequent questions that he wanted complete details of everything we had seen, heard and done on the Appian Way. He didn't call his secretary to take notes, apparently preferring to hold the relevant details in his head and to keep the information entirely to himself. I held very little back from him. We had struck a bargain, after all. The payment he had offered could never make up for the days I had lost in captivity, but he had fulfilled his guarantee to keep my family safe while I was gone.

About certain points, especially regarding the actual encounter between Milo and Clodius, he questioned us intently. Eco and I had gone over the

evidence so many times in our captivity that we could have answered his questions in our sleep. Indeed, I was sick of talking and thinking about it, and Pompey apparently sensed this, for now and then he would sit back and fall into easy conversation for a while, asking if we had enjoyed the amenities of his Alban villa and the skills of his cook, before delving back into our discoveries along the Appian Way. The conversation assumed a certain rhythm, intense for a while and then relaxed, and before I realized it the entire morning had passed. Pompey was not a great orator, but he was a skilled interrogator. Long experience as a general had taught him how to brief and debrief his men. No wonder his judicial reforms had placed greater emphasis on questioning witnesses and less on rhetorical summations. If anything I reported startled or alarmed him, including the details of our incarceration, he had the control not to show it.

I ended my report with a brief account of our escape and a few words about our stay at Caesar's headquarters in Ravenna. Pompey seemed impressed that we had met with the commander himself.

'He said that I should convey to you his warmest regards,' I said.

'Did he?' Pompey seemed vaguely amused. 'Tell me, how did he treat Cicero?'

While I was considering how to answer this, Pompey noticed the smirk on Eco's face and nodded knowingly. 'Pretty shabbily, then?'

'Caesar seemed to be very busy, and kept putting him off,' I said carefully.

'Ha! You mean he did everything he could to make Cicero feel like an idiot. It's because I sent him, of course.'

'I beg your pardon, Great One?'

'Cicero was there to represent me. You didn't realize that, Finder? What, did he tell you he was acting all on his own?'

'Not exactly . . .'

'He fooled you, then. Admit it! Well, Cicero has fooled all of us at one time or another, so why not you, too? What a fox he is. I'm sure he put on quite an air, acting the great saviour of the state who must dash here and there, making sense of all the strife and linking everything together. The fact is, I sent Cicero to Ravenna, to bargain with Caesar for me. Right now, you see, I have the power I need to do certain things that need doing. But Caesar's faction in the Senate could still cause me an awful lot of headaches. They're wary of me. They fret about this sole consulship of mine. To balance things out, they insist that Caesar have a chance to stand for consul next year, even if he's absent in Gaul. Well, why not? Caelius was the sticking point, threatening to veto the special exemption for Caesar. That made things interesting. Then there's this new uprising among the Gauls; Caesar is eager to tidy things up in Rome before he heads north. That made things even more interesting. Oh, I'll give Caesar what he wants, of course, but one must always negotiate a bit. So I thought, who better to send as my envoy than Cicero? There's Caesar, harried and pressed and getting ready to leave on a

473

dangerous campaign, and who should show up for an audience but a man he absolutely can't stand, Marcus Cicero! Caesar will take out his irritation on poor Cicero, but at the same time he'll have to acknowledge that I've done him a favour. Meanwhile, Cicero will have a chance to feel that he's powerful and important, since he's the only person who can knock any sense into that blockhead, Caelius, and he'll feel absurdly beholden to me for giving him such a grave responsibility – letting him into the game, making him a mediator between Caesar and myself. And if nothing else, the trip has got Cicero out of my hair for a while!'

I blinked and nodded, thinking that I really had no understanding of politics and politicians at all.

'Well, Finder, I appreciate your honesty and thoroughness. I also appreciate your suffering at the hands of your captors. If you were a soldier, I would say that you had served beyond the call of duty. You shall be rewarded. I don't forget these things.'

'Thank you, Great One.'

'If you wish, you may keep my guards at your house.'

'I would appreciate that, Great One. For how long?'

'For the duration of the current crisis. There will be a resolution rather soon now, I think.' He took a long sip of wine. 'You know, Finder, you and your son are not the only ones who've faced danger in the last month or so. I've had my own small adventures, trying to keep my head attached to

my shoulders. I dare say I could have used a man of your skills here in Rome to help me make sense of it all.'

'Adventures, Great One?'

'There are those who say Milo is quite determined to do me in.'

'Really?'

'Don't blanch, Finder! I won't assign you to investigate Milo's intentions. I have enough people looking into that already, and you deserve a rest. Still, I rather wish you had been here to help me deal with the episode of Licinius the butcher-priest.'

'I beg your pardon, Great One?'

'Licinius; the man's a butcher and a priest. He's a popa, the one who actually cuts an animal's throat when the priests make a sacrifice; this Licinius does the bloody work while the others tend to the chanting and incense. But in his own time, he runs a butcher shop in the arcade along the Circus Maximus. Convenient, eh? I dare say some of the flesh that's been sacrificed to the gods one day ends up being sold to mere hungry mortals the next. But the fellow seems to be fairly respectable, for a priest. My dealings with him started a few days before the Senate voted to make me sole consul. Licinius showed up at my door one night, explaining who he was and begging to see me, for the sake of my own safety, he said. I had to think twice before admitting a professional slaughterer into my presence!'

He took a sip of wine. 'Licinius apparently has a regular clientele of bodyguards and gladiators from

the Circus – his place is something of a gathering place for big meat-eaters. That day a group came in to gorge themselves on blood sausages and wine. They got very drunk, on the blood as much as the wine, Licinius said, and let it slip that they were part of a plot by Milo to assassinate me. When they realized the butcher was listening, they backed him against a wall and put a knife to his ribs, saying they'd kill him if he told anyone.

'After he closed up his shop for the day he came here, quite distraught. I heard him out, then summoned Cicero, to see what he had to say in Milo's defence. Before Licinius was halfway through his story, Cicero launched into a blistering assault on the man's character. Called him a butcher masquerading as a priest, said he'd drawn more blood with his knife than any of the men he was accusing, said he was likely to be a paid assassin himself because he was bankrupt and desperate for money, and on and on.

'Do you see the lapse in logic, Finder? How was it that Cicero happened to know so much about this obscure butcher from the Circus Maximus? How was it that he arrived at my house already armed with arguments against him – unless there really was a plot and Cicero already knew something about it? I don't accuse Cicero; I don't believe he would actively take part in a conspiracy to kill me. But I think Milo's gladiators must have warned Milo that the butcher had overheard them, and Milo must have mentioned it to Cicero, so that Cicero wasn't entirely surprised when he saw

Licinius. When the butcher lifted up his tunic to show where the gladiator's dagger had been pushed against his ribs, Cicero brayed like a donkey. 'That little scratch? Do you expect us to be impressed with that? You want us to believe a big, strong gladiator made that tiny scratch? You've obviously used one of your wife's hairpins and scratched yourself, and even then not much. For a butcher you've awfully squeamish about drawing any of your own blood!'

'Then, while Cicero was still ranting, a man claiming to be a friend of the butcher showed up, wanting to see him. I let Licinius meet the fellow in the anteroom, but of course I had the anteroom watched, and a moment later a guard came in to tell me that Licinius's so-called friend was trying to bribe him to keep his mouth shut. Right here, under my own roof! That was quite enough for one day. I sent Licinius home under guard, I locked up the fellow who tried to bribe him – who was a mere errand runner and knew nothing – and I told Cicero to get out of my sight before I throttled him.'

'And what came of all this?' I said.

'Eventually I put the evidence before the Senate. When Milo spoke he claimed that he'd never seen most of the gladiators in question. Some of them he admitted to having owned at one time, but he said he had manumitted them long ago and was no longer responsible for them. As citizens, they couldn't be tortured for evidence, of course, and they kept their mouths shut. Milo suggested that

Licinius the butcher had overheard a drunken fantasy and misunderstood most of it. I had no real proof to the contrary. And that's where the matter rests . . . for now.' Pompey gazed at the city below. 'Perhaps I could have used your help to get at the truth of the matter, Finder, but you weren't here.'

'Believe me, Great One, I would much rather have been here than where I was.'

'Yes, yes, I know that you faced great hardship. I don't dismiss your suffering. But I tell you, some days it isn't easy being Pompey the Great.'

I spent the next few days undisturbed. Eco and I passed the time by looking through every scroll and scrap of parchment in our two houses, trying to find a match to the handwriting in the note to Bethesda. We were unsuccessful, but after a while, sorting through mementos and old correspondence became an end in itself, a nostalgic respite from the world. I needed this period of distraction. I was being reunited with my life. I had thought, falsely, that once I was back in Rome I could get on with my business without missing a step, but the experience in the pit had frightened and disturbed me more than I could acknowledge at the time. I found myself in a sort of twilight state, not yet ready to move on.

From Bethesda I could not have asked for more comfort and support. She never once said a word of blame for my having placed myself in such great danger. She never called me a vain, thoughtless fool, as I had called myself a thousand times while I

was in the pit. She saw that I needed her complete attention and unconditional affection, and she gave it to me. I began to think that I had married a goddess.

Diana was more problematic. If she had been angry with me for putting her through so much worry, for making her feel abandoned and bereft, I might have understood, but her behaviour was more puzzling than that. She had always been inscrutable to me, even more so than her mother. Past experience had taught me, sometimes with a rude shock, that she was capable of thoughts and actions I could not possibly anticipate. So I tried not to worry overmuch about her seeming coolness, her brooding melancholy, her new habit of staring into the middle distance.

Davus was equally perplexing. I had thought that my whispered conversation with him in the garden had put everything right and that he would stop skulking about and avoiding my gaze. Instead, this guilty behaviour only became worse. What was wrong with him?

Just when I was beginning to feel fully settled again, and fully engaged in these family concerns, distraction arrived in the form of a red and white striped litter.

It was inevitable that Clodia would call on me sooner or later, just as a summons from Pompey had been inevitable. There was even a part of me that had been looking forward to her arrival with a certain impatience. When Davus showed in the same haughty slave who had summoned me to her

litter before, I tried to suppress a smile. Eco was away that day tending to his own affairs; what choice did I have but to go by myself? As I was leaving through the foyer, I met Bethesda coming in from outside. She had surely seen the litter and knew where I was going. I held my breath, but she only smiled as we passed and said, 'Take care of yourself, husband.' Then she stopped, pulled my face to hers, and gave me a long, deep kiss. She laughed as she walked away. Pompey's politics, Bethesda's sense of humour, my seventeen-year-old daughter's moods: what else did I need to add to the list of things I would never, ever comprehend?

A moment later I was beside Clodia in her litter, moving through the streets of the Palatine. She took my hand and gave me a sidelong, soulful look. 'Gordianus, the rumours we've heard about you – so awful! Such an ordeal for your family! Tell me everything.'

I shook my head. 'No. I'm in much too good a mood to spoil it with unpleasant talk.'

'Is it so painful for you to remember?' She drew her eyebrows together. It had to be a trick of the soft, filtered light that there was not a wrinkle on her face. 'Gordianus, what are you grinning at?'

'The light inside this litter. The warmth of your body. That elusive, unforgettable scent of yours. Men live and die, nations rise and fall, but some things never change.'

'Gordianus . . .'

'What an extraordinary woman you are,

Clodia. Shall I live and die and never make love to you?'

'Gordianus!' Did she actually blush? No, that was impossible; Clodia was beyond blushing. It had to be a trick of the light, like the perfection of her skin. 'Gordianus, I've come on behalf of Fulvia; you must know that.' She tried to make her voice businesslike, but she couldn't help smiling.

'Is that what you told my wife, when she looked into the litter to say hello to you?'

'Of course. Then we talked about the weather. Don't you love an early spring?'

'My wife is a goddess, you know. Any mortal woman would be insanely jealous of you.'

She tilted her head. 'I agree, she must be divine; any man married to a mere mortal would have succumbed to me long ago. But I thought perhaps you considered me a goddess.'

'Oh, no, Clodia. I most definitely consider you a woman. There is no question of that . . .'

We smiled at each other. Then our smiles wavered. A cloud obscured the sun, changing the light inside the litter. Neither of us looked away.

'Is something about to happen, Gordianus?' said Clodia. I hardly recognized her voice.

I took a deep breath and squeezed her hand. After a moment she pulled it away, able to read my touch. I shrugged. 'If something were to happen between us, Clodia, then everything would change. The play of light inside this litter, the

481

warmth of your body, that elusive, unforgettable scent. They would never be the same again, and I want them never to change.'

She seemed to tremble, then laughed softly. 'Men!' she said, in a disparaging but not unfriendly way. For a moment I thought I had hurt her, and felt a strange thrill. Then I realized I was being absurd. A few moments alone with Clodia could bring out the peacock in any man.

'What did you discover, then, on the Appian Way?' Her voice was casual again. 'Anything new of importance?'

'I hardly know where to start. We're almost at Fulvia's house, aren't we? Why don't you come in with me, and listen along with Fulvia?'

The look on her face made it clear that this was not possible. 'Perhaps afterwards, on the way home, you can give me a private report,' she said.

'Yes, if you wish.'

Her litter deposited me on the steps leading up to the entrance. A guard showed me inside. The lofty rooms were still unfinished and haphazardly furnished. Without its master and its architect, the house of Clodius was frozen in time.

The room where Fulvia and her mother awaited me was brighter and warmer than before, but Sempronia still kept a blanket over her lap and gave me an icy look. I sensed that there were others in the room, and felt a unexpected thrill of relief as Fulvia introduced them.

'Gordianus, I think you already know Felicia, keeper of the shrine of the Good Goddess on the

Appian Way, and her brother Felix, attendant to the altar of Jupiter in Bovillae.'

'You took my advice, then?' I said to Felicia.

'My brother and I discussed it for all of an hour, then gathered up what we needed and headed for Rome before dawn the next morning. We've hardly left this house since.' Felicia was as striking as ever. Even as a suppliant in another woman's home she carried herself with the same intriguing, infuriating nonchalance.

'I won't let them leave,' said Fulvia. 'They're too valuable as witnesses. And too vulnerable; Milo must have heard by now that there were witnesses to his crimes. Felix and Felicia are safe with me, and quite comfortable.'

'Quite, quite comfortable,' agreed Felix, whose face looked fuller than I remembered it.

'Witnesses?' I said. 'Is there to be a trial?'

'Oh, yes,' said Fulvia. 'There have been delays. Pompey had to reorganize the courts to his liking, and Milo has made a bigger spectacle of himself than he ever put on with his gladiators, stalling and blustering and using every kind of legal manoeuvre to wriggle his way out of the inevitable. But my nephew Appius is finally ready to bring the case. Once the charges are officially filed, it will be only a matter of days until we crush the bastard for good.'

Sempronia ground her teeth and spat on the floor.

'We heard of your misfortune,' said Fulvia.

'Please, as I just told your sister-in-law, I have no more stomach for talking about it.'

483

'Good,' said Fulvia bluntly. 'I'm sick of mulling over misfortunes myself. It's the future I want to think about now. Felix, Felicia, please leave us.' Felix crept out obsequiously. His sister followed behind him, flashing a very inappropriate smile at me.

Fulvia made a face. 'What trash those people are! My skin crawls every time they're near me.'

'The man eats like a pig,' said Sempronia, 'and the woman snoops everywhere, then pretends to be a halfwit when I catch her at it.'

'Utter trash!' declared Fulvia.

'I should think your late husband's wide circle of friends must have acquainted you with many people no better or worse,' I said.

'Watch your tongue, Finder!' snapped Sempronia.

Fulvia waved a hand to caution her mother. 'Gordianus is our guest. And we have unfinished business with him.'

'Do we?' I said.

'I realize that you never formally agreed to the proposition I made to you. Yet you set out to investigate my husband's death, anyway. I suspect you must have been employed by a certain other person; how else to explain the presence of his bodyguards at your house? But in light of the fact that you directed valuable witnesses to come to my house for protection −'

'I did it as much for their sake as for yours,' I said.

She paused, taken aback by my bluntness. 'Maybe so, but the action still marks you as a friend

to our cause. Did you accept my proposition, after all? Do you have anything to report to me?'

'About Marc Antony, you mean?'

'Yes.'

I hesitated. 'What was the figure you promised?'

She named the sum.

'I'll settle for half that amount,' I said. 'To make up the difference, I want you to give me two of your slaves.'

She looked dubious. 'If you're looking for more bodyguards, I should tell you that the best of my men are each worth considerably more than the sum I just named.'

'No, Fulvia, it's not protectors I'm looking for. I only want two small boys who reside at your Alban villa. Brothers; their names are Mopsus and Androcles.'

'What, the stableboys?'

Sempronia smirked. 'Is that how your tastes run, Finder? Clodia must be telling the truth when she says that you've never tried to touch her, despite all her rubbing up against you.'

I bit my tongue. I sighed and shrugged. 'I can only say that I intend to put the boys to better use than you have, Fulvia. Did you realize that they saved your son's life when Milo and his men stormed the villa?'

'What, because they happened to be in that secret passageway with him and managed to keep from blubbering?'

'Is that how your son explained it? I think neither of you give the boys enough credit.'

485

'They're only stableboys, Gordianus.'

'Perhaps, but I'll wager that they grow up twice as clever and resourceful as anyone else in your household.'

Fulvia raised an eyebrow. 'If you want the two slaves as part of your payment, Gordianus, you may have them.'

'Good. Shall I make my report?'

'Yes.'

'Marc Antony had nothing whatever to do with your husband's death.'

'As simple as that?'

'You have my word.'

'Your word?' said Sempronia icily. Fulvia began to pace before the open windows.

'What else can I offer you? Certainty is a strange thing. Aristotle showed that no man can prove that a particular thing did not happen. I carried your question with me everywhere on the Appian Way, Fulvia, and into the pit where I resided for forty days, and even to Antony himself in Ravenna. I travelled back to Rome beside him, making my own judgment. Antony is completely innocent of spilling your husband's blood, despite his feelings for you.'

Sempronia looked disgusted. 'The scoundrel seduced you, then, as well!'

Fulvia glared at her. 'Leave the room, Mother.'

Sempronia made a great show of gathering up her blanket and straightening her weary limbs. She did not deign to look at me as she left.

For the first time, I found myself alone with

Fulvia. I sensed a difference in her at once. When she stopped her pacing and turned towards me, her face seemed to belong to a different woman, younger and more vulnerable. 'You're sure of this, Finder?'

'Antony is innocent, of this crime at least.'

She smiled, but there were also tears in her eyes. What emotions raged inside her, always held in check to keep others from seeing? 'There's hope, then. I may have a future, after all.'

'With Antony? But he's already married, to his cousin. Does he intend to divorce Antonia?'

'No, that's impossible. A divorce now would destroy him. He's suggested that I consider marrying Curio instead.'

'His boyhood friend?'

'His boyhood lover. You can say the word. I think of the two of them as fabled Greek warriors, like Achilles and Patroclus.'

'But would you settle for being Briseis?'

She looked at me blankly. The allusion escaped her, and so failed to insult her. She was not the literary type.

'Are you thinking of marriage again so soon?' I said.

'Curio and I shall wait until an appropriate time.'

'But such a marriage —'

'Why not? The two of us love Antony and always have. And Antony loves the two of us, more than anything else. Certainly more than he loves Antonia.'

'But Clodius —'

487

'Clodius is dead,' she said grimly, 'and I intend to see him revenged. But Antony is alive. And Curio is alive, and unmarried. I have to think of the days to come. Who knows what the future will bring?' Her smile was gone. So were her tears. 'Do you want your payment now?'

'Yes, thank you.'

'I'll have the silver brought up and counted. And the two stableboys?'

'I'll collect them at my leisure.'

I left Fulvia's house in high spirits. It was the ebullience of being free again after having been captive, of being back in the city where I was known and others had need of me. The heft and jingle of new silver in my purse also helped, as did the satisfaction of having acted on pure impulse when I requested the two boys from Fulvia. I felt quite content with myself and with my place in the world at that moment.

My mood changed abruptly when I saw that Clodia's litter was gone.

Her haughty, handsome young slave remained, along with a sufficient bodyguard to see me safely home. 'I hope you won't mind walking,' he said, practically sneering.

'But where is Clodia?'

'She remembered more pressing business.'

'But I had things to tell her. Things she wanted very much to hear.'

'I suppose she decided they weren't so important after all.' The slave was absurdly patronizing. 'Shall

we be going? You can manage the walk, can't you? Or shall I send someone to hire a litter?' Now he was being deliberately insulting.

I considered giving him a friendly lecture. He was young and beautiful now, and he had his mistress's favour. But for how long? Had he seen what became of the long line of those who had pleased his mistress before him?

But what was the point? The slave was simply deluded. What he took to be my humiliation, Clodia's abrupt departure, was precisely the opposite. I had wounded her after all, so badly that she fled. I, Gordianus, had hurt Clodia. It was a triumph, I told myself; and answered myself, yes, of the sort that Pyrrhus was famous for. The light inside the litter, the warmth of her body, that elusive, unforgettable scent — something told me I would never experience these things again.

# XXIX

Over the next few days, as had been the case all through the period of our absence from Rome, there were continual contios in the Forum at which the radical tribunes railed against Milo. I myself stayed safely bolted behind the doors of my own house, but Eco, who made a point of attending these contios, assured me that they were peaceable affairs, kept that way by the presence of Pompey's troops.

'I don't know which would dismay me more,' I told him, 'seeing a contio erupt into a riot, or seeing Roman citizens being cowed by Roman soldiers.'

'Papa, something had to be done about the violence.'

'Then we might as well have a king. That's what it feels like now, seeing soldiers in the streets – it's like being in Alexandria, where you see King Ptolemy's men everywhere you go.'

'Well, let's hope Pompey's soldiers do a better job of keeping the peace,' said Eco. 'Really, Papa, you sound almost nostalgic for the good old days of blood in the streets.'

'I'm not sentimental about the past, Eco, only fearful for the future.'

'Meanwhile, Papa, the rest of us are living in the present. Nobody else objects to seeing a few soldiers in the Forum.'

'Not yet.'

When I told Bethesda about my acquisition of Mopsus and Androcles, she took the news that there would soon be two more mouths to feed – children, no less, and boy-children, at that! – with more equanimity than I expected. Did I seem so frail that she felt obliged to indulge me, no matter what madness I came up with? Had the spirit of Minerva entered her when the statue fell and broke, making her permanently serene?

Her own explanation was simpler. She had always enjoyed Eco and Meto when they were boys, she said. If the Fates had led two more boys to my household, then she would do her best to welcome them. Managing to feed the household had always been a challenge – especially at present, since Davus seemed to eat even more than Belbo had – but she would manage.

Diana's reaction was even more surprising. She had hated it when Eco and Menenia's twins supplanted her as the baby of the family, but she had matured a great deal since then, and I had no

intention of making her accept Mopsus and Androcles as little brothers; they would simply be household servants. Still, I anticipated that Diana might be diffident or even averse to the idea. I had no idea that it would cause her to break into tears and run from the room.

'What in Jupiter's name was that about?' I said to Eco.

'She doesn't seem to like the idea.'

'But why the tears?'

'She's seventeen. She'll cry at anything.'

'Bethesda says Diana never shed a tear while we were gone.'

'Then I should have said: she's seventeen, she'll cry at nothing. You know, it's time she married, Papa. That's probably what it's about. The idea of new children in the house makes her realize that she probably won't be here much longer herself.'

'Do you really think that's it?'

'I have no idea. Have you given any thought to finding her a husband lately?'

'Eco, when have I had time? You're the one who's been out and about, going to all these contios.'

'I hardly think I'll find a fit husband for my little sister among that rabble.'

'Maybe Menenia has a cousin the right age,' I suggested.

'Or maybe Meto knows of an officer who's eligible.'

'I suppose it is something we need to start working on,' I admitted. 'But you know what I

really need to get done? I need to have the statue of Minerva repaired . . .'

A few mornings later, one of Eco's bodyguards returned to the house in a state of great excitement. Davus showed him into my study. 'There's a contio about to start down in the Forum,' he said, a little out of breath from running up the Ramp, 'and the master says you must come.'

'But why?'

'He only says that you must. He's waiting for you there.'

Davus and I followed the man back to the Forum.

A considerable crowd had gathered. The tribune Plancus was already speaking. Not far from the Rostra, a squadron of armed soldiers were stationed on the steps of the ruined Senate House. The sight of them did lend a certain gravity to the proceedings, I had to admit.

We found Eco in the crowd. 'What's this about?' I whispered.

'If the rumours are true, Plancus is going to introduce – but look, he's just brought them onto the platform with him.' Four men led by another walked onto the Rostra, all of them looking nervous and out of place.

Plancus reached for the leader and pulled him to the centre of the platform. 'Citizen, tell these good men your name.'

The man answered with an inaudible mumble. The crowd jeered and laughed. 'Citizen,' said

Plancus good-naturedly, 'you'll have to speak up. See those soldiers over on the Senate House steps? Pretend you're speaking to them.'

'My name is Marcus Aemilius Philemon!' the man shouted. There was a round of cheering and applause.

'Tell us, Philemon,' said Plancus, 'do you remember where you were on the day that Publius Clodius was murdered?'

'Indeed I do. I was with these four other men on the Appian Way. We were travelling on foot, headed for Neapolis.'

'And how far did you get that day?'

'To Bovillae.'

'What happened there?'

'We came upon what looked like a battle.'

'Where was this?'

'At the inn.' The crowd now listened with rapt attention. Philemon cleared his throat and continued. 'There seemed to be a group inside the inn and a group outside, and the ones outside were after the ones inside. They'd broken down the door. They kept forcing their way in and dragging out the men one at a time and stabbing them to death, right there in the road. There was blood all over the place.'

'A horrifying sight, I'm sure,' said Plancus. 'What did you do?'

'We shouted at them, 'What are you doing?' And they said, 'We've got Publius Clodius trapped like a rat and we're going to cut his tail off!' They were laughing quite a lot, having a good time of it.'

' "They", you say. Did you recognize any of these men?'

'I knew two of them right away. We all did. Those two famous gladiators of Milo's, Eudamus and Birria. They were the ones who seemed to be doing most of the killing. Blood all over them.'

'What did you do then?'

'We shouted at them to stop what they were doing. I may be only a freedman, but I wasn't going to stand by and watch while slaves murdered a citizen!'

This elicited noises of approval from the crowd.

'Freedman you may be,' said Plancus, 'but it's a worthy citizen who'll stand up for his fellow Roman. You tried to stop this atrocity, then?'

'My friends and I went at them, but I'll tell you, not one of us has ever been a soldier or a gladiator. They beat us back. Then they chased after us. We had daggers, but these fellows were gladiators and armed with swords. I won't say I did a brave thing, turning and running, but I'll challenge any man here to stand nose to nose with the likes of Eudamus or Birria and not flinch.' This elicited some sympathetic murmurs.

'Still, you did a brave thing, citizen, you and your fine friends here. I should hope that if ever some scoundrel like Milo sends his slaves after me or my loved ones, there'll be citizens like you to come to my rescue!' Plancus led the crowd in an outburst of cheering and applause.

'But Philemon,' Plancus continued, 'how is it that we're only now hearing about this? Why did

you not come forward before, when we were all in a state of confusion about what happened on the Appian Way?'

'Because we've only now had the chance to come forward. For two months, we were all held prisoner by Milo at his villa in Lanuvium.'

This created a great stir in the crowd.

'Explain, Philemon,' said Plancus.

'When Eudamus and Birria and their men came after us, we all split up and headed away from the road. We thought we might be able to lose them in the hills and the woods. But there were plenty of them after us, and they caught us one by one until they'd rounded up all five of us. They tied us up and herded us like prisoners back through Bovillae and up the Appian Way.'

'Slaves did this? To citizens?'

Men in the crowd shook their fists and shouted curses at Milo. 'Burn his house!' someone shouted. 'Burn down the villain's house!' I looked uneasily at the soldiers who stood rigidly at attention on the Senate House steps.

Plancus quieted the crowd so that Philemon could go on. 'They took us up the hill to Milo. He was standing in the road with a lot of men around him. When he saw us he stamped his foot and had a tantrum like a child. I thought that was the end of us, that they'd kill us right there in the road. But Milo ordered his men to gag us and put bags over our heads. Then we were shoved into some sort of wagon or carriage and they took us to a place a few miles away – Milo's own villa in

Lanuvium, as it turned out. They locked us in an underground storage room. And that's where we stayed for two long months while they fed us on kitchen scraps and mouldy bread. Then we heard from one of the men guarding us that Milo had finally made up his mind to have us killed. I don't want to say too much about how we escaped, as there were those in Milo's villa who helped us do it.'

'You said you were prisoners for two months,' yelled someone in the crowd. 'But it's been more like three months since Clodius was killed. What have you been doing in the month since you escaped? Why haven't we heard from you before?'

'I can answer that,' said Plancus. 'These men have been lying low. Are you surprised? Milo spared their lives once, but what would stop him from killing them if he could catch them a second time? Now it finally looks as if Milo will be brought to justice after all, and so these men have come forward. Truth bides its time.'

'But is it the truth?' shouted another man in the crowd. 'The whole story sounds suspicious to me. You Clodians looked everywhere and you never could find anybody who saw the actual killing, and now you've suddenly come up with five witnesses who claim they were there on the spot! And if it seems a bit funny that we haven't heard from them in all this time, oh, that's because they just happen to have been held prisoner for a couple of months! It's all a bit incredible, if you ask me. Do they have any proof that Milo held them captive?'

One of the four men ran to the front of the platform and shook his fist. 'Proof? You want proof of something? I can think of a way to prove whether or not you have blood in your veins!'

There were more shouts and threats. The mood began to turn ugly. I looked towards the soldiers. Was it my imagination, or had they all moved a few steps closer? Plancus shook his head and gestured for calm, but more and more shouting matches began to break out. I nudged Eco, who nodded his consent, and we made our way out of the crowd.

'So, Papa, the mystery of the prisoners on the road is solved.'

I nodded. 'Not Clodius's men after all, just hapless travellers who happened to stumble upon the fracas.'

'I can see why Eudamus and Birria hunted them down, but why didn't they kill them on the spot? Why did they spare them?'

'Their recklessness had already got their master into enough trouble for one day. Who knew who these five fellows were, or whether some powerful patron might be offended if they were killed? Milo must have thought it was better to simply hold them prisoner until the storm passed. Instead, the storm only kept building. You heard what Philemon said: just before they escaped, Milo had finally made up his mind to get rid of them. Probably some slave in Milo's villa took pity on them and helped them get away.'

'There were sceptics in the crowd. I suppose it is a rather incredible story.'

'But it all sounds only too credible to us, eh, Eco?'

The next morning, Pompey's legislation to reform the law courts, proposed a month before, was officially voted on and approved by the Senate. Immediately, Appius Claudius brought formal charges against Milo, accusing him of the crime of political violence in the murder of their uncle. Under Pompey's new rules for the courts, each side was allowed ten days to prepare for the trial. Rome held its breath.

If convicted, Milo would be subject to immediate, permanent exile and the confiscation of almost all his possessions. He would be disgraced and dispossessed. He would be finished in Rome forever.

But what if he was absolved? I tried to imagine the reaction in the city. I could envision only endless flames, rubble and bloodshed. Could even Pompey with his troops contain such a whirlwind? Reason, morality and simple pragmatism argued that any verdict other than guilty was impossible, except . . .

Except that Milo had Cicero on his side. And as I had learned from long, sometimes bitter experience, with Cicero for the defence, anything was possible.

# XXX

The trial of Titus Annius Milo began on the morning of the fourth day of the month of Aprilis, with the examination of witnesses in the courtyard of the Temple of Liberty. Presiding over the court from a raised tribunal was the former consul Lucius Domitius Ahenobarbus, a grim-jawed, humourless former consul hand-picked by Pompey himself and, purely as a formality, approved by a vote of the people's assembly. Testimony was given before a panel of 360 potential jurors who sat on raised benches on either side of the courtyard. This panel had been selected from a list of eligible senators and men of property drawn up by Pompey. Of these, eighty-one would ultimately be chosen by lot to make up the jury.

Milo and his advocates, Cicero and Marcus Claudius Marcellus, sat with their secretaries on benches facing the tribunal, as did the prosecutors,

Clodius's nephew Appius Claudius, Publius Valerius Nepos, and Marc Antony. Also present were numerous officers of the court, including a battery of secretaries to record the testimony in Tironian shorthand.

A huge crowd gathered at the open end of the courtyard to view the proceedings. Those with foresight sent slaves ahead to save places for them. Eco and I, with our long experience of trials, had managed to secure excellent seats in the tenth row; Davus and one of his fellow bodyguards had arrived well before dawn with our folding chairs, and dozed on them until we arrived. Latecomers without chairs crowded into every vacant nook and cranny and continually tried to push their way in from the Forum.

Pompey was not present. Nor were Pompey's soldiers, who seemed so omnipresent everywhere else in the city. Even Pompey would not dare to post armed troops at a Roman trial. Surely they would not be needed; even the Clodians would not dare to disrupt a Roman trial. A political gathering was one thing. A public trial, the most sacred of Roman institutions, the cornerstone of Roman justice, was another matter.

The first witness to be called was Gaius Causinius Schola, one of the men who had accompanied Clodius on horseback that day on the Appian Way. He testified that Clodius's party had met and passed Milo's larger party close to the tenth hour of the day; that a scuffle had broken out among the rearguard of the two parties, for reasons

he did not know, though he suspected that Milo's men had started it; that when Clodius turned and cast a dark look at Birria, the gladiator hurled a spear at Clodius and wounded him, knocking him from his horse. Fighting broke out, and Schola himself was knocked from his horse and driven into the woods by Milo's slaves. He remained in hiding until well after dark, then made his way to Clodius's villa, where he found that the place was in shambles and that the foreman and the tutor Halicor had been murdered. The next day he returned to Rome.

In essentials, Schola's story matched what I had learned from Felicia, though in the finer details he cast Clodius in an even more innocent light.

When the time for cross-examination arrived, a thrill of anticipation passed through the crowd as Milo, Cicero and Marcellus conferred. Milo and Cicero remained seated. Their colleague Marcellus stepped forward.

Someone in the crowd shouted, 'Let's see Cicero!'

'No, let's see Milo – with his head on a stick!'

Marcellus ignored them. He was a seasoned orator, used to the give and take of debates in the Senate and catcalls from the rabble at trials. 'So, Schola,' he began, 'you claim that the incident on the Appian Way occurred at the tenth hour of the day. And yet –'

There was an eruption of jeering from the crowd, drowning him out. Marcellus scowled and waited for the noise to subside, but as soon as he opened his mouth again, the jeering

recommenced, even louder. He opened his arms in an appeal to Domitius on the tribunal, then gave a start as a stone the size of a child's fist came hurtling through the air and struck him in the back. He whirled about and stared at the crowd with a look of utter shock on his face.

The mob, still screaming and jeering, began to rush towards the tribunal, pouring in along the sides of the seated crowd, knocking down bystanders and stampeding over broken folding chairs. Eco and I seemed to be safe enough, since we were seated near the centre of the seated spectators with plenty of occupied chairs all around us. Then a group of men came scrambling right through the midst of the seated crowd, stepping on people's laps and shoulders.

Domitius rose to his feet and shouted furiously at the prosecutors. They shrugged helplessly, making an elaborate mime of being unable to hear him and equally unable to do anything about the unruly crowd. The panel of potential jurors, men of substance who were not easily intimidated, shook their heads and looked thoroughly disgusted. Milo, Cicero and Marcellus, together with their secretaries, gathered up armfuls of scrolls and wax tablets and rushed to join Domitius on the tribunal. As the mob drew closer and showed no sign of stopping, Milo and his party retreated into the Temple of Liberty, leaving Domitius to stand with his hands on his hips, defying the mob to violate a sacred temple. But the mob seemed satisfied to have silenced Marcellus and driven Milo to flight. They

occupied the tribunal and in a jubilant mood began to stamp their feet and recite lewd chants about Milo's wife Fausta. When it became evident that order was not going to be restored, jurors and peaceful spectators who had not already fled began to disperse. Eventually there was a rumour that Pompey was coming with a troop of armed soldiers. This caused the mob to abandon the tribunal and scatter in all directions.

Thus ended the first day of Milo's trial.

The next day began much as the first, except that the room for spectators was more constricted, thanks to the soldiers who now flanked the courtyard on either side. At Domitius's insistence, Pompey had assigned troops to keep order during the trial. Roman justice would be carried out with the assistance of Roman steel.

The hearing of witnesses resumed with the testimony of various persons from the vicinity of Bovillae, beginning with Felicia. Like an actor finally allowed to have a major role, she seemed determined to make the most of her time as a witness. She flashed her incongruous smile and projected her sultry demeanour while the advocates examined and cross-examined her; many of the spectators, meanwhile, seemed to be examining her in another way. The day was off to an appropriately bizarre beginning.

Her brother Felix testified next, about the comings and goings of the victims and their pursuers, including the bound prisoners, who were now

known to be Philemon and his companions. Philemon himself testified, reiterating the story he had told at the contio. The wife of the slain innkeeper at Bovillae did not appear; she was still in seclusion down in Rhegium, I assumed. Her sister and brother-in-law, the current keepers of the inn, gave secondhand testimony about what the widow had told them and described the gory aftermath.

The Virgo Maxima told of the visit by an unknown woman offering thanks to the goddess for the death of Publius Clodius. This account so inflamed the Clodians that for a while it seemed there might be another disturbance. Pompey's soldiers eventually moved to drive off some of the more vocal agitators. Order was restored, but by this point Domitius was ready to adjourn the court for the day.

The third day of testimony began with the last of the witnesses from the vicinity of Bovillae. Senator Sextus Tedius was called. He rose from the front row of spectators and hobbled before the court, using a cane and dragging his lame left leg. I was in the second row of spectators that day and was close enough to see his daughter Tedia sitting next to the chair he had vacated, looking after him with a worried expression. Normally she would have assisted him, I thought. Probably he did not care to be seen accepting a woman's help in front of the court.

Senator Tedius repeated the story he had told me: that he had left for Rome in his litter accompanied by his daughter and some slaves, that he had

encountered Milo, who warned him of fictitious bandits, but had pressed on to Bovillae, where he found Clodius's abandoned body in the road, apparently dragged there by his killers, and had sent it on to Rome in his litter. It was now evident that Tedius must have arrived while Eudamus and Birria and their men were off in the woods hunting for Philemon and his companions. After dispatching Clodius to Rome, Tedius returned by foot towards Aricia, and told of seeing the prisoners being marched up the road while he rested at a spot close to the new House of the Vestals.

A man named Quintus Arrius, a colleague of Clodius, testified that he had helped to interrogate Clodius's slaves after the incident. One of them, a personal secretary, had confessed under torture that for months he had provided information on Clodius's movements to an agent of Milo's. Therefore, Arrius suggested, Milo was regularly kept apprised of Clodius's comings and goings, and could have premeditated the apparently chance encounter on the Appian Way. Cicero, during cross-examination, scoffed at this idea, pointing out that Schola had testified on the first day that Clodius left his villa suddenly, upon hearing the news of the death of Cyrus the architect; therefore, how could Milo, even with an inside source, have predicted their encounter?

Then Cicero called a witness himself: Marcus Cato, who descended from the raised benches where the potential jurors sat. Cato, perhaps the only person in the court even more staid and

conservative than Domitius the judge, gave second-hand testimony to the effect that a certain Marcus Favonius had passed along a remark to him which Clodius had made exactly three days before the fatal incident.

'And what was this remark, this jewel, this bit of wisdom from the lips of Publius Clodius?' said Cicero.

Cato looked at Domitius and the panel of jurors. 'Clodius told Favonius that Titus Annius Milo would be dead within three days.'

There was a stir of excitement in the court. 'Cato's a liar and a drunk!' someone yelled. 'What's he doing sitting with the jury if he's a witness?'

Cicero spun about. 'Who impugns the judgment of Pompey? It was the Great One himself who personally selected Marcus Cato to sit among the jurors, and why? Because Cato's integrity and honesty are absolutely beyond doubt. Any man who says otherwise only shows himself to be a fool.'

This was true enough. Whatever one thought of his politics, Cato was not a man to lie. But the story he told was only secondhand; Clodius supposedly said something to Favonius, who said something to Cato. And Cicero, I noticed, made no refutation of the accusation that Cato was a drunkard. A lifetime of hard drinking showed in the statesman's rheumy eyes.

Whatever effect Cicero had hoped to achieve by Cato's testimony was entirely negated by what followed.

507

The last witnesses to be heard were Sempronia and Fulvia. Each told how Clodius's body had arrived at his house on the Palatine borne in a stranger's litter, unaccompanied by friends or any sort of explanation. They described the shocking condition of his corpse. They explained how the surviving friends and slaves who had been with him made their way back to Rome one by one, each adding another horrifying detail to the catastrophe that had occurred on the Appian Way. They spoke of Clodius's young son, Publius, who was missing and unaccounted for all that night, and of their grief and worry when they learned of the slaughter at Clodius's Alban villa. Sempronia – dour, smug Sempronia – broke down and wept, and seemed to become the image of every man's anxious, fretful grandmother. Fulvia, who began with a stiff, emotionless recitation of the facts, ended with a shrieking lament that eclipsed even her agony on the night of her husband's death. She wept, pulled at her hair and tore her stola.

I heard more weeping nearby, and saw that the daughter of Sextus Tedius had covered her face with her hands. Her father stared straight ahead, apparently embarrassed by such a display.

But Tedia was not the only one who shed tears. I thought it could only be a miracle that kept the Clodians from erupting into another riot, until I looked around and saw that many of them were weeping uncontrollably.

Cicero did not dare to cross-examine the women. The court adjourned at the tenth hour.

Thus ended the third day of Milo's trial, and the last day of testimony. One hundred days had passed since the death of Publius Clodius. One more day, and the fate of Titus Annius Milo would be decided.

Late that afternoon, the tribune Plancus held a final contio on the subject of Clodius's death. He urged Clodius's followers to come out in force the next morning to hear the actual pleading of the case. The speeches for the prosecution and defence would be delivered in the open Forum, which would accommodate a great many more spectators than the courtyard of the Temple of Liberty. Those who had loved Clodius must make themselves seen and heard, said Plancus, so that the jurors could know the will of the people, and they must encircle the court completely, so that once the outcome of the trial became evident, the treacherous coward Milo would have no opportunity to slip away before the verdict was announced.

That night, over dinner, Eco and I gave Bethesda a full account of the day's events. She seemed to approve of Fulvia's performance. 'A woman's grief is sometimes the only weapon she has. Think of Hecuba and the Trojan women. Fulvia has used her grief where it will have the most effect.'

'I wonder why they didn't call Clodia to testify,' said Diana, who had been so listless throughout the meal that I thought she wasn't listening.

'That would only have detracted from Fulvia's

grief,' said Eco. 'And it would have distracted the jurors, reminding them of certain rumours of what went on between Clodia and her brother.'

'And after what Cicero did to her the last time she appeared at a trial, I should be surprised if she ever appeared at one again,' said Bethesda. 'Has she attended this trial?'

'I haven't seen her,' I said, and changed the subject.

Like many people in Rome that night, I imagine, I had a hard time sleeping. I tossed and turned and finally got out of bed. I went to my study and looked for something to read. I scanned the little title tags that hung from the scrolls in their pigeon-holes, muttering to myself.

'Now what is the play that has that famous quote, about the gods bringing about an unexpected end? Euripides, isn't it? And why is it on my mind tonight? Oh, yes, I know. Because it always reminds me of the trial of Sextus Roscius, when I first worked for Cicero; his first great triumph in the courts. And when it was all over – almost over – I remember quoting that bit of Euripides to Tiro. Tiro was so young then, only a boy! I was so young then, too . . .

'But what is the play? Not *The Trojan Women* or *Hecuba* – that was Bethesda, who mentioned Hecuba at dinner tonight. No, it's from . . . *The Bacchae!*'

And there it was at my fingertips. I pulled it from the hole, found some weights and unrolled it on a table.

It was one of the oldest books I owned, but was still in good condition. The passage I was thinking of was at the very end, delivered by the chorus of frenzied Dionysian revellers:

> The gods have many guises.
> The gods bring crises to climax
> while man surmises.
> The end anticipated
> has not been consummated.
> But god has found a way
> for what no man expected.
> So ends the play.

What no man expected . . .

Could Cicero pull it off? Could he deliver a speech – one of those famous, logic-twisting, doubt-defying, hilarious, wrenching speeches of his – that would actually convince the jurors to declare Milo not guilty? It seemed impossible. But so had many another case where Cicero had snatched triumph from despair. If anyone could do it . . .

As I was rolling up the scroll, I ripped a bit of parchment at the top. I cursed. It was such an old scroll. When and where had I got it? Ah, yes: Cicero himself had given it to me, as he had given me many books since. This had been the first. He had even inscribed it, as I recalled.

I unrolled it enough to read the message he had written across the top, in his own hand:

> To Gordianus, fondly, with bright hopes for
> the future.

My blood froze. I had known all along, of
course. Still, to see the proof before me . . .

I found the message that had been left for
Bethesda and put it side by side with the
scroll.

> Do not fear for Gordianus and his son. They
> have not been harmed. They will be returned
> to you in time.

There could be no doubt. The proof was there in
the peculiar shape of the letter G – indeed, in the
way my name was written in each case.

I had looked at other messages from Cicero in
my possession, but not one of them had been in his
own hand. They had all been written by Tiro or
some other secretary. But the dedication on *The
Bacchae* was assuredly in his hand, for I had been
there when he inscribed it.

Davus mumbled in his sleep when I shook him.
The other bodyguards stirred in their beds.

'Davus, wake up.'

'What?' He blinked, then gave a start and jerked
away from me as if I were a monster. 'Master,
please!' His voice cracked like a boy's. What in
Hades was wrong with him?

'Davus, it's only me. Wake up. I need you. I'm
going out.'

The walk to Cicero's house had never seemed so

long. My blood pounded in my ears. I didn't wake Eco to come with me, though he had as great a grievance against Cicero as I did. What I had to say to Cicero I would say by myself.

# XXXI

Cicero's doorkeeper perused me through the peep-hole. A little later he opened the door for me, allowing Davus to enter and wait in the foyer. The interior of the house was ablaze with lights. No one would be abed early in Cicero's house on this night.

As I was led to the study, I heard Cicero's voice echoing down the hallway, and then Tiro, laughing out loud.

I was shown into the room. Cicero and Tiro both greeted me with a smile.

'Gordianus!' Cicero stepped forward and embraced me before I could stop him. It was a politician's embrace; he seemed to encircle me completely and yet hardly touched me anywhere. He stepped back and looked at me like a shepherd at a lost lamb. 'So, at the very last moment, you've come to me. Can I dare to hope, Gordianus, that this means you've come to your senses at last?'

'Oh, yes, Cicero. I have definitely come to my senses.' My mouth was suddenly so dry that I could hardly speak.

'You sound like you need something to drink.' Cicero nodded to the doorkeeper, who disappeared. 'I should tell you, the speech is already pretty much done. But it's not set in stone. Better late than never.'

'What are you talking about?'

'Well, with the way you've been running back and forth to Fulvia's house, and all that time you spent with Marc Antony on the road, you must be well up on what the prosecution has in mind for tomorrow. I can use that sort of information to make sure that all my rebuttals are on target. The fewer surprises they're able to spring on me, the better. Oh, Gordianus, you gave me a scare this time. I thought we had lost you for good. But here you are, back where you belong!'

I looked around the room. Tiro sat amid masses of rolled and rumpled parchment. 'Is Caelius here? Where's Milo?' Merely saying his name made me clench my fists. I took a deep breath.

'Caelius is home, at his father's house, probably sleeping like a baby.'

'Shouldn't he be here with you, working on his speech?'

'Actually . . . ah, here's something to wet your throat! Tiro, would you like a cup as well?'

I thought of refusing, but I needed the drink. I raised an eyebrow as it passed my lips. It must have

515

been the best vintage in the house. 'Isn't it a bit premature to be celebrating, Cicero?'

'Ah, you appreciate the Falernian. Good. Your appearance in my house is adequate cause for celebration, Gordianus.'

'Where's Milo?' I said.

'Not here, as you can see. He's at home with Fausta, I imagine, dreaming sweet dreams of the consulship that will be his next year. Did you especially want to see him?'

That was a difficult question to answer. 'No,' I said. I wanted to keep my head, and that might not be possible in Milo's presence. I finished my cup of wine.

'Gordianus, you look a fright! We must finish our business as quickly as we can, so that you can go home and get some sleep. Now, you asked about Caelius giving a speech. Actually, only one advocate will speak for Milo tomorrow: myself.'

'The rest have all run scared, then? Even Caelius?'

I had finally managed to dampen his ebullience. 'That's not the case at all. This idea that his friends have all deserted Milo is a vicious rumour put about by the Clodians, the same people who keep claiming that Milo wants to assassinate Pompey and bring down the state. They hope to make me look like a fool and to intimidate everyone else into abandoning Milo. But I'll tell you, the best men in Rome are still solidly behind Milo and would gladly have appeared as character witnesses on his behalf. But Pompey's reforms eliminated character witnesses! I

could have had former magistrates and consuls lined up the whole length of the Forum, reciting Milo's virtues for hours. But Pompey wants only material witnesses to speak – people like that parade of disreputable characters we've had to put up with for the last three days.'

'If Milo's friends are still behind him, why are you the only one giving a speech for him?'

'Again, Pompey's reforms! The defence is allowed only three hours – three hours! – to make a case. You know how it was before; a man usually had two or three advocates all speaking for as long as they wished. I hardly need to tell you that I'm usually just beginning to warm up after three hours. The simple truth is, I didn't want to share the time with anyone else. It's even worse for the prosecution; they have only two hours. Well, let their three advocates go tripping over one another, rushing through their notes. They'll make hasty, confused speeches, and then I shall use my time to draw the jurors slowly, steadily, irresistibly into our camp.'

He poured himself a straight cup of the Falernian. When had Cicero begun to drink like other men? 'Don't think I can't do it,' he went on. 'Wait until you hear the speech. It's my masterpiece, Gordianus. Am I boasting, Tiro, or am I simply telling the truth?'

Tiro smiled. 'It's a very fine speech.'

'I have never written a finer one! And my powers of delivery have never been greater. I shall seize the jurors from the first words, I shall clutch them to me like a lover until I have nothing more to say, and

after I'm done I'll defy any man to take a stand against Milo.'

Wine and curiosity had cooled my anger. I decided to listen for a while, bide my time and hear him out. It was the last time I would ever do so. Once I'd said what I'd come to say, there would never again be words between us of any sort. 'How will you do it, Cicero? How will you seduce the jurors?'

'Well, I can't go through the whole speech for you right now; there isn't time.' He smiled crookedly. 'Besides, you might yet be a spy for the enemy, Gordianus. Have you come to ferret out my puns and double meanings before they're ready? I won't have my metaphors and historical allusions anticipated and headed off by the prosecutors! But I'll give you a general outline. Perhaps it will give you some ideas of how you might help me.'

'Help you?'

'Perhaps there's a weak point in the prosecution that I've missed, something you know of that I don't; some point they intend to emphasize that I haven't foreseen. You've probably been privy to information which even my spies have missed. All that lolling about in Clodia's litter, making camp with Antony – you're a valuable man to know, Gordianus! I've always said so. And I've never turned my back on you, no matter how wrongheaded you've been from time to time. I can't tell you how glad I was when the doorkeeper came to say that you were here. I can think of no one I had

rather see on this night. Gordianus the Finder, always full of surprises. 'He shall help me add the final crowning touches to my masterpiece' – I said those very words, did I not, Tiro?'

'You did indeed.' Tiro looked very weary. With his delicate constitution, he should have been in bed, I thought. Or did he blink and lower his eyes to avoid looking at me? Had Tiro been part of the plot against me? The idea sickened me, but Tiro's loyalty to Cicero had always eclipsed everything else in his life.

'The main thrust of my argument,' Cicero went on, full of excitement, 'will be that it was Clodius who planned an ambush on Milo, and that Milo had no choice but to defend himself. It was justifiable homicide!'

'And what about the facts, Cicero?' I said.

'Oh, I shall remind the jury of certain facts – such as the fact that Clodius had a long history of criminal behaviour against the gods and the state. And the fact that even as he was setting out on the Appian Way, he had legislation in the works to reorganize the voting system so as to give himself and his rabble of freedmen even greater power. And I certainly shall not let anyone forget the fact that Clodius was one of the most lecherous and debauched men ever to plague this city.'

'But Clodius did not ambush Milo. Must I say it more slowly? Clodius . . . did not . . . ambush Milo.'

Cicero paused. 'This matter of an ambush, who plotted against whom, who was lying in wait – it's

all academic in a way, don't you see? Consider it a literary device. My young friend Marcus Brutus says that I should argue from the assumption that Milo assassinated Clodius intentionally, knowingly and with foresight, and declare that the homicide was justifiable on the grounds that Milo acted to save the state from a dangerous man. Well, Brutus might get away with that argument, but not me. It would only remind the listeners of my own handling of Catilina and his supporters. Milo must not suffer for the controversies of my own consulship. So that line of defence is closed to us. On the other hand, I might argue that neither Milo nor his men were ultimately responsible for Clodius's death, at least not technically. That may well be the case, as I'm sure you discovered for yourself in your investigations –'

'What are you talking about?'

'Don't be coy with me, Gordianus. It's much too late for that. However, to argue for Milo's outright innocence, I would have to introduce some rather arcane reasoning, and besides, that approach would fail to make any thematic sense; it would neglect the most persuasive argument of all, that Clodius was an immediate danger to Milo and a perennial danger to the state. No, I shall use the argument of an ambush –'

'Cicero, there was no ambush, by either side.'

'Yes, but how do you know that, Gordianus?'

'Because I went there. I saw the place. I spoke to the witnesses.'

'Ah, you went, you saw, you spoke – but the

jurors will have done none of these things. It is up to me to shape their perceptions.'

'But the jurors have already heard the witnesses.'

'Yes, and that's unfortunate. These innovations of Pompey! The traditional sequence is for the advocates to make their arguments first, and shape the juror's opinions before they ever hear a witness. But never mind. Do you think the jurors will still be thinking about that whore of a priestess and her pathetic brother, or that incredibly common woman from the inn, after they've heard me plead Milo's case for three hours? I think not.' He saw the look of consternation on my face and smiled. 'You fail to understand, I see. You doubt that any speech could be so persuasive. But believe me, this is my best speech, by far the finest piece of oratory I've ever devised. You can't imagine the labour that's gone into it.'

'The guile, you mean.'

'Gordianus!' He shook his head, not in disgust – he was too ebullient for that – but in dismay. 'Very well, then, guile. Composition, craft, guile, call it what you will! Where did you ever come by this naive, overweening reverence for the absolute and utter truth? This peculiar obsession – where has it ever got you? If simple truth alone could send armies into battle and sway jurors, if men could be made to respond as they should by telling them the truth, do you think I would use any other tool? It would all be so easy, then. But truth is not enough; often it's the very worst thing for a man

with a cause! And so we have oratory. The beauty, the power of words! Thank the gods for the gift of oratory, and thank the gods for men who are clever enough, and wise enough, to bend the truth a bit every once in a while in order to keep the state free and in one piece. The important thing about tomorrow's hearing is not to determine who did what to whom on the Appian Way. The important thing, the absolutely vital thing, is that at the end of the day, Milo must go free. If the truth hinders that objective, then it must be dispensed with. It serves no purpose. Can't you see that, Gordianus? It's such an elementary matter.'

I had heard enough. 'And my captivity? Was that an elementary matter?'

Cicero's face went blank. 'What do you mean?'

'While I was trapped in that stinking pit, someone wrote an anonymous note to my wife, telling her not to worry. I found another bit of writing – an old, old inscription in a scroll – that matched the handwriting of that note exactly. You wrote the note, Cicero. Do you deny it?'

He clasped his hands behind his back and began to pace. He glanced at Tiro, who watched him expectantly with furrowed brows. 'I wrote the note to your wife, yes.'

'What was your part? Did you know from the beginning? Did you plan the attack on me?'

He made a face, like a man who must step into something soft and smelly. 'When we learned that you had set out for Bovillae, Milo became convinced that you had become a danger to him. It was

all he talked about for days. Who knew what you would find out? For whom were you really working? I tried to dissuade him, but Milo is a stubborn man. He became determined to remove you —'

'To kill me, you mean?'

'To prevent you from returning to Rome. Yes, his first intention was to have you killed. I forbade it. Do you hear me, Gordianus? I forbade him to kill you and your son. I reminded him of the men he was keeping locked up at his villa in Lanuvium, the witnesses his men had captured on the Appian Way. If he could hold those men prisoner, then why not you and your son? I insisted that you be spared, do you understand? Milo compromised, and agreed merely to detain you, and only until the crisis was over. Then you and Eco would be released unharmed.'

'The men who escaped from Lanuvium said that Milo had made up his mind to kill them.'

'That was only a rumour. Even if it was true, it had nothing to do with you. I had Milo's word that you would come to no harm.'

'Milo's word!'

'Did you come to harm? Were you badly treated? There, you see! He kept his word to me. Even so, I felt deeply concerned for your family, knowing how dear you are to them, how much they would miss you and worry about you. I was not so hard and cold that I could ignore that! So I wrote that note to your wife, to allay her fears. I wrote it with my own hand, and had it delivered by an illiterate slave. I should have known you would find

me out in the end, Gordianus. Nothing escapes you! But it was the right thing to do. I can't regret having done it, even now.'

He stood erect with his chin up, like an officer whose honour had been impugned over an act of bravery. I gaped at him. 'You're actually proud of yourself, aren't you? Proud because you browbeat Milo into kidnapping me instead of murdering me —'

'I saved your life, Gordianus!'

'And proud of yourself for writing two lines to my wife instead of setting me free.'

He sighed at my obstinacy. 'Sometimes, Gordianus, in defence of liberty, actions which might otherwise be reprehensible become not only justified but unavoidable.'

I shook my head. 'Tiro, did you hear that? Are you copying it down? Surely your master can use that in his speech tomorrow!'

Cicero pressed his fingertips together. 'Gordianus, some day you will reflect on this episode and realize that you were called upon to make a sacrifice for the good of the state. It may have been a misjudgment on Milo's part, thinking he had to get you out of the way for a short while. You should be flattered that he thought you so dangerous! But consider the greater context. Ultimately, it is a good thing – an exceedingly good thing – that Clodius is dead, and it will be an unmitigated disaster if Milo's enemies succeed in sending him into exile.'

'A disaster for Milo, you mean.'

'Yes! And a disaster for me – and for anyone who

cares about preserving Rome as a republic. We need men like Milo, and Cato, and yes, like myself. There are none of us to spare! You've dealt with Pompey now. You're acquainted with Caesar. Do you really wish to leave everything up to them? If it comes to that, if all the good men are picked off one by one and the power of the Senate dwindles to nothing, and Caesar and Pompey are the only men left standing, how long do you think their partnership will last? Can you imagine another civil war, Gordianus? You're old enough to remember Marius and Sulla. How much more terrible would it be this time, with the whole world in flames? Who will be left to pick up the pieces?'

He bowed his head, as if the hour suddenly weighed on him. 'Everything I do, everything, is to avert that course of events. Consider that, Gordianus, and then consider this little thing, this little injustice that Milo has done you, that you were detained for a few days of your life. Do you wish to be repaid somehow? Is it restitution that you want? Would that satisfy you? Or can you make the effort to see the greater picture and to arrive at some sense of proportion about your part in it? This trial is not just about Milo and Clodius. It's about the future of the Republic. If the truth must be bent, if you and your family must suffer a bit in the name of that cause, then so be it!'

He lifted his head and stared at me steadily, waiting for my reaction.

' 'The beauty, the power of words!' ' I finally said, mocking him. 'Curse the gods who gave us

oratory! And curse the clever men like you who make a travesty of words like liberty and justice! This matter is not finished between us, Marcus Cicero. As for Milo, hopefully my grievance with him will be settled for me, when the court decides his fate tomorrow.'

I turned to leave, then looked back at Tiro. He had remained silent and averted his eyes during the whole exchange. 'Did you know of this?' I said.

When Tiro hesitated, Cicero answered for him. 'Tiro knew nothing about the kidnapping. Milo and I never discussed it in his presence. The fact is, I didn't trust him to keep his mouth shut about it. Tiro has always had a soft spot for you, Gordianus. Even I weakened, and wrote that note to your wife. Tiro might have been even more foolish. He knew nothing.'

I stared at Tiro, who still would not look me in the eye. 'So you deceived Tiro as well. I can believe that. He's not the actor you are, Cicero; his surprise and relief when we met on the Flaminian Way were too genuine to be a pretence. But Tiro – Tiro, look at me! You must have suspected something. Who else but Milo had a reason to kidnap us? How could Cicero not have known?'

Tiro bit his lower lip. 'The thought did occur to me. But I simply didn't ask. I suppose I didn't really want to know. There's been a great deal else on my mind . . .'

'Tell me just one thing, then, Tiro. Only one thing, and the absolute truth. Will you do that for me?'

Tiro looked at me rather forlornly.

'This speech for Milo – is it as good as Cicero claims it is? Or is that only his vanity speaking? Tell me what you really think.'

'The truth, Gordianus?'

'Nothing else.'

'Cicero's speech for Milo is . . .' Tiro sighed. 'Cicero has never written a better speech. No one has. That is my honest opinion. If anything can save Milo, this is the speech to do it. The jurors will weep. It will be Cicero's finest hour.'

This was not what I wanted to hear. May the gods help us all, I thought, as I hurried from the room and left them to go about their work.

As I made my way home, some of Cicero's phrases kept ringing in my head, try as I might to shut them out. All of it had been nonsense, of course, but some had been more nonsensical than the rest. I might argue that neither Milo nor his men were ultimately responsible for Clodius's death, at least not technically. That may well be the case, as I'm sure you discovered for yourself in your investigations . . . However, to argue for Milo's outright innocence, I would have to introduce some rather arcane reasoning . . .'

What in Hades could he have meant by that? I almost wished I had kept a cooler head and asked him; there was no turning back now. He had probably meant nothing at all, I told myself, but was simply spinning words, filling me with doubt, throwing dust in my eyes, just as he would try to do to the jurors in the morning.

# XXXII

On the fourth and final day of Milo's trial I awoke to birdsong in the garden. New flowers had bloomed overnight. Bees and butterflies were already at work, doting on the blossoms. I was tempted to forget the trial and stay home. Why not spend the day enjoying the warm sunshine of Aprilis in my garden? But the plaintive eyes of the staring, broken Minerva would not let me forget what was about to transpire in the Forum.

Davus and a fellow bodyguard had risen long before cockcrow to go down with folding chairs to save places for us. It was a good thing, for I had never seen the Forum so thronged with spectators. By order of Pompey, all taverns were closed for the day. Pompey no doubt intended to head off the threat of drunken rioters, but the radical tribunes must have been pleased for their own reasons; with the taverns closed, even their least civic-minded

supporters had nowhere better to be than in the Forum attending the trial. Despite the crush, Davus had doggedly held on to our seats near the front of the crowd.

Dominating everything were Pompey's troops. Wherever there was an elevated place – temple steps or a bit of wall or ramp or pedestal – the soldiers had already occupied it the night before. A ring of troops completely encircled the Forum. At the various points of entry they pulled aside perfectly peaceable citizens to search for concealed weapons. Pompey himself was said to be in his stronghold in the treasury building, from which he would not stir until a verdict was announced. I felt as if I had awakened in some other city that morning, a place ruled by a military autocrat – except that autocrats do not allow public trials. There was a sense of confusion and uncertainty in the air, almost of unreality.

And yet, everything proceeded smoothly. Milo and Cicero had shown up before most of the crowd, travelling in a plain, closed litter so that their arrival went unnoticed, which was no doubt as they wished it. They stayed out of sight in the litter, ringed by bodyguards, until it was almost time for the trial to begin. The three prosecutors arrived on foot to a great deal of cheering, surrounded by an entourage of secretaries and bodyguards. The officials of the court brought out three large urns; these contained the wooden balls on which each potential juror had written his name. Balls were chosen by lot until eighty-one jurors had been selected,

among them Marcus Cato, I noticed. After the speeches by the prosecution and the defence, each side would be allowed to remove fifteen more jurors, leaving fifty-one men to decide the verdict.

Domitius called the court to order. The prosecutors commenced with their arguments at once.

As Cicero had predicted, their three orations seemed unduly short, more like synopses than full-blown speeches. They were potent, nonetheless. In typical fashion, the prosecutors divided various aspects of the case between them, according to their skills and dispositions.

I knew little about Valerius Nepos, but I had heard that his forte was narrative, and so was not surprised that he gave the opening argument. He described the actual incident with dramatic flourish, using the full range of his ringing voice and dwelling on gruesome details to elicit groans and cries of outrage from the spectators. His final lament was so full of grief that it seemed all he could do to keep from tearing out his hair. Nepos would have made quite a performer on the stage, I thought, bringing blind Oedipus or the tormented Ajax to life.

Marc Antony, the tactician, delivered the middle speech. He made the case that Milo had deliberately plotted to murder Clodius, citing evidence that Milo had spies among Clodius's slaves and going over and over the complicated chronology of Milo's and Clodius's movements on the day of the murder. Antony was the right man for a speech that dwelled, by necessity, on such a concentration of details. A more emotional speaker like Nepos,

wailing over timetables, would have risked looking absurd. A staid orator like Pompey would have put his listeners to sleep. Antony's blend of soldierly gruffness with an innate sincerity of purpose kept the jurors' full attention.

Appius Claudius, the dead man's nephew, delivered the emotional finale, a eulogy full of pathos. Seemingly overcome by grief, he was often choked with tears and had to struggle to regain his composure. In a ringing summation, he made proud references to the greatness of Clodius's forebears and to the poignant irony that he should have met such a brutal death on the famous road which Appius Claudius Caecus had built and along which stood the tombs and shrines of so many members of his noble family.

During these speeches, I looked to see the reactions of Milo and Cicero. Most defendants bring a horde of family members to cluster around them during the trial, but Milo sat alone, his arms tightly crossed. Granted, his parents were dead, but where was his wife? It would count against him that Fausta Cornelia was nowhere to be seen during her husband's ordeal. Given her reputation, I could imagine the sort of jokes the Clodians would come up with to explain her absence.

And what was Milo thinking, to show up at his own trial in a snow-white toga without even a loose stitch, much less a tear in it? His hair looked freshly clipped and combed, and his jaw was so clean-shaven that he must have seen his barber that very morning before he left his house. I had to

shake my head at such audacity. Even the always sardonic Caelius, at his trial, had had the sense (drummed into him by Cicero) to wear an old, threadbare toga and to look at least a bit dishevelled, and Caelius's parents had shown up in torn clothes with their eyes red from crying and baggy from lack of sleep. A Roman defendant is expected to look as wretched as he possibly can, in order to play upon the sympathy of the jurors. This is often merely a formality, but everyone goes along with it out of respect for legal tradition. By showing up looking as if he were paying court to a widow or posing for his portrait, Milo was deliberately thumbing his nose not only at the jury but at the whole judicial process.

Perhaps this was one of the things on his advocate's mind that day. Cicero looked uncommonly distracted, and completely transformed from the previous night. Where was his excitement, his ebullience? His eyes were shifty, his jaw tight, and he gave a start at every unexpected noise from the crowd. He fiddled with scraps of parchment, scribbled notes on a wax tablet, kept whispering to Tiro, and seemed hardly to listen to the prosecutors. Only once did he seem to come to life, during Antony's speech. Antony was trying to imply that Milo paused to water his horses in Bovillae to kill time while he waited for a report that Clodius had left his villa and was on his way, so that Milo could be sure to pass Clodius on the road in order to stage a deliberate attack on him. To frame his accusation, Antony needed to establish

the exact hour at which the incident took place, and stressed the point by repeatedly asking, 'When was Clodius killed? When, I ask you – when was Clodius killed?'

Cicero, in a loud voice, quipped, 'Not nearly soon enough!'

In the immediate silence that followed there was some scattered laughter, but also expressions of shock among the jurors, and then a sudden welling of outrage among the spectators. Cicero's icy grin vanished. Milo stiffened. Even Antony, who had faced barbarians in battle and had no cause to feel threatened by the crowd, backed away from the Rostra and turned pale. I looked behind me to see what they saw: a sea of upraised fists and angry, shouting faces. The fury on those faces was not of the opportunistic sort one sees on looters or soldiers; it had a kind of fiery purity, like the madness of religious ecstatics. It was a fearsome thing; even some of Pompey's soldiers visibly flinched to see it. These were Clodius's people, the angry and dispossessed, the degraded, the hopeless. They were a force to be reckoned with.

I thought in that instant that the trial was about to come to an abrupt end. There would be a riot, murder, mayhem, massive bloodshed, no matter that Pompey's troops were everywhere; the crowd would swallow up the soldiers along with everyone else. But even in the act of cursing and shaking their fists, the Clodians restrained their violence. The climax of the day promised them a deeper satisfaction: their dead leader's vindication and the final

destruction of Milo. The soldiers banged the butts of their spears against the paving stones and clanged their swords against their greaves until the crowd eventually quieted down.

Antony managed a smile. 'The time, in fact, Cicero, was the tenth hour of the day.' The crowd roared with laughter. Cicero's face was like wax.

Antony finished his speech. Appius Claudius delivered his encomium to his uncle, which drove much of the crowd, and even some of the jurors, to tears. Better that they should grieve than riot, I thought.

And then it was time for Cicero to speak.

Surely it must be some sort of ruse, I thought, as Cicero knocked his wax tablet to the ground and stumbled against his chair. Was he feigning clumsiness in a bid for sympathy from a hostile audience? The same people who had been weeping only moments before began to laugh and make catcalls. Milo scowled, crossed his arms tightly across his chest and rolled his eyes up to heaven. Tiro bit his lower lip and pressed his hands against the sides of his face, then seemed to realize what he was doing, drew back his hands and made his face like a statue's.

Cicero's voice shook as he began his speech. It had quavered in just that way the first time I heard him speak in public, at the trial of Sextus Roscius; but that had been a lifetime ago, and since then Cicero had become the leading orator of his time, moving from triumph to triumph. Even in his darkest days, when Clodius was working to have

him exiled, his defiance and sense of self-righteousness had always given him a steady voice, if not always steady friends.

But now his voice shook. 'Distinguished jurors! Distinguished . . . what an opportunity you have today! What a vital decision is yours to make . . . yours to make, and yours alone. Shall a good man, an upstanding citizen, an untiring servant of the state . . . should he be forced to pine away in miserable hardship . . . indeed, shall Rome herself be made to suffer endless, ongoing humiliations . . . or shall you put an end . . . that is, by your staunch, courageous, wise decision, shall you put an end to the long persecution of both the man and his city by lawless hooligans?'

There was another outburst from the crowd. The noise was almost like a physical assault. Cicero appeared to quail before it, shrinking back on the Rostra. Where was the strutting cock who tended to swagger rather than fret before a hostile crowd? I was still inclined to think that his timidity was some sort of pose. What other possibility was there?

The furore at last quieted enough for him to continue. 'When my client . . . and myself . . . when we first took up politics . . .'

'Yes, but when will you give it up?' shouted someone in the crowd.

'Not soon enough!' answered a chorus of voices, to raucous laughter.

'When we first took up politics,' Cicero went on at a higher pitch, 'we held high hopes that honourable rewards for honourable service would come

our way. Instead we suffer a constant burden of fear. Milo has always been especially vulnerable, for he has deliberately . . . deliberately and bravely . . . placed himself on the foremost . . . I mean to say, in the forefront . . . in the struggle of true patriots against enemies of the state —'

There was another outburst, so loud it hurt my ears. Milo had sunk so low in his chair and hugged himself so tightly that he appeared to have melted. His expression was one of utter disgust. Tiro flinched every time Cicero stammered, and began to bite his nails.

From that point on the roar of the crowd was almost constant. Whenever Cicero did manage to make himself heard, he seemed to be uttering confused fragments from more than one speech. On several occasions he clearly lost his place, muttered to himself, and started at some point he had already covered. His voice continually shook. Even knowing his general intention — to accuse Clodius of an ambush and to exonerate Milo completely — it was impossible for me to make any sense of his argument. From the looks on their faces, the jurors were equally confounded.

Cicero's orations had roused many reactions in me over the years — outrage at his willingness to twist the truth, admiration approaching awe at his ability to construct a logical argument, simple wonder at his prodigious ego, grudging respect for his loyalty to his friends, dismay at his shameless demagoguery, for Cicero was always ready to exploit his listeners' religious sentiments and sexual

prejudices to his own ends. Now I began to feel something I had never felt before, something I would have thought impossible: I began to feel embarrassed for Cicero.

This should have been his finest hour. When he defended Sextus Roscius and risked offending the dictator Sulla, he had been too young to know better; inciting the people against Catilina had been almost too easy; destroying Clodia in his speech for Marcus Caelius had been an act of personal vengeance. This was a situation that required true bravery and heroic stamina. If he could have stood his ground against the angry mob, if he could have stared them down and by the sheer power of his oratory compelled them to listen, what a crowning accomplishment that would have been, whether he won the case or not. He could have attained a kind of glory even in failure.

Instead, he was the very portrait of a man cowed by fear. He stuttered, averted his eyes, broke out in a sweat, stumbled over his lines. He was like an actor crippled by stage fright. No man could be blamed for being intimidated by that crowd, but from Cicero such a reaction was difficult to stomach. The wretchedness of his performance robbed his words of any weight they might have possessed. The few audible portions of his speech seemed disconnected, forced, artificial, insincere. I seemed to be watching a second-rate actor doing a poor parody of Cicero. More than feeling embarrassed, I almost felt pity for him.

Milo became increasingly agitated until he

seemed about to come out of his skin. He kept jumping towards Tiro, engaging him in whispered arguments. Milo, I suspected, wanted to call Cicero from the Rostra and speak extemporaneously in his own defence; Tiro managed to argue him out of it.

The crowd soon learned to make a game of their outbursts. I have seldom seen a mass of people act with such seeming single-mindedness. They would grow just quiet enough to allow Cicero to be heard, then would laugh when he stuttered or misspoke, then would wait until the critical moment of the point he was making and let out a deafening roar. Their performance was uncanny, as if orchestrated by an invisible hand. The spirit of Clodius himself seemed to guide them that day.

The debacle seemed to go on forever. In fact, it lasted for considerably less than the three hours allotted for the defence. Eventually Cicero neared the end of his speech. 'Milo was born to serve his country. Surely it cannot be right that he should be forbidden to die within her boundaries –'

'Then let him take his own life, right now!' someone shouted.

'Distinguished jurors, can you possibly see fit to banish him from our soil? Send a man such as Milo into exile, and he would be eagerly welcomed by every other city in the world –'

'Then send him! Send him! Exile! Exile!' The word became a chant that echoed all through the Forum.

Cicero did not wait for the chant to die down in order to finish his speech. He continued in a hoarse

voice amid the growing roar of the crowd. I strained to hear him. 'Urgently I ask you, honourable jurors, when you cast your votes, be brave enough to act as you truly think is right. Do that, and believe me, your integrity . . . and courage . . . and sense of justice will surely please the one who chose this jury by fixing on the best and bravest and wisest men in Rome.'

Was that, then, the ultimate appeal? That a vote to acquit Milo would be pleasing to the Great One, the sole consul and selector of judges and juries? If that was his final argument, it was just as well that Cicero's voice was drowned out by the mob.

Once the speeches were finished, each side was allowed to excuse fifteen of the jurors. This was done quickly, as both prosecution and defence had already drawn up their lists of those they considered undesirable.

All that remained was for the fifty-one remaining jurors to vote. Each was given a tablet with wax on each side, with the letter A (for absolve) stamped on one side and the letter C (for condemn) stamped on the other. The juror wiped out one of the letters, leaving the other to show his judgment. These were collected before they were counted, so that the vote of each juror was kept secret. Domitius presided over the counting of the tablets as they were separated into two groups. From where I sat, I could see that one group was about three times higher than the other.

Domitius announced the results. The vote to

condemn was thirty-eight. The vote to absolve was thirteen.

The defeat was crushing. Even so, Milo had gathered more support from the jury than I expected. Strangely enough, I felt a sudden twinge of sympathy for him. He was responsible for some of the darkest days of my life; he had deliberately separated me from my family and treated me like an animal. Yet the time I had spent in captivity had also made me consider the harsh reality of the exile's existence, cut off forever from his heartland, from the places of his childhood and the people he loves, from the only life he has known, forbidden ever to return, even in death. I had had a taste of that despondency, at Milo's hand. Now Milo's world was at an end. Just as I had almost felt pity for Cicero, I almost felt it for Milo.

There was an outcry of triumph from the crowd. Expressionless, Milo rose stiffly from his chair and went directly to the closed litter in which he had arrived. Cicero, looking dazed, followed him. In addition to their own bodyguards, Pompey's soldiers formed a cordon around the litter to ensure its safe passage out of the Forum.

Pompey must be pleased, I thought. After a shaky beginning on the first day of the trial, he had managed to establish order, and order, of a sort, had prevailed to the end. The question of Milo had been settled; Milo would trouble him no more, and neither would Cicero, at least for a while. Now the Great One could turn his attention to the Clodian radicals. What punishment would be appropriate

for those who instigated the burning of the Senate House? Rome craved law and order, and Rome was about to get it — in the short term, at least.

Taverns reopened as soon as the trial was over. The Clodians would drink to celebrate. Milo's supporters would drink to drown their misery. I decided to stay behind locked doors.

Over dinner, I revealed to the family what I had discovered the previous night regarding Milo's responsibility for abducting Eco and me, and Cicero's knowledge of it. Eco was not surprised. Bethesda and Menenia were outraged. Diana began to cry and left the room.

We discussed the trial, which had done the job of punishing Milo for us; he was already being penalized to the full extent of the law, and there was nothing more that we could do to him. As for Cicero, Bethesda vowed to put an Egyptian curse on him. I myself was less certain about how to deal with him. Certainly, there could be no more friendly commerce of any kind between our houses ever again. I had come close to making a full break with Cicero in the past; now it was done. But beyond that, it was difficult to see what sort of satisfaction we might obtain against him, at least for the time being.

We discussed and argued long into the night. The lamps grew dim and the slaves refilled them. We had eaten our fill, but gradually grew hungry again. Bethesda produced another course. We discussed and argued some more. At some point I

realized how inexplicably happy I was. I was safe in my home, in the heart of the city, content with my family, finally out of harm's way. Was everyone else in Rome like myself, heaving a great sigh of relief?

The world had been turned upside down and given a great rattling shake. Soldiers had been given the run of a Roman court, a man who called himself sole consul was acting suspiciously like a dictator, and Cicero – Cicero! – had fallen apart during the most important speech of his life. These were grave omens, surely more meaningful and menacing than the usual run of omens, those dubious fires and strange cloud formations seen in the sky by professional mystics. But now I felt that the world was at last right side up again, and my feet were finally back on solid ground. The immediate, overwhelming problem of Milo had been taken care of, however messily. Things could only get better.

Even Bethesda looked especially beautiful that night. Perhaps some of this was the glow of the wine, or even the glow of her warm cooking in my belly. Looking at her in the lamplight made me think of Diana. Where was Diana?

I would send Davus to go and find her, I thought, but Davus wasn't in the room either. I would go and find her myself.

I knocked on the wall outside her curtained door. There was no answer. I thought she must be asleep or not in the room at all, but as I pushed the curtain aside there was a shuffling noise. The room was dimly lit by a single lamp. Diana seemed

to be in the act of throwing a coverlet off her bed. She slipped back onto the bed and sat against the wall. 'Papa, what are you doing here?'

'Daughter, only a few moments ago you were weeping for all that Eco and I suffered. Are you so unhappy to see me now?'

'Oh, Papa, it's not that.'

'Then what is it, Diana? You've seemed so unhappy, ever since I came back. I might almost think you weren't glad to see me at all.' I said it as a joke, but the look on her face gave me pause. 'What's the matter, Diana? Eco thinks it's because you want to get married and leave home, or don't want to get married and leave home . . .'

'Oh, Papa!' She turned her face away.

'Have you at least talked to your mother about it, whatever it is?'

She shook her head.

'Diana, I know I've been away, and since I came back I've been more preoccupied than I should be, but these are not normal times. I hope things will be better now. But your mother is always here, and I know she cares –'

'Mother would kill me!' Diana whispered hoarsely. 'Oh, she's the last person I can tell!'

This took me aback. Was the problem really as great as Diana imagined, or was it a trifle that a young girl had blown out of all proportion? As I wondered how to proceed, I walked around her bed and glimpsed the chamber pot. Though I looked away from it almost at once, the dim lamplight happened to fall on it in such a way that

I saw its contents in an instant. 'Diana! Are you sick? Have you been throwing up?'

She realized what I had seen and tried, too late, to push the pot out of sight with her foot. At the same time I was startled by another sound behind me and turned to see Davus. How had he entered the room so quietly?

'Davus, what are you doing here? No one called you. Go away. This doesn't involve you.'

'Oh, yes,' said Diana. 'It does.'

'No, Diana —'

'But it does involve Davus, Papa. It does!'

Then I realized the obvious. So did Bethesda, I imagine, who stood in the doorway wearing a look that could turn a man to stone.

# XXXIII

I needed a drink.

More than that, I needed to get away from my house. I could take only so much of Diana weeping, Bethesda stamping her feet, the broken Minerva staring at me. I did not want to overhear the whisper of my slaves saying, 'What's to be done with her?' or 'What's to be done with him?' or 'I knew it all along!'

Where can a man go to forget his cares in the middle of the night?

I had not set foot in the place the poet Catullus called the Salacious Tavern in almost exactly four years, since the final day of another trial, that of Marcus Caelius. Eco and I found it easily enough, tramping through the warehouse district to the northwest of the Palatine Hill accompanied by his bodyguards (without Davus, of course) until we came to the upright pillar in the shape of a

phallus, and the door lit up by a phallus-shaped lamp.

The place had not changed a bit. It reeked of smoke from cheap lamp oil and the fumes of cheap wine. The general roar was punctuated every now and again by the rattle of dice and the cries of winners and losers. The few women in the place were clearly for sale. Most of the men appeared to be in a good mood. Insofar as the clientele of the Salacious Tavern had any interest in politics, they were likely to be Clodian sympathizers.

While Eco and I looked for a bench to accommodate ourselves and our bodyguards, I overheard several snatches of conversation.

'Cicero might as well have had his tongue cut out – maybe that'll be next, if Pompey ever has the guts to make himself dictator and starts handing out some real justice!'

'The idea of Milo heading off for Massilia, where he'll stuff himself with mussels and wallow with Gaulish whores – what kind of punishment is that?'

'Did Antony's speech make any sense to you at all?'

'Only a little more than Cicero's!'

'I wept, I tell you, wept when his nephew talked about him dying alone and bleeding on the Appian Way. He was a great man –'

We finally found a place. A serving boy brought us wine at once. The vintage was as foul as the service was quick.

'Eco, what am I going to do with them?'

'A good question, Papa.'

'How did it happen?'

'I think you know how it's done, Papa.'

'You know what I mean!'

'Is she absolutely certain about . . . her condition?'

'She seems to be. So was Bethesda, after she questioned her.'

'When did it happen, Papa? The first time, I mean . . . assuming there was more than one occasion . . .'

'Do you remember the day the contio turned into a riot, and Belbo was killed, and the next day you and I decided to merge our households? You brought your bodyguards along with you, and gave me Davus to replace Belbo. Apparently, that very first night he was under my roof –'

'Oh, no!'

'Yes! What in Hades are you smiling at?'

'Am I? Well, it's just – at least, Davus wasn't my slave any longer when it happened, technically. Thank the gods for that. I'd given him to you, to be your personal bodyguard.'

'So you're saying none of this is your concern?'

'No, Papa, that's not what I meant. I'm concerned, of course. But deciding what to do with Davus is entirely up to you.'

'Thank you very much!'

The serving boy made a fortuitous appearance to refill our cups.

'He saved my life that day, you know,' I said.

'What's that?'

547

'The riot, the massacre in the Forum. When Milo and Caelius escaped dressed up like slaves. I came very close to being killed myself. It was Davus who plucked me out of the crowd. He's no coward, that's for sure.'

'I'll say. It takes a brave man to fiddle with his master's daughter right under his roof, and on his first day in the house. What could he have been thinking?'

'What was he thinking with, you mean. Not with his head! Diana claims it's not his fault, of course.'

'I think some of it must be his fault, Papa.'

'I know what she means, and so do you. She says that she was the one who . . . initiated the matter.'

'You make it sound like a legal contract! She may have 'initiated' it, but he was the one who should have refused. I told you Diana was starting to have an eye for young men. I told you it was time for her to marry.'

'An eye for young men . . .' I nodded. 'You'll have to admit, Davus is just what they like. Big as Hercules. Handsome as Apollo.'

'And as stupid as an ox. An ox in rut, at that! Where in Hades is that serving boy? Do you feel like doing some gambling, Papa?'

I had to laugh out loud. 'Eco, I feel like I've been doing nothing but gambling for months now. I think I'd like to stop gambling for a while!'

'And just drink!'

'Exactly! Just drink!'

The serving boy arrived. We complained that the

tavern's cups were absurdly small. He made a face to show that he had heard this before.

'So Diana is absolutely certain?' said Eco. His speech was beginning to slur.

'Yes. I didn't inquire for the precise details, Eco, but it's been over three months since the two of them met, and Bethesda says that Diana's schedule is considerably more reliable than the Roman calendar —'

'No leap-months!' For some reason Eco found this hilarious. I waited for him to finish cackling.

'Anyway, it's all a great mess.'

'So you mean, all the time Davus was with us on the Appian Way —'

'He was thinking about Diana, no doubt! Just as you were missing Menenia, and I . . .'

'And afterwards, when we were abducted, and he was thrown from his horse and then came to his senses and went back to the house —'

'Yes, Eco. The two of them were under the same roof every day, all day, and can you believe that Bethesda never noticed? Of course, Bethesda was distraught over the two of us, and busy managing Pompey's guards and trying to keep the household running. Diana was probably her least worry.'

'Still, how could Bethesda not have smelled something brewing? I think what this means, Papa, is that Diana has proved herself to be more clever and conniving than her mother!'

'Actually, I think I knew that already. Yes, Diana outwitted Bethesda. She hid her trysts with Davus —'

'All those days we were gone . . . and all the days we've been back!'

'Please, Eco, I don't want to think about it. And she also managed to hide her condition from Bethesda, which was quite a feat. Of course, that couldn't go on forever. All this time, she's been growing more and more miserable –'

'And Davus has been acting like the treasury slave caught with his hand in the coffer . . . so to speak.'

'Yes, I could tell he was guilty of something. It's a terrible betrayal, isn't it? He was supposed to be guarding me and my family, and instead . . .'

'Papa, Davus is a man. And Diana, like it or not, is a woman.'

'Davus is my slave, and Diana is my daughter!'

'Meto was a slave, before you adopted him. And Bethesda was a slave, before you set her free and married her.'

'But Eco was only a little boy, and Bethesda was carrying Diana. What was I to do, have my daughter born a slave?'

'You could set Davus free. Make him a citizen. Then he could –'

'Out of the question! Reward him for what he's done?'

'Then the only alternative, short of putting him to death, is to sell him, preferably to a new master somewhere far, far away. Or you could sell him to the galleys or mines if you really wanted to punish him; he's young and strong enough that he'd probably survive a few years of that. Most men

would have had him beaten senseless and put in chains the moment they found out, and done something almost as bad if not worse to the daughter involved. In the old days, a good father would have had both parties put to death on the spot and never have blinked an eye –'

'Eco, stop! Oh, all this smoke is giving me a headache. I don't want to think about it any more. Look, isn't that . . . ?' I peered through the orange reek of hazy lamplight. 'Over there in the corner – it is! Who would have thought it?'

I got up and walked, not entirely in a straight line, across the room. Sitting alone in the corner was Tiro.

'Exercising your rights as a freedman to go out drinking and whoring in the middle of the night?' I said. 'Surely Cicero wouldn't approve.'

Tiro looked up at me bleakly but didn't speak.

'The atmosphere in this place can hardly be good for your health,' I said. 'And this wine would rot anybody's stomach. Is there room on that bench for me?'

'I can't stop you from sitting wherever you want, citizen.'

'Tiro, let's have no hard feelings between you and me.' I put my arm around him.

'Gordianus, you're drunk.'

'And you will be, too, soon enough. Do you come here often?'

He finally smiled a bit. 'Every now and then. Sometimes I just have to get away. And

sometimes . . .' I saw that he was looking at one of the women for sale.

'Tiro, you dog. Are you telling me that you have a secret life that Cicero wouldn't approve of?'

'Why not? He's done things behind my back that I don't approve of, hasn't he? Gordianus, if I had known at the time, if there had been any way for me to stop it —'

'No, Tiro, not another word about that. Not tonight! I have too much else on my mind that I'm trying to forget.' I summoned the serving boy to refill Tiro's cup. 'I couldn't believe your master's performance today.'

'He's not my master any longer. You know that.'

'Sorry; habit. What in Hades was wrong with him? He seemed so sure of himself last night, so confident. He was pure Cicero. I wanted to strangle him!'

'When you saw him, yes. But he's been up and down for days now. Giddy and sure of himself one moment, blind with despair the next. You have no idea how this crisis weighed on him. How many friends deserted him over Milo. How shabbily Pompey and Caesar have been treating him. You know his Achilles' heel, his digestion; he's hardly been able to eat a thing for days. He wakes up in the middle of the night with cramps. It's been a terrible ordeal, a crushing burden. What he allowed Milo to do to you — I know you said not to speak of it, but I have to — that was out of character for him, and you know it. Just as out of character as what happened today. Thank the gods it's over, at least!'

'I've seen Cicero under pressure, but I've never seen any orator fall apart as he did today. What a spectacle.'

'You sound as though you enjoyed it, Gordianus.'

'Oddly enough, I actually felt a bit sorry for him. But a great many people appeared to relish it.'

'That mob! Cicero was right to be afraid of them.'

'Pompey's troops were there to keep order.'

'Oh, really? And would they have protected Cicero, if someone had started throwing stones at him?'

'What do you mean?'

'Who knows what secret orders Pompey gave to his men?'

'I can't believe –'

'Pompey was ready to be rid of Milo. He'd just as soon be rid of Cicero, too, if there was an easy way. Would his soldiers have defended Cicero, if it had come to that? Or would they have looked the other way, just for a few moments? Can you think of a more convenient way to get rid of Cicero for good, with no blame attached to the Great One himself? You shake your head, Gordianus, but believe me, Cicero had good reason to be frightened for his life today.'

'He simply panicked, then?'

'Something like that. Oh, it was excruciating to watch.'

'Yes, I saw you squirming all through the speech.'

'And Milo was practically frothing at the mouth! Now he talks as if it's Cicero's fault that he was convicted.'

'That's nonsense.'

'He says they should have explained the full circumstances and argued for his technical innocence, no matter how embarrassing it might have looked, or how unlikely.'

My head was muddled with wine. Tiro seemed to be echoing something Cicero had said the night before. I hadn't understood Cicero either. 'What are you talking about, technical innocence –'

'And I know what you'll ask next: was the speech really that good? That's the truly painful thing. All the hours we put into that speech, and then to have it blown away like dust in the wind. It just might have got Milo off. Who knows? You can judge for yourself when we publish it. There'll have to be revisions, of course. Then the world can see Cicero's case for Milo laid out in all its perfection, without the distraction of that howling mob!'

'Alas, too late for Milo. Tiro, what was that you said about –'

'By Hercules, there's someone I don't care to see! It was good talking to you, Gordianus.' As he rose from the bench, I squinted through the orange haze to see who had arrived. I didn't recognize him at first, until I heard someone call his name: 'Philemon!'

I felt an impulse to introduce myself. I looked around for Eco, but couldn't find him in the haze. Was I that drunk? At last I spotted him off in a little

anteroom, playing at dice. Faintly, above the roar, I heard him cry Menenia's name for luck.

Philemon was looking for a place to sit. I waved him over.

'Do I know you, citizen?'

I couldn't blame him for being wary. 'Not yet, but we have something in common.'

'We both like cheap whores and rancid wine?'

'A bit more than that. Sit. I'll buy you a cup.'

'I'd rather you bought me a whore.'

'Maybe I will! I suppose it wasn't easy, doing without for all that time.'

'What, while I was stuck in Milo's villa? At least that swine will never spend another holiday there!'

'I suppose not. Have you finished that cup already? You must have another.' Philemon was behind me in inebriation, but he quickly caught up. He seemed to revel in repeating the story that had made him one of the prosecution's chief witnesses. He launched into the tale with no prompting from me. The wine seemed to loosen his lips.

'All right,' he said at one point, 'the way I told it in court, I made us out to be a bit more heroic than we were; there, I've admitted it.'

'What do you mean?'

'Well, it's true enough that when we came upon Eudamus and Birria, and realized what they were up to, boasting about trying to kill Clodius, we shouted at them to stop.'

'Yes, and then you said you and your friends rushed at them, but they beat you back and pursued you.'

He laughed sheepishly. 'Right! Except that we never rushed at them. I mean, this was Eudamus and Birria, grinning and covered with blood! Rush at them? I think not. We turned tail and ran, and they came after us.'

'It's nothing to be ashamed of,' I assured him.

'No, but try telling it that way in front of a crowd of a few thousand people!'

'Did you sweeten the truth about anything else?'

He shook his head, then shuddered. 'You can't imagine it, being tied up at the mercy of creatures like that. My blood was like iced water. The first big fight they had, when they marched us through Bovillae, I thought I'd empty my bowels.'

'A fight? What do you mean?'

'An argument, among themselves. Pretty fierce. I thought maybe they'd kill each other and leave us alone. Something about where to go next and what to do about Clodius. I suppose they were arguing over what to do with his body.'

'But his body was already gone. Senator Tedius had arrived on the scene, loaded it into his litter and sent it on to Rome.'

'Ah, yes, that's right. Maybe that's what they were arguing about, then – wondering where the body had gone. I suppose that gave them a start! Yes, I suppose that's what Milo was so furious about when they brought him the news. What, do you think he wanted them to bring back Clodius's head for a trophy?'

'He appears to have ended up with Clodius's ring. That should have been enough, I'd think.' I

imagined Eudamus or Birria slipping it off the corpse's finger. I swallowed hard. 'I wonder if Milo intends to take the ring to Massilia with him – a comfort for his exile?'

Philemon wasn't listening. 'Yes, Senator Tedius. I saw him testify at the trial today. We passed him in the road, you know, between Bovillae and the place where Milo was waiting. Just sitting by the side of the road with his bodyguards, looking pleased with the world. You'd think he might have helped us!'

'He thought you were the bandits who'd killed Clodius, and that Milo's men had simply rounded you up!'

'Ha! It's a joke of the gods, isn't it!'

'Did you ask him for help?'

'A lot of good that would have done. He practically saluted those two monster gladiators as we passed by. I felt like a trussed-up Gaul in some general's triumphal parade.'

'Maybe you should have appealed to his daughter for help.'

'His daughter?' Philemon looked at me blearily and shook his head. I took it I had offended him by suggesting he might have appealed to a woman for help.

Even fathers of errant daughters and husbands of imperious wives must go home some time; and so, before the first hour of the day, Eco and I departed from the shelter of the Salacious Tavern and made our way up the Palatine Hill. I remember very little

557

of that walk, except that far too much of it was far too steep. Like old Sextus Tedius labouring up the Appian Way, I kept having to sit and catch my breath. Growing older is a torment, and being drunk is a comfort only to a point, after which it becomes a torment, too.

With sunrise would come a new day. Everything would be put back as it was. Eco and Menenia and the twins would return to the house on the Esquiline. I would send home Pompey's guards with heartfelt thanks and a sigh of relief. Of course, some things could not be so easily undone . . .

At least the crisis of the last few months was over. I washed my hands of everyone concerned! Milo, Clodia, Fulvia, Cicero and their respective satellites could all join Clodius in Hades. An end had been put to that story for good.

So I thought, wending my way up the Palatine Hill. It was that hour of day when a man can still see only dimly, though dawn is near at hand; but in my befuddled state, I didn't even realize that I was still in the dark, or that a light would soon be breaking.

# Part Four

## *Ring*

# XXXIV

'It can be fixed, of course,' said the artisan. 'But . . .'

'But it will cost me,' I said.

'That goes without saying. The materials, the labour – the highly trained labour, I remind you – these things involve considerable expense.'

'Then why the hesitation?'

He shook his head. 'I can't guarantee that the work will keep. In fact, to be honest with you, I don't think that the breaks in the statue can be repaired in a . . . fully satisfactory . . . manner.'

'Satisfactory?'

'In a way that would be both artistically pleasing and structurally sound. You see, if you look here, at the point where the break began, you can see the traces of a tiny fissure that was there to start with –'

'You're saying that the statue had a flaw all along?'

'Oh, yes. Here, where the metal's so thin. See

how the lip of the break shears in a different pattern? That shows there was already a thin spot with a hairline crack. You would never have noticed it from the outside, of course. It looked perfectly sound. But it was obviously cast with a flaw. Granted, no statue should be pushed from its pedestal, but given such an unfortunate event, this was the weakest point, and this is where the breakage inevitably occurred. Then it ran up along this thin spot, where the folds of the goddess's robes are thinnest, then across the top of her hips . . .'

After all the bloodshed I had seen in my life, it seemed foolish to be squeamish about a statue. But there was something gruesome about the scarred, chipped metal that showed along the rupture that had torn her in half, and something distasteful about examining her so intimately from the inside out. On the surface, she was so serenely perfect, gleaming, seemingly indestructible. On the hollow inner surface, she was all a mass of protruding plugs and rough spots and blisters. And all the time she had towered on her lofty pedestal overlooking my garden, radiating wisdom, there had been a terrible flaw inside her. A murderous mob had knocked her from her pedestal, and the flaw had torn her apart. Now the artisan was telling me that there was no satisfactory way to put her back together again.

'But I can't just leave her lying here in the garden like this, staring up at me every time I pass.' Wisdom in two pieces, with weeds growing up around her!

'The statue could always be melted down. Of

course you wouldn't recover more than a small fraction of the value . . .'

I shook my head. 'Out of the question.' The statue, like the house, was a legacy of my old patrician patron, Lucius Claudius. Cicero himself had envied her. Melt her down? Never! But what was to be done? I had slept for only a few hours after returning from the tavern, but the moment I awoke, to the exclusion of all other problems, my mind had settled on the Minerva. Nothing would really seem right until she was back on her pedestal.

The artisan rubbed his chin thoughtfully. There was said to be no man in Rome who knew more about casting bronze. He was a small bearded fellow, a Greek, the property of a foundry owner for whom I had once solved a problem involving a missing slave and a statue that seemed too heavy.

'You might be able to make a bust out of her,' the Greek suggested.

'What!'

'If you made a clean cut, straight across below her breasts . . .'

It was clear that the fellow might be a skilled artisan, but he was no artist. Nor did he seem to have any religious respect for the statue at all. I suppose it was a hazard of his work, dealing so much with the malleability and tensile strength of various alloys, that he should lose touch with the mystery inside the metal.

'I simply want her put back into one piece again. Can it be done or not?'

'Oh, it can be done.' The Greek turned aside for

a moment. I knew he was rolling his eyes at my Roman wilfulness. 'But you'll be able to see the patch if you look for it, and it won't hold forever. A sharp knock, an earthquake –'

'Let's do it.'

'As I said, it will be expensive.'

'Are you authorized to bid for your master?'

'I am.'

'Then let's bargain.'

The lowest figure the man would settle for was still too much for the household coffers to bear. But I would get the money somehow. I dismissed him and stepped from the garden into my study. What was next for the day? I felt surprisingly energetic for having whiled away so many drunken hours the night before, and peculiarly sanguine, considering the storm clouds that had burst in my own home. When such a bright mood comes to a man of my years, I think it is best to enjoy it without question.

Pompey's guards had already left, while I slept. Eco and Menenia were busy transporting their household back to the Esquiline; it was remarkable how many objects had gravitated from their house to mine during their stay. I would miss seeing the twins' toys – little painted ships and carved chariots and Egyptian board games with brightly coloured pebbles – but I would not miss tripping over them. Bethesda felt obliged to oversee the move. She had apparently said whatever she had to say to Diana the night before. Diana herself stayed out of sight. Davus had apparently decided that there was an

urgent need for a lookout on the roof, and had stationed himself there, conveniently out of the way.

I clapped my hands. One of the slaves who was helping Eco stopped and looked into the room. 'Do you know where my daughter is?' I said.

'In her room . . . I think . . . Master.' He looked uncomfortable. They all knew about Diana by now, of course.

'Go and tell her I wish to see her.'

'Yes, Master!'

My heart sank when she stepped into the room. She looked much too haggard for a girl of seventeen who was carrying a child. I felt many things – anger, apprehension, regret – but nothing as strong as the impulse to put my arms around her and simply stand that way for a moment, pressing her to me. It was Diana who broke the embrace and stepped away, averting her eyes.

'Was it awful, after I left last night?' I said.

'Mother, you mean?' She managed a little smile. 'Not as awful as I expected. She blustered and shrieked at first. But once she calmed down, she acted more disappointed than angry. I don't understand her. She was born a slave herself. Now she acts as if I was born to marry a patrician, and I've spoiled it.'

'It is precisely because your mother was born a slave that she wants you to marry well.'

'I suppose. Today she's simply ignoring me.'

I sighed. 'I know how that feels, all too well. But Diana, how is your health? I know less than I should

of what's to be expected with such things. Your mother would know —'

'That was her first concern, after her tantrum last night. She asked me a lot of questions. Everything seems to be as it should be, though I do feel wretched much of the time. That's been the worst thing about all this – worrying and wanting to talk to her about it, and wanting to talk to you, Papa, and being afraid to. At least that's over.'

I fiddled with a stylus. 'Perhaps you're not fit for this pregnancy. Again, I'm woefully ignorant of specifics, but I'm sure your mother knows of ways to —'

'No, Papa. I don't want to end it.'

'What is it that you do want, Diana?'

'Papa, don't you understand? I'm in love with Davus.' She shuddered and blinked. Her lips trembled.

'Diana, please don't cry any more. Your eyes are red enough as it is. But whatever idea you may have in your mind concerning Davus, dismiss it.'

'But Davus and I —'

'Impossible, Diana!'

'But why not? Mother was a slave. You married her, didn't you? And that was because she was pregnant with me, wasn't it? Meto was a slave when he was a little boy, and Eco was hardly better, a street urchin, but you adopted them. Why should it be any different —'

'Diana, no!'

The tears came at full flood. 'Oh, you're no better than she is! What hypocrites you both are.

566

Well, I'm not a Vestal Virgin! You can't bury me alive just because I love a man! I'm not ashamed that I'm carrying his child!'

'Why don't you yell a bit louder, so they can hear you at Cicero's house? Now I suppose you'll go running from the room.'

'No. Why should I? It doesn't matter where I am. I'm miserable! You're a man, you can't know how miserable I am. I'd want to die, if it wasn't for the baby . . .'

So much for my sanguine mood. 'Diana, we'll talk more about this when I get back.'

'Where are you going?'

'The day is still young. I have an errand to run, down the Appian Way. If nothing else, it will give me an excuse to spend another night away from this house.'

Diana retreated back to her room. I stepped into the garden, avoided Minerva's accusing stare and climbed the ladder to the roof. I came upon Davus near the front of the house, sitting with his arms around his knees. When he heard me he gave such a start I thought he might fall to the street below.

'By Hercules, Belbo, be careful!'

'Davus,' he mumbled, hurriedly righting himself and standing.

'What?'

'Davus, Master. Not Belbo.'

'Oh. Of course. What was I thinking? Belbo had the common sense to be careful on a rooftop. And he never took advantage of a member of my family.'

'Oh, Master!' Davus dropped to his knees. Those in the room below must have flinched at the concussion. He bowed his head and clasped his hands. 'Have mercy on me! Don't torture me, Master — kill me outright if you must. Torture is worse for big, strong fellows like me. Every slave knows that. Little weaklings are tortured for a while and then they die. But with a man like me, it could go on for days and days. I'm not afraid to die, Master, but I beg you —'

'And how would you prefer to be executed, Davus?'

He turned pale and swallowed. 'Cut off my head, Master.'

'That is not the part of you which has offended me.'

He shuddered and looked up at me with wide eyes. 'Don't geld me, Master! I couldn't stand to be a eunuch! Oh, have pity on me!'

'Stop, Davus! Stop, stop, stop. Whatever am I going to do with you? Do you seriously imagine that I might have you killed?'

'What else can I hope for, Master? It's the best punishment I can expect.'

'Then what are you doing here?'

'Master?'

'Why are you still here, waiting for your fate? Why haven't you jumped off the roof and run away? You wouldn't have much chance of escaping, but it's better than death. Stow away on a boat leaving Ostia. Go into exile, like Milo. Why didn't you run away last night?'

'Because . . .'

'Yes?'

'Because of . . .'

'What, Davus? What's kept you here to face your punishment?'

'Master, must you make me say it? It's because of her. Diana. I can't leave as long as she's here. Where else would I go? What would be the point? I should die without her.'

'Oh, Davus!' I shook my head. Minerva lay in pieces in my household, and Venus reigned supreme.

We set out on the Appian Way at the sixth hour of the day, when the sun was straight overhead. Pompey's stableman agreed to lend me horses, after I reminded him who I was and told him I still had business to do for his master. This was a small, harmless lie, since my business with Pompey was done. Or so I thought at the time.

The stableman, with a broad grin, brought out three horses. I was startled to see that they were the very same horses we had ridden before. All three mounts, it turned out, had returned to the stable together and riderless on the day we were attacked. I felt at once reassured and a little apprehensive to be setting out from Rome astride the same beast as before. I was not sure what to make of the omen, but I was determined to go ahead.

The objective of the trip was simple: I wanted to collect Mopsus and Androcles, the two stableboys I had acquired from Fulvia. I left Eco behind and took only Davus with me. The third horse was for

the boys to share on the ride back. I expected that we would spend the night at the inn in Bovillae.

Davus was as quiet as a mute until we passed the Monument of Basilius. He wore a deep frown and grew increasingly agitated. 'Master — Master, are you sure . . . ?'

'Sure of what, Davus?'

'Are you sure that you want me with you? Why not one of the other bodyguards?'

'Are you afraid of the horse, Davus? You can't claim to have no experience of riding now. This is your second trip on the same horse! This beast threw you, true, but when a man's been thrown, the only thing to do is to get back on.'

'It's not the horse, Master. I like this horse, actually. I think she trusts me.'

'Let's hope you give her no cause to regret that.'

Davus frowned.

'Besides,' I went on, 'I could hardly leave you at home in my absence, given the circumstances, could I?'

'You mean . . . because of your daughter —'

'No, because of my wife. I shouldn't care to return home and find that Bethesda had killed you while I was gone.'

Davus swallowed hard. 'Still, Master, I don't understand why you're taking me with you, just the two of us.'

'I don't quite understand that myself. Reason has fled; I give myself over to impulse. We shall see where the road takes us.'

'But Master, we already know that.'

'Do we?'

'It leads yonder to Mount Alba.'

I laughed out loud. 'What a remarkable wit you have, Davus!'

Davus laughed, too, but only halfheartedly. Was that because he feared me, or because he did not quite grasp the joke?

It was springtime on the Appian Way. The weather was mild and there was birdsong on the air. The grass was green along the road and spangled with flowers. Slaves and oxen laboured in the fields. There was a great deal of traffic in both directions – sheep and cattle being led to market, messengers on horseback, the litters and carriages of the rich. The whole world seemed to be awakening from a cold dream of winter.

I was hungry by the time we passed through Bovillae, but I decided to press on to Clodius's villa. As we passed the altar of Jupiter, I caught a glimpse of Felix sitting against an oak tree, dozing in the dappled shade. We passed the road leading up to the new House of the Vestals, and farther on, on the opposite side of the way, the shrine of the Good Goddess. There appeared to be a gathering of women inside, to judge from the litters and carriages and idle attendants outside. As we passed I heard chanting from within, and recognized Felicia's whimsical singsong. Perhaps nothing much had changed in her world, despite the bloody scene that had unfolded before her eyes and all the commotion it had caused.

We approached Clodius's villa this time by the road leading up to it, and were seen and challenged long before we reached the top. When a group of very rough-looking slaves barred our way, I produced the scrip from Fulvia transferring ownership of the two stableboys. Fortunately, one of the slaves could read, if barely. He slowly mouthed each word, then handed the square of parchment back to me.

'Good riddance, I say! Those two are nothing but trouble. Always getting above themselves. Taking them back to the city, are you?'

'That's my intention.'

He shook his head. 'There'll be no end of trouble for them to get into there. Well, come on. They'll be in the stable, I imagine.'

The boys remembered us at once. They seemed especially delighted to see Davus (or the elephant, as Mopsus called him). When I told them they no longer belonged to their mistress, but to me, they were puzzled at first, but together they mounted the third horse readily enough. As we set out, they seemed suddenly to realize that they were leaving for good. Mopsus turned about and hooked his thumbnail under his front teeth to make a clicking sound at the older slaves they were leaving behind. 'Goodbye, you no-good drunkards!' His little brother copied him, and the insults degenerated into references to various bodily functions. The slaves standing in the road watching the departure feigned outrage and pretended to look about for stones to throw. Some of them laughed out loud.

How had I described to Bethesda the new acquisitions for the household? 'Two high-spirited boys, and very clever. They'll put new life in the house.' That was before I realized that new life was already on the way, thanks to Diana and Davus. And I had assumed that the woman who tamed Pompey's bodyguards would have no trouble controlling two boys; now I began to wonder.

Davus seemed finally to relax a bit. I realized that he felt safer with Mopsus and Androcles along; surely I would not try to murder him in front of two laughing boys.

It was late in the afternoon when we returned to Bovillae. I wanted nothing more than some of the hostess's excellent cooking and a reasonably clean place to sleep. We would make an early bed and be up and ready to leave before dawn.

At first I thought that our hostess had lost weight and changed her hair somehow, then I realized it was a different woman behind the counter. She had the same eyes but was thinner and prettier, or would have been except for her drawn expression. I told her we needed accommodation for the night.

'You're early for that,' she said, smiling wanly. 'The first of the day. So you can have first pick.'

'Is there much choice?'

'Not really. It's all one room, but some folks prefer to be against the wall instead of out in the middle, or closer to the stairs or the window. Come up, and I'll show you. Then you can bring up your things to mark your places.'

I followed her up the stairs. The upper floor of

the inn was much as I expected – a single room with a few small windows and some pallets for sleeping. 'This will do,' I said. 'Davus, take the boys and see that the horses are properly tended to at the stable up the way.'

'Yes, Master.' He clomped heavily down the stairs. Mopsus and Androcles slipped past him and flew down the steps as if they were all in a race.

The woman moved to the head of the stairs and smiled wistfully after them. 'I have a little boy myself,' she said. 'Only a baby. Well, if you're satisfied, then I'll be –'

'This must have been the window where you stood and watched,' I said, walking to the open shutters and gazing out.

'What do you mean?'

'After the battle was over, and you dared to come out from under the bedding. Your sister told me that you went to the window to have a look, and saw that everyone had already left, except for Sextus Tedius, who must have just arrived.' I peered out the window, imagining the scene: dead bodies and pools of blood scattered about, the litter and its attendants, Sextus Tedius and his daughter discovering Clodius's body.

'Who are you?' There was a tremor in her voice.

'My name is Gordianus. I came this way on a mission from the widow Fulvia, in Februarius. I spoke to your sister. She told me what she had learned from you, about the battle between Milo

and Clodius. You are the innkeeper's widow, aren't you?'

She relaxed a little. 'Yes. My sister told me about you. And about your handsome young bodyguard – that must have been him with you just now.'

I smiled. 'Yes, I remember she took a liking to Davus. It seems she's not the only one . . .'

'What's that?'

'Never mind. Tell me, did you really go all the way to Rhegium to stay with an aunt?'

The woman looked at me cautiously. 'No. That's just what we decided to tell people.'

'Then your sister wasn't completely candid when I asked if I could talk to you.'

'I was out of my head for a long time. My sister wanted to protect me. If she told you that you couldn't see me, that was the truth.'

'I wanted very much to ask you about what you saw that day.'

'So did others. My sister kept them all away. She wasn't afraid to testify to the court herself. Someone would have to come forward, she said. But she protected me.'

'And now the trial is over, and here you are again. Back from Rhegium, so to speak.'

'Yes. Back from Rhegium.' She gave me a weak smile. 'It feels good to be here, to be working again. I always loved it before. Working with Marcus . . .'

'What you saw that day –'

She shook her head. 'I still can't talk about it.'

'Not at all?'

She gripped the stair railing and drew several

quick breaths. 'I never talk about it. I only told my sister about it once, right after it happened. After that, neither of us could bear to talk about it again.'

'I understand.' Her sister's judgment had been correct; the woman would have been useless to the court as a witness. She was shaking now. It was hard to imagine her giving testimony in the heated atmosphere that had stifled even Cicero's tongue.

She looked down the stairway. 'Even now, every time I go down these stairs, I think I'll find him, as I found him that day . . .'

'Your husband?'

'Yes! All bloody and still . . .'

'Do you need my help, to walk down the stairs?'

'Perhaps. But not yet. I don't want to move.'

'Shall I go find your sister, or her husband?'

'No! They must be sick of me by now, but not half as sick of me as I am of them,' she said with sudden vehemence. 'The way they moved in and took over this place – all for the sake of my little boy, they say, keeping it in trust for him. But they act as if it's their tavern now. As if Marcus never existed. They won't even say his name, for fear of upsetting me. Oh, if only everything could be as it was before! Curse Milo and Clodius both! Curse the gods.'

I thought she would weep, but her eyes remained dry. She steadied herself and breathed deeply. 'What was it you wanted to know?'

I wrinkled my brow. 'Can you speak about that day, or not?'

'Why don't you ask me and find out?'

I looked out the window. Up the road, Davus

and the boys had finished stabling the horses and were playing some sort of game with a leather ball, all three of them laughing like children. What sort of father would Davus make?

I looked back to the widow. What was left to ask her? It seemed that all the missing details had been supplied. The events of that day had been discovered, one by one, and put in order. The incident on the Appian Way had been fully documented and justice had been dispensed. Her testimony had not been needed after all. Still . . .

'What did you see when you looked out this window, after the battle?'

She lowered her eyes. 'Bodies. Blood. The senator and his daughter, and their retinue. The senator's litter.'

'Eudamus and Birria? Milo's men?'

'No. They were all gone. I don't know where.'

'They were off chasing a fellow called Philemon and some friends of his who had the bad fortune to stumble upon the scene.'

'Oh? I never heard about that.'

'Your sister didn't tell you? Philemon testified, on the same day she did.'

The widow shook her head. 'She was afraid of upsetting me, I suppose. Go on. What else do you want to know?' She had a grim, determined look on her face.

'You looked out this window. You saw Tedius and his daughter, the litter, the retinue. And Clodius?'

'Yes. They were leaning over him.'

'And you knew it was Clodius?'

'Yes.'

'How?'

She shrugged. 'By his face.'

'You could see his face? He must have been lying on his back, then.'

'Yes, he was. On his back, looking up at them.'

The skin prickled at the base of my skull. 'What did you say?'

'Clodius was on his back, looking up at the senator and his daughter.'

'You mean his eyes were open and staring in death?'

'No. I mean what I say. He was looking at them, and they were looking at him.' She frowned, trying to remember. 'They talked a bit, back and forth. Then Tedius and his daughter helped Clodius stand up and get into the litter.'

I looked down at the road, picturing the scene, then turned to the widow. It was possible, of course, that grief had made her mad. 'Are you saying that Clodius was alive?'

'Yes. Only barely, I suppose.'

'But your sister made it seem that Clodius was dead when Tedius found him. That was the way she told it, to me and to the court. She said that you saw the senator and his daughter put Clodius into their litter, but she said nothing to indicate that Clodius was still alive.' I tried to remember exactly what she had said . . .

'He was alive,' the widow said. 'Probably she misunderstood me. I was raving when I told her

578

what had happened, what I'd seen. I hardly knew what I was saying. Perhaps the way I told it to her, it was unclear.'

'Perhaps. You and your sister seem to have been unclear with each other on a number of points. But Sextus Tedius told the story the same way. He made no mention of Clodius being alive when he found him.'

'But Clodius was alive. He was stiff and limping and bloody, and they had to help him into the litter – but he was alive, I assure you, unless dead men can walk and talk. He was still alive! And my husband was dead, lying at the foot of these stairs. Why are you doing this to me?' Suddenly she turned and ran down the stairs, weeping at last.

I looked out the window, staring hard at the empty road, as if by concentration alone I could conjure up the lemures of the dead to re-enact their final moments of life. Oh, what a grand and terrible power that would be!

# XXXV

It was twilight when we arrived at the house of Sextus Tedius. I was very hungry and very tired of riding. I told the boys to watch the horses and sent Davus ahead of me to rap on the door.

The doorkeeper took a long time to answer, and even longer to confer with his master and return. At last I was invited inside.

Sextus Tedius received me in the same room as before. The windows were opened to show the town of Aricia below, a pool of pale blue shadows surmounted by rooftops glinting with the last of the day's sunlight. Tedius sat upright in his old-fashioned backless chair. Despite the warmth of the day, a blanket was thrown over his legs. It was the left leg that was crippled, I remembered. He ran a dark, leathery hand through his white hair and appraised me shrewdly.

'I remember you,' he said. 'Pompey's man.

The one who came around asking all the questions.'

'Not all the questions I should have asked, apparently.'

'Have you come here again, 'on behalf of the Great One', as I believe you put it before?'

'In a way, yes. Pompey hired me to find out everything I could about the incident on the Appian Way. I thought I had done that, but I appear to have been mistaken.'

'Speak plainly.'

'I intend to. I hope you'll do the same, Sextus Tedius.' He raised an eyebrow at this, but said nothing. 'Is your daughter here?' I asked.

'I can't imagine that my daughter's whereabouts could be of any concern to you.'

'Nonetheless, I should like very much to speak to both of you together.'

He lowered his white brows and studied me for a long moment. 'You know something, don't you?'

'I know more now than I did an hour ago. I should like to know everything.'

'Ah, to know everything! What a curse that would be for a mortal. Tedia!' He raised his voice. 'Tedia, come into the room and join us.'

His daughter emerged from the hallway. She was dressed as I had seen her before, without jewellery or makeup and wearing a white linen mantle over her head, tied with a blue ribbon at the back. She stood rigidly upright with a grim look on her face.

'Tedia always eavesdrops on my conversations,'

581

said Sextus Tedius. 'It makes it much easier for me to remember all the details afterwards.'

'My father and I have no secrets from one another.' She stood behind him and laid her hands on his shoulders.

'I saw your father testify at the trial, repeating the same story he told to me. I thought you were determined to keep him away from the trial, Tedia.'

'In the end it seemed better to make an appearance,' she said. 'Clodius was sent back to Rome in our litter, after all. To have refused to explain how that occurred could have excited . . . comment.'

'I see. And the story you told, Tedius, was entirely credible, after all. You merely left out certain details, such as the fact that Clodius was alive when you came upon him.'

'How do you know that?' said Tedia. She began to knead her father's shoulder, in the same way that I had seen her nervously wring her hands at our first meeting. 'If one of our slaves has talked —'

'Your slaves are loyal. There was another witness.'

'Not at the trial.'

'No, the witness was away from Rome that day — down in Rhegium, I was told.'

Sextus Tedius winced almost imperceptibly. His daughter had squeezed his shoulder too hard. 'Clodius deserved to die,' she said.

'Perhaps. Yet I saw you weep when Fulvia testified.'

'A woman can feel pity for a widow without feeling sorry that her husband is dead.'

'I see. And how, exactly, did Clodius die?'

I held my breath. I had no means to compel her to speak, if she chose not to. Her father reached up and clutched one of her hands with a gesture of restraint, but she seemed not to notice. Her face was adamant.

'I killed him,' she said.

'But how? Why?'

'Why?' Her voice rose. 'Because a more impious man never blighted the earth. You must have learned of his crimes when you were pestering everyone on this mountain. He cut down the sacred grove of Jupiter, merely to add some rooms to his house. Imagine, evicting a god to make room for himself! And what he did to the Vestals was unspeakable, driving them from their ancient house, defrauding them, treating them like common business rivals to be cheated and driven into the dirt. Did he think he could commit such crimes and go unpunished?'

'Publius Clodius had been committing many crimes of many sorts for years, without being punished,' I said.

'All the more reason that the time had come,' said Tedia sternly.

'He was alive when you came upon him at the inn . . .'

'Very much alive.'

'But near death, surely.'

'How can you say that? Were you there to judge? I shall tell you how it was –'

'Daughter!' Sextus Tedius scowled and shook his head.

'Father, I have nothing to be ashamed of, and nothing to fear. It began as my father told you – we were on our way to Rome, we came upon Milo in the aftermath of the skirmish, he lied and told us there were bandits about. I was afraid and wanted to turn back, but my father insisted that we press on, and so we did. The goddess Vesta was guiding us that day, I have no doubt of that. We arrived at the inn in Bovillae and saw the carnage there. I thought I would faint from fright, I felt such a tremor and a coldness inside me. Now I know it was only the goddess stirring in me, preparing me for the task at hand.

'There were bodies scattered in the road, blood everywhere. It was strange, to come to a place one has seen so many times and passed without a thought – such a common, familiar, ordinary place – and to witness such horror and devastation. Everything seemed unreal, as if I were delirious with fever. I helped my father from the litter and we walked among the bodies. There was no one to be helped; they were all dead.

'Then we heard a voice from inside the tavern, a thin, weak cry for help. Clodius appeared at the door. His clothes were torn. He was wounded. He clutched a blood-soaked rag to his shoulder. He spoke through gritted teeth. 'Help me,' he said.'

'All the others had died defending him, you see,' said Sextus Tedius. 'His men were loyal, no one can deny that.'

'He staggered out of the tavern,' Tedia continued. 'He tripped and dropped to his knees, then rolled onto his back, groaning and keeping his shoulder from touching the ground. He seemed comfortable that way, lying on his back. We leaned over him. His voice was hoarse and strained, hardly more than a whisper. 'Take me home,' he said. 'Not back to the villa – they'll look for me there. Take me to Rome in your litter. Hide me from them!' 'From the bandits?' said my father. And Clodius laughed! A hissing, hateful laugh – what perfect white teeth he had! 'The only bandits on this road are Milo's gladiators,' he said. 'They chased me here and tried to kill me, but something scared them off. Quickly, hide me in your litter!' So we helped him to his feet and then into the litter. I could see that my father was uncertain what to do next. I drew him aside, where the slaves couldn't hear.'

Tedius grunted. 'I'd have sent him back to his villa, whether he wanted to go there or not, but Milo was in the way. I had no intention of trying to slip by Milo, making myself a spy in the service of that jackal Clodius. Nor did I wish to hand Clodius over to that liar Milo. Perhaps if we'd left him there, he'd simply have bled to death, or Milo's men would have come back and finished him off. But there he was in our litter, getting blood on the pillows . . .'

'I made the decision,' said Tedia. Her voice was like cold iron. 'It came to me all at once. I happened to look up at the inn, and saw her in the window of

the upper storey. Her face seemed to hover there, like a portrait in a frame. I saw the face of Vesta and I knew what to do.'

I shook my head. 'The face you saw was the poor, terrified widow of the innkeeper.'

Tedia looked at me disparagingly. 'How do you know what I saw? Were you there?'

I saw no point in contradicting her. 'How did you kill him?'

She removed her hands from her father's shoulders and reached up to undo the blue ribbon that secured the linen mantle at the back of her head. She wound the ends of the ribbon around her strong, supple hands and pulled it taut. 'I killed him with this. I only wish the goddess could have watched, but I had to do it inside the litter, out of sight. The slaves were there; they had no business seeing. I climbed into the litter and moved behind him. Father climbed in after me and we let the curtains drop. I slipped the ribbon over his neck. Father held him from the front.'

'We could never have managed it if he hadn't already been weakened by his wounds,' said Tedius matter-of-factly. 'Look at us — an old, crippled man and a woman. But we managed it.'

'I saw the body,' I said. 'The wound at his shoulder was deep. He probably would have died anyway.'

'Don't be so sure,' said Tedius. 'I've seen plenty of battles, and plenty of soldiers who looked to be in worse condition than Clodius did, who none-theless recovered. There was a surprising amount of

life still left in that jackal. I know; I watched the last
of it leave him. Unmolested, he might very well
have survived the trip back to Rome. He would still
be alive today.'

'You claim credit for his death, then. You seem
to be proud of it.'

'I'm proud of my daughter, yes! You have a
son, don't you, Gordianus? I remember, he was
with you when you last came here. Well, I'm like
every other man — I would like to have had a son,
to watch him grow to manhood, to see him prove
his courage in battle and show his convictions in
the Forum. But I had no son. I only had a
daughter. But that daughter has always been
faithful to me and never disappointed me, and
when her mother died, she willingly took her
place. No man could ask for a better daughter.
And now look what she's done! She accomplished
what no man was able to do either by battle or by
using the law: she put an end to Publius Clodius.
An enemy of the state, a menace to decency, a
blight on the Republic, a disgrace to his ancestors.
And it was my daughter who finally put an end to
him! The gods and goddesses manifest their wills
in mysterious ways, Gordianus. They'd had
enough of Publius Clodius, and snuffed him
out. Who am I, an old, lame senator, to question
their choice of a vessel?'

I studied the two of them, so grimly self-satisfied,
models of stern Roman virtue. 'Why didn't you
push his body from the litter and leave him by the
road, then? Why did you send him on to Rome?'

'The litter was polluted by his blood and offal,' said Tedia. 'I could never enter it again.'

'It was his last request of us, to send him home,' her father said. 'It's as I said to you before: once a man is dead, what use is there in despising him? No, I wouldn't leave him lying in the road, like a dead dog. I sent his body on to Rome, and told the bearers to deliver it with great respect into the care of his widow.'

'His ring,' I said, remembering. 'His body arrived without his ring. Did you take it from him?'

Tedia lowered her eyes. 'That was a mistake. I thought it would be pleasing to the goddess.'

'You were the woman who went to the House of the Vestals and offered Clodius's ring for a prayer of thanksgiving?'

'Yes.'

I suddenly understood the strange look I had seen on Philemon's face in the Salacious Tavern. I had asked why he had not appealed to Tedius's daughter for help when he was herded in bondage up the Appian Way, past the place where Tedius was resting below the House of the Vestals. What I had taken for offence was merely puzzlement. Philemon had never seen Tedia, for Tedia had been up at the House of the Vestals.

'You hid your face from the Virgo Maxima,' I said. 'You disguised your voice.'

'Yes. Otherwise the Vestals would have known me.'

'Weren't you proud of what you'd done?'

'I felt no need to boast or show my face. I was a

mere vessel for the goddess, and it was to the goddess alone that I wished to offer the ring. But the Virgo Maxima refused to take it. She said that such an offering would be impious.'

I shook my head. 'Everyone thinks it was Milo's wife who –'

Tedia laughed. I could tell she was not accustomed to laughing. 'Fausta Cornelia? That blasphemous cow? It's hard to imagine her making a prayer for anything, except perhaps for the gods to bring her a new lover every day. What a great joke, that anyone should have mistaken her for me.'

'Where is the ring now?'

'Why do you ask?'

'Because I should like to return it to the family. You admit that taking it was a mistake. The goddess has no use for it. To keep it as a trophy surely would be hubris, a curse on your own house.'

Tedia considered this and seemed about to speak, but her father shook his head. 'The ring is the only real evidence against us. All that we've told you is only a story from our own lips. Your witness at the tavern – that girl in the window, I suppose – may have seen that Clodius was still alive, but she couldn't have seen into the litter. No one saw the actual moment of his death except my daughter and me. The Vestals know that a woman brought them Clodius's ring, but they never saw the woman's face. Only the fact that we possess the ring offers any proof of what we did. Why should we give it up to you, Gordianus? What will you tell the family of Clodius, that you recovered the ring

589

from the true killers of their beloved, a woman and a lame old man? Shall we have to suffer their revenge?'

'What should I tell them, that I happened to find it by the side of the road? Think, Tedia, of the tears you shed when you heard the testimony of Fulvia. Do you really want to keep the ring?'

She took a breath and began to move, but her father clutched her arm.

'Only if you make an oath, Gordianus,' said Tedius.

'No promises!'

'There will be, if you want the ring. You'll make an oath never to repeat what you heard here today, and in return we shall give it to you. Think, Gordianus, what purpose will it serve to incite the Clodians against my daughter and me? The mob has finally been assuaged by Milo's conviction; you'll simply make fools of them and set them rioting again. Think how irritated Pompey will be, to discover that his court failed to find the whole truth and that the conviction of Milo is flawed! Rome has been ripped apart by what happened here on the Appian Way. But now the people have been pacified and the wicked on both sides have been punished – Clodius is dead, Milo is exiled. What purpose could there possibly be in delivering a last revelation, except to massage your own vanity, to show off your perseverance and cleverness? Make the oath I require; return the ring to the one who loved Clodius best, and leave the rest to the gods.'

I walked to the window. Below, the town of Aricia, where Clodius had given his final address, had darkened to a jumble of deep blue shadows. I thought for a long time. What did I owe to Milo, who had committed such a grievous offence against me, and would have killed me outright if Cicero had not restrained him? What did I owe to Cicero, who acquiesced to my abduction? Or to the friends and heirs of Clodius, who instigated the riots that resulted in the sacking of my house and the death of Belbo? What did I owe to Rome itself – for who could say any longer what Rome was, or would become in the next few years? All was in flux, all was chaos and confusion. I found myself confronted by what I most craved, the truth, but I also found myself utterly alone; even Eco was not there to share the discovery or advise me. That was just as well; I doubted that he would have approved of the decision I made. I turned back to Sextus Tedius.

'You have my word; I swear by the shade of my father that I'll keep your secret. Bring me the ring.'

Tedia left the room. While she was gone, a slave entered with a burning taper and lit the lamps, dispelling the growing darkness. Tedia returned and dropped the ring into my open palm, looking glad to be rid of it.

It was heavy, made of solid gold. I saw the name p. clodius pulcher engraved on it, but was at a loss to see any other ornament. Surely there should be some reference to the glories of his illustrious ancestors? Then I held it to the light and noticed the honeycomb pattern scored into the glittering

surface of the ring itself, inside and out, little interlocking polygons like the perfectly fitted stones which paved the Appian Way. The ring was the very image of the great road, cast in a circle without beginning or end, a homage to the place where its wearer had fallen to his enemies and breathed his last with a blue ribbon wound tight around his throat.

That night we slept in an inn in Aricia. The tavern below was loud and smoky, and the bedding had ticks in it, but I slept better there than I should have in Bovillae, with all its phantoms, living and dead.

I was up before dawn, and woke the boys. All three of us had to shake Davus to get him up. We were on the road before the first hour, and made swift progress. We reached the city before midday. I had three last calls to pay, and then I could turn my back for good on all that had happened on the Appian Way.

# XXXVI

Mopsus and Androcles grew increasingly excited as we made our way through the Forum and up the Ramp to the Palatine. Both were wide-eyed at the sight of so many buildings and people. Davus put on a slightly snobbish air – the city slave condescending to the country slaves. I remembered his own consternation at finding himself in the countryside for the first time in his life, but said nothing.

All three of them grew quiet as we neared the house. Davus's face grew long. The boys drew closer together. We had hardly stepped into the foyer before Bethesda appeared.

'So these are the new slaves,' she said, ignoring Davus.

'Yes, this is Mopsus, and this is his brother, Androcles. Boys, this is your new mistress.'

The boys lowered their eyes and sneaked glances

at her. Androcles whispered in his older brother's ear, 'She's beautiful!'

Bethesda's lips almost formed a smile. She was resplendent in a saffron-coloured stola and a simple silver necklace, with hair done up very high on her head in such a way that the strands of grey looked like white veins snaking through shimmering black marble. I was almost as awed by her as the boys were.

'You both look agile and energetic,' she said, making the words sound more like a judgment than a compliment. 'I suppose we shall find ways to keep you busy. You might be good at carrying messages, I imagine, except that you must be ignorant of the city. You shall have to do a great deal of exploring in the next few days, to acquaint yourselves with the seven hills. Right now, you must be hungry after your trip. Davus will show you where the kitchen is — won't you, Davus?'

'Yes, Mistress.' Davus was the most awed by her of anyone. It was remarkable how small a space such a large fellow could seem to occupy, and how quickly he could make his exit from a room.

Bethesda and I were left alone.

'Husband, I did a great deal of thinking yesterday.'

'So did I.'

'You and I must have a serious talk.'

'Can it wait? I have a few more errands to finish today, and then —'

'I suppose. But by the end of the day, I want a resolution to this matter of Diana and your . . . and Davus.'

'I agree. Shall we talk this evening, then?'

'Yes.' Our eyes met, and it hardly seemed necessary to talk at all. We were agreed about what to do. I had lived with her long enough to be able to read that much from her eyes.

I ate a quick meal of olives, cheese and fresh bread, then headed out again. I took Davus with me, though a protector hardly seemed necessary. The streets seemed almost preternaturally calm after the furore of recent days.

The Great One had moved into the city and was in residence at his house in the Carinae district, as I had hoped. He agreed to see me almost at once.

The house in the Carinae was a sprawling old villa surrounded by newer, taller buildings. It had been owned by Pompey's family for generations. There was a musty smell everywhere in the house, and in the room where Pompey gave audiences there were no fabulous views, only a glimpse of an inner courtyard with a modest fountain. The room was full of old trophies from various military campaigns, some brought back by Pompey from the East, some acquired by his father – exotic weapons and bits of armour, statuettes of obscure gods, shadow puppets from the Parthian borderlands and antique theatre masks from Greece. Lurking discreetly in the corners and shadows, as always, were the soldiers responsible for his safety.

Pompey sat beside a little table stacked high with scrolls. At my approach, he put aside the document he was reading. 'Finder! I was surprised when the

doorkeeper announced you. I didn't expect to see you again.'

'And I didn't expect to be able to see you so soon.'

'You happen to have come at the one hour of the day when I do not already have some prior obligation. Do we have unfinished business?'

'I came to ask a favour, Great One.'

'Good. I always like it when I'm asked for favours, whether I grant them or not. It gives me a chance to live up to my name. What is it you want, Finder?'

'I understand that a part of the penalty against Milo will be the confiscation of his estate.'

'Not quite his entire estate; I think we may allow him to take along a few personal slaves and such to begin his new life in Massilia. First, everything's to be liquidated to pay off his creditors, which number into legions. After that, we shall see how much is left for the treasury. The estate shall be picked quite clean before the scavenging is finished.'

'I should like to be listed among his creditors.'

'Oh? I have a hard time imagining that you lent him money, Finder. Or did you render services that were never paid for?'

'Neither of those things. I have a grievance against Milo. He was the man responsible for abducting me and my son and holding us prisoner for over a month. Since I last spoke to you, I acquired proof of this.'

'I see. Practically speaking, you have no legal recourse against him. The man's been convicted

and will soon be gone for good. He wouldn't be here to stand trial if you did bring charges against him.'

'I realize that, which is why I came to you, Great One.'

'I see. What is it you want?'

'I wish to be recognized by the state as one of Milo's creditors. I want a settlement from his estate.'

'And what is the price for what you and your son suffered at his hands?'

'That can hardly be estimated. But there is an amount I'll settle for.' I named it.

'A rather precise sum,' said Pompey. 'How did you come by it?'

'During the worst of the Clodian riots, my house was ransacked. A statue of Minerva in my garden was overturned and damaged. That's the cost to repair it.'

'I see. Is that fair, asking Milo to pay for damage that was done by his enemies?'

'Not fair in a legal sense, true. But perhaps I could paraphrase something you once said, Great One.'

'What's that?'

' "Stop quoting laws to us. We carry past-due bills." '

Pompey found this richly amusing. 'I like you, Finder. In coming years, I should like to think that you will be on my side.'

'I don't understand, Great One.'

'Oh, I think you do. Very well, then, how shall we do this?' He called for a secretary, who com-

597

posed a memorandum in duplicate. One copy was pressed flat and added to an already high stack in a cabinet against the wall. Pompey signed the other. His secretary rolled it tightly and applied a daub of red wax into which Pompey pressed his ring. 'There, have that delivered to Milo's house. Good luck collecting it. There are quite a few rather important people ahead of you. On the other hand, yours is likely to be the smallest bill. Perhaps the estate will pay it off first, simply to get rid of it.'

'Thank you, Great One.'

'Certainly.' He smiled, made a gesture of dismissal and strolled across the room. A moment later he turned back, surprised to see that I was still there. 'What now, Finder?'

'I feel a certain conflict, Great One, between an oath I took, and a prior obligation to yourself.'

'Yes?'

'Now that the trial of Milo is done, do you have any further interest in discovering what happened on the Appian Way?'

'I'm not sure what you mean.'

'If I were to tell you that Milo's men gravely, perhaps fatally, wounded Clodius, but that someone else — someone entirely removed from their mutual sphere of enmity — actually finished him off . . .'

'Are you saying that the final blow was delivered by a third party?'

'I have taken an oath not to speak of the details.'

'I see.' Pompey considered this. 'Then I suggest that you keep your mouth shut.'

'Should I, Great One?'

'Yes. By all means, don't break an oath on my account. Clodius is dead and burned to ashes. Milo is ruined and about to leave Rome for good. So much for those two. My next task shall be seeing to the punishment of the parties responsible for burning the Senate House. The state must deal evenly with all disturbers of the peace, you see, or there can be no law and order. Could this revelation of yours have any effect on that?'

'I think not, Great One.'

'Then it's irrelevant and of no interest to me. The murder of Clodius is old business. Do you understand, Finder?' There was a note almost of menace in his voice.

'Yes, Great One, I think I do.'

The inside of Milo's house seemed oddly familiar, though I had never been there before. The mosaics on the floor, the pale ochre colour of the walls, as well as various objects in the foyer and what I could glimpse of the nearby rooms reminded me at once of Cicero's house. Having no sense for such things himself, Milo had slavishly emulated his great friend's impeccable taste.

The place also reminded me, in an odd way, of Clodius's great house on the Palatine, for it was clearly in a state of chaos. But where I had seen Clodius's house in the process of being decorated and refurbished, Milo's house was the reverse, in the process of being undecorated and dismantled. Paintings had been removed from the walls and

stacked upright. Precious objects were being boxed up. Curtains had been removed from doorways and neatly folded on little tables.

Like Clodius's mansion on the night of his murder, there was an air of distraction and abandonment in Milo's house. Occasionally a slave would pass by on some errand, looking unhappy and hardly glancing at me. I began to think I had been forgotten. Finally, the slave who had admitted me returned and gestured for me to follow him deeper into the house.

Was I a fool, leaving Davus outside and going to face Milo alone? I braced myself for the confrontation. I was not sure how I would feel when I saw him. He had done me a great wrong, and I had every reason to despise him, and yet, oddly, the experience of my incarceration made me feel a kind of sympathy for him. It is a terrible thing, for a man to lose all his dreams, to have everything taken away from him except the bare means of sustenance. Milo had risen from obscurity to a position of great power. The consulship itself had been within his grasp – then his world had been shattered in a moment and his destiny had gone spiralling out of his control. He had played a dangerous game, and in the end had lost everything. Whether he deserved his fate or not, the totality of his ruin moved me. Nevertheless, I intended to tell him what I thought of his treatment of me, and to demand restitution.

The slave showed me to a room with a decidedly feminine atmosphere. The walls were painted with

scenes of peacocks in full fan strutting across wildly blooming gardens. A low dresser was covered with little cosmetics boxes, jewellery cases, brushes and burnished hand mirrors all made of fine woods and metals inlaid with precious stones. Across the room, a riot of colourful gowns and stolas spilled from an open wardrobe. Dominating the room was a large sleeping couch with a diaphanous red canopy. The air was scented with jasmine and musk.

Sounds of splashing and laughter came from a doorway at the far side of the room, which evidently led to a private bath. I could hear both male and female voices. Where had the doorkeeper taken me, and why had he gone off without announcing me? I cleared my throat as loudly as I could.

The laughter and splashing stopped. There was dead silence. I cleared my throat again and called out, 'Milo?' The response was silence, then a burst of laughter and splashing louder than before.

'Wait there,' called a woman's voice. I heard whispered conversation and more laughter. Finally she appeared in the doorway, wearing a loose, unbelted gown which did very little to conceal the plump, voluptuous contours of her body. Masses of ginger-coloured hair were piled and pinned atop her head. Whatever she had been doing in her bath, she had managed not to get her hair wet.

I had met her father once long ago. The dictator Sulla had been near the end of his life; Fausta Cornelia must have been no more than a child

601

then. Thirty years later, she was still too young to show the ravages of severe dissipation, which had ruined her father's looks, but there was a decided family resemblance – the same fair complexion, the same carnivorous smile, the same wilful fire behind the eyes. She was not graceful; when she moved, some part of her body always seemed to jiggle or sway. Instead of grace, she exuded a ripe fleshiness, and even from a considerable distance I could feel the radiant heat of her body, flushed and pink from her hot bath. Her high birth had attracted two promising husbands; other attributes had attracted a steady string of lovers, and I was being given a good look at them.

'So, you're the Finder,' she said.

'Yes. I came to see your husband on a matter of business.'

'My husband isn't here.'

'No?' I looked towards the door to the bath. I could still hear an occasional splash and the sound of voices.

'If Milo were here, do you think I'd be taking a bath with two of his gladiators?'

She looked to see if her candour would shock me. I did my best to keep a blank expression.

'I realize that Milo must be very busy during his last days in Rome,' I said. 'It isn't absolutely necessary that I see him face to face, but I do want to make sure that he receives this.' I held up the little scroll with Pompey's seal.

She rolled her eyes. 'Oh, not another bill! Thank the gods I kept my own income, even if it is in my

brother's name.' She took the scroll from me and walked down a short hallway. She jiggled a good deal behind as well, I noticed. We came to a cluttered room filled with documents. 'My husband's study,' she announced, with an air of distaste. 'From here, he was going to run the Republic. What a joke that turned out to be! I suppose there'll never be another man like my father, a real man who can bring this unruly town to heel.'

'I'm not so sure of that,' I said quietly, thinking of Pompey, and of Caesar.

She didn't hear. 'This is the latest pile of bills,' she said, indicating a tall box overflowing with scrolls and scraps of parchment. 'Shall we toss yours on top? There. But don't be surprised if it gets moved to the bottom, or lost altogether.'

'Who's attending to sorting out all these bills? Is your husband doing it himself?'

'Gods, no! Milo's a wreckage; he can hardly sort out which shoe to put on first in the morning. One peek inside this room and he's reduced to a blubbering baby. No, this will all be dealt with after he leaves. Cicero will take care of it. Or Tiro will, I should say; Tiro is a wonder at organizing things.'

'I see. Here, then, let's put my request aside from all the rest. If you would, tell Cicero to honour it first. Tell him that Gordianus the Finder insists. Cicero will know why. So will Tiro.'

She looked at me wryly. 'And you think I don't? I know who you are, Finder. I'm more aware of my husband's affairs than you seem to think. He was

quite bent on killing you, you know. It was all he talked about for days.'

'Really?' Her candour about her lovers was not nearly as startling as her candour about her husband's plots.

'Oh, yes. Milo considered you to be quite a menace. You should be honoured, I suppose. Of course, towards the end, he was seeing an assassin in every cupboard and a spy behind every bush. You obsessed him for a while. Cicero kept telling him that he was blowing any threat you posed out of all proportion. Cicero said that your reputation was grossly inflated, that you were barely competent, really, and that Milo should stop worrying about you.'

'How kind of Cicero.'

'He was trying to protect you, you fool. But Milo was determined to see you dead, in a cold sweat about it. In the end Cicero made him agree to a compromise, and Milo simply had you abducted. But you must be as clever and persevering as he thought – you escaped before the trial came up. By Hercules, what a fright you must have given Cicero when you popped up on the road right in front of him!' She emitted a short, barking laugh.

'I only wish I could have appreciated the humour at the time.'

'Can't we all say that, in retrospect? If only I'd known that marrying Milo would turn into such a joke! And that horrible day on the Appian Way, when I thought I was living through a nightmare, it was really all a grotesque farce from beginning to

end. The cruellest irony of all was that Milo never intended to kill Clodius. The fight broke out on its own, and when Milo sent his men after Clodius, he ordered them to spare him! The gladiators still swear that they didn't touch Clodius at the inn.'

'Is that a fact?'

'Do you doubt it? Come, I'll let them tell you the story themselves.' She took me back to her room. 'Boys! You can come out of the bath now. My visitor has promised not to bite you.'

First one appeared, then the other; the two of them could not possibly have fitted through the door at once. They wore loincloths but were otherwise naked and still damp from their bath, two great steaming masses of hairy flesh, each of them twice the size of an ordinary man. I noticed that they were nicked with little scars here and there, but were mostly unmarked, as one might expect of gladiators who had never lost a match. They moved with surprising lightness and grace considering their bulk. Unlike Fausta, nothing shook or jiggled when they walked; for all their fleshiness, their muscles were as solid as marble.

I winced to see their famously ugly faces so close. 'Eudamus and Birria,' I whispered.

They walked across the room with supreme nonchalance, pushed aside the diaphanous drapery and lay down side by side on Fausta's sleeping couch. The frame groaned and sagged under their weight.

'My husband intends to take them with him to Massilia,' said Fausta wistfully. 'He'll need protec-

tion, of course. But gods, I shall miss the two of them!'

'I take it that you don't intend to accompany your husband into exile?'

'Follow Milo to Massilia, to live among Greeks and Gauls and washed-up Roman windbags? I had sooner live out my days on Milo's pig farm down in Lanuvium.'

I looked at Eudamus and Birria warily. 'Are you sure they can talk?'

'It seems almost too much to expect, doesn't it, given all their other talents? But yes, they can actually speak – though it's Birria who does all the talking. Eudamus is the shy one, because he's so much prettier, I suppose.' The less repulsive of the two made a simpering smile and actually blushed. The uglier one wrinkled his nose and grunted. 'Boys, this is Gordianus. I was telling him a few things about the day that Clodius died, and he didn't believe me.'

'Do you want us to tear his head off his shoulders?'

'No, Birria. Perhaps some other time. Do you remember how the fight started that day?'

'Of course.' Birria crossed his arms behind his head, showing off biceps as big as his head. 'We met that fool Clodius on the road, which might have been trouble right off, but we passed without a hitch, everything as smooth as silk. But the fool couldn't let the opportunity pass to shout an insult at us at the last moment.'

'And you lost your temper, didn't you?' Fausta commiserated.

'I did. I threw my spear at him. I meant it to whizz by his head, but he made a move and it hit his shoulder.' Birria laughed. 'Knocked him clean off his horse, and I didn't even mean to. Then it was Mars in charge and every man for himself. We got the best of them. Pretty soon they were running like rabbits into the woods and down the road.'

'Then the master sent you after them,' prompted Fausta.

'After he threw his tantrum,' agreed Birria.

'And what were his instructions?'

Birria stretched on the couch. His legs reached so far over the end that he was almost able to touch his toes to the floor. 'The master said, 'Kill all the rest if you have to, but take Clodius alive. Don't harm a hair on his head, or I'll send the lot of you off to the mines.' So we chased the fool down to Bovillae, where he was holed up inside the inn. We had to go in and drag his men out, one by one. The stupid innkeeper got in the way; Eudamus took care of him. We had the situation under control, and all that was left was to drag Clodius out of the inn by the scruff of his neck. Then that fellow Philemon and his friends came along. He pitched a fit, shouted some threats and shook his fist at us, but as soon as we took two steps towards him he let out a squeal and turned tail. He and his friends scattered all over the place. So we went after them. What else could we do? Eudamus chased one, I chased another, and all our men followed along. You'd think that someone would have had the sense to stay and keep a watch on

Clodius, but no one thought to.' He shrugged, bunching a great mass of muscles around his oxlike neck. 'Everything was crazy that day.'

I shook my head at the simplemindedness of it. 'And when you finally rounded up the witnesses and came back —'

'Clodius was gone.'

I nodded. 'Because Sextus Tedius had already come along and dispatched him to Rome in his litter, while you were off chasing Philemon . . .'

'Yes, but we didn't know that,' protested Birria. 'When we got back to the inn, we couldn't figure out where in Hades Clodius had got to.'

'So you argued about it for a while; that was the hushed argument Philemon only half overheard without understanding.'

Birria shrugged. 'We decided to head back and ask the master what to do. Clodius was wounded. We figured he couldn't get far.'

'And on the way, you passed Sextus Tedius, resting below the House of the Vestals, and he saluted you, while his daughter —'

'We just ignored the old senator and hurried back to the master. He took one look at the prisoners, saw that we didn't have Clodius, and threw another tantrum. While he paced up and down we loaded the prisoners into a wagon and sent them on to the master's villa at Lanuvium, along with the mistress. Then the master decided that Clodius would probably make a run back to his villa on the mountain, so that's where we headed.'

'But when you got there, you didn't find Clodius.'

'We searched everywhere – in the stable, behind the rock piles, all through the house. We started threatening the slaves in charge, the foreman and that fellow Halicor. 'Where's Publius Clodius?' the master kept yelling.'

'You were looking for Clodius at the villa – not for his son!'

'That was a dirty lie the Clodians put out afterwards, saying the master went on a hunt for Clodius's little boy. What would we have done with him? We didn't even know the boy was there, and we certainly never saw him. It was Clodius himself we were hunting for. The master was frantic that we couldn't find him. He kept asking us how badly Clodius was wounded. He figured that Clodius must be hiding in the hills –'

'And my dear husband dreaded what would happen next,' added Fausta, 'now that blood had been spilled and Clodius would be mad for revenge. Milo didn't know that Clodius was dead until he sneaked back into the city the next day. Then of course we heard the story about how Sextus Tedius had found the body, and we figured out what must have happened.'

'Did you really?' I said. 'And the next step was for Milo to concoct his own fanciful version of the incident – all that nonsense about Clodius setting an ambush for him.'

'It was a good try,' said Fausta wistfully. 'But there was no way for him to wriggle out of it in the

609

end, was there? Not even with Cicero on his side –
and what a mess he made of things! The irony, you
see, is that Milo never intended to have Clodius
killed, nor to harm his little boy. Once Clodius was
wounded – by you, Birria, you very, very naughty
boy – Milo simply wanted Clodius to be taken
alive, to keep him safe and quiet until we could
figure out what to do next. But Philemon drew the
men away from the inn. Either Clodius's wounds
were worse than everyone thought, or else . . .'

'Yes?'

'Milo suggested to Cicero that someone else
might have actually finished him off.'

'How could that have happened?'

'Clodius had plenty of enemies on Mount Alba.
He'd stirred up a lot of trouble. Any local person
passing by, who happened to see that Clodius was
wounded and alone, might have been tempted to
take advantage of the situation. And there were
reports that Clodius had strangulation marks on his
throat – you mentioned them yourself, to Cicero.
Eudamus and Birria both swear that they never
touched his throat – so where did those marks come
from, unless some unknown party throttled Clodius
while they were off chasing Philemon? That would
explain why Sextus Tedius found him lying dead in
the road, when he was still alive in the tavern when
Birria and Eudamus took after Philemon.' She
sighed, sounding more bored than weary. 'That
was a theory that Milo proposed, anyway, but
Cicero said there was no use in pursuing it.
'Why try to convince the jury that you're techni-

cally innocent by some convoluted logic, saying your men only wounded Clodius and someone else killed him? They'll never believe it, whether it's true or not. Make no apologies and argue self-defence!' If Philemon hadn't appeared, we might have taken Clodius alive. But Sextus Tedius showed up at just the wrong moment, and then he sent the body on its way to Rome without our knowing it. Do you grasp the irony, Gordianus?'

'Oh, yes,' I said. 'More than you know.'

Fausta sighed. 'All this dwelling on the past is depressing me. You should run along now, Gordianus. I'd just finished my bath when you arrived, and now it's time for my massage.' She brightened. 'Unless you'd like to join me . . .'

'I think not.'

'Are you sure? Eudamus and Birria give quite an extraordinary massage. Twenty fingers between them – nineteen actually, since Eudamus lost one in a fight – and such power! They could break me in two like a twig, but they leave me feeling as light and airy as a cloud. They could handle two of us as easily as one. It might be rather interesting.' The look on her face left no doubt about her meaning.

'And your husband?'

'He won't be back for hours.'

'Are you certain?'

'Reasonably certain . . .'

I remembered Fausta Cornelia's penchant for getting caught in compromising positions, and imagined Milo walking in on the four of us. It was not the kind of confrontation I cared to have

with Milo on the eve of his exile, though it might have amused Fausta Cornelia a great deal.

'Alas, I have a final errand I must attend to before the day is done.'

She pouted her lips and shrugged. 'Regrets, then, Gordianus. Shall I tell my husband that you came by to bid him farewell?'

'Please do.'

# XXXVII

On such a magnificent spring afternoon, with flowers in bloom and the sun spreading warmth from a cloudless sky, I knew where I would find her.

We made our way through the cattle market west of the Palatine and across the old wooden bridge. 'Where are we going, Master?' said Davus.

'To the other side of the Tiber. I should have thought that was obvious.'

Davus frowned. It was time for me to stop teasing him, I thought. I would not be his master much longer. I would miss the particular relationship that had grown up between us.

'Actually, Davus, we're going to a garden villa on the west bank of the Tiber across from the Field of Mars. A beautiful spot with a rustic little villa and a green meadow surrounded by tall trees, and a strip of land on the riverbank excellent for swimming. I would prefer that you told no one of this visit, not

even Eco. And certainly not Bethesda. Can you keep a secret?'

'I should have thought that was obvious, Master,' he said with a sigh.

After a while we left the road. We passed beneath a shade-dappled canopy of berry bushes and emerged onto a wide green meadow alive with hovering insects and butterflies. The long villa was to the left, just as I remembered. But she would not stay inside on a day such as this. I told Davus to find a shady place to wait for me and I crossed the meadow, the high grass pulling at my feet. Through a stand of tall trees I glimpsed fleeting patches of sunlight on the river. I also saw her tent on the riverbank with its red and white stripes shivering in the breeze, and nearby the matching red and white stripes of her litter where it had been set down on higher ground. If the litter was here, then so was she.

No one noticed my approach; no one was posted to watch. All her litter bearers and bodyguards were down in the river, swimming and splashing each other and playing some sort of game with a leather ball. I came to the tent and circled around to the side which faced the river and the swimmers. All the flaps had been rolled up to let in the breeze and the view. She half sat, half reclined on a high, pillow-strewn couch, swathed in a gown made of some diaphanous golden fabric, with a cup of wine in her hand and a forlorn expression on her face. She looked as if she might be watching a tragic play instead of a group of naked slaves cavorting in the water.

She saw me and gave a start, then recognized me and managed a wan smile.

A handmaiden seated on the rug at the foot of her couch scrambled to her feet as I approached, then looked to her mistress for instructions. At a nod from Clodia, the girl left the tent.

'Gordianus,' said Clodia. Her voice was like the languid music of the river. Her scent, of spikenard and crocus-oil, suffused the warm air inside the tent. Her flesh seemed to glow in the soft filtered light.

'I hurt your feelings the other day,' I said.

'Did you?' She turned her eyes back to the bathers.

'I think so. For that, I apologize.'

'No need. I'd already forgotten. Pains and pleasures have all been dulled for me, since –'

'Since your brother died?'

She lowered her eyes. 'The one pain that never grows less sharp.'

'I suppose you must take some comfort from what happened at the trial.'

'I have no taste for trials any more.'

'But Milo was punished, and Cicero barely stumbled through his speech.'

She laughed softly and nodded. 'Yes, I should like to have seen that. But none of this will bring him back to me.'

'No. But sometimes people are willing to settle for justice, or revenge.'

'I learned my lesson when I tried to take revenge on Marcus Caelius. What use is any of it, in the end?'

I spoke carefully. 'Taking vengeance on those

who killed him – would that bring you no satisfaction?'

'Why do you keep bringing this up, Gordianus? I have no appetite for revenge.' She took a deep breath and exhaled it. 'My brother gave a great many people a great many reasons to want him dead. I'm not a fool, or blind; I know the way he was and the life he lived. I loved Publius, more than anything else in the world. There was nothing about him I would have changed. But sooner or later, given the game he played and the rules he broke, a bad end was waiting for him. They're all playing the same game, and I suspect they shall all meet a violent end – Pompey and Caesar, Caelius and Antony . . . even Cicero. So long as Publius was a player, I had some interest in the contest. But now . . .' She sighed. 'I simply lie here and watch my beautiful young men enjoy themselves in the water. I don't even see the young men any more; I watch the water, the way it sparkles and slides off them. The way it flows towards the sea, never stopping, never turning back. It all used to mean something to me, I think, but I can't remember what.'

'Are you so miserable, Clodia?'

'Miserable? That seems too strong a word. I seldom weep any more, or wake up from nightmares about his death. I just feel very tired.' She smiled crookedly. 'I must look frightful.'

'No, Clodia. You look beautiful. Unspeakably beautiful.'

She reached for my hand. I looked into her eyes for a moment, then had to look away. I watched

the bathers, in the way that she watched them, abstractly and without really seeing them, only their movements and the play of light on their wet flesh. Then the abstract became concrete. I suddenly recognized one of them.

'By Hercules!'

'What is it, Gordianus?'

'One of your men, the one with the red face . . . and ice blue eyes . . .' The man was diving for the leather ball. He screwed his face up, just as he did on that night he confronted me on the Palatine Hill after ransacking my house.

'You know him?' said Clodia.

'He was one of the looters who plundered my house and wrecked my statue of Minerva. One of the men who murdered my slave, Belbo.'

'I wouldn't be surprised. The fellow's a former gladiator. Clodius owned him, then freed him so he could go on the grain dole. Since then he's been passed around the family as a bodyguard. He caused some sort of trouble among my nephew's slaves. I ended up with him only a few days ago. They thought I should like looking at him, I suppose. But you say he wrecked your house?'

'And killed a man very dear to me.'

'I see. What shall we do about it?'

'I have no proof. No one was there to see him do it, except his friends. Maybe it was one of his friends who killed Belbo. Perhaps he's innocent, though he seemed to be the leader.'

'Why worry over details? This isn't a court. We both know his sort. I'm sure he's done something

or other he deserves to die for. Shall I take care of it for you, Gordianus?'

'What do you mean?'

'I could have the fellow drowned, right here and now. It would only take a word to my chief bodyguard. A man like that would put up quite a struggle, I imagine, but between my bodyguards and litter bearers there are enough strong men out there to hold him down for however long it takes. You could have the pleasure of watching. Shall I give the order?'

'You're serious, aren't you?'

'Yes. But only if you want it. Shall I give the order?'

I considered it. In a single afternoon, I had been invited by Fausta Cornelia to take part in an orgy and by Clodia to watch a man die by my order. Such opportunities were the prerogatives of kings and emperors; why should I refuse? Perhaps I had never really known the meaning of justice or truth, but once I thought I did, and the illusion had comforted me. Now everything had changed. All my bearings had slipped out of sight. I felt dizzy and disoriented. Was the world spinning out of control, or was it only me?

'No,' I finally said. 'Your brother is dead, and so is Belbo, and no amount of killing will bring them back. The river flows only forwards.'

Clodia smiled ruefully. 'Very well. The fellow shall never know how close he came to being drowned like a dog. But I'll remember what you told me. I shall keep a close eye on him from now on.'

'Clodia —'

'Yes.'

'Hold out your hand.'

She did so with an arched eyebrow, expecting some trick. I placed her brother's ring on her open palm.

She sighed, shuddered, sobbed, and caught a breath to steady herself. 'Where did you find it?'

'If I say that I found it lying beside the Appian Way, will you be satisfied?'

She looked at the ring for a long time, with an expression of such tenderness that I realized how foolish I was to think that I could hurt her. What could she feel for me, or for any man, compared to what she had felt for her brother?

'Why did you bring it to me? Why not to Fulvia? She's his widow.'

'Yes, but Fulvia has already moved on. She's planning her next marriage — and perhaps the next marriage after that. She's looking towards the future, not the past.'

'But Publius's son, his little boy . . .'

'If you think your nephew should have the ring, I leave that decision to you. I decided to return it to the one who loved him most.'

She closed her hand tightly around it and shut her eyes. A single tear ran down her cheek.

I turned and retraced my footsteps in the soft earth, going back the way I had come. At the corner of the tent I turned back. She blinked her eyes open. 'I almost forgot.' I said. 'I want to invite you to a wedding.'

'A wedding? In your family? Don't tell me it's your daughter, Diana!'

'I'm afraid so.'

'But she's only a child.'

'Not any longer. Time flies.'

'But I shouldn't come. I'm not related, and hardly close enough to the family. It would be most unconventional.'

'All the better. I suspect it will be a most unconventional marriage.'

'Your daughter is following after her father, then.'

The thought gave me pause. 'Farewell, Clodia.'

'Farewell, Gordianus.' She gave me a parting glance, then leaned back among the pillows, holding the ring to her breast.

I walked back across the meadow to Davus. Clodia had it exactly right: Diana was following after me. They were all following after me.

If only I knew where I was going . . .

If only I had the vaguest idea of what was in store for any of us . . .

Davus was resting in the shade of an oak tree. At my approach he rose to his feet and brushed himself off. 'If only I knew where I was going,' I muttered, thinking aloud.

'But, Master, I should have thought that was obvious.'

'What?'

He smiled. 'We're going home now, aren't we?'

I heaved a sigh of great relief. 'Yes, Davus. Home!'

# AUTHOR'S NOTE

The sources for the murder of Clodius and Milo's trial are remarkable in themselves. The text of Cicero's oration for Milo which has come down to us – most likely an idealized version of the speech he intended to give, prettied up for publication – gives us one view of events, and a clearly prejudiced and deliberately skewed one at that. If it was all we had to go on, it would still make a great story, but we should have no idea of what really happened on the Appian Way.

(And if Cicero had been able to deliver the speech intact, things might have turned out differently – such, at least, was the substance of a bitter jest by Milo. When Cicero proudly sent him a copy, Milo remarked that it was a good thing the orator had not been able to deliver such a stirring speech – otherwise Milo would still be back in Rome, and not in exile in Massilia enjoying the excellent mullets.)

Fortunately, in the next century the scholar Quintus Asconius Pedianus wrote some study guides for his sons to use when reading Cicero's orations, and one of these surviving commentaries analyses the Pro Milone. It reads today as a sort of precursor to the 'true crime' genre. Asconius gives us fascinating details about the desperate parliamentary manoeuvres and frantic damage control by both sides in the wake of Clodius's death. He describes the nuts-and-bolts conduct of the trial, including the selection of the jury. Most important, he gives us an account of the murder completely at odds with the one Cicero puts forth.

In Cicero's day, as now, defence lawyers were not ashamed to come up with fanciful, even outrageous angles to absolve their clients. Then, as now, courtroom sideshows and overlong trials were a serious problem, though Pompey's one-day solution might strike even the most television-weary American as too extreme.

The Pro Milone is available in the Penguin edition of *Selected Political Speeches of Cicero*, translated by Michael Grant, and in volume 14 of the Loeb Classical Library editions of Cicero, translated by N. H. Watts, who also includes an abbreviated version of Asconius's commentary. The complete text of Asconius can be found in *Commentaries on Five Speeches of Cicero*, edited and translated by Simon Squires (Bristol Classical Press and Bolchazy-Carducci Publishers, 1990). Our knowledge of the tumultuous events of 52 BC comes from numerous sources which vary greatly in importance

and reliability, including the histories and commentaries of Appian, Caesar, Velleius Paterculus, Plutarch, Quintilian and Dio Cassius, and the letters of Cicero.

Crucial to any depiction of the murder and trial is an unravelling of the conflicting details and the tangled sequence of events. Three works by modern historians have done much to sort things out: Albert C. Clark's annotated edition of the Pro Milone (Oxford at the Clarendon Press, 1895), A. W. Lintott's 'Cicero and Milo' (*Journal of Roman Studies* 64, 1974) and James S. Reubel's 'The Trial of Milo in 52 BC: A Chronological Study' (*Transactions of the American Philological Association* 109, 1979). In deference to his scholarship (and for the sake of consistency), I have chiefly relied on Reubel's chronology.

How crucial was the murder of Clodius to subsequent events? As the assassination of Archduke Francis Ferdinand in Sarajevo in 1914 is generally regarded as the spark that ignited World War I, so the murder of Clodius can be regarded as precipitating a chain of events that led to civil war between Pompey and Caesar and the final dissolution of the Roman Republic. As Michael Grant notes, the Pro Milone 'casts a lurid light upon the savage chaos and vendetta which signalized these last moribund years of the Republic, and helped to make it inevitable that this once mighty institution should come to an end and be replaced by an autocracy.'

Claude Nicolet argues the point even more explicitly in *The World of the Citizen in Republican*

*Rome* (University of California Press, 1988): 'The intervention of Pompey's troops was indeed prophetic: it sounded the knell of the free Republic and, by the same token, of Roman political and forensic eloquence. The Roman mob thought it had gained a victory by intimidating Cicero and driving Milo into exile; but all it had done was to prepare the way for civil war and thereby the Empire.'

Most of my research was conducted at Doe Library and (somewhat surreptitiously) in the Classics Reading Room at the University of California at Berkeley. I want to express my personal thanks to Penni Kimmel for reading the manuscript; to Rick Solomon for various sorts of indulgence and inspiration; to Pat Urquhart, for his technical assistance with the map; to Terri Odom, for reading the galleys; and to my editor at St Martin's Press, Keith Kahla.

# Steven Saylor Roma sub Rosa Series

| No. of copies | Title | Price (incl. p&p) | Total |
|---|---|---|---|
| | Catilina's Riddle | £6.99 | |
| | Roman Blood | £6.99 | |
| | Arms of Nemesis | £6.99 | |
| | The Judgement of Caesar | £6.99 | |
| | A Gladiator Dies Only Once (hardback) | £16.99 | |
| | The Venus Throw | £6.99 | |
| | **Available from 29 September 05** | | |
| | Rubicon | £6.99 | |
| | Last Seen in Massilia | £6.99 | |
| | **Available from 24 November 05** | | |
| | A Mist of Prophecies | £6.99 | |
| | The House of the Vestals | £6.99 | |
| | **Grand Total** | | £ |

Name: _____

Address: _____

_____ Postcode: _____

Daytime Tel. No. / E-mail

_____

(in case of query)

Three ways to pay:

1. **For express service telephone the TBS order line on 01206 255 800 and quote 'CRBK'. Order lines are open Monday – Friday 8:30am – 5:30pm**

2. I enclose a cheque made payable to **TBS Ltd** for £_____

3. Please charge my ☐ Visa ☐ Mastercard ☐ Amex ☐ Switch (switch issue no._____) £_____

   Card number: _____

   Expiry date: _____    Signature _____
   (your signature is essential when paying by credit card)

**Please return forms (*no stamp required*) to, Constable & Robinson Ltd, FREEPOST NAT6619, 3 The Lanchesters, 162 Fulham Palace Road, London W6 9BR.**

**Enquiries to readers@constablerobinson.com.**
www.constablerobinson.com